Praise for John Keeble's novel *Nocturnal America*

"This is a real writer, with an authenticity of place and character." —Robert Olen Butler, Pulitzer Prize–winning author of *A Good Scent from a Strange Mountain*

"Keeble's Pacific Northwest [is] a rich and desolate landscape that yields a limitless trove of both peril and passion. . . . Keeble is adept at speaking from either the male or female point of view. . . . Daily existence is a wild and precarious dance in Keeble's world, where lives gingerly balance between hope and grief." —Carol Haggas, *Booklist*

"Like the setting, this book is rich and rewarding." —*Publishers Weekly*

"A haunting and touching look at love and life in the Pacific Northwest." —Kellie Gillespie, *Library Journal*

"[Keeble] succeeds in building an entire community, with a history that haunts and sustains and explains the present-day generation. *Nocturnal America* is a remarkably involving work." —Barbara McMichael, *Olympian* (Olympia WA)

"[Keeble] is absolutely convincing in the viewpoints of both men and women and has a lovely ability to drop luminous observation into an apparently mundane moment of the narrative." —Janet Burroway, author of *Raw Silk* and *Writing Fiction*

Prairie Schooner Book Prize in Fiction   Editor: Kwame Dawes

Nocturnal ✦ America

John Keeble

University of Nebraska Press

Lincoln and London

∞

Library of Congress Cataloging-in-Publication Data
Keeble, John, 1944–
Nocturnal America / John Keeble
p. cm. — (Prairie schooner book prize in fiction)
ISBN-13: 978-0-8032-2777-4 (cloth: alk. paper)
ISBN-10: 0-8032-2777-9 (cloth: alk. paper)
ISBN-13: 978-0-8032-7177-7 (paper: alk. paper)
1. Community life—Fiction. I. Title. II. Series.
PS3561.E3N63 2006   813'.54—dc22
2006005908

This book is for Jonathan, Zeke,
Carson, Sue, the next Carson,
Alexander, Bryson, and whosoever
may follow. They will know why.

CONTENTS

ACKNOWLEDGMENTS

Thanks to Gordon Bleeker, Gillian Conoley, Elizabeth Cook-Lynn, Laura Furman, David Grimes, Christopher Howell, Sandy Huss, Jonathan Johnson, Howard Junker, Fred Newberry, Ladette Randolph, Hilda Raz, Diane Roberts, Kim and Blaine Roberts, Lois Rosenthal, Denise Shannon, Dan Sisson, Ted Solotaroff, Ruben Trejo, and John Witte.

"The Chasm" was originally published in *Prairie Schooner* 67, no. 2 (Summer 1993). Reprinted in *Best American Short Stories*, ed. by Tobias Wolff and Katrina Kennison (Boston: Houghton Mifflin, 1994).

"The Transmission" was originally published in *American Review* no. 25 (1976). Reprinted in *From Timberline to Tidepool: Contemporary Fiction from the Northwest*, ed. by Rich Ives (Seattle: Owl Creek Press, 1986).

"The Fishers" was originally published in *American Short Fiction* 2, no. 8 (Winter 1992).

"Zeta's House" was originally published in *Northwest Review* 29, no. 2 (1991). Reprinted in *Reflections from the Island's Edge*, ed. by Carolyn Servid (Graywolf Press, 1994).

"Chickens" originally appeared under the title "The Messenger from the Fallen State" in *Volt: A Magazine of the Arts* no. 1 (Summer 1993).

"I Could Love You (If I Wanted)" was originally published in *Story* (Summer 1992). Reprinted in *Dreamers and Desperadoes: An Anthology of Contemporary Writers of the American West*, ed. by C. Lesley and K. Stavrakis (New York: Dell Publishing Co., 1993).

"The Cross" was originally published in ZYZZYVA 9, no. 4 (Winter 1993).

"Nocturnal America" originally appeared under the title "NBound" in ZYZZYVA 20, no. 1 (Spring, 2004).

All previously published stories have received revisions.

Nocturnal America

The Chasm

IN WINTER the glazed bunchgrass and wild oats tuft the road-sides and edges of fields. In spring the exhausted grass will still be there, a blond whiskering to the green. Through summer the dry stalks of last year's grass memorialize winter, the pale of the dead fringing the alive in this place that has become Jim Blood's country. In the heat of the summer, it takes a powerful leap of the imagination to remember the snow that covered the fields. So it is. Usually, the winters in eastern Washington are kind enough, but not too many years ago the cold came early. A northerly from the Gulf of Alaska found a trough between the mountain ranges to howl down. For a solid month, record low temperatures were broken daily. Before it was done, Jim found cause for the first time in years to reflect upon the small Saskatchewan town he'd come from.

That was a hard place. He remembered it as crystalline and white. He remembered voices ringing in the cold like metal. His infant sister had died there. He remembered the bright sound the tiny coffin made when it struck the ice at the bottom of the grave. He remembered his parents in the graveyard and how his father, the only minister for miles around, had conducted the service himself. He remembered how his father seemed to stand straight against this trouble, while his mother had bent under it. That was then. He'd been a boy to whom the many common and uncommon things in life were equal in their power to astonish him.

❦

Now, he lived here with his wife, Diane, and their three sons. They were trying to start up a ranch. They'd moved out to the place late last spring to finish building a house. They had few neighbors. By their driveway, the distance from the house to the county road was nearly a mile, and when they drove out they emerged from the woods onto a rise from which they could look northward across the fields to the Lanattos' place, and then westerly and further north to the Holisters' where there were two houses and the network of outbuildings that went with a dairy. To the south was the canyon. That was all. Phil Lanatto was a dentist, but he and his wife worked an alfalfa crop, too. Bob Holister was a farm cooperative executive. He and his wife lived in a house near the road. Their son and daughter-in-law, Lem and Judy, lived in the back house.

It was the younger Holisters' dairy operation. Lem and Judy worked as X-ray technicians in a hospital in the city. Judy worked swing, Lem graveyard, and by day they ran the dairy, which they were establishing with the greatest care. Like Phil Lanatto, Lem was a veteran. Gradually, Jim had come to know how long the other two had been in Vietnam, whereabouts, and in what capacity they served: Lem had been a helicopter gunner and Phil a surgical dentist. When Phil and Lem talked about Vietnam, about the jungle, Jim felt uneasy, and yet he felt drawn to the scorching he could almost smell on them like burnt hair.

Jim met Lem early in the summer when he dropped by the Holisters' place to introduce himself. He found Lem loading calves. A trim man with black hair and sharp eyes, Lem drove the calves into a pen and then coaxed them up the chute and into a closed, two-ton truck by clucking softly and flicking them with a switch. These were excess calves headed for a feedlot. It was June. The flies had just hatched and the air was thick with them. The calves did not balk at the loading but crowded anxiously into the head of the box, their glossy eyes and white and black coats flashing in the dark. Jim and Lem leaned against the chute, and occasionally Lem reached over with the switch to make a calf move. The two men continually brushed flies away from their faces. They spoke little. Lem grinned and said, "It's hard to talk when you have to keep your teeth shut."

Jim saw Lem again in July. Jim was doing roadwork with his old crawler tractor. The tractor had a boom on it and a blade for dozing. His road had a low spot near the front gate, a sink that became a pond in the spring and would make a hard place to plow the snow in winter. He pushed rocks into the hole, then scraped dirt off the rise to cover the rock. The blade snagged on an outcropping near the bottom and the tracks on the left side spun. He lifted the blade and tried to back the tractor off. The tracks didn't grab. He looked down and saw that he was in mud, that it wasn't just a hole or a runoff pond he was filling but an underground spring, and that he'd chewed off the crust with the tracks. He tried to move the tractor forward and backward. He tried to turn it to drive it out. The left side only dug itself in. He got out to look and instantly sank knee-deep in the mire. He scrambled onto the outcropping and looked.

The side of the tractor was sinking, slowly but visibly sinking. It was not a small tractor. An antiquated behemoth, a D-14, it weighed five tons, and it was tipping. Something had to be done right away. Diane and the telephone were too far away, and the Lanattos' house was a half-mile across the field. The Holisters' place was farther yet. If Jim tried to move the tractor and failed, digging it in deeper, the situation would quickly change from grave to desperate. He pictured the tractor listing until it dropped to its side. He told himself to calm down.

The tractor had two winches, one to operate a boom and the other to run a set of long tongs. One cable might be disconnected and used to winch the tractor out if he could find something to tie it to. He looked for a tree in front or in back of the tractor. They were all too small. They would snap under the weight. There was a tree to the right, a big one. He stared at it. There was no way to pull the tractor out sideways. He walked around and studied the tractor. He could see the mud inching up the tracks on the left side. He looked at the tree again, then at the boom, which could be swiveled. As he considered this, the shiny nose of Lem's black pickup appeared.

Lem came over. "Saw you from the road," he said, and then he squinted at Jim. "It's that bad?"

"It's not good."

"It won't move?"

"Down."

Lem squatted and scrutinized the buried track, then stood and looked the tractor over. He looked at the boom, then at the tree Jim had been considering.

"You were thinking about the tree."

Jim nodded. "The boom."

"I'd try it."

"I don't know if the boom can lift up half of that tractor. I don't know, maybe the right side will just sink."

"The cable'll go first. Do you know anybody with a bigger cat than this one?"

Jim looked down at his boots, covered with mud.

"If you have to hire somebody's cat, it'll cost you a small fortune."

Jim nodded.

"You drive," Lem said.

Jim didn't like it. He didn't like the thought of the cable snapping, but he got in and swiveled the boom around to the right until it was perpendicular to the tractor body and let down the tongs. Lem grabbed them, wrapped the cable twice around the tree, and secured it by closing the tongs onto the trunk. Jim winched in the cable, then paused. He'd seen the tongs go rigid. He didn't like the thought of anything breaking – boom, tongs, or cable – with him sitting there in the open cab. Lem grinned and gestured with his thumbs up. Jim didn't like the fear he felt, either. He wound the winch in a little more. He watched the cable cut into the bark of the tree and felt the left side of the tractor rise. He glanced down at the right side. The track hadn't sunk. He winched in more. If the cable snapped, he would be in the line of fire, and a whipping cable could slice him in half. He took a deep breath and winched in the cable until the left track cleared the ground. The cable held.

Lem motioned to back the tractor up. Jim got about a foot before the left track touched again because of the incline. Lem motioned to winch in more. Jim did so. They used the same method again and again, five times lifting the left track and backing up on the right until the tractor was clear. Jim let the cable out and Lem

4

unhooked it from the tree. Jim wound it back, moved the tractor up the hill, stopped, and turned it off. The silence boomed in his ears. He sat still, balanced with his hands on his knees.

Lem grinned. "You had it from the start."

"I had the idea. That's all." He thought – the idea, I had the idea, but the execution of it scared me.

"Hell," Lem said, "that machine could pull itself up a tree if you found one big enough. You could hook it up to its own engine, and it'd pull out its guts."

ℱ❧

Lem and Judy had no children but planned to adopt a baby. It had taken them three years of waiting. The baby was to come home with them the Friday before Christmas. Over roughly the same period, Jim and Diane had felled trees, trimmed, hauled, peeled, milled, set, and notched them to make the walls of their house. They were building with logs. When the two couples talked, they were struck by the mirror in their lives. One couple had children, which the second couple desired. The second couple had their farming enterprise well under way, which the first couple had just begun. Though they did not spend that much time together, they had spoken of this – the waiting they shared, the expectation, the work – and a sense of luminousness that cast away their differences fell upon them.

For the first two and a half years, Jim and Diane had used the nearby city of Spokane as a home base and traveled to the ranch to work. They used chain saws to cut and trim the logs, and the tractor's boom to lift them; but otherwise, it was an extended exercise in hand labor – socket slick, chisels, sledge, augers, froe. This was an economy, but the use of primitive methods also came from Jim's desire for the cleansing touch of simple tools and natural materials.

Diane didn't believe in such things as fervently as he did. She wished to live in this place in approximately this fashion, but she wondered why he had to do everything the hard way. She'd said that maybe what he really wanted was to vanish into the woods of North Idaho like some of the others had, to become a neo-mountain man. Or to go to Alaska, maybe. "What are you trying to overcome?" she asked him one day. They were working their way through the last group of logs on the ground, peeling them with bark spuds.

Jim couldn't answer. He thought that Diane knew about the touch of the hand to things – nail, spike, bar, and wedge, the yellow pine – and about the spirits that had their roots in the material world. She was a musician, a cellist. She understood that the bow drawn across the strings activated the atoms in the air. But in another way he realized that Diane's question went deeper, that the images of impeccability he pursued were striking a crazy, precarious balance with a chaotic thing he couldn't name. He stuck the blade of his bark spud into a log and looked at Diane. She was staring deeply into him with her bright green eyes. The true answer to her question seemed just out of his reach. The answer was like a word remembered for its feel on the tongue, but which he couldn't raise to his mind.

During the second year of work, Jim's parents moved out from the Midwest. Everyone lived in Jim and Diane's rented house in the city and planned to move together to the ranch when the new house was ready. This became the plan, a closing of ranks following Jim's father's retirement. Funds were pooled. The new house expanded and then took shape, but at the same time, the couples were learning that they could not live together. Relations grew strained, then fragile. The more fragile relations became, the more far-fetched were the dreams. Life together was like a web, intricately woven, but cut loose from its moorings and floating away crazily on the wind.

There was a scene. Jim's father corrected his middle grandson, a five-year-old, at the dinner table. In itself it was nothing, but Jim told his father to let the boy be. His father, one who by profession had given comfort to others, called the child despicable. Hot words were exchanged. Several months' worth of resentment suddenly broke the surface: when to make noise and when not, in what order to use the bathroom, how clean to keep the kitchen, who should wash dishes. . . . Jim's mother slammed a glass on the table, shattered it, cut her hand, rose, and vented a flood of accusations. Who did Jim and Diane think they were to bring them to this? There were too many children here, too many people, too much junk. Her face was white, and her eyes blazed in the way Jim hadn't seen since he was a boy – blue, young-looking, glinting like knives in the old face. Heedless of her bleeding hand, she cursed her son, this house, and the one under construction. Why weren't they left where they had been to die? Or sent away to a retirement home in California? She cursed herself, her husband, and her long life of disappointment.

The oldest boy, a nine-year-old, watched his grandmother in amazement as the room rang with her voice. The baby was silent. The five-year-old – who believed, his parents would learn, that he had caused his grandmother to cut her hand – began to cry frantically. Jim felt drawn into the center of a dynamo of his own making, and yet he was also on the edge of it, watching as it spun and broke apart. He couldn't swallow the chunk of bread in his mouth. His mother's blood dotted the white tablecloth like wine. Diane, whose face showed her burden winding tight on its spool, picked up the five-year-old and carried him away. His cries receded and then grew louder again from behind a closed door. They sounded piteous and made Jim's body wrench. His father had his hands folded on the table, and he stared at them with an expression of great solemnity.

֍

In June of the third year, Jim, Diane, and the boys moved into tents at the ranch. Jim's parents bought their own house in Spokane. Jim kept on building. The two older boys helped as they could. Diane managed the household, which consisted of two tents pitched under trees, and a table, a rickety shelf, and an old wood-burning cookstove set up on the porch of the small tool shed. She helped with the building, but because she was a musician, there were certain things she shouldn't do. She needed time to practice, too, and to go to rehearsals and concerts with the symphony in the city. For his part, Jim had taken time off from his job to build. Sometimes Diane practiced outside as he worked. The notes were whipped around by the breeze. They seemed to shatter into pieces and to fly at him like a flock of birds bursting out of a tree.

When the work was heavy, friends might come out. By September the log raising was completed, by October the floors were finished, and by November half the roof was up. It snowed. The family spent a great deal of time huddled around the cookstove. The two older boys were happy to go to school where it was warm. By Thanksgiving they had electricity in the house, a door, temporary windows, a temporary wall erected between the half of the house they would live in and the half that would remain uninhabitable through the winter, and two temporary chimneys, one for a potbelly stove in the bedroom and one for the cookstove in the kitchen. They moved in. They shared the bedroom, all five of them. Diane found a corner for practicing. As he worked, Jim liked to feel bass notes throbbing in the wood.

By December they had plumbing: the copper pipe run under the house, up into the water heater and down again, then up into the bathroom. One night early in December, everybody took a bath, each of the boys separately, then all three together. Their laughter rang in the house. For six months they'd bathed in the spring just down the hill. For three months the water heater had stood waiting in its crate, an article of faith. Diane took a bath and emerged with her flushed legs shining behind the slit in her bathrobe. Jim took a bath and lay in it, astounded, then came out looking for Diane. They put the boys to bed, waited for them to go to sleep, and threw a blanket down on the subfloor in the kitchen and made love. Afterward, Diane sat up and leaned toward Jim, grasping his leg. Her hair was disheveled. Her eyes gleamed. She said, "It's okay for you to be a mountain man, so long as you come out of your cave once in a while."

Several nights later a hard north wind blew down the chimney to the potbelly stove in the bedroom and the house filled with smoke. They had to open the door to the cold. Jim went out to fix the chimney. It was dark and the wind bit through his coat. He stood on a twenty-foot ladder with a flashlight in his mouth while Diane steadied the pipes from inside. He had to rejoin the sections of pipe and secure the whole with wires fastened to the roof. He couldn't work with gloves on, but with them off his fingers went numb. The flashlight stuck to his lips. Every few minutes he climbed down the ladder, ran back into the house, and stood before the working cookstove with his hands out.

Diane stood on a chair in order to hold up the pipe. Jim went out and came back repeatedly. His fingers became numb more quickly with each trip. Standing at the cookstove, he saw that Diane had the pipe balanced on her shoulder. She'd put on a tattered coat over her blue nightgown and had her hands in the pockets. Her mind had gone off somewhere else. She was dreaming. The soot that masked her face made her look like a ceremonial creature. She turned her eyes to him. Provoked by her calm, he swore at her. Her eyes suddenly narrowed, and she said, "Not me. It's not me."

"Then what?" he said.

"Right now, it's you."

He went out and stayed until he had the chimney reassembled, then moved around the snow-covered roof to secure the wires. He lay flat and moved with great caution to keep from plummeting off. He slipped once but caught himself by grabbing hold of a lath with his fingertips. He discovered himself laughing. He felt himself surrounded by his own crazy, scared laughter. Alarmed, he stopped laughing, pulled the wires taut, tacked them down, and stayed for a moment straddling the ridge, staring at the night, listening to the vibration of the metal chimney and the wind singing in the wires.

Diane had started a fire in the potbelly stove, and they sat down on the floor in front of it. The fire was hot, but their legs were cold. They'd only just begun to apply insulation in the house. Jim's fingers were white. When he had first come in and touched the wall with one hand, he found the hand dead as a block of wood. He rubbed his hands together under a stream of cool water. Now, he squeezed them under his armpits and bent double with pain as the blood filled his fingers. He thought about the water trench that had to be covered before the line froze and the vulnerability of the copper lines in the house. Diane touched his back under his shirt. As he bent and unbent his fingers, he apologized for swearing.

"It's hard," Diane said. They often said this to one another. To say it was to speak the truth, and so it was a ritual form of reassurance. "But please don't take it out on me. It's not just you struggling here."

"You're right," he said. He looked over at the three boys sleeping side by side on a double mattress on the floor under layers of blankets: The oldest was now ten, the next was six, and the baby was just over a year. The two older boys slept on the outsides, and the baby, in the middle, snuggled up close to the six-year-old. The six-year-old slept on his side with one arm stretched out, touching the ten-year-old's head. Their faces were filled with the calm of sleep, the tenderness, the perfect innocence of youth. Jim longed for the power to keep them so forever. He looked at Diane. Firelight flickered through the vent and danced on her soot-streaked face. She smelled of carbon. It made her alluring.

He touched her knee. "Why are we doing this?"

She answered more quickly than he had expected. "It's like you're making a monument."

He looked down at the floor, at the plywood, which was already shiny from wear. He reached out and ran his finger along a whorl in the grain. "To what?"

"When you get obsessive, the rest of us are closed out."

"The chimney had to be fixed."

"Yes."

"I have to get jacked up to take care of these things."

"But your energy's too strong. You're rushing at something. It's like you're trying to smother something, not just fix it and go forward."

Exasperated, he said, "Smother what?"

"Look," she said. "I love this place, and the garden we'll have, the fields we're supposed to plant, all of it. I don't mind the work, and even trying to bring your parents in was fine, but they're not my parents."

He thought about her parents, who were different from his and maybe wiser in their refusal to compromise their separation from their children. It galled him to think that. He said, "It's the ideas."

"What ideas?"

"Like that. Providing for the old instead of having to send them off. Raising our kids with their grandparents around. That's why."

"It didn't work."

"But the idea was worth trying."

"All right. I supported it. I liked your parents."

"Also, raising the kids in a place where they'll be in touch with wild things, building our own house, and not going into debt to do it." He could have gone on. He had in his mind a litany of objectives they had dreamed of fulfilling.

"We're not hippies."

"Maybe not, but they had some good ideas. Ideas can change the world."

"Not if they don't fit the world. If something doesn't fit, it's destructive." Diane paused, and then asked, "Is it guilt?"

Startled, he said, "Guilt?"

Diane didn't respond but leaned up against him and grasped his arm. Though they were arguing, he felt comforted by her touch, even aroused. He stared at the stove, remembering when they'd "picked rocks" from a field the Holisters planned to seed to hay the following spring. That was September. The weeds had crackled underfoot because of the long, dry spell that had begun back in August. All of them were there. Judy drove a wheel tractor with a loading bucket. She kept the bucket poised so that Lem, Jim, and the two older boys could toss rocks into it. Diane drove a one-ton flatbed, and she had the baby in the cab with her.

Each time Judy dumped a load into the truck, a thin cloud of dust lifted into the air. A cocoon of dust followed the tractor. It rose in tiny puffs from the footfalls of the men and boys.

When the truck had a load, the boys jumped into the back and Diane drove out of the field, down the gravel road, and along the lane to the house. Dust trailed the truck and hung above the road. Diane and the boys would unload above the house, where Jim planned to build a riprap reinforcement to an embankment. It was necessary to do this to keep the bank from washing out in the springtime. Lem and Judy wanted to get the rocks out of the field to avoid damaging their swather. In each case – Jim had thought – that present action was directed against trouble several seasons distant. It had pleased him to realize that. Even now, it made him feel better to think of it – that one good thing done.

They had established a pace in the field. The truck came and went and returned and waited for its load. The boys jumped out and rejoined Lem and Jim. The tractor followed the men, who sought out the rocks, the basalt, the granite. It was hot, dusty, pleasurable work in the blazing sun. Lem and Jim fell in and out of conversation. Lem talked about Vietnam. He said he could still see the jungle beneath the helicopter, the charred sectors like scars, and the green again, rushing by. There was no green in the world like it. The actual air seemed green. But the veins of the jungle ran with death.

Jim had asked how he felt about that, living through the death. "You mean guilt?" Lem said. Jim hadn't meant that at all, but Lem went on and said that the soldiers who never saw action felt guilt, the ones who went to Germany or who came near but were spared from fighting for one reason or another. They felt guiltier than the ones who did the killing – for what they'd narrowly escaped, for what happened to the others. "I was a helicopter gunner, for God's sake," Lem said.

Jim stood there, cradling a rock against his belly. He had never before considered guilt in quite this way – that cleansing might come from entering the demon's bowels. He felt foolish.

"What about you?" Lem asked.

"I guess I was a protestor."

"Of course," Lem said. He grinned. "A lot of us were torn between wanting to waste you guys and wishing you'd get on with it and shorten up our calendars."

Jim looked down at his boots, which were coated with dust. The cuffs of his jeans were brown. Behind them, the tractor's engine rumbled. The flatbed came up the road. The two boys clung to the rack behind the cab. Jim looked back at Lem. "Some protestors were antisoldier," he said. "I wasn't. That was a mind-fuck."

"Right," Lem said. He picked a weed and stuck the stem between his teeth. "We got burned. But you sure can't feel guilty for wasting somebody who'd waste you the first chance they got. Most everything was elusive there, but that one thing was not."

"Yes," Jim said, meaning to acknowledge that he heard. "I spent time in jail." He wanted to say that he hadn't had to do that, that it was his choice, that he'd had a child and so was exempt, practically speaking, that he was Canadian by birth, that he could have returned to Canada any time he wanted to, that he'd almost enlisted anyway, that he supposed he felt some guilt over the greater suffering of others, but that he still believed what he'd done was right. Between himself and Lem there were boundaries and, at times, an edginess, so he didn't say any of that.

The truck pulled up. The boys jumped out and walked toward the men. When Jim threw his rock in the loader, the steel clanged. He looked over at the baby, whose mouth and chin were covered with dirt that had stuck to the juice he'd been drinking. The baby clutched the edge of the partially rolled-up truck window, bounced ecstatically up and down, and screeched at his father. "I guess we had a few things in common with the protestors, though," Lem said, grinning again. "Jimi Hendrix and the hash pipe." Jim grunted. They went on, picking rocks and tossing them into the bucket. Over toward his place, Jim could see the pine trees that encircled the hole where the tractor had almost sunk. The trees raked the sky. Heat waves pulsed above the pale earth. Dry weeds tufted the roadsides. Everything was absolutely still. There was not a breath of wind, not a drop of moisture. The dust went up and slowly came straight down.

Here in the house, in the cold, Diane said, "Forget I said that. Fuck guilt."

"Okay," Jim said.

The stove ticked as it cooled. He swung around to his knees, pulled the stove door open, put in a chunk of wood, and shut the door. The stove sucked air. The ticking accelerated as the metal expanded with renewed heat. He sat back down and rested his hand on his oldest boy's foot. Diane put her hand on Jim's thigh. They were all touching each other, Diane and himself, the oldest boy, snuggled up baby, and the six-year-old. They were silent, being that way in a chain. Finally, Jim said, "I hope the boys remember this well."

Diane sighed. "If we quit, they won't. If we keep on, at least they'll know that such things can be done. But we have to do one thing at a time and then the next."

"If we hadn't started, they wouldn't have to bother with this."

"There'd be something else. It's all right for them to know this." She stopped. Without looking at her, Jim could tell she was going to make a joke. "Maybe we are trying to be like the hippies," she said. "But what I don't understand is where they get off being so damn cheerful all the time."

They went into the bathroom and made love against the wall. He hiked her up and she wrapped her legs around him. They sank to the floor and made love there from various angles of pursuit and repose. It seemed ornate. Diane whispered, "Is this how the hippies do it?"

"This is guilt we're fucking," he said. Diane laughed. He felt the laughing like a shuddering that came all through her body to the point where they were joined.

℘

Because of the push to make the house livable, they'd acquired no store of wood. Daily they dug wood out of the snow, chopped

14

it, and stacked it inside to dry. Jim dozed the piles of dirt into the water trench, finishing one night when the temperature was predicted to fall to fifteen degrees. A few hours later, a switch in the pump house froze. The pump house roof hadn't been insulated yet. The next day, he did that and replaced the switch. The bathtub trap froze every night. He thawed it with candles, a torch, and finally worked out a dangerous system with an electric heater placed inside a makeshift tent. He insulated the floor. He cut the bats and shoved them under the house, crawled after them, dragged them around, and placed them up between the joists. It took a week. At night he coughed up the fiberglass filaments. The bottom of the house was open, and the wind blew through it. A plastic vapor shield had to be stapled over the insulation. The plastic was as cold as metal and the temperature kept dropping – ten degrees, zero, ten below, twenty below.

When Jenny Lanatto called on Christmas Eve they were applying insulation to the ceiling. It was a cathedral ceiling and Jim had laid planks across the beams to sit on while he stapled insulation between rafters. Diane cut the bats and passed them up. The boys slept in a row on the floor. The Christmas tree was alight and the gifts, wrapped. When Diane answered the phone, Jim waited with his legs dangling ten feet above the floor. It was fine up there, heady and warm, for the insulation had begun to take effect, and it was a vantage point from which to survey the work – logs, floor, children, wood stack, and gifts. But then Diane's voice changed tone. She asked if there was anything she could do. She mentioned the Holisters. Jim thought it must have been the adopted baby girl, who had arrived the day before: the baby was unwell or there'd been a legal complication. Diane hung up and said that Lem had been in a wreck. In his excitement over the baby, he'd hardly slept before going to work Friday night, and on his way home, he'd fallen asleep at the wheel. His car had been found in a ditch. His back was broken and he'd nearly frozen to death.

Jim stared blankly at the wall opposite him, then climbed down the ladder. He went over and stood next to Diane at the stove. Jim thought about Lem in the ditch, in his car. He wondered who'd found Lem. He thought about how, in the country, relations between neighbors grew firm when they were good and how they were like the country itself with its points to which one fastened – the house, the barn, the spring, gates to open and close, a neighbor's place, turns in the road. He thought about how the space between points was never truly disconnected, but material in differing ways – joined by earth and air as if by filaments in a web. The space was treacherous if one was hurt and alone or when a cow out in the pasture calved in the breech. The space was made for surprise because of the detail with which one knew it. It allowed people to show their good side and for things like this to hurtle at one out of nowhere.

Diane turned her back to the stove. Jim turned. Their hips and shoulders touched. They didn't talk. Jim remembered the last time he'd seen Lem. It wasn't long after they'd moved in. Lem rode over on his horse. He'd looked the house over and spoken about the logwork in the fashion of the truly polite, of those with the power to reflect upon someone else's life and to speak kindly of it. He sat in the kitchen, drank coffee, admired the notchwork and the two-by-twelve roof joists, and joked about the overkill in the construction. "You expecting an invasion?" he'd asked, poking Jim in the arm.

Jim remembered how he'd stood out in the yard to see Lem off and how Lem had looked going away – the straight figure of the warrior on the black horse, leather chaps, spurs on his boots, brown hat and bright blue shirt. He crossed a meadow of sage and straw-colored bunchgrass and climbed the rise, just black horse, hat, and blue shirt showing, and then just the blue shirt like a flag as he rode into the trees.

ॐ

Jim and Diane were to drive to his parents' place for Christmas. Before they left the next morning, Diane called the Lanattos to check on Lem. He'd improved during the night. At first, it hadn't been thought he would walk again, but now it was thought that he would. He might be ready for visitors tomorrow. Tomorrow then, Jim decided, he would go to see Lem. The boys were waiting outside, and they cried at their parents to hurry. Their voices sounded thin in the cold air.

They headed for town. Jim's parents had bought an old house on a hill. Two walls of their living room were lined with leaded glass doors. In the glass, the windows, and in the mirror over the mantel, the Christmas tree was reflected, broken up into parts and reflected again and again, scattered across the room. Jim's parents sat on the sofa near the tree, and they could be seen, too, all around the room in the mirror, the windows, the glass. Their images were everywhere, lit by Christmas tree lights. Jim's mother liked light and glass for it to shine through and mirrors to reflect it. She liked to be surrounded by light. They ate nuts and fruit and the pastries Jim's mother prepared every Christmas – coconut drops, chocolate chip cookies, sugar cookies cut into shapes, shortbread, and fruitcake steeped in rum. But they ate in moderation because they'd seen the elaborately laid out table in the dining room, the carrot and celery sticks, pickles, and chutney already set on the linen cloth, and the broccoli and peas in the kitchen, ready to be cooked, and the makings for Yorkshire pudding and gravy, the giblets chopped up and stewed, and they could smell the goose roasting in the oven, the potatoes, and the rich aroma of plum pudding, steaming in a double-boiler.

They exchanged gifts. Jim and Diane sat on the floor and watched the children. Diane was mainly silent. Jim conversed with the old ones about the cold, about the pipes that had burst and flooded the new county courthouse. Talk turned to the ranch, to that cold, those water pipes, and then stopped abruptly. It was the rift between them that blunted exchange when it neared the delicate ground. It seemed that the grandparents still wished to come into the house once it was finished. This was intimated, but just when or how and according to what agreements, remained quite unclear. Jim felt hung between two worlds. In one he was father and husband; in the other, a son. He knew well which one required his first loyalty, but he couldn't extricate himself from the other one. No one ever spoke directly of any of this. Surely, no one spoke of the rift itself – the wound, which was to the belly – but chose to address it by attending the extremities. It was so that Jim's mother had prepared Christmas dinner in all its detail and that Jim, Diane, and the boys were here.

The baby played with a stuffed bear, lay on his back, and held the toy up with his feet. The six-year-old sat in a corner, engrossed by a set of plastic blocks. The ten-year-old had received a brass compass. He read the directions for charting a course then looked up to ask a question, but he didn't ask it, struck perhaps by the heavy silence that had fallen over the adults. His face became somber. The boy looked at his father then at his mother. Jim followed the progression. The boy looked at his grandfather, who was staring at the rug and who, despite his sixty-seven years, was as hale as many men of forty-five. But he had also come to need comforting more than Jim could ever remember his needing it, and yet by his nature and the pride of his profession, he was a hard one to comfort. The boy looked at his grandmother. She had back troubles and had been plagued lately by one minor infirmity after another: Her body seemed to express both her and her husband's trouble, their aging, their sense perhaps of their error in having come out west, and she accepted her husband's comfort so that he might be comforted in giving it. She dwelt on death. She'd become fanatic about her grandchildren's affection, as had he about the ranch, Jim thought – a fanaticism pulled taut over the rips.

Jim's father bent and picked up the directions to the compass from the floor then sat with his elbows on his knees, reading. His mother leaned forward and smiled at her grandson in a way that seemed would break her face. The boy smiled back wanly, holding his compass. It was a crèche.

Shaken by the powerful sense of emotional wreckage, Jim leaned back and stared into a pane of glass that collected the reflection from the mirror on the mantel. He saw all of them there:

the baby, the two boys, the grandfather reading as if to answer the question the boy still hadn't asked, and the grandmother's white face locked in what seemed an aghast expression, and Diane, and himself, a reduced, doubly removed crèche. Everyone was frozen in position – waiting, waiting. . . .

Jim had a glimmer of how his oldest boy saw the people – in stronger, purer outline, and not so cluttered, the old ones a little forbidding in their frailty. He considered that where he saw entanglement the boy saw obscurity. Where he saw the need for comfort, the pride, the dwelling on death, and the quirks of character twisting toward strangeness, the boy saw mystery. He further considered that the boy received all this truly, and yet in his youth, he still had the freedom not to judge it. Jim hung onto his glimmering of the boy's way of seeing and kept staring into the glass, and out of this emerged the small Saskatchewan town in which he'd grown up. It rose slowly in his memory then filled his mind: the cold, the crystalline brightness of ice and snow, the town buried to the eaves in drifts, the tunnel-like pathways shoveled from one place to the next. His body jerked when he remembered the car that was buried in a snow-filled ditch and the frozen body of a townsman that was found inside it during the spring thaw. Then he remembered the graveyard, the half-dozen icy graves pre-dug in the fall against the averages, and his sister's tiny coffin going down to the bottom of one of them, and his father, stoic and formal, a tuft of his hair rising and falling in the breeze.

It seemed to Jim that his father had conducted the funeral as if it were for anyone, not for his own daughter. He remembered his mother's torment, how she clutched her arms together and bent as if she were about to dive into the grave. His father was strong, Jim supposed. In a manner of speaking, his mother was weak. But the rigid strength of his father contained his mother's weakness, and within the weakness of his mother was the love that was not afraid to show itself and so was open to assault. It made the strength of his father possible. In the strength was weakness, and rising from the weakness, the greater strength. Jim remembered being in church the next Sunday and hearing the women's choir singing "Rock of Ages," and how when he had closed his eyes and leaned his head against his mother's shoulder, the voices seemed to be coming like distant laughter from the snow-covered graveyard.

He was transfixed by all he had remembered, and then he felt a need to say something. No one in the room had moved. He wanted to say that it would be all right, to tell himself that, and his sons, his family. He wanted desperately to claim the substance of mystery for everyone, to draw it over the weirdness like a cloak, but he couldn't speak. He had words with which to begin the naming – death, dream, laughter – but he couldn't break the silence.

ॐ

The route back home was Lem Holister's daily route to and from work. The road took them through a small town that had built up between the municipal airport and a Strategic Air Command base. Lem had crashed just beyond the town. It was night, but the town, which did nearly as much business by night as by day, was brightly lit.

The two boys slept in the back seat. The baby slept on Diane's lap. They passed the base, where the atmosphere above was orange colored from the lights, as if with fire. The hangars were dark. In daytime the b-52s cruised over the ranch, tipping ponderously to turn. They drove by a place where the snow in the ditch appeared to have been gouged out by a car, a deepening of shadow in the ditch and bank. Without speaking of it, Jim and Diane had been looking for such a place. When he glanced at her, she looked back with a searching expression.

He tried to tell her about the town in Saskatchewan, how he'd recalled it in his parents' living room, but he stumbled on his words.

"There was a moment there," Diane said, "when you looked like you'd seen a ghost."

"It was what I was remembering."

"And?"

He couldn't go on. He was bewildered by his inability to speak sensibly.

"And your mother," she said. "You scared her, the way you looked. Did you see her face?"

"Yes. She lost a daughter there. My sister. Maybe it's a hole in her life that sucked her in and kept her. I haven't thought of it in years. I remembered it tonight. Maybe it was a ghost."

Diane murmured and then said, "Maybe we both have to give your folks a little more room."

He stared into the rearview mirror at the fire-colored light above the base. "You weren't exactly kicking up your heels."

"I hated it," she said, "and I hated myself for hating it so. Now I feel guilty."

Jim said, "The bad thing about guilt is that it makes you into a stranger to yourself."

They turned onto the gravel road. Diane said, "We have to give them more room. Beginning with the way we think of them."

"You're generous."

"No. It's the only alternative. Maybe it's not as damn complicated as we're making it."

Tomorrow – he reminded himself – he would go see Lem. He didn't want to. Or he did want to. But he didn't want to see Lem broken. They turned onto the gravel road. The way was desolate, the sky black, and the earth white. When they walked in the doorway of their house, the telephone was ringing. It was Jenny Lanatto calling to tell them that Lem was dead. A blood clot, she said.

๙๖

The bathtub drain froze that night. The line into the water heater froze. Jim thawed them out the next day. Nothing had burst. Diane baked bread and took it over to the Holisters.

The next night they had more snow and then cold – twenty-five below – and a wind that tore down power lines. They awoke Tuesday morning to darkness and cold. The fire had burned out. They had no water. With no power the pump had stopped. Jim started both fires in the house. The logs and rafters creaked as they expanded. The baby awoke crying. Diane stood hunched over the stove and cooked eggs.

Jim walked out to check the pump house. The sky was absolutely blue. The snow squeaked under his boots. In the pump house, he crouched and shined the flashlight and ran his fingers along the pipes, seeking ice oozed out of a break, but found none. He walked to the shed, got the Coleman lantern, took it to the pump house, lit it, and closed the door on it, hoping that when the heat thawed the pipes he would still find no breaks. He knew he'd have to crawl under the house to check the pipes. He didn't want to. When he got back to the house, he crawled under, pulled down the insulation, and found what he feared.

There was ice everywhere. The piping was ruptured. He lay back and looked at the bathtub and toilet drains, which dropped through the holes he'd cut in the plywood subfloor. He looked at the plywood itself, nailed to the joists that were attached to the stringers he'd bolted to the lower logs of the house, and at the insulation and the plastic vapor shield he'd carefully pulled taut and stapled all along the bottoms of the joists. Now the bathtub and toilet drains were cracked, the vapor shield bulged with ice and had torn loose, and he could see that the plywood had buckled under the toilet. Ice was packed against the joists and piled up like stalagmites on the ground. It was a cave of ice. It was cold. He felt helpless. His toes and fingers were going numb.

He crawled out, went inside, found the bottle of whiskey, and took a belt.

"It's that bad?" Diane said.

"The hell with it."

"No," she said.

"The hell with the whole damn thing."

"No," she said. "Eat your eggs." She handed him his eggs. He turned his back on her. The boys were in the other room by the potbelly stove, keeping warm, eating eggs, and keeping their distance. "So, what is it?" she asked.

"The bathroom's wrecked."

"So?"

"So!" he said, turning to face her. "I mean wrecked. Destroyed." Wildness thrashed inside him.

"And?"

"And? What do you mean, 'And'!"

"And what else?"

"What else, the hell."

"So what is it with you about Lem?"

Angry, he couldn't respond to that.

"Listen," Diane said. "What happened is awful, but it's got nothing to do with the bathroom. There's no connection except the cold." The way she held the iron frying pan with both hands looked menacing. "We're lucky," she said. She looked like she was about to cry.

He didn't speak.

"Lem lived up the road," she said. "Not here. We're lucky, do you hear? Look at us."

He moved away toward a window. Behind him the frying pan clattered violently against the stove. He stood, squinting out at the blinding world. The earth was white. The grass, weeds, and trees were encased in ice. Flakes of ice floated in the air. He thought of the day in the hay field, so unlike this day. Lem had gone on to say that sometimes when he fired on the enemy, the figures disappeared. "Just popped out of there," Lem had said, "like they were puppets." That was the worst part, he'd said – not the actual slaughter, not even the wrecked bodies of his own buddies, but the enemy that vanished, whose invisibility he sometimes kept on strafing, the deaths he did not witness, the deaths that may or may not have occurred, the death that was everywhere. "That's what I mean by elusive," he'd said. "Being there, you had to join the dead."

In his desolation at this moment, Jim took that to mean the death that was always near, the inescapable end of everything. He turned back to Diane and said, "I'm sorry. I can't adjust so quickly."

"Adjust! My God, we chose to chase ourselves out here half-cocked," she said. "But that's okay. I can live with not being ready, just so long as we see that taking care of these things, all these daily things as they occur, is the only path."

He took a deep breath then let it out. "All right."

Diane picked up the frying pan and delicately set it down again. "What happened to all the good reasons for being here?"

"They keep going into hiding."

She gazed at him and then walked into the other room to check on the boys. Jim moved to the stove and ate his egg. He thought about the Holisters, of Lem's cows, of the lack of power, and the automatic waterers in their barn, of the electric milkers. He considered that he should go over there despite their assurances that they could manage – because they had seven grown children, some of whom had wives and husbands, all of whom would come out for the funeral. He decided that he would drive over.

When Diane returned he told her so.

"Yes," she said. "And I'm sorry. I'm upset about the bathroom, too. Truly, I am."

"No," he said. "That's fine."

"It's good to check on them."

"Look," he said. "Lem and Judy were very different from us, but I liked him. He was wise in his way."

"All right."

"Now he's dead."

"Yes," Diane said.

"He was in the clear. Now he's dead for God's sake. Just snipped off."

Diane reached up and held his face between her hands. "Yes, awful."

He went. The Holisters' driveway was crowded with cars. Jim went into the barn and found Bob Holister with two of his sons, his daughter, and Phil Lanatto. They were carrying water from a hydrant that was attached to a line that ran to a diesel-fueled pump at their pond. Jim found the foresight in this impressive. He thought of that – foresight, Lem's foresight, his competence. Lem, Phil Lanatto, and he had planned to go quail hunting the week after Christmas. Now they would not.

He helped carry water. A bucket was filled in one place, emptied in another, and it was good work to calm one down. Then, there wasn't anything to do. Phil and Jim stood and watched the Holisters milk. The Holisters knew what they were about. They moved from one cow to the next and emptied the brimming pails of milk into a large stainless steel canister. Light seeped through the walls of the barn. Lem's Holsteins, standing at the troughs in four rows, were handsome animals, well-built, well-conditioned. The white on their flanks was as white as their milk. They stomped sometimes and chewed, and there was the rhythmic sound of milk squirting into the four metal pails, slower or faster according to how close a cow was to being milked out. It made a counterpoint, the milk hitting the empty pails, and the tone of it deepened as the pails filled, but they didn't all fill at the same pace, so in addition to the intricate rhythm, there was a melody. And there was the sound of metal clinking and the gush when a pail was emptied into the canister and footsteps and the soft words of the three men and one woman, an occasional murmuring. There was that music, the very substance of mystery, a requiem. There was the sweet smell of alfalfa and straw and manure. Vapor rose from the pails, from the breath of the people, and from the ground when a cow urinated. There was an air of peace, of spiritual calm attending the work. After a time Jim and Phil left quietly.

As they walked up the drive to their cars, Jim glanced over at Lem and Judy's place. Just then Judy came up to the front window. Her shape, obscured by the dimness within, moved close to the glass. She didn't seem to notice them. She was cradling a baby, holding it against her shoulder. She seemed to be looking across the fields in the direction of the road that ran toward the trees, as if she expected to see Lem drive up it. Jim glanced at Phil. Phil was looking straight ahead. They walked on in step.

The Chasm

On Wednesday Jim and Diane gathered wood and then drove through the snow to Lem's funeral mass, taking with them a loaf of sweet bread Diane had made for Judy. During the eulogy it struck Jim that dreams and personal acts – Lem and Judy's dairy, his and Diane's ranch – always left wreckage. There was hazard to a good idea and to family. This morning, as she hugged an ice-encrusted hunk of pine, Diane had said that it would honor Lem to use him as a conduit, not as a blockage heavy as stone.

"Exactly," Jim had said. He plunged a steel pry bar through the crust of a snow bank. He hoped to find another log end hidden there. He said, "I've been thinking maybe my problem is that I can't face death." Diane gave him a quizzical look, as if to say, "You and who else?" It made him smile. It made him feel immeasurably grateful to her for her refusal at times to bend. He began to laugh. Diane chuckled and rocked back and forth. Jim wondered – what the hell? He probed with the pry bar, felt resistance, and leaned on the bar. There was a crack. Suddenly, the dark edge of a chunk of pine tipped up through the snow. Jim straightened. "Maybe it was my sister – the death that got slipped to me and the guilt that came with it, being a survivor of something I had little to do with except by being alive. I didn't understand that at the time, not even enough to know how to mourn her. Maybe, in my head I got it mixed up with everything else just like the politicians do, sitting around with their heads up each others' assholes. Lem said that Vietnam was about as real as Disneyland, only Mickey was passing out M-16s instead of balloons."

Now Jim stared at the priest in the pulpit, scarcely hearing the words. He was thinking about how he had opposed the war in Vietnam and yet not his comrades who suffered in it, and about how that suffering took so long to come home to him, how it would still never be truly his because there was no actual wound, but how he was required to carry what of it he could and not ever to either claim or deny it, only to hold close its pain. It was a contradiction from which there was no escape, like the war itself, which opened a chasm in the nation for the charlatans to enter. It was the same with the fury he felt toward his father for the insult leveled at a five-year-old boy. He must not become a charlatan in his own chasm, must not pit himself against himself, and must not be afraid.

On Thursday it snowed, helping to bring the temperature up to ten below. Winter had scarcely begun. Jim capped off the water line to the house. They would have to use the outdoor stock hydrant until spring. As the baby napped, Diane practiced. The older boys were at school. Jim went out to plow the road with the crawler. He found a Christmas card in the mailbox at the end of the drive. The card had a note from Judy Holister, thanking them for the bread, their help, and their support.

The utter lack of bitterness in the note made him sit for a long time up high on the seat of the crawler. Below, the mailbox door hung open. He stared across the fields, then into the white sky that swirled with flakes. He discovered himself weeping. The singing of women came again just as he had heard it when he was a boy – the sound, eerie and distant and beautiful. The music turned into laughter and back again to music coming out of ice, and then, when he turned a little and looked toward the trees, he saw something in the darkness: the shape of a horse, its hooves kicking shimmers of snow off the bunchgrass, and one gleaming spur, and the bright blue shirt of a rider, flashing in and out of sight behind the black trunks, going southward deeper into the woods.

The Transmission

I WAS TO HAVE slaughtered the wether, the yearling goat, but I didn't mind going next door to the Crofoots'. For one thing, slaughtering the wether was a chore, and not a chore I relished. For another, it was necessary that I learn to go anywhere, anytime, and to take things as they came. This amounted to a moral maxim. Louis Crofoot had asked me to come, said he must have me. Just as I was sharpening the knives, I heard the pounding on the door and then Louis's shout. He opened the door before I had a chance to move and stuck his head in and shouted again. From the kitchen, I saw the brim of his Stetson cocked like the bill of a goose. I didn't mind.

Each thing in its place as each thing occurred: have patience, allow patience the time to do its work so that I might be calm, entire, and wanting nothing. Since I was on the cure, that was the second maxim.

Louis, a trucker, had wanted to trade in his old International Loadstar tractor on a new one. He said the time spent repairing the old tractor, bought used, was holding him back. He said he wanted to expand his route, but Bird, his wife, said he just wanted the flash. They had fought last night and drawn this line: Louis would pull the blown transmission and trade it, work off his overhead on the old truck, take on a partner to drive it, then buy the new truck – tractor and trailer. It was a risk either way; I could see that. I'd been in the same position with more than one old car – whether to junk it or sink money into it – but Bird and Louis were dealing in thousands, with their livelihood, not with a few hundred dollars. "She don't know it yet," Louis said to me as we walked in the thin rain from my place to his toward the tractor, transmission, and the old man, his father, "but after this you can be damn sure I'm moving my route to Montana for a while."

Bird would know it, I figured. I'd have bet that now she would forget the whole thing – old tractor, transmission, and all – and let Louis trade them deep into hock if she could find a way that

29

would make Louis come back as far her direction as she went his. Failing that, though, she would settle for the truck in her name and a hired man to drive it for her. When pushed, they grew mulish, the both of them.

The child, a four-year-old girl, was too young to understand all this but old enough to know full well by feel when a home has been brutalized. Early in the morning, in the dark, the shouting had begun, the stomping through rooms and in and out the front door. Louis drove the truck up and down the hill, gears clashing like a tin roof blown apart, the tremor of the engine enough to shake a picture off a wall. When he switched it off, the shouting resumed, Louis from the truck across the road, and Bird from the front door of the house. Louis stalked the house. The two silhouettes postured and arms broke loose to punctuate the curses. Back inside, still shouting, they hurled appliances, or furniture, or themselves, or something big enough to resound when it hit the walls. I sat on my bed, peering out the window. Through the lilac bushes, I saw the child's face, pale and lantern shaped in the corner of her bedroom window, looking out of the action in my direction.

And now in daylight, the tractor was in the garage, the cab jacked up, tipped forward, and bulging from the doorway like a bull squeezed into a dog house. The child's folks, blunted and remote and relentless, had crawled back into themselves. The child stood under the eave against the screen door, pulling the screen taut with the weight of her body. Her grandfather was outside, waiting, and her father was outside, too, walking forward with me, but her mother was inside, and the child kept sentry on the margin. She was motionless: her hands quiet at her sides, her skirt limp above her dirty knees, her flat, dark hair clinging to her head, her round face compact, her eyes the bright covert eyes of a small furry beast scrutinizing our approach.

The old man, I would learn, would rather be home at his job outside Omak than here, moving a thousand-pound transmission. At home he was a ditch-walker, a waterer of orchards; here he had put up his peace of mind to stand against his son's fury.

The Transmission

The old man wore a bowler hat, a ragged slicker, and under that a threadbare suit. He looked like an augur with his feet crossed and one arm outstretched, leaning, gripping the pry bar, which was driven into the ground and wedged against the transmission. He held the transmission steady on two ten-by-two planks that spanned the ground and the bed of a pickup truck. It was a piece of iron, all right, the transmission. Louis and the old man had eviscerated it from the Loadstar, drawn it down on hydraulic jacks, and winched it out from under the tractor to the pickup. The planks sagged under the weight. When we stopped, the old man smiled, making the dark furrows around his mouth shine.

"You can't know Louie too good if he got you out for this," he said, touching the brim of his hat.

At my side Louis grunted.

I saw what I was needed for. I picked up a six-foot four-by-four and wedged it under the transmission on the side opposite the old man. Louis vaulted into the bed of the pickup and cranked the hand winch. Immediately, at the first upward shift of the transmission, the ten-by-two plank on my side cracked through the center, and then the winch jammed, the transmission stopped dead, and my plank cracked again. I felt weight come down on my four-by-four, felt that it could be awesome, beyond my powers. My scalp prickled.

"It's giving!" I said.

Louis cursed and jumped out of the pickup and leaned into the four-by-four with me. Slowly, we lifted my side of the transmission clear of the spoiled plank, lifted it up to where it stood poised with most of the weight on the good plank, on the old man's side. The old man accepted the weight and balanced it with the pry bar, which he had braced against his shoulder. My four-by-four went light. Louis let loose of it and walked out of sight behind the garage in search of a sound plank.

The old man's strength – despite being a small man probably pushing seventy – made me rue what I expected to lack at his age. His legs, though, had begun to tremble. "Louis!" he called. The transmission listed toward him. His arms shook, as did his head.

I was frozen in place. Quickly he hopped, resetting his feet. I saw the transmission drop quite definitely, but he caught it and leaned, his body the other side of an isosceles to the bar, and he shoved weight back onto my four-by-four. The plank on my side cracked again, the transmission wobbled, and my breath caught in my throat. The plank held. The old man gave me a toothy grin and raised his eyebrows, then called out, his voice thick, "Goddamn it, Louie!"

He was echoed from within the house by Bird: "Louis!"

Louis didn't respond. I bent and unbent my knees and carefully shifted position so the four-by-four wouldn't dig into my shoulder. The old man stared over my head at the sky, his expression uneasy and rigid and patient and feral. Between us was the transmission, balanced, a pig of a load. I rested my cheek against the four-by-four and looked past the old man, down into the shallow valley, through the gray, the stinted rain.

It was August, a rare time of year for rain here. Trails of mist hung about the dun-colored hills and pine stands. The Crofoots and I, the Parslows from Oklahoma, and two fatherless welfare families who lived in Parslow's duplex rental had a perspective on the small town that lay below, which was veiled and opaque looking. The homes and establishments seemed like dislodged vertebrae at the neck of the valley. We lived on the rise to the east. The town was an early settlement in eastern Washington. Before that, as is the way, it was a native encampment, then in 1858 the site of the last in a hundred-mile procession of battles between the army and allied tribes. The Indians, outmanned and outarmed, were pushed onto the plain and picked off; even the prisoners shot upon the command of Colonel George Wright. Later, Wright, who distilled the force of post-Civil War fury into a personal mission – brutal and fraught with religiosity – saw that the truce bearers were summarily hung. Nez Percés had fought on both sides of the battle as army scouts and as "belligerents." My neighbors, the Crofoots, as transplanted Nez Percés, were now the only Indian residents of the town, and I believed that they were somehow a living vestige of the history. In so believing, I inclined to make more and less of them than they were.

The Transmission

There was a crash from behind the garage – planks, probably, jerked from a heap of scrap. The old man blinked as if awakened from sleep.

In fact, the Crofoots lived here because Interstate 90 passed just north of us, reaching east and west and giving Louis direct access to his routes. The Interstate was not visible where we lived, but from it came the incessant hum of trucks. There is great violence in the freeway's presence: At the nearby turnoff, on one side of chain link are the ruins of half a log building, and on the other side are two decrepit maple trees from the old homestead. Between us and the freeway was a lake, dark as a gland, bounded by a stone ridge, and shrouded in mist. A girl riding a spotted horse bareback galloped up the ridge, bright as if embossed against the mist – mane, tail, hair, yellow jacket flying.

Louis burst from around the side of the garage, carrying a fresh ten-by-two and gulping whiskey from a pint. He wiped his mouth on his sleeve.

"Okay," he said. "Pull that plank out."

I looked at him.

"Goddamn it, Louie," the old man said.

Louis laughed, dropped the plank, and stuffed the bottle into his hip pocket. He crouched, reaching under my four-by-four brace, and yanked on the split plank. It wouldn't budge. Louis came up beside me, and again we tipped the transmission. I looked at the old man with dismay as he edged back, narrowing the angle of his body to the earth. The weight passed entirely away from my four-by-four. Louis let go and vaulted back into the pickup, abandoning the old man and me. Everything rocked when his feet hit the steel – truck, chains, transmission, planks, old man, and my head. Louis set to work on the winch.

The old man's voice came out a croak, "Get that ten-by loose. Now!"

I tugged on the ten-by-two. It wouldn't budge. "Louis," I said. "Hey . . ."

"For Christ's sake, boy, kick it out!" the old man said.

I kicked. I turned away and lifted my leg and kicked the splin-

33

tered plank with my boot heel, shattering the plank. I then
turned back and pulled it free in pieces. I raised the fresh ten-by-
two and tried, and failed, to force it into place.

A wave of helplessness swept over me as I clutched the four-
by-four lever. I was moving, not stopped, turning around and
moving fast. My eyes took in everything: the landform and Louis
with his back to us, hunched and furious over the jammed winch
like a spider venomizing a kill. The child was inside now but still
at the door, a great moth denting the screen outward. Across
from me, the old man's body was braced beneath the flaps of his
slicker, and his face, under the water-beaded bowler hat, lost
color from the strain. The tab collar of his pinstriped shirt was
buttoned up snug. Once, Louis had proudly told me that his father was a direct, first-generation descendent from the Hundred
Fifty, the remnant of the five-month war of 1877 who were captured and sent to Fort Leavenworth, then, sick and dying, sent on
to Indian Territory, and then shipped back west again, but along
with the Nez Percé chief, Joseph, designated as "hostiles," kept
separate from the rest of their tribe in Lapwai, Idaho, and exiled
to Nespelem in Washington. The old man was certainly not
old enough to have witnessed Joseph's death in 1904, but well old
enough to know what was past and what was present. The hat
and the band of his collar around his neck under the harrowed,
solemn face made him look preposterously like a preacher.

To force the plank under the transmission, I struck it repeatedly with the butt of the four-by-four, filling my fingers with
splinters. My hands stung with each blow. The plank didn't
move. I went down on my knees and peered, cold with fear, feeling the ponderousness of the iron that hung over my head. The
plank was caught, the water-saturated wood indented and hung
on a housing bolt.

"I need another quarter-inch," I said, standing up. I looked at
Louis, but already the old man was inching back, taking more
weight, allowing the transmission to tip farther toward him.
"Jesus!" I said. "Louis. Bird!"

The old man was set and quivering against the load, tapping

his resistance and remaining strength. From the expression of terrific frailty on his face – the hard, ashen, angular pitch of skin on bone – and his stupefied eyes, it seemed just a narrow line of pure will was supporting him. I hoped to God that he was ready to fall clear should he buckle under the weight. Incredibly, out of the corner of my eye, I saw the girl on the spotted horse galloping crazily up the ridge again, or her reflection, galloping through the waters of the lake.

The old man looked straight at me. "Goddamn it, Louie, get that thing working. Goddamn it, don't get your hand crushed." He was panting. I was still hefting the four-by-four. He made no sense, talking to me and cursing Louis. "Goddamn it, Louie," he said, "if this thing gives . . ."

Louis jerked the winch lever, tugged on the chain, and looked up. His eyebrows wrenched, crabbing his round face under the Stetson brim. "Huh?"

"Now!" the old man barked. "Knock that plank in."

I was already swinging. I rammed the plank with the four-by-four and the plank slapped to, flush with the other plank. "Done," I said, but I looked up quickly at a cry from Bird. The old man's knees quivered, and his hands, gripping the bar, were colorless, and the whites of his eyes were lunuled beneath the irises. I jumped around and jammed the four-by-four under the transmission next to the old man's bar and leaned. Bird was there, too. Together, Bird and the old man and I eased the transmission back past the fulcrum point until it became light, having dropped onto the fresh plank where it rolled and teetered on both planks, which creaked but held. The transmission came to rest, safe.

"Take it," the old man said. "Support those planks."

When the old man withdrew his bar, I grunted and my body rocked forward. The old man grinned. Louis looked down and laughed. Bird backed toward the house, her elbows out like wings. The edges of the four-by-four dug into my hands. The old man laid the hauling chain straight up the planks into the pickup bed with the air of one to whom nothing is extraordinary. He picked up his bar and balanced the transmission opposite me. Under the eave of the house, Bird cradled the little girl's head with one hand, holding the child's face flat against her mother's thigh. The child's eyes were dull while Bird's eyes, sharp in her angular face, winnowed us.

"Louie," the old man said.

"Okay," Louis said. "It's clear."

"Easy."

Louis wound the chains taut. The winch was suspended crotch-high in the center of the bed, one length of chain to the transmission, and two to short pipes dropped into the post slots up next to the pickup cab. Louis cranked, and as each link was swallowed, the winch jumped and the chains vibrated. When Louis increased his speed, one of the pipes juggled upward in the slot.

"Louie, goddamn it, slow down!" the old man cried.

Louis shoved the pipe deeper into the slot and cranked faster than before, standing spread eagle, rain dripping from his hat brim, sweat from his chin. The transmission slid past the edge of the plank on my side, then a split jumped the length of my plank. It was too late to do anything. Louis wound like a wild man. He got the transmission to the lip of the pickup where it hung up, the lower end lifting from the planks and the ends of the planks dancing crazily in mid-air.

"Louie!"

"It'll jump!"

Bird was back out on the lawn: "Louis, stop it!"

The old man and I pried desperately under the base of the transmission, but from the ends of our levers for fear of the transmission breaking loose entirely. Abruptly, the transmission bounced into the bed. The pickup sagged. Louis whooped and kept cranking, hauling the transmission into the center of the bed. I stood up straight, my shoulders tingling. The old man let the pry bar drop and leaned against the fender, bowing.

Louis leaped to the ground and moved for the garage. He sidestepped when he came up to Bird, who raised her hands and stepped back, startled. They rebounded, as if their anger made the space between them pneumatic. Louis's body hung, and then he walked into the garage. Bird eyed his back and walked into the house and slammed the door. The little girl moved after her mother but stopped, her hand at the door. It was a moment, a pantomime emblazing a day of fury.

Confused as to whether I should stay or leave, I had stepped up on the tailgate. It was quiet now except for the dripping of water from an eave to a sheet of tin. I stared into the transmission through the inspection hole at the bright, rain-dotted gears. Curious, I put my hand inside to search out the fault. To do so, I had to force my wrist down, and when my fingers hit bottom, pain shot up to my elbow. I jerked my hand back, but my wrist caught. Embarrassed, I looked around.

No one saw. The child squatted against the house under the eave, safe from the rain. She had her knees drawn up to her ears and her eyes were blank. At my side the old man coughed, his head jumping. A ratchet resonated inside the Loadstar's engine compartment. One of Louis's legs stuck out, jerking with each backswing. A trucker since he was eighteen, he had nylon in his knee and a stainless steel patch riveted to his skull and, therefore, a bald spot on the back of his head where the skin from his thigh had been grafted. It itched often, hence his characteristic gesture: two fingers slipped under his hat and a sudden thrash of the elbow. The injury came from a load of logs crashing straight through the cab when he drove into a sand bank. Bird, riding with him, broke her leg in three places. It was before they had married, before Louis switched to hauling grain. On better days than this, I had gone down to the town bar with them and listened as they laughed and contested over weather forecasts, she sounding the string of leg mends, Louis gauging his itch.

❧

An old Impala pulled up in front of the house, and six men and women piled out – Louis's brother Sam, a blonde woman, and the Blues, cousins of Louis. But for the blonde woman, I had seen them all before. They lived nearby in Spokane. The Blues were a heavy people. The women dressed in long skirts, their hair braided, and the men in bright shirts and Levis. They all wore thick silver jewelry and beads. They seemed costumed and aware of the picture they cut. The Blues moved onto the lawn, one of the men carrying a case of beer. The blonde woman hung back, posing in front of the car in her red jumpsuit with one hip hiked up. Sam Crofoot, a tall man, handsome and elegant in matching denims, was a dealer in jewelry, curios, and artifacts, and I'd heard he was a bookie of sorts at the local racetrack. He walked toward the old man and me as I was easing my hand up and down, pulling and twisting it to and fro inside the transmission.

The old man hacked, bent, stood up, hacked again, and spat into the pickup bed. The globe of pink-colored phlegm slid slowly past my toe on the wet sheet metal. "Are you all right?" I asked, stretching for the old man's shoulder. I couldn't reach him.

The old man gripped the ledge of the bed. "Hell yes." His voice was husky. He hacked again and then swallowed hard, his eyes dense with water. Sam, with us now, grasped his father's arm. The old man jerked back out of reach, squinting, nodding rapidly: an old cock. Then he stopped. His eyes widened. As he looked at me, a smile crept to his lips.

"I thought we were going to move that thing at six," Sam said to the old man.

"You know Louie," the old man said. "He won't wait for nothing."

"You and Louie loaded that by yourselves?"

I wondered what the hell he thought I was doing here.

"Me and Louie and Pete, there," the old man said. "Pete's a live one," he added, pointing at my arm. He winked at me.

Sam scrutinized my arm calmly, his lips curling: "Keeping it warm?"

The old man barked. I felt myself flush. I looked down at my hand. It was the thumb bone; I could have pulled it loose if it weren't for the thumb bone.

The Transmission

An iron brace rang when it dropped from the tractor to the concrete. The screen door slapped and Bird came out with a six-pack and a plate of cheese sandwiches and deviled eggs, covered with wax paper. She handed an egg to the little girl. The Blues rambled toward Bird but stopped, perplexed, as she went right by them across the lawn, her anger in her legs now, and her legs like twigs.

The old man peered closely at my arm. "Were you looking for something?" He looked up at my face and giggled.

Bird passed a beer to the old man, then one to me, which I took with my free hand. Sam, she ignored.

"Give the man a sandwich," the old man said, suddenly somber.

Bird held out a sandwich, which I attempted to take between two fingers of the hand that already held the beer. Bird looked down at my arm. At first she smiled, but then the smile dissolved as she looked into my eyes, her eyes aggressive, sexual, hard as hooks, examining the intruder, seeking out the soft spot. I felt exposed and bigger than life up on top of the transmission, a strange out-of-place beast, an ostrich, a gnu.

The old man turned and called, "Louie, come out here."

Louis grunted. His leg was straight out and wagging parallel to the ground as he struggled with a bolt.

"It went in. It won't come out," I explained to Bird. "Maybe some soap . . ."

The old man doffed his hat. "How much for a transmission with a hand in it?"

Sam laughed. Bird tugged on her hair, which was brown at the roots and blackened with cheap dye. I wished she would laugh, too. I found myself gazing at her breasts, apple sized beneath her damp shirt.

There was a sharp crack from within the Loadstar's engine compartment and Louis's leg swung, then the ratchet's ticking resumed.

"Why'd you put it in there?" Bird asked.

"I don't know. I wanted to feel what was wrong, maybe."

The Transmission

The old man cocked his head and looked at me with mock gravity from the corners of his eyes. His humor was infectious, and I chuckled at my own stupidity but stopped because of Bird's baleful stare. I wished she would smile.

Louis scrambled out from under the tractor and drank from the pint as he carried the braces over to the pickup. The old man, antic, gestured at me and began to speak, but he was cut short when Louis dropped the braces into the bed. Louis greeted his brother by heading straight for the blonde woman. "Hey, hey," Louis said. "Hey, Sam, where'd you get the muff?" The blonde hiked herself back further on the fender of the Impala.

"Parslow was here," Bird snapped. It took me aback. "And you're drunk already."

"What?" I said.

"He wants fifty dollars more a month," Bird said. "It's the truck, he says, being parked here." She still looked toward me, not straight at me, but just over my shoulder. These people had a habit of addressing one person while they spoke to another. I saw what she was doing and also the anger against Louis crowding her face. Out of feeling for her, I wished I had a way to mend the rift before it widened into a crevasse, but I had no such power.

Louis swaggered and said something to make the Blues laugh. The blonde sat absolutely still on the fender. Louis clutched her arm, spun on his heel, and shouted, "Hey, hey, Sam! What's this?"

Bird's hair clung to her skull. Keeper of the books and cross-hatched with rancor, she moved into the center of the yard. Ledger sheets, licenses, and permits bought, deliveries made and taken, machines and bills, her life was enclosed in a rolltop desk that she said her grandmother had left her: tires, an axle, the drive shaft, next the transmission blown on the used truck and costing an even dollar a pound, and her husband, dispenser of goods, her medium of exchange, turned against her, and she, the wife now to what another wife had been to him five years before. She knew that Louis most likely had yet another medium of exchange in a kitchen somewhere else off the highway.

For distraction the Blues turned back upon me. They pressed

in close, their presence lugubrious. I could feel their breath. They pointed at my arm and gently chuckled.

They hovered, Sam and the Blues, and now Louis, too, while the blonde woman stayed where she'd been. The Blues rose and settled like great owls – feet up on the tailgate, elbows on the rail of the bed. One of them, Fanny Blue, reached out, grasped my wrist, ran her finger slowly down into the hollow of my palm, and looked at me with large brown eyes. She murmured. I leaned forward, signaling that I hadn't understood. She stepped back, smiling broadly. Her husband laughed and put his arm around her shoulders and handed me a beer. I had two now. The cheese sandwich, soaked with rain, lay beside my swallowed hand.

"Maybe some soap," I repeated. Meant as a joke, it came out nervous sounding, yet the people laughed, except for Bird and the old man, who stood next to each other some fifteen feet away. Bird was steamed. The old man was still and erect, his eyes snapping here and there. The laughter of the others fed upon itself and grew. Even the child laughed shrilly and coldly from her place against the wall of the house.

"And you still owe him for that check you forgot to sign," Bird said.

"Parslow's a vulture," Louis growled.

The people fell silent and edged away, leaving a cavity for Bird and Louis to talk across. The old man walked into the garage, vanishing behind the tractor.

Bird stood square. "You're too drunk to drive this transmission into town."

"Goddamn you, Bird," Louis said, tonguing the egg in his cheek.

"You and me need to talk, Louis."

"Talk to Parslow!"

"That's right!" Bird said. "He's bleeding us."

The old man came out of the garage, his body pitched sideways by the five-gallon oilcan he carried in one hand.

"Sam, we needed you an hour ago, not now." Bird said.

Sam looked over at the old man. The old man held his free

41

hand up, telling Sam to desist. The blonde had moved into the back seat of the Impala and was looking away, down the road to the water. The Blues were motionless. They held their beer cans before them and watched Bird. There was solidity, tolerance, and grave indifference in their manner.

Bird rocked back on her heels and gazed at the sky. Raindrops spattered against her face. "Louis, Louis, you've overdrawn the bank." It was plaintive, almost a moan.

"The bank can fuck," Louis snarled. "It's got its head up its ass." He walked to the tractor in the garage. Bird glared after him.

The old man stepped up on the tailgate and poured a quantity of oil through the inspection hole. The oil soaked my shirtsleeve and spilled over one pant leg. "Try it," the old man said gently.

I twisted my arm and my hand slid free. I held it in my other hand like a dead mouse, oil soaked, bleeding at the fingertips, which bristled with steel shavings. I wiped the hand on my trousers and laid it down on my knee and stared at it. "Thank you," I said.

"You can fuck!" Louis said. He was leaning against the tractor, his hands in his pockets.

Bird whirled and went into the house, slamming the screen again. The child stared after her. For a moment it was silent, then a pop-top sprang, then another. The people began to move about. Louis stepped out next to Sam. He was grinning and talking in a low voice while Sam, six inches the taller, stared expressionlessly over his brother's head.

I liked Louis. God knows, I liked him by instinct, but he didn't know when to leave a thing alone. I slid off the transmission and walked the hundred yards up to my place, picking gingerly at the needles in my fingertips. I looked back once and saw Bird staring at me from the window behind the lilac bush.

෴

It was too late to slaughter. Out back in the shed, the air smelled of ammonia so I pitched out the straw bedding for compost. I had a heap of it just outside the doorway, and the nanny goat stood on it with her neck craned over the young doe. All four bulbous eyes peered at me as I worked. The wether, George – castrated and kept for meat – was in the shed worrying me. The rain hissed on the tin roof. Gloved, I worked steadily until I had a sweat. I used a rake and a scoop shovel to loosen layers, then the fork to pitch, grunting softly with the strokes. There was six months' worth of straw, the fresh strewn over the old for as long as I'd lived here, a short archaeology. At the bottom the straw was saturated with seepage and urine, packed in thin sheets, and heavy with rot. Once the floor was scraped clean, I drew down a bale from the loft and spread fresh straw over the boards, in all corners, and under the trough where George would sleep his last. I filled the trough with chow and the bucket with water, then stepped through the doorway and hunkered against the back wall of the shed for a smoke. I inhaled deeply in an attempt to fight off my other need.

I removed the glove from my right hand and picked at the remaining steel slivers, but they were hopelessly embedded. Beyond the fence line at the far end of the pasture was a stand of pines. Half were snags, hampered by better than fifty of Parslow's wrecked cars and scabs of volcanic rock. It had been a strange year. There were still wild flowers out there in snatches, shots of color against the wet gray and green and rusted steel – daisy, dandelion, mullein, lupine, grass widow. The clouds were separating. Shafts of light slapped down. The setting sun was a fiery yolk in the west. Parslow, dressed in loose overalls and a skullcap, crawled through the window of a wheel-less Edsel, in search of a part, I figured – door lap, knob or pinion, hex screw – to help string together the matching Edsel he had out front. Parslow vanished. The doe cavorted in the pen while the nanny stretched over the fence for a pine bough, which she had already nibbled just beyond reach. Pine needles, or the turpentine in them, can be lethal to unborn kids; but it hadn't been so this time.

The wether nuzzled at my back. I jerked him out and pushed him away. I wanted nothing to do with him. He came back, personable and undaunted, innocent of my fear of his innocence.

Parslow appeared suddenly in the trunk of the Edsel, standing with his overalls folded down as he pissed.

I slipped away and discovered Bird in my kitchen, leaning against the electric stove. "I want to borrow your pickup," she said. "I want to borrow it tonight."

I didn't know what to say.

"I'm moving out. That's why." She teetered on her toes. "I'm through. I've had enough. Five years and I've given all I've got to give."

"You need a woman to talk to," I said lamely.

"Talk to!"

"To confide in," I said. "I'm no good for that."

"Confide?" Bird said. "What's that? I need a truck." She glared at me. Then her eyes softened, or the skin around them softened, covering more of the white as she kept looking at me. It made me feel awkward. She gripped her belt buckle with one hand, a crab at the center, and looked down.

"I can lend you," I said softly, "but I'm not helping any woman move out of anybody's house."

"I'm not asking you to."

She left with my keys. I washed my hands, nursing the cut fingertips. I fried up eggs and trout and wolfed the food down standing. I went into the living room, which was barren of furniture except for the piano and potbelly stove and mattress. It was not cold enough to warrant a fire. The piano was here when I moved in – the bench, filled with old pop tunes. I had played while I was growing up and now had taken on the instrument again to fill the evening hours. I sat down and fumbled with chords, but I knew what was coming. I hated what was coming. But the day had weakened my will and given me cause, I imagined, for the veil of white.

I tried to play the piano with the fingers of my right hand cocked sideways to the keys. It was no good. I stopped, stood, let down the keyboard cover, opened up the bench, and took out the little powder I had saved, not for taking, but as a temptation to be denied. I poured out a small heap onto the piano case, dipped a finger, and rubbed my gums. The numbing brought back the sense of my old self before I'd moved here to collect my wits – a dog lost in a hiatus, nursing a cyst in the weeds at the side of the road. I'd been a junior officer in the Navy after getting my university degree. A relationship had gone bad. Each of my parents died while I was in the service, one after another . . . too young. They were too young for that. I wanted to go back to the university. The life I'd slipped into wasn't the way my life was supposed to be. Nothing was lining up. Everything seemed awry and jagged. I needed a future. I had to be clean.

But now that my mouth was medicated, my throat went dry with anticipation. It had been two months. "It doesn't matter now," I told myself. Just this once. I split the heap in two and snorted it. I'd never believed cocaine was addictive. It was the sense of determinism that was so hard to give up. The night turned to water. A freight train zoomed through the valley. Outside the window at my right, there were muffled shouts, a scoop of laughter over at the Crofoots. If I had looked, I could have seen them – the odd body passing under the storm light, in and out, like geese on a pond. I'd seen them thus before. A halo seeped through my head. I heard the old man's loaded pickup depart, the Blues' Impala, then, after a time, my own pickup passing down the drive. I stripped, lay down, slept, and dreamed of a hundred albinos risen from the dead, dressed in sheets and busy mixing concrete in the snow. I was awakened by the sense of a shape like a fetus hung up in a womb, denser than the dark.

"I brought your keys back."

"All right," I mumbled. My eyes were filled with seeds. I looked at the woman poised on her knees, her straight shoulders, and the axe of hair outlined in the moonlight. She didn't move. Like an insect, she was watching me without breath. I shook my head. "All right."

"I took the color TV. I'm packed up and moved out, and I'm going to claim the truck." She paused. "I knew it was going to happen."

I struggled to prop myself up and felt along the floor for my cigarettes.

"And I took the color TV," she said.

45

"You said that."

"I took it."

I held the pack out toward her. "Cigarette?"

She accepted one and smoked it sitting up. I smoked on my back, letting the cloud settle in my lungs. The little girl was on the floor beside her, asleep in a blanket. Bird talked: She told me how she and Louis had argued over the transmission, how Louis had two more children by another wife, how he'd done the same thing to them as he was doing to her daughter, how he didn't love her, how he couldn't stay put, how he was a damn drunken Indian.

I listened. What could I say? She was half Nez Percé, she'd informed me before with great pride.

She told me how she'd called the old man to come down with his pickup from Omak to haul the old transmission into Spokane and the new one back out. The old man had asked about Louis's pickup, but like the one-man helicopter out back and the shelves in the basement, the old Ford pickup, bought for just that purpose – hauling parts – was a project begun and abandoned by Louis. I knew the pickup. It sat out in the field across from the house with a dead battery, a broken starter, and two flat tires. The hood was askew on broken hinges.

"How come you didn't borrow my pickup?" I asked her.

"Family."

I raised my head and looked at her.

"He's not family, now."

I put my head back down and closed my eyes. She leaned toward me when I touched her leg with my hand. Her words filled the room: She told me how the old man had said he had work in Omak, how it was a 200-mile drive, how he'd asked about the Blues and Sam helping, how the old man, knowing what she wanted, had told her that he couldn't do a thing with any of his boys. She'd called the old man in the first place, she said, not for the pickup, not to help move the transmission, but because it was a step to be taken, because the old man was more family to her than her husband, because she wanted to have him here with her. "I love that old guy," she said. She said she wished she'd never

46

called him because all of it had come out wrong, because she was ashamed for the old man's shame and for the piece she'd taken out of him and out of Louis, because it had been she who'd done the taking. When she stopped talking, the space of the room swelled around us.

"I could have called him after Louis and I were through with it," Bird added. Her voice broke and her head dropped.

I rolled to my side. "Hey," I said, touching her hand.

She curled up beside me and wept into my neck. She smelled like work and axle grease. She was all knees and elbows, her hands the hands of a chemist. Her sweater chafed my chest. I grasped the back of her neck and gazed at the blank wall with great, sudden confusion. She felt like the germ to my plague of white arms and legs. She stopped weeping and pressed her chin against my shoulder. Her hair fell across my face. My moral doubt, my knowledge of how I was prone to trouble, and yet my inability to determine the right action, all left me locked in my lonesomeness. She shifted her weight and stretched out, her body blooming against mine and mine rising upon her.

Afterward she left with the child by the back door. I listened to her footsteps. When I heard them stop, I kicked free of the knotted sheet, sitting up and peering through the window at her. She stood at the mouth of my driveway with the child in her arms. She stared at her husband's grain trailer out in the field, still loaded with wheat. The sky had cleared. The metal ribbing on the side of the long box and the taut rubber lacing that secured the canvas cover stood out in the moonlight. Bird's head was thrown slightly back – a counterweight to the little girl – her back arched, her left leg cocked, standing as if in appalled prayer for what would not be. I lay back and looked at the ceiling, at the dark. The room began to sway gently like a boat on a pond.

෯෧

Her car was gone when I checked the window early in the morning, but the old man's pickup with its skirt of planks was back, as were Sam's Impala and a Lincoln Continental that I hadn't seen before. The yard was full again, but of men only. The two Blues hung over the chains that dragged the new implement-orange transmission. The winch was reversed, hooked up now to the chassis of the Loadstar. Louis was out of sight, under the cab cranking. Sam followed the transmission at a snail's pace. The old man sat up on the lip of the pickup bed, against the cab window. He looked serene in his suit and bowler hat and faintly amused, a pipe between his teeth. It was a backward cameo of where I had been yesterday. The day was bright.

My hand was swollen, the fingertips red and raw to the touch. My arm ached from favoring it in sleep and my head was thick. I went into the kitchen and finished sharpening the knives, stroking them slowly on the stone, using my fingers, trying to draw some of the pain back to the butt of my hand. When the knives were sharp, I took one and carefully lacerated the festered nubs on three of my fingers. My head reeled. The blood ran down my hand and under my sleeve. I heated tweezers and probed, digging out what of the steel needles I could find, then turned on the electric stove and cauterized the wounds by touching my fingers down on a red-hot burner. I felt the back of my head tip for the floor but caught myself and stumbled to the sink and turned on the cold water over my head.

Gasping, I slid to my knees and banged my head against the steel cupboard. I pressed my forehead against the steel. Water streamed down my neck. I clutched my hands together and pressed them into my stomach and whispered a beseechment of curses. And then I walked to the piano bench and ate the last of the cocaine.

Outside, I set the knives and bone saw and ball peen hammer down at the trunk of a cottonwood, which was dead at the top but alive and green from the middle down. I threw the ends of a rope over two high limbs, high enough to allow me to pull the meat up and let it hang. I shut the nanny and young doe inside the shed and led George out to the tree on the grass at the side of the house. I felt cold and large. The day, the sky, was dazzling. The wether danced sideways and nipped at my trouser leg. I scooped up the hammer and hit the wether, hard, between the horn stubs. The wether screamed, jerked loose of my grasp, and staggered away.

This was not supposed to happen. It should be silent. I chased the wether across the grass. The nanny knocked the shed door open and broke into the pen, bleating desperately. That was not supposed to happen, either. I had the wether down; I had my knees on him. Angry now, I hit it twice on the head. It passed out, kicking.

I dropped the hammer and ran to the tree for a knife and came back and slit the wether's jugular. Then, with blood spurting over my shoes and trouser cuffs, I dragged it to the tree, looped the hind feet, and hoisted it up. I had the rope wrapped behind my back, yet still it was a struggle to lift the weight. My right hand, the three fingers bound in a rag, throbbed violently. I fixed the ropes and leaned against the tree. I felt sick. The goat swung lightly, the head dripping.

Three neighborhood dogs gathered and circled warily at a distance. One began lapping at the grass where I had cut the goat's throat. I slit down the belly and scooped the innards into the box at my feet. I pushed the box toward the dogs. They scattered, then returned. The biggest dog pulled the large intestine away and lay down with it, while the remaining two snarled at each other from either side of the box. Just down the road, I heard Louis's Loadstar catch and roar, shaking the air. It came out of the garage to shouts of approval. I cut and drew the hide down the hind legs, working the tissue free with the skinning knife. The nanny was bleating. I breathed more easily, though, because the skinning transformed the life into meat. I heard the gate open and shut, and then, as I pulled the hide free of the ribs, his first question: "You cut yourself that badly?"

I looked at the blood-soaked rag and grunted.

"You don't want to get any hair on the meat."

I had the forelegs clean. I twirled the goat, eased the hide over the tail and down the back, and knelt and pulled and cut, stripping the head. I hung the hide over a limb so as to save it from the dogs and turned to Louis. He'd changed into fresh jeans and shirt, new cowboy boots, and a stiff white Stetson. He was shaven and spiffy, but drunk again, or still drunk; his eyes were bloodshot. He grinned and scratched under his hat.

"You see my car?"

"The Continental?"

"Yeah. I bought me that in town last night."

"Yeah?"

"I got home and turned around and drove back into town and bought it off a mechanic I know. Class, hey?" His eyes glittered.

I turned back to the wether and notched the penis.

"You don't want to get any piss on the meat, Pete," Louis said.

The penis popped free when I pried at its root.

"You don't want to get any piss on yourself, either," Louis said.

I picked up the bone saw and pushed the carcass against the tree with my knee and sawed into the neck.

"Any more than you've already got on you," Louis said.

I turned back to him. The look of hostility we exchanged carried much more than either of us would say about each other, and more than we knew, too. Neither of us wanted to know anything more. Louis spat on the grass and turned away, his body swaying, and left. I stood still for a while, ruminating upon guilt, pain, the habit of causing it, and the ever-elusive cure for it all as the saw hung from my hand. I didn't mind! My body shuddered when I sighed. The nanny and the doe grazed peacefully in the pen, as if nothing had happened. A magpie landed on the roof and chattered.

I finished cutting through the neck. When the head fell, it rolled against my boot. I picked it up by the lip and heaved it toward the dogs, making them jump back. They regathered with their necks bristled and their lips flicking as they snarled at each other. The big dog snatched the head by an ear and trotted off, leaving the intestine for the other two to fight over. I cut off the hooves and hauled the carcass up into the cottonwood to let it cure. The white lines of the rib cage arched into the spine so that it looked like a fancy kite against the blue sky, lightly swinging amongst the cottonwood's dead limbs.

The Fishers

LOUISE CAME FROM TACOMA. Years ago she'd received a scholarship to attend an Ivy League college, but her parents couldn't bear having her so far away. She attended a public university on the eastern side of the state. She met Ed Erickson, married him, moved to his farm, and thus was drawn into the weave of life at the edge of the high desert. She came to know the dances at the Grange Hall, the potlucks, mothering, the short winter days and the long yellow light of summer, drought, fire, coyotes, porcupines, and the white-tailed deer that grazed along the edges of the grain fields near the hem of the dark woods.

Her three children went through school in the small country town of R———. For years she and Ed were active in the town's Lutheran church. She was a vivacious woman with a quick smile and a gift for coming near to share another person's happiness or trouble. She was one of those rare few who, just by being there, brought pleasure into the lives of others, but ever since Ed had passed on, some of her friends believed she'd taken too deeply to cover. She and Ed had been married for forty years. To her mind, her life still gathered around his lost presence, but at the same time, she was seeking out a wider, more lightly propelled orbit than that of her former life.

Her son lived in California. Her two daughters and a sister lived in Seattle. She often spoke with them by telephone and sometimes flew to see them. She indulged her love for classical music. She bought a compact disc player and marveled at its brilliance. She attended concerts in the city of Spokane, twenty miles to the east. She liked sitting among people she didn't know. She shopped in the malls at the busiest times so she could be lost in the throng. She signed all her checks, Mrs. Edward Erickson. She'd come to feel she was most herself when she was a complete stranger.

The town of R——— was six miles west of her farm, dug in amongst the wheat fields. To this day the school is the town's

51

leading employer. After it come the cooperative grain exchange, the Cenex outlet, the grocery store, the gas station, the café, and the tavern. There are three churches, but half the buildings along the main street have been boarded up for years. It gives the place a grim look. An old motel is sinking into the ground, and the International dealer is gone. What is now a drab community hall with vinyl walls was once a rooming house and saloon with a twenty-foot bar, brass cuspidors, and a rowdy reputation. Wild stories persist that touch upon the ancestors of some of the present citizens – a giant of a man named John Kolb who terrorized the community, a barmaid from Chicago who traded her way into land holdings. Years ago the stone railway station was razed.

The old days are gone. Fast cars and highway improvements brought people to the malls and equipment outlets in the city. Louise entered midstream into the change back in the late fifties. She and Ed had watched the number of farms dwindle. The money passed increasingly into the hands of a few educated farmers, who – besides holding the land and the knowledge of it handed down to them – became adept at buying up more real estate and playing the subsidy programs against their investments. But the old days linger as a memory and exert a force upon the imagination of the people. There is a form of deeply held dreaming that continues, inspired by this memory as if by a living relic.

Kindergarten through twelfth grade, fewer than four hundred kids attend the school. In the days before consolidation, there had been forty one-room schools in the same area. Now, some children ride the bus for an hour each way. The children enter into the exchange with modern times – computers, MTV, ESPN, cell phones, and bitter jokes about AIDS – but even from them, there emanates a powerful tribal spirit, a hardy innocence. The people are devoted to the children. It's because of the children that the town remains a gathering place. Many of the children never truly leave. They may graduate, go to a nearby college, or join the army, but then return to be laced back into local life.

The Fishers

There are two forces at work. One says, "Leave this dying place." The other says, "Come home." The relic resides in all the children, imprinting them with the memory of what they themselves never knew. Louise had slowly come to understand all this.

Once, she thought that high school basketball was the binding agent. Between them, the girls' and boys' teams have been Class B State Champions twelve times. Each time, the town has been filled with revelry into the early morning hours. Carloads of kids cruise back and forth, shouting and honking wildly in the chill late-winter night. The next day there will be a short parade in the snow-lined streets: the Scouts and high school band marching in formation, the cheerleaders and team members riding in open cars, followed by an equestrian unit. At the end come the men of the Lions Club, sitting precariously on folding chairs on a flatbed truck. After the parade everyone retires to the community hall for a pancake feed. Nothing matters at this moment but the unanimity to which victory has stripped the people.

It's a winter tradition, basketball. Other seasonal sports are followed with less intensity although Ed and Louise's son had preferred baseball. In the fall the farms are finishing harvest. In spring the seeding and spraying begin. During winter the fields are covered with snow. The snow fills the barrow pits and swales. The machinery waits in the barns.

Louise and Ed attended the games, Ed the local boy and Louise the newcomer. The stands that lined the gymnasium overflowed with parents and children, the recent graduates, and even those whose school days went back to the time before consolidation. The old folks came to see their grandchildren. The grandmothers had watchful eyes. The grandfathers' hands were discolored with liver spots and thick from years of labor. At crucial moments in the games, the gymnasium thundered with voices. At other moments while the kids shouted school chants, Louise, still a young woman then, would find her eyes drawn to the old folks, whose faces grew stolid and sometimes strangely wry and distant.

When her eldest daughter reached high school, Louise re-

53

mained baffled by the grip of basketball but fell into its thrall. The scores, the victories, and the championship meant nothing to her. She liked to watch her children and their friends pound up and down the court, weaving in and out. She liked the way their faces brimmed with health. She liked to see the body of a child she knew suddenly poised in the air after rising from a tangle of arms and legs and then the ball sailing toward the hoop.

Not until her second child, her son, had become a player, did it strike her that success at basketball spoke of a contradiction in the people. It reaffirmed their savvy and raw power – the way they pulled a fence line taut, or worked a bull into a squeeze chute, thrived in a house at the end of a country road. But it also offered them relief from the deep sense of chanciness that came from their balance sheets and endless planning, from the cold, from being alone.

As her third child neared graduation, Louise's sympathy for the old folks sharpened. She sensed a stirring beneath the raucous pleasure in the gymnasium, an undercurrent emanating from the old ones' stolid presence. It was a whispering that said the fervor for basketball was a last, desperate defense against a crumbling world and a ritual that, though beloved, grew more and more flimsy with each passing year. Soon the ritual would be as small and delicate as a wheat husk held in the fingers.

She wondered about the children who put on their uniforms for every game and never left the bench. She wondered about the unnoticed gifts of the children. Her care for her own children enlarged into a desire to improve things for all. This was her nature. Also, it was a time of impoverishment for education. Before her youngest graduated, Louise stood up at a school board meeting and suggested that, in addition to sports, money should be put toward the science fair. The children needed to be prepared for lives filled with change, she said. She spoke longer and with more intensity than she'd expected. It was as if someone else had suddenly been turned loose inside her. When she finished, the people were utterly silent. Louise's chair creaked noisily as she sat down. She felt her blood pounding in her arms. Before she could recover, the meeting moved on to another subject.

On the way home, Ed said, "That took nerve."

Louise didn't respond at first. She'd been shaken by the meeting. Now, she gazed out the car window. It was April. The snow was melting. In the moonlight the fields were black-and-white. The white followed the gullies. The black was strong on the crests of the slopes and like a fine etching along the ridges of all the plowed furrows where the winter wheat was planted. As the car sped by, it was an ever-shifting cagework of black-and-white. Louise had come to love this stark region for the fine detail through which it made itself known. It comforted her to look at it. "Half the people in the room are wondering the same thing," she said. "Why don't they speak up?"

"They're proud," Ed said. "They don't like to be questioned. They can't think of what might be wrong. They live through their kids."

"Good heavens, don't we all?" Louise said.

"Their grandparents settled this country." Ed's teeth and eyes caught light from the dashboard. "They have that to live up to. Some of them still hate the Indians, for God's sake. But look, those kids respect authority. Our people believe they're bringing the kids up right."

"They need to consider other things," Louise said.

"They see their kids as themselves," Ed said, "coming into the life that's taken so much effort to make and that's hardly lasted any time at all. It's like they're holding an egg, all of them together, as carefully as they can, and if they get the slightest crack in it, everything's lost. You have to be gentle. They want to keep on going the way they are so it won't hurt any more than it does already."

"And going and going. It drives a person crazy."

"They're farmers. It takes years to get the weeds out of a field. Monotony is their idea of a good time." Ed chuckled because Louise accused him of that when she wanted to go to the Grange on a Friday night to dance. She loved dancing.

She looked out at the fields. "Maybe I'll take up quilting."

"Oh Lord, no," Ed said.

55

Louise turned back to him. He had smile lines in his cheeks. His lower lip drooped. He had a kind face and a quiet way of speaking. The words seemed to have been rolled around in his mouth like hard candy before they came softly out.

"Besides," he said, "chances are more folks paid heed than you think. You have to give them rope. They like to turn an idea over and look at its belly side for a while."

It starts in grade school, the coming and going. The kids will play on grade school teams, and then there are spring track meets, baseball in the summer, football, scouts all year long, band concerts, church youth groups. And basketball. The parents go down to the café for coffee while they wait, or sit in the gymnasium in small groups, talking about the kids, the weather. It has always taken patience. For a family whose kids were spread out in age like Louise's were, this can continue for years. It was so that she learned who was who in the town and in the miles of farmland. Early on when she might ask about a certain person, the people she was with would sometimes fall silent and take on the wry expressions of the old folks. Louise supposed she'd blundered into a trouble – divorce, teenage pregnancy, bankruptcy, an old enmity. She felt she'd broken a taboo.

They were a good people, though. There was a bus driver, a troubled woman who took her life with a pistol after she was abandoned by her husband,. A couple was killed on the highway just outside town, hit by a semitruck at night while they were walking home. In each case kids were left behind. One bunch moved in with their aunt and the other with their grandparents. But everybody kept an eye out for them. A boy was killed and his sister injured in another accident. The sister, who was a classmate of Louise's youngest child, spent three weeks in a hospital in the city. The nurses had to bring out extra chairs to accommodate the folks keeping vigil. The nurses said they'd never seen anything like it. If a farmer took sick during harvest, there would be a dozen combines in his fields the next day. Scores would turn out for memorial services, spilling out of the sanctuary to the lawn. The people in their goodness huddled up to smother the trouble that tore at them.

The Fishers

It was the same with fires. In the summer most anything could start one: a spark from a passing train, heat lightening, chaff stuck up in the undercarriage of a combine. By August the pine needles in the woods were dry a foot down. At harvest time fires could rip through wheat fields. The Ferguson girl got caught in a field with a load of wheat once. When the fire came at her, she jumped out of her truck and ran through the flames. The truck exploded, the force knocked her flat, then she got up and ran again. She had burned her legs and her feet right through the boots. But the people watched out for her and she was all right.

Ed Erickson was a volunteer fireman. Louise used to ride along with him. She'd pitch in with a shovel, which caused folks to admire her from the start. Her dark hair shone and her cheeks flushed in the heat. Her eyes flashed. As often as not, she'd find herself shoveling a fire line next to somebody she knew. It might be anyone. She felt enriched by the steadiness of the work and the conversations about how deep to dig and in what direction. Then, as the fire came under control, she enjoyed the idle talk of other fires in other years: the one up at Four Mound two years before, the one out at Rattlesnake Crick in '92, the one out at the Bodines' dairy, the one that took the Groenig place way back in the sixties – house, barn, silo, and all, everything except the metal posts. At the same time, though, Louise wondered how one could be with these people in a way that truly counted, how the deep chords of discovery that came with friendship could be struck.

"It's hard," Ed would tell her. "They've got a few of their cupboards locked up."

"Don't they gossip?" she once asked him. This was when their oldest child was but twelve.

"It takes a lot to get them to turn on one of their own," Ed said. "Much of the time, they'd rather not know enough to make them turn on someone. But if they do, watch out."

She knew there was gossip, of course: the clergyman with the alcohol problem, the teacher with Roman hands, and the young wife who inexplicably left the house every morning after her husband headed for the fields. But that wasn't what she meant.

"When you gossip you're sounding out the same possibilities in yourself, even at the worst. At best it's the talking that finds openings. It's what gives meaning to conversation and makes you feel for others."

Ed looked steadily at her. "You're right."

They were in the kitchen, cleaning up. The children were in bed. Louise had turned on the stereo in the living room. Strains of a Strauss waltz drifted into the kitchen. She loved the Strauss waltzes for their sailing, melancholy melodies set against a strong rhythm. She smiled impishly at Ed. He rocked sideways and chuckled.

"Don't you see?" he said. "It's your spirit. It runs hard. People are wary of you. They're afraid they'll get toted off somewhere they don't know and they'll never find their way back. Like me. Like that music," he said, tipping his head toward the living room. "You've got me liking it."

Louise set down her dishrag and pressed against him. They began to dance. They moved along the kitchen counters and by the refrigerator. Ed's touch was soft. He kept his body straight. He wouldn't admit it but he was a good dancer. The stereo was turned low. They moved lightly so as not to wake the children. Louise was filled with passion. At the same time, she was thinking that even when pleasure was most intense there was sadness in it just like this music, that pleasure was ephemeral, that even in the heat of it one knew it would soon be over. They whirled into the living room. They probed the extremities of the room. A tautness came over their motions. The intensity of the music increased. Her hair grew damp against her temples. She threw back her head and felt her throat fill with wildness.

Eventually, the last of their children graduated from school. They had all gone away to college – one to Seattle, one to California, and the third had gone east to the very school Louise had considered attending years ago. Everyone knew that Ed would be the last Erickson to work the farm. Louise sometimes blamed herself for this, but Ed said that she should not, that they'd done their duty by the farm, that the kids should go their own way. He said that farming would continue on a larger and larger scale. What made him sorry was that the mix of people and work would soon disappear forever. There would be no small farmers, fewer mechanics, fewer supply outlets. Someday there would be just the big farmers, and all the trade would go to city dealerships or shipping centers. County lines would mean nothing at all. "That's what we're afraid of," he once said. "That we'll lose everything we know, every small thing in our life and maybe even our memory, just like the Indians. All the things we valued are jumping away and scattering in all directions. You can't blame yourself for freeing our children to survive in that world."

But Louise knew that, for Ed, the children had been torn away from the very fabric of who he was. Sometimes when they spoke of their grown-up children, he would abruptly turn away, his eyes growing moist. She felt helpless to console him. Six years ago she lost him.

At first, the ladies of the community dropped by to sit with her or invited her out for coffee, but then as time passed she visited less and less frequently. Her church attendance lapsed. She felt herself becoming an absence in the life she had previously lived, but she hoped her old friends would remember her well from the basketball games, from cleaning up after the Blue and Gold banquets, from the fire lines, even from the time she stood up in front of the school board. She hoped they remembered her as a good Christian woman, as one of the few outsiders whom they had accepted as their own.

She saw her neighbors sometimes, slowing as they drove by the house, their heads turning to give her place a good look. Her house rested on high ground just south of the bluff that overlooked a canyon. At the bottom of the canyon was a creek. White-tailed deer worked the margins of field and wood. There were badgers, marmots, raccoons, and squirrels. The basalt cliffs were favored nesting places for birds, snakes, and porcupines – too many porcupines. Once, cougars had prowled the canyon. In a dry summer a lone cougar might still drop down into the watershed. Louise had heard one long ago at dawn, its bloodcur-

dling howl like the scream of a woman. It brought her bolt upright in bed. Next to her Ed slept soundly. When she told him
about it the next morning, he didn't believe her at first, but then
he said, "Wait. Maybe. Maybe I remember dreaming something
like that."

There were coyotes. They sang at night, yipping back and forth
from the fields, sending messages that way, or howling over a kill.
The worse the weather got, either in the cold or the heat, the
harder they sang. In her solitude, Louise came to admire them. It
was as if they reveled in trouble: drought, snow, furious hunters,
encroaching civilization. Louise thought that, in their power to
sustain themselves, even to multiply in the midst of violent
change, they were the fittest of all God's creatures. When their
singing filled the night, she thought they'd captured the angels
from the heart of music.

Hers was an old house with gables. There were bare patches in
the lawn where she had shorn it to the root. An ancient backhoe
stood next to a low spot in the front lane. Before he died Ed had
parked it there in preparation for laying out a culvert. Weeds had
grown up around the axles. On the south side of the house was
the greenhouse, its glass encrusted with pine pollen. A barn
stood on the other side of the house next to the woods that
stretched to the cliffs. Out back a file of farm implements told the
story of the Erickson generations. The house needed paint. The
woods had grown tangled. A "For Sale" sign began appearing at
the end of the lane every spring, only to be removed in the fall.

One day last year – before the sign was up for the season – a
newcomer to the area knocked at the door. Louise scrutinized the
young man through the screen. She'd been listening to Brahms.
After the Strauss family, she loved Brahms, Schubert, Schumann,
and Beethoven, even Mahler, all the German romantics.

"Brahms," the man said.

"Yes, it is." She stepped outside. The music became muted. A
woman in her sixties now, her hair was liberally salted with gray.
She had no idea who this person was. He wore jeans and a dusty
plaid shirt. He'd been working. She was mildly surprised that he

The Fishers

could look that way and know Brahms, but then her own son might have been so. This man was deeply tanned and had dark eyes.

He explained that he was digging a water trench, that he'd seen her backhoe and wondered about renting it. The tractor didn't work, she said. It hadn't worked for years. The young man suggested that maybe he could get it running, but the offer struck her as being too complicated, even risky. She said, "It's been too long."

"This is a beautiful place," the man said, looking toward the canyon.

"Yes," she said. "Thank you." She saw him peering through her doorway. Struck, she looked inside herself. Her heavy furniture was visible as was a wall full of books. It looked like a lair. Music soared from deep within. She looked back at the man. His dark eyes seemed to burn into her.

Not long after that, the "For Sale" sign reappeared at the end of the lane. In the fall it disappeared. The next spring a new sign appeared, listing a different realtor. Real estate had its own way. Out toward the highway, south of the creek, was an area favored by officers from the nearby air force base. They lived on five-acre "estates" that constantly went on and off the market. The old farm families lived out on the flats, striving to stay solvent by endlessly expanding their production, and often enough by holding down extra jobs in the city. In between were the rest of the folk, working people with small acreages, professional people, and even a few trying against all odds to break into farming. In the midst of this, the real estate agents ranged across the land and ran skirmishes from the county assessor's office. Sneaky as skin cancer, they turned up in the fields with survey crews in tow.

Ed Erickson had been a Swede. To the west, around the town of R——, was the prime dryland wheat country. The Germans and English moved out there. Here and stretching northward was mixed timber and farmland. The Swedes, good with timber, had settled here. Through the years, Ed and Louise had made a narrow living out of five hundred acres of field and four hundred of timber. Sometimes they pastured cattle. They would have been cutting it close if they had tilled a thousand acres, but Ed never considered mortgaging his holdings for the sake of investing in more land. What he had, he husbanded, and with it he had the touch. But Louise came to feel he'd had a sense of doom all along that attached itself to her inclination – not ever advocated, exactly, but born of her longing and surely expressed in her nature – to see that the children got away.

The timber stand was of yellow pine and some Douglas fir. During winters Ed had worked the woods, thinning and culling. He sold this as firewood during the succeeding falls, and every five years he picked a section and logged out the topped-off and forked trees. He felled, trimmed, and skidded with his crawler, and hauled out the logs in his truck. Louise helped. Each of the children helped when they were big enough. The income from the woods was seed money, often the difference between staying afloat and going under.

They had fire to worry about in the trees, and beetles and porcupines. The place was lousy with porcupines. During breeding season the porcupines talked to each other from tree to tree at night, their calls resonant like wet timbers rubbing against each other in the wind. Wanton feeders, the porcupines chewed through the bark of the trees to the cambium. The smell of the sap brought the red turpentine beetles, which bored into the trunks and laid their eggs. Red sap bled through the holes, and that smell attracted the pine beetles. They laid their eggs, their larvae girdled the trees, and newly hatched beetles emerged to attack more trees. The ips beetles, whose larvae ate out the tips of limbs, were always there, rising and falling in numbers. It was an elaborate conversation carried on amongst the elements that could turn into a fission. When that happened, there was no remedy except to clear, truck out, and burn.

Ed studied all this and came to consider the porcupines the perpetrators of destruction, so he carried a .22 with him when he drove around during the day. At night he kept it and a high-powered flashlight next to the back door. The porcupines were easiest to locate when they talked after dark or when their urine encircled the tree trunks after a fresh snow in winter. He found them at sunset sometimes, the dark clumps of quill up in the trees against the glowing sky. Rarely he encountered one on the ground, making its way from one tree to the next in a motion like a small oil barrel rolling slowly over the rocks. More than once he came back and told Louise how he'd been in the woods and heard the clicking sound of porcupines eating at the bark all around him but couldn't find them. He hated porcupines.

There was once the fisher. The last of them had lived here during Ed's boyhood. Not long after Ed and Louise married and moved back to the farm, both his parents died, one after the other. He talked to Louise about his family, and he remembered the fisher one night and fell into a passion. He told her about how it had been trapped for its pelt, how it was big, smoke-colored, how it was the quickest tree-traveling animal he'd ever seen. It liked to meet a porcupine on a limb, he said. It was the porcupine's truest natural enemy. Porcupine quills did not infect its skin. The porcupine was slow. The fisher was agile. The porcupine looked clumsy. The fisher was sleek and focused. Everything in its musculature, its sinew, its long, flowing tail, and its very life seemed drawn like a gun sight to a bead. The porcupine seemed ancient and at home nowhere, hardly even in the trees, while the fisher was adept everywhere. Ed considered it a creature sprung from God. It swam like an otter. While the porcupine was thick, ugly, and stupid, the fisher was like mercury, like lightening. It dissolved into the woods and came out suddenly to kill.

Ed told Louise about the time he'd seen one when he was twelve. He'd been hunting birds and had stopped to rest on a stump when, out of nowhere, a fisher tore up a tree trunk right in front of him. He heard snarling and scratching. He spotted them – the porcupine backed up on a limb and the fisher facing it. The fisher lunged and bit into the porcupine's face. The porcupine's body swung sideways, tumbled through the limbs, and thudded against the ground. The front of its skull was crushed. The fisher flashed back down the trunk and leaped at the porcupine. Ed

hardly dared to breathe as he watched the fisher eat the porcupine's brain and then tear into the belly, disgorging it.

Not long after this conversation, Ed located two litters of fishers up in Canada. He sneaked six of them across the border and
raised them in pens. Two died. He carefully nurtured the remaining four. He expanded their pen and fed them live rabbits. As
they flourished, their fur became luxurious. Years later Louise
would realize that, for Ed, the fishers tapped into a lost time
when violence lurked much nearer to the surface of life, along
with the other kinds of meaning he valued. She had helped with
the feeding and watched as the fishers ceaselessly prowled the
perimeters of the pen. The four of them wove intricate paths.
They moved along the fence line, turned, slinked past each other,
went behind the water trough and came out, turned, moved di-
agonally, and then started over again at the fence line. They wove
themselves into a design that appeared as a maze in the ground.
It was hypnotic. The wildness in them twisted toward lunacy. Finally, Ed opened the gate and left it open, giving them the freedom of the pen and the woods. For several days the fishers ventured out but returned to look for food. Then they disappeared.

A couple of months later, Ed found one killed on the road not
far from the house. At a Grange meeting, he and Louise over-
heard a man saying he'd found a porcupine carcass with a
crushed skull. Nearly a year passed, and then they heard that a
farmer up the road had trapped a fisher by his creek. People
started talking about porcupine bodies found here and there,
and more trapped fishers, and others shot breaking into chicken
pens. Ed said that the bulk of these had to be rumors, another
scattering soon to pass into the dust. But maybe there were a
couple fishers out there, absorbed somehow into the wild
scheme of things, he would say wistfully. Maybe they'd had a lit-
ter. Or maybe all the fishers were lost. He didn't know.

He died in the winter. He'd been skidding logs. When he didn't
return before dark, Louise set out on foot to find him. She came
up to the loading deck where he had a pile of trimmed logs and
played her flashlight around the clearing. The truck was there.

She listened for the sound of the crawler engine but heard nothing – only the distant hoot of an owl in the icy air. It was February. There'd been a thaw, then more snow. The skim of ice under the snow snapped beneath her feet. She passed the stumps of freshly cut trees along the skid trail and, with an increasing sense of foreboding, neared the cliffs. She could see where Ed had been skidding off the slope. She stopped at the rim. The chill from the bottom rose to her. For a moment she didn't shine the beam down – out of fear, out of the knowledge that logging was dangerous, and out of a reluctance to probe what her imagination had long ago learned to feed her fear. At last, she turned the beam downward and the light glinted against the metal tracks of the overturned crawler.

A neighbor found her late that night, weaving along the road that ran beside the creek. She was scratched and bruised from making her way down to the canyon bottom and wet from breaking through the ice in the creek as she crossed to the road. She'd found her husband at the tractor, crushed beneath it. She was hypothermic, numbed by the weblike closing in of shock and cold.

Ed had rolled his crawler. It's still there, lying on its side at the base of the cliff where it was left by the crew that retrieved the body. One man offered to pay Louise for the salvage, but she declined. She wanted it to stay, gradually sinking into the earth, overgrown with the softness of nettles, hemlock, and willow.

During these last years, the disappearing and reappearing "For Sale" sign expressed Louise's quandary. She leased out the fields. One year she hired a logging crew to work the woods. They cut more trees than they should have and in their heedlessness left a mess – slash strewn everywhere. Her children wanted her to sell and use the money to travel. She had always dreamed of journeys, it was true, and she now felt drawn more strongly than ever to the anonymity of the traveler, to being no one. She wished to sleep in white, empty rooms, to escape the disorder of her memories. She came to love airports, sitting in them surrounded by unnamed, unknown people, all of whom were suspended and waiting as if at the portal of sleep. But she also wished to be free to come home when she was done. She didn't understand how her children could forget that last part. They seemed to have become of a piece with the distant, shimmering places to which she might travel.

When she listed the farm and people inquired, she always asked too much, insuring that no one would buy. She had one offer to buy at her price, but it was from a California developer. For Ed's sake, she couldn't sell to a developer – not that, not by her hand. At times she thought that if she could find the right buyer, someone who would keep the place intact, then she would sell in an instant. At other times she didn't want to sell at all. She felt trapped. She believed she herself had become a relic. She worried about the way she was forgetting small matters. Her entire life seemed to heap up in every moment. All manner of physical things were coming apart on her.

She was sure the man to whom she had leased the fields was shorting her on the income. Two panes of glass in the greenhouse broke inexplicably. The lawnmower balked. The barn needed a new roof. Chunks of kitchen linoleum tore loose. One day this last spring as she was emptying garbage out behind the house, she glimpsed a movement at the corner of her eye. Turning, she saw a porcupine. It was huge, the size of a large dog. It skirted the field, and then cut in toward the woods. Its footfalls seemed delicate. Its body bent sinuously. It seemed agile like no porcupine she'd ever seen, as if it were a bobcat inside the big porcupine body. It receded and vanished into a burrow. She stared into the woods and wondered if she'd seen a phantom. When she picked up her garbage pail, her hands were shaking.

That afternoon as she was setting out for town, she backed into the ditch at the end of the lane. The newcomer came by soon after in his flatbed truck. A whole family was wedged into the cab – the man, his wife, and their three children. Heads swayed and tipped like heavy flowers, watching as the newcomer backed up to the ditch, then got out. Louise admired his deft, strong hands as he hooked a chain to the bumpers. The woman drove the truck and the man steered Louise's car free. Because the new-comer's gaze seemed to burn into her when he asked if she was still listening to Brahms and because he chuckled and shook his head when she offered to pay him, Louise considered giving him the backhoe. She even wondered if she should ask if he and his wife would be interested in buying her farm. She considered carrying the contract herself for them, but then she caught hold of herself. She thought she was becoming like those old ladies who gave their life's earnings to television preachers.

This August Louise was heading for the grocery store. She started her car, but it died before she had it out of the garage. The gas gauge registered empty. She poured gas from a can into the tank and tried again, but the engine wouldn't start. The car was a Buick she'd had for years, and she remembered seeing Ed prime the carburetor when an engine ran dry. She lifted the hood, removed the air cleaner, and poured gas into the carburetor. Later, she would say that she must have put too much in. Also, she left the open gas can sitting on top of the radiator. When she started the car, fire flared out of the carburetor and leaped to the gas can. Flames rushed straight up to the rafters. The can fell to the floor and burst. Shocked, Louise didn't move.

The flames licked toward the benches that stood against the wall. Beneath the benches were five-gallon cans of oil that Ed had stored there. At last she got out of the car. She saw the flames encircling one can, then another. Frantically she searched the shelves for a fire extinguisher, but then ran outside, turned on a tap, and dragged a hose toward the garage. She heard deep, popping sounds as the oil cans caught. Suddenly, flames roared through the garage roof. The cedar shingles on the adjacent barn ignited. The fire moved through the cedar as if it were paper. The heat forced Louise back. The barn roof collapsed, and the remains of the hay that had been left there since Ed had died caught. The walls fell inward. The flames shot skyward and the air turned orange.

From the barn the wind blew the fire through the dry grass to the slash in the woods. Fire then jumped into the trees – the dead ones, the sick ones, the leaners – that Ed had always kept cleared for exactly this reason. Fire moved simultaneously along the ground and from treetop to treetop. In tree after tree the sap-filled needles burst into plumes of flame. Louise dropped the hose and backed toward her house.

Someone called in the fire. The volunteer department arrived. Neighbors came with their shovels. The Department of Natural Resources brought a dozer to cut breaks and a helicopter to drop retardant. The house was spared. At first the neighbors had thought Louise was away, but the newcomer, who was among them, noticed the running hose and went into the house. He found her sitting at the kitchen table.

She was staring out the window toward where the garage and barn had been. There was an entirely new vista through the charred, smoking trees. It was twilight. The fire was under control. The dark shapes of the fire fighters could be seen, as could the hulking forms of the trucks. In the distance a line of low flames licked toward the bluffs. A row of neighbors had formed just outside. Elbow to elbow, they marched slowly in the direction of the house. Their shovels glinted and clinked. As they came nearer, she made some of them out as people she knew from the old days. Their eyes looked hollow. Their gaunt, smudged faces appeared masked. They moved awkwardly as if in addition to grasping their shovels they were struggling between them to hold a large thing they'd found in the woods, something as fragile as a cocoon.

She jerked when she heard the newcomer's footfalls in the kitchen. Recognizing him, she smiled weakly. The newcomer came near and put his hand lightly on her shoulder. She reached up, clutched his hand, then sobbed, "I burned it! It's gone!"

૪ઽ

She disappeared without a word to anyone. Before fall set in, the farm changed hands. The machinery that remained was auctioned off. The newcomer got a call one morning from an equipment outlet, telling him that the backhoe that had been left for him was repaired and ready to be delivered. The bill had been prepaid. He located the address of a daughter in Seattle and wrote to Louise there, offering to sell the backhoe if she wished, but he never received a reply.

Where Louise had gone, no one could tell him for certain – maybe to Seattle or to California, maybe even off to Europe. After all, people said, the land was unencumbered and that made her a millionaire. He observed as the place down the road that had belonged to her husband's family, and finally to her, was broken up. The fields were sold to a wheat farmer. Flanks of bright orange survey flags appeared in the blackened woods. The house was sold separately. The pleasure and trouble of being neighborly, of raising children, of putting them through school, of keeping everything running, of laboring – all that fell to the others, now, and to him.

He thought about this as he stood outside one winter day, looking at the backhoe. Its armature was cocked and its bucket, tucked close to the front axle, touched the ground. Dark, the tractor stood against a snow-whitened field. It looked as if it had been etched into thin air. He heard a porcupine calling. There was only one tree nearby. When the newcomer looked up, the sound ceased. He saw no porcupine. Snow weighed down the branches. The newcomer thought about enduring the rips that tore through one's life as one labored, about the world that sometimes seemed to swallow up all the details of lives passed in it. A second porcupine called from the distance, its voice faint and eerie. The newcomer looked up expectantly into the tree near him.

Zeta's House

IT WAS LATE AFTERNOON when I arrived, but as usual I wondered at the last minute if I had taken a wrong turn. The color of the house was like the changing coat of a coyote that took up the red, brown, yellow, and silver of the earth, as changeable as that. One could look at such a coyote standing in a field, and look away, and look back and not see it, then look away and look back again and find it there, just where it had been. It was this way with the house. Although it was hardly a small place, it could seem invisible until one came right upon it. Suddenly, it was there, rising from among the rock and tree and bush.

I got out of my car. On the deck, I had to maneuver around a large food dryer and several bushel baskets filled with unhusked corn. I found the front door thrown open. A wasp flew in. I had seen the nests of the mud daubers cemented to the soffits above my head as I passed, as well as openings straight into the eaves made by swallows. I peered through the doorway and discovered my friend Zeta and one of his sons sitting at a large table in the living room. The table was heaped with corn. The large room was filled with light. The light was filled with motes. The two gazed expectantly at me, and then my friend motioned to me to come in. I went and sat with them.

Zeta explained that Nona, his wife, and the other children were pressing cider at a neighbor's place. The apples had come in early. It was hot. Zeta's house was located at the edge of a long valley that ran northward across the Canadian border. Even here, near the border, a seemingly displaced microclimate allowed for the cultivation of apples, plums, peaches, and apricots. Snows fell during the winter but the summers were desertlike. Water for irrigation came from a nearby river, and drinking water from deep, expensive wells. The kitchen was open to the living room, and in it I could see a glass pitcher filled with water and ice. The pitcher stood on a counter. It glittered in a shaft of sunlight. Nona had put it there, I thought, in a place of honor.

Not long ago a daughter in the family had died. I came to be with my friend, to comfort him with my presence. We hadn't spoken yet of the death, but of our families otherwise, our work, the pennant races, the weather. As we spoke, Zeta's son, a fifteen-year-old, moved his eyes watchfully from one of us to the other.

The two of them were shelling corn. They took up the corn from the center of the table, husked it, dropped the husks onto a pile on the floor, and stripped the kernels from the cobs with knives. The kernels went into a large basin that rested on the floor between them. It was a variety of corn with hard yellow seeds for making meal. Several wasps buzzed above the table, but the steady movement of hands kept them at bay. I understood from the start what Zeta and his son were doing and I wished to help. It was always good to mix work with pleasure and talk. Zeta brought me a knife and a small basin. When I filled my basin with kernels, I emptied it into theirs. From here the corn would be carted out to the dryer. Later it would be ground into flour. Nona and Zeta would then make tamales on special occasions throughout the year.

I had eaten their tamales. Last March my family had brought a pig's head to them. We boiled it over a fire in the yard. It was cold. A cloud of steam suffused the air. We drew out the brain of the pig for soup and stripped the cheeks of meat. In the kitchen we stewed the meat in broth with peppers, made a cornmeal mush, and spooned the mush into corn husks, and then the meat, folded the husks into envelopes, and cooked the tamales in a steamer. The delicate smell of the corn on the table before us now brought it all back to me: beans, rice, soup, tamales, the people laughing and working, our children running back and forth from the house to the snow that still lay in patches under the trees, or to the coals of the fire, and my wife there, and Nona in her dark blue skirt moving quickly from one thing to the next.

The daughter that the family would lose was in the kitchen, seated on the end of a counter. She was six years old. Her eyes looked unnaturally large, too bright, and her hands seemed too long, too thin. She was dying. Her family treated her with deference but not so much as to force her into herself. She observed everything closely, and at times her face brightened at the antics of the other children. Once, she forgot herself and slid down from the counter in an effort to join the children who were flooding by on their way to the living room. She lost her balance and nearly fell. But she caught hold of the edge of the counter and turned, tottering weakly.

A hush moved from those of us who had seen her to the others. The children stopped and came back toward her. The daughter smiled shyly and said, "Don't worry." One of her brothers — this one, the stripling who sat shucking corn with his father — moved to her and placed his arm gently around her. She put her head against his waist. "It sounds like it's raining," she said. Everyone listened. In fact, it was clear outside. The stars were brilliant in a black sky. But in the quiet of the kitchen, the refrigerator made a ticking noise like the sound of water dripping from an eave, and a bubbling pot on the stove sounded exactly like a spring rain driven against the roof. For a moment we all entered the phantasm. Having her there seemed a gift. It was as if she'd been sent to us to stand watch for a time at the entrance to the other, adjacent world.

Here at the table, I selected an ear of corn and pulled back the husk, then glanced upward at the heavy timbers that bound the walls together and said, "This is a fine house." It was the best I could manage.

"Yes," Zeta said. "It holds all the things we leave behind, the marks and gouges, the wear." He smiled and, as if he'd read my thoughts, added, "It holds the grief for us."

We fell silent and continued working. Not far from our table lay a large black dog with a grizzled muzzle. The dog had raised its head when I came in and then fell back to sleep. Occasionally, it grunted in its dreams. Next to it lay the shadow of a branch from a fir tree, elongated yet precisely articulated. At the far side of the kitchen was a doorway that led to other rooms. The door was open, and through it I could see a cage hanging from a rafter. In the cage were two parakeets. Every once in a while, magpies could be heard chattering outside, and each time they did, the parakeets talked back from the other end of the house. This exchange became an irregular measure of our wordlessness and our work. The sounds of the shucking, of knives tearing softly along the cobs, and the papery whisper of leaves falling to the floor measured the work. The heap on the floor was a measure. Every so often Zeta or his son would carry the basin of kernels out to the dryer, cart in more corn, or get up to sharpen a knife. Those were measures.

The son had an electric glue gun at the table. He was making a construction out of scraps of metal: screws, bolts, spokes, little gearwheels, and small engine parts. Every so often he paused in his work with the corn, fished through his box of parts, and glued on another piece. The scent of epoxy snaked through the air. The construction had begun compactly. At first it looked like a mechanical root, then an animal form, a human, and then it grew abstract. The son was tied to the work we shared, but at the same time, the construction bespoke his separateness. This was another measure, one of his own time and out of it his relation to his father.

At dusk when the last of the corn dwindled on the table, the shadow of something large flitted by a window. The son went out the door, then reappeared with a crow perched on his wrist. He took the bird to a corner of the living room and set it gently on a small peeled limb that had been screwed to the wall. The crow cawed once and the dog snapped up its head. Its collar jangled. The parakeets answered from the other room. Zeta and his son looked across at each another and chuckled. The crow preened its wings. A gray cat appeared and stalked the crow. The crow glared at the cat with its black eyes. The cat stopped to roll in the dust.

Zeta told me how they had insulated the north wall of the loft with old books. It wasn't the best insulation, but he liked the idea of the wall loaded with words. It made him think of all the words afloat in the house – the talking, the murmuring in the night, the crying of children awoken from a troubled sleep, the moans, the laughter. Sometimes he heard his lost daughter calling him, her voice as clear as if she were still here. The house held every word uttered in it as well as the softness of hands, the weariness of legs, and the terror. It held the pain and every bit of the decomposable, flimsy, true substance of life.

I wanted to say something to him but I could not. I felt I had unexpectedly tumbled to an obscure ledge within myself, a place of hazard. It struck me that I had come seeking Zeta's comfort for something that had yet to happen to me, that he was not awaiting mine for what had happened to him.

At that moment a bat flew through the doorway. It circled the living room again and again in the characteristic, ragged flight of its kind. Our work was complete and we watched the bat. Soon Nona and the children would arrive, and I wished to greet them before setting out on my journey home, to see the flurry when they all came in and the way their energy would change everything. The son had gone off. He returned with a tennis racquet, closed the front door, and stood up on a chair. Each time the bat circled, he swung. Outside were more bats and swallows gliding in graceful loops, eating the twilight insects. Finally, the son hit this bat and sent it hurtling way across the kitchen and through the open doorway to the other room. We heard it ping against something hard. The son went to retrieve it.

Zeta leaned toward me. A metal button on his vest clinked against the table edge, and he nodded in the direction his son had taken. "That one was the most affected by his sister's death. He was her companion." He explained that, in his daughter's pain and through the long trial of being carted in and out of hospitals, she came to believe in reasons. He said, "She told her brother that God was taking her for a reason she would soon learn." Between us was the son's construction, which had grown even more abstract, having exploded into pure geometry. It shimmered in the fading light like a constellation afloat in space. "It's true. Our house is a refuge," Zeta said, "and yet the world comes in. We are never safe here, but we are never alone."

Chickens

THE TOWN OF G—— lay at the head of a shallow depression in the Saskatchewan prairie. At the east end of town, the concrete grain elevator towered above everything. At the west end, the fire station and the Church of Canada faced each other from either side of Main Street. The fire station was made of granite, and joined to it was a smaller building that served as the headquarters of the Cooperative Commonwealth Federation. Across the street stood the church and parsonage, and the boy's home. The boy was seven. From his upstairs window he could see all the way down the street to the elevator, or look straight across at the fire station, which appeared to be gray, although he knew that the cream-colored feldspar was dotted with black hornblende crystals and bright bits of mica. He had examined the building with his father and found all the granite blocks to be the same – beveled, bedded in mortar, an army of interlocked pieces – and yet within each were worlds of black and light like separate constellations.

His father had explained that years ago, before what was called the dustbowl, the fire station and the CCF headquarters had been a Catholic church and rectory. The boy loved to hear it – the names of minerals and of things in history that formed paths along which his mind might run. There was still a bronze plaque implanted in stone at the side entryway to the station:

SAINT ANNE'S PARISH.

ROMAN CATHOLIC.

ERECTED 1914

At the front of the building, two large openings had been made. Doors hung from steel hinges that had rusted and bled onto the adjacent stonework. If the doors swung open, two fire trucks might burst from the shadows and roar into the street. The interior of the church – the narthex, his father had told him, the nave, chancel, apse, and sacristy – had been emptied long ago. Much later in the boy's life, when he became a man, he would remember this and ponder the grim satisfaction the citizens of the farm country, beset by drought and collapsing prices, must have taken as they ripped out the false walls and disemboweled the sanctuary of its pews, rails, icons, altars, and pulpits in order to house the engines.

Space had been made for the town government and police headquarters, too. Sometimes the boy would see Sergeant MacLeod, the Mountie, standing behind his window at the corner of the building with his thumbs stuck behind his black suspenders. The boy had been taught that Sergeant MacLeod, who had a ruddy face, stood for what was right. The building had a slate roof and a blunt tower through the lattices of which could be seen the dark outline of a huge bell. At times, when he gazed across at the building, the boy felt a sense of inexpressible heaviness. Once when the bell had been rung to sound an alarm, he was astonished to discover the deep tones throbbing through his bedroom floor to the soles of his feet.

His house and his father's church had white clapboard on the outside. The church had a narrow spire that pointed straight up. It did not appear heavy at all but more like a paper fold-up that might sail off at any moment. The boy's father was also pastor to three congregations in three other, smaller towns some distance away, and in the absence of a priest, who might be hundreds of miles removed, he sometimes administered holy events for Catholics, too – holiday services as well as ceremonies of marriage and internment. He called himself a circuit rider.

The boy had thought about that word – circuit.

Circle.

Circulation.

Circus.

The words were all about rings. In the winter his house had circulation, too much air moving through it, his mother said, but too little in the summer. He longed to go to a circus. He kept a book on the shelf next to his window that had pictures of one. Trapeze artists flew above the rings marked on the ground.

Chickens

Clowns did tricks in them. Animals came inside them to dance. More animals looked on from behind the bars of their cages. Circus people traveled by train, but the boy had never seen them on the trains that passed through his town. In electricity, his father had explained, a circuit might be closed, which was right, or it might be open, which was wrong. The idea of a circuit needing to be closed forever to be right frightened the boy.

During the early hours of summer days, the grain elevator's shadow filled Main Street to the brim. During winter the shadow skittered over the white earth like the second hand of a clock. To one side of the elevator was the ice house, and just behind it, the coal burning electric plant. Since the rationing times of the war, the plant had run for only two three-hour periods a day until just this fall when Hugo Goettinger persuaded the town government to operate it from six in the morning until ten at night. The boy heard that Hugo had said the ladies needed the light to prepare their kitchens in the morning and the children required it for their studies at night. It would be good for business, Hugo had argued, and many townspeople agreed though they believed that Hugo was mainly interested in his chickens. The boy knew this from the talk that spun among the men who gathered after Sunday morning services. "It's high time," he'd heard one man say. "It ought to run without ever stopping, but thanks to us who've put in the years and paid for it, not him."

Now, the buildings along Main Street – the equipment dealer, pharmacy, hardware, and mercantile – kept their electric lights on all day. The hotel, which was situated next to the school building halfway between the boy's house and the grain elevator, no longer had to switch from electric to kerosene lamps. In the evenings, the boy could see the hard white light in the hotel windows instead of the soft amber color. There was talk that the movie house might show evening features in addition to the usual ones on Saturday morning. Everything changed. At nightfall the town blazed with light. It cut from the windows to the ground. As the boy fell asleep, it crept through his eyelids. It was in this way that he came to consider electricity.

Chickens

Behind the elevator stood the Canadian Pacific Railroad Station. The trains picked up loads of grain and delivered coal and goods and sometimes people. It was 1949. The boy learned in school that the tracks extended to the shores of the seas. Hugo Goettinger arrived by train last spring. Carl Krains, the stationmaster – a small man who turned his hands into fists when he spoke – reported to the men of the church that Hugo had disembarked with a large trunk and headed straight off with it perched on his shoulder. Hugo was the most impressive man the boy had ever seen – tall, solid as a post, and powerful. He had blazing blue eyes, skin as pale as snow, and a shock of hair the color of sunlight and as stiff as a brush. His cheekbones protruded like two bullets laid on their sides. The boy liked to think about how Hugo must have appeared the day he arrived – dressed in the loose navy blue suit he wore to church, tossing up the big trunk as if it were nothing, and striding without so much as a single inquiry directly to the house at the southern edge of town where Ilse Goettinger lived. Hugo was the son of Ilse's brother-in-law from the old country across the Atlantic Ocean. The country was named Germany.

Ilse's husband had passed on, and the rest of her family lived out on the Goettinger farms. It was a custom among farm people to move into town when they retired or became ill or widowed. The boy knew Ilse as a plump lady with a quick smile who brought strudel to church occasions. The layers upon layers of pastry as thin and crisp as parchment, drenched with honey and rolled again and again around fruit and nuts were best eaten hot in a bowl of cool cream.

On Sundays Hugo joined Ilse in the Goettinger pew. The boy sat next to his mother and waited for his father to turn his back to pray. Freed from the hold of his father's eyes – soft and gray and flecked with bright like the granite – the boy could steal glances across the aisle. He was fascinated by Hugo's hair, and by his eyebrows as pale as his skin, by the rigid jaw and the cords in his neck. Even as the boy's father stood before the cross with his arms spread, Hugo sat stock upright and wide eyed in the pew. Most of all, the boy was fascinated by the impression Hugo gave that absolutely nothing that anyone thought or said about him mattered in the least.

Once, not long after Hugo's arrival, the boy's father delivered a sermon, using marbles in a milk bottle as a demonstration. His father had borrowed four red marbles from the boy's collection. The scripture for the sermon was taken from the General Epistle of James: "For as the body without spirit is dead, so faith without works is dead also." In the midst of the sermon, his father, who was tall and lithe and dark haired, stepped out from behind the pulpit and crouched just above the steps to the sanctuary. The arms of his black robe touched the wooden floor. He dropped the marbles one at a time into the milk bottle. They made a ringing sound in the hushed church. He said that the marbles represented Christians. He began to roll the marbles around in the bottle, then turned the bottle upside-down and kept rolling the marbles so that they wouldn't fall through the open mouth. The sound of the marbles filled the church, resounding against the bare walls. The people began to smile. Pews creaked as people shifted in order to see. His father said that the milk bottle represented the church, that the Christians were in the fold of the church, that their motion represented their good works, that the need for good works – as with faith – was never ending unto death. If they ceased their good works, his father said, the Christians fell away from the fold. At that moment his father stopped revolving the bottle. The marbles tumbled out and rolled noisily down the steps and under the first line of pews. A murmur of approval rippled through the congregation.

Suddenly, a deep voice rang out: "Ja! Ja!" It was Hugo. He leaned forward and clutched the back of the pew before him. A broad smile was fixed to his face, and as if he were attending a musical performance, he called out, "Bravo!"

The congregation fell silent. The boy's father smiled gently at Hugo, but his eyes had grown alert. People looked at Hugo and the atmosphere became tense. Ilse shrank. Hugo had gone too far. It was wrong to speak out like that in church.

❧

Chickens

Throughout the spring, Hugo received deliveries at the train station: a panel truck, then a war surplus flatbed with a plow mounted on the front and tracks like a Caterpillar instead of wheels. It roared as it crept forward. The hinged cap on the exhaust stack clanged as it flapped up and down. The boy was forbidden to go out of sight from his house without permission, not even to the park behind the school. But if he heard the wail of the train's horn and the train itself rumbling into town after school or on weekends, he would stand out front of his house and watch for the truck to make its way to the station. If it did, he would run to the edge of the lot at the back to watch as the truck reappeared from behind the line of houses and parked at Ilse's place. He saw Hugo's distant figure leap from the truck, bolt back and forth, and lift things bigger than he was himself. Within two weeks Hugo had a small tractor with a scoop, several truck loads of concrete block, mortar, cement, sand, and lumber. After a time a shipment of steel cages arrived.

Even in the cool of autumn, the boy spent hours at the edge of the lot, where he built tunnels, canals, mountains, and a labyrinth of roads, or threw a ball against a large stone and caught it when it came back. From there he sometimes heard his mother playing the piano in the living room – the Chopin ballades and nocturnes that she loved, hymns, and Stephen Foster tunes. She always ended with "Beautiful Dreamer." At other times, he heard her in the kitchen – the sounds of pots and dishes rattling, the hum of the electric mixer she prized, or her voice, which was clear and penetrating, speaking to his father. If he looked back, he might see her peering out the window at him. She might hold his baby brother up for him to wave at. He enjoyed the comfort of having his mother in the kitchen – near, but not too near. He could watch Hugo working amongst his supplies, digging, pouring concrete, laying the block. Once, Hugo stopped his work, stood erect, and shaded his eyes to look back at the town. The boy sensed a secret ring of power formed by the watching – his mother watching him from the kitchen, himself watching Hugo, and Hugo's head turning their direction.

Chickens

The kitchen was the center of activity in the parsonage. The boy's bedroom was upstairs, above his parents' bedroom. In time his brother would also come upstairs, but for now he slept in a tiny cubicle just off his parents' room. The living room was used to entertain church visitors, and so even the baby crept into it at peril. The Knabe spinet stood against one wall. There was a study off the living room. Its walls were lined with books, and the door was kept closed. Behind the door, the boy's father prepared sermons and consulted with parishioners on private matters. The kitchen, however, was open to all. It had a coal-burning cookstove that was kept lit all year long. Water was heated on it for baths since the house had only the hand-driven cold water pump mounted above the kitchen sink. Aromas of baked goods, vegetables, and meat suffused the kitchen and seeped into the other rooms. When it was very cold, the family hovered around the stove. The boy would read or play near it. His brother napped by it. There had been another child, an infant sister who died the previous year, and the boy recalled her, also, tucked into a wicker cradle near the stove. During summer the stove was an uncomfortable necessity. During winter it was the heart of the household.

After the boy went to bed at night, he could hear his parents talking in the kitchen and the clanking sounds of the stove as it was stoked. Like the aroma of food, the sound of the voices seeped up the stairwell to his room. It was a comfort to hear his parents talking, although sometimes it was evident that not all was well. His mother's voice might grow strained. She didn't like this Saskatchewan town. She was from Vancouver. Her dead father had been a judge. Before the depression, her family had been rich. His mother considered this place too cold, too primitive. The boy's father, who had never been rich, consoled his mother. He told her that she needed more rest, that she carried her worries too heavily, that soon the church authorities would find another "call" for him. He reminded her that he had entered his request to return to Vancouver. The thought of life ending in this place and then resuming in another thrilled the boy. It would be like leaving one room, shutting the door, and finding himself in another room he'd never imagined before.

His parents spoke of church matters, the treasury, the hope that the house could soon be wired for an electric stove, and of people, some of whom brought only trouble. The talk told the boy that the world was a precarious place. Later in his life, he would understand that his parents, as pastor and pastor's wife, were positioned at the core of the town. He would realize that it was especially hard for the wife, who had always to appear upright, even to serve as her husband's confessor and yet never receive the honor accorded him. All things kind and cruel passed through the both of them. They were the spiritual sieves and the last wall of defense against the chaos of personal trouble and gossip. The talk the boy heard was often like a story, a tale of what this person did, what someone else did, and what another person thought of that – what was said and how it passed to other people and made them angry. Hugo and Ilse's names entered the stories. The parishioners were worried about Ilse. Some resented that Hugo hadn't purchased his materials through the local merchants. They wondered where his money came from. Some didn't like him driving his truck over the town's streets. The tracks were chewing up the pavement, and the boy learned that a delegation of men had asked Sergeant MacLeod to speak to Hugo about this. The stories never had endings since the boy always fell asleep. The people in the stories drifted in and out of his dreams, creating new stories. Hugo and Ilse joined in . . . the tall, pale, electric man dressed in blue and the small, round woman.

One afternoon the boy heard the train, then saw Hugo's truck head down the gravel road that led eastward into the fields. The sound of the clanging exhaust cap and creaking tracks dwindled and vanished. After a time the truck became audible again from the other side of town. Like needles, its sound pierced the throbbing of the train's engines. The boy saw a thin line of dark exhaust drift into view from behind the elevator and slip into the paler cloud that hung above the waiting train cars. The truck had stopped at the station. Soon, the train drew away, roaring and crashing as its wheels turned on the tracks. Its horn howled. All its variously colored cars turned into one dark snake in the westward fields and soon disappeared. The noise of Hugo's exhaust cap took dominion again, then receded to the east, and finally came back. From that time on, Hugo received his shipments in this roundabout fashion.

The man labored from dawn to dusk, and the boy watched as the concrete block rose to make a long, gray building. Hugo did everything alone. By late May he had the walls finished. In June he nailed on a galvanized roof and installed a chimney. Along the roof's peak were five vents that revolved and glinted in the sun. Hugo painted the door and window frames white. He dug trenches, laid pipe, spread gravel all around the building, and moved the stack of steel cages inside. In the heat of July he received a load of wooden crates filled with chicken poults. Now it wasn't just the boy watching, moving from the front to the back of his yard; townspeople also came out to see. Hugo made four trips with his truck, passing in and out of sight, and then parking and carrying the crates inside. Faintly, the boy could hear the high din of hundreds of poults, emanating from within the barn. As time passed, the timbre of the noise deepened, and resonant cries sometimes tore loose like shrieks of laughter.

The harvest crews that worked the Midwest from Oklahoma to the Canadian Plains arrived in August. While the combines harvested the outlying fields, the town was in a fever of activity. Trucks carted loads to the elevator. Trains stopped. The gondolas were filled to the brim with wheat. Cars came and went, and draft horses appeared, pulling carts laden with equipment. More trucks lined the streets. Farm wives pulled away from the mercantile with huge loads of groceries. The doors of the fire station were hooked open, and the big engines waited, glittering in the shadows. Most anyone could become a farmhand during this time. Schoolteachers and even the boy's father drove trucks, hauling goods or wheat or making runs to Regina for parts. The boy watched from the front of his yard. He liked the machinery, the racket it made, and the sharp smell of diesel exhaust. Some of the workers teamed up to take hotel rooms. At night the boy heard voices from the street. He could look out his window and see dark figures moving through the shadows. Forgetting that he might not be here for long, the boy dreamed of a time when he would be part of the harvest and come home with his clothes so filled with dust that his mother would make him strip before entering the house.

One evening after supper, he heard cries from the street. He went outside and saw a crowd of men in front of the hotel. In the glow of a sunset that turned the fields, street, and storefronts a luminous pink, the closely packed bodies appeared like a stockade. The boy looked back at his house. No one was looking. The piano was tinkling, which meant his mother had finished in the kitchen. His father was watching the boy's brother. The boy slipped through the gate and darted across the street, thinking — Wrong, this is wrong.

As he moved toward the crowd, the ring of men bulged one direction, then another. Low voices curled from the center. More people were watching from the hotel, their heads outlined in the lit windows. Many of the men in the crowd were harvesters — Americans. They could be told by their wide-brimmed hats. He smelled them as he moved nearer — the dark odor of sweat, petroleum, and soil. On the other side of their murmuring — the low, humming malevolence — he heard distinct grunts and blows, one blow following another. He stopped a few feet away. Between the bodies, he glimpsed one head higher than all the others. The pink light filled its shock of pale hair like fire. The head cocked back, then lunged forward, and there was the sound of a single, sharp blow and the thud of a body collapsing to the ground. Then everything stopped. The men stood still. Their silence made a hole in the night. The boy felt himself trembling. A passage opened in the crowd and Hugo burst through it. His face was blotched. The boy felt himself being passed as if by a bright field of energy. Hugo strode rapidly away. Through the passage, the boy glimpsed a young American on the ground. He had dark hair, as dark as the boy's own, and a twisted, sun-darkened face.

He lay prone and another man knelt over him. The boy looked back along Main Street. Sergeant MacLeod appeared, pulling his suspenders over his shoulders, but down the side street that led to Ilse's house Hugo's silhouette had already grown small.

That night after he went to bed, the boy listened to the stirring of his parents' voices. They didn't know what he'd seen. "It was the accent," his father said. "They mocked it. They mocked where he was from."

His mother said, "There are people here from the same place with the same accent."

"Yes," his father said, "but maybe they know how to keep out of harm's way when there's bad feeling."

To the boy's surprise, his mother seemed to be defending Hugo. "But why should they? The war's over. Germany's in ashes."

"It's the Americans," his father said. "They're prideful. They won't let up."

"Yes." His mother's voice, clear as a flute, swooped downward and took on a burnish. "They're savages and outlaws, every one of them."

There was a silence, then footsteps. The boy knew it was his father moving, that he was pacing a loop from the kitchen to the living room as he thought, and that he would then turn back and speak. The boy lay still with his hands at his sides, rigid as a board. He heard his father's footfalls on the kitchen linoleum, then the words: "Listen. Our people were there. Even the CCF committeemen. They should know to stop the like in their town."

"Yes," his mother said, "and I'm glad it was the American who got hurt. When they're here, the mothers are afraid to let their daughters go outside."

After church that Sunday, the boy stood on the lawn near a group of men. By then the harvesters had moved on, and the men were talking about the fight. The boy poked at the ground with the toe of his shoe as he listened. "He was pushed into it," Sven Johanessen said.

"Maybe," said another man, whom the boy knew as Otto,

the butcher. "But he could have stopped before he broke the American's jaw."

The stationmaster, Krains, said, "What about the midnight marches?"

A fourth man said, "I heard the jaw was shattered like glass. It is not a good thing." This man was Louis Carpenter, who was so successful that he'd bought into the equipment outlet. He wore a gold watch chain, and his deep, resonant voice brimmed with conviction. He was the church treasurer and the first to run his own combines. It was said that he owned thousands of acres and that before long the party would put him up for Parliament.

Johanessen spoke up again: "I've never seen such a punch."

"Easy now," Louis Carpenter said softly.

Otto said, "No, it was not necessary to hit the American like that."

The stationmaster held his two fists poised in front of his belt and said, "What about those marches, eh? What about that? Have you seen him? Have you looked at Ilse lately?"

The others were not listening to Krains. The group of them shifted away from him. They came nearer the boy, who looked down at the little trench he'd dug with his toe but held his ground. He heard Johanessen's voice, husky, swelling with admiration: "It was as though he hit him with a hammer." It was true. As the boy remembered, it was as if a chime had been struck.

※

Following harvest, the town had a festival. The parade in the afternoon began at the train station behind the elevator and ran just beyond the church and fire station. Half the town lined the two sides of the street to watch the other half go by. There were flag bearers, farm machinery, trucks, horses pulling carts, and two Model T Fords. The church choir wore its long, white robes and sang "Oh, Sacred Head" a cappella. The boy's mother had joined the choir for the parade, and when she passed where he stood watching, she inclined her head forward and raised her eyebrows questioningly at him. He glanced into the perambulator at his side. His brother was there, sleeping under a flannel blanket. The boy had been told he was in charge of his brother during the parade, although he also believed he was being overseen by the doctor's wife, Mrs. Pruitt. A person as wide as she was tall, Mrs. Pruitt had no children of her own. She stood several steps away – all flowered cloth, pansies on a field of white, the block of this bisected by a belt with a big steel buckle. The boy's authority, he sensed, was fragile.

Nevertheless, he looked back at his mother and nodded gravely. His mother's eyes flashed. She smiled. She was small and strong, and she skipped lightly to rejoin the pace of the choir. Her red hair shone in the sun. A matched team of four white oxen followed, pulling a long, flat wagon on which was mounted Louis Carpenter's portable sawmill. The mill's diesel engine was running. It overwhelmed the strains of the hymn from the choir. Dark puffs of exhaust floated to the rooflines, then sailed down the street. Louis Carpenter himself drove the team. He wore overalls and a red shirt, and it seemed odd to the boy that the everyday apparel looked like a costume on him. The engine's flywheel spun, the belt narrowed to the drive wheel, and the big blade whirled. When it passed, the boy looked across the street at Hugo, who stood by himself on the far side of the hotel. Hugo leaned forward and scrutinized Louis Carpenter's machine with such ferocity that it seemed he might leap out of his skin.

Children not much older than the boy rode decorated bicycles. Behind them came a group of mothers dressed in white skirts and blouses with big red maple leaves on their fronts and backs. The community band followed, playing "God Save The Queen," with the Boy Scout troop and the banker, Horace Jones, in his chocolate-colored Packard in tow. The boy's father sat next to Horace Jones in the front seat. Two schoolteachers carried a slate on which had been written in yellow chalk, "Our Youth! Our Future!" The two fire engines passed with their bells ringing furiously. Periodically, their sirens knifed through the air. At the end came Sergeant MacLeod in his scarlet coat on his motorcycle. He had a sled dog beside him in a sidecar. Each time the sirens went off, the dog began to howl. Each time the dog howled, the boy saw Hugo rock back on his heels and grin, and then, sliding his gaze to the alley at the side of the hotel, the boy saw a family, dark-skinned and darkly clad. They became a mobile darkness in the shadows, father, mother, two children, and a spotted horse. The father turned the horse, which pulled a travois. They moved away down the alley. *Piegans,* the boy had heard such named. He saw them again later from the front of the church at twilight as they angled away from the two gleaming lines of the train rails and moved into the distance across a wheat field. They were a ragged snarl of darkness vanishing into the blonde stubble, and the boy wondered – Where? Going where?

At nightfall the oil lamps mounted on posts were lit, and then a bank of electric lights, too, mounted on stands. Tables heavily laden with food stretched across the street from the churchyard to the fire station. Mrs. Pruitt and the boy's mother saw to it that he had a heap of bean salad to go with his grilled pork and scalloped potatoes. A beer keg was tapped. There was dancing to the tuba, bass drum, clarinet, and two violins of a polka band. The people thronged the street, whirling and bumping up against each other. The women's long skirts snapped as they swung. In the center the stamping feet reverberated in the earth. The air was thick with the smell of food and dust and with sound, the throbbing music and the grunts of the dancers. The boy's head pounded and his skin tingled with excitement. It was as if he had entered the pulsing heart of music. When he saw Ilse Goettinger's strudel appear on one of the tables, he sidled up to it, took a large helping in a bowl, drenched it with cream from a white pitcher, and then retreated to the edge of the crowd. He ate slowly, deliberately closing his teeth on each bite through the parchment of pastry to the sweet honey and fruit. He was transported by the taste. From where he stood, the music became reedy sounding as it dissipated into the air. Thin layers of dust hung above the lamps.

When he saw his mother cradling his brother against her shoulder, he edged deeper into the shadows near the steps of his father's church. He came upon a group of men there, standing in a circle. They held plates heaped with food. Among them were Louis Carpenter, Krains, and Stan Fassbinder, a large man with a spoon-shaped nose. Several Catholics were there. They talked about Hugo. One farmer, a Catholic named Kowalski, complained about raising animals for commercial purposes in town. "It's not the custom," he said.

Louis Carpenter said, "But it's something, the way he has the pens set up. The eggs roll into a catch. He keeps charts. He has temperature controls and a contract with a soup company to take the hens that don't yield."

Krains, the stationmaster, said he'd learned over the wire that Hugo had been in prison. A heavy silence fell over the others as they turned to Krains. "Don't you understand?" Krains asked.

"Easy," Louis Carpenter said. The men looked around as if to see who might be listening. The boy felt their eyes pass over where he stood in the darkness as if he were nothing. He was nothing, merely a boy.

The men ate for a moment, their forks clinking against the plates. The boy tipped his bowl to his mouth and drank down the last of the cream. Out in the street, the bass drum thumped the start of another tune. The stationmaster's voice rose. His body was rigid. He spoke of war – bombing raids, gas chambers.

"Now, Carl," Louis Carpenter said, reaching out to grasp the stationmaster's arm. "Easy."

Fassbinder said, "Louis is right. We've been through this in this town. Not again. It's torn us apart once already. It causes pain."

But again Krains spoke up, and the boy heard exotic-sounding names: *Düsseldorf, Liege, Argentina.* When he finished, the men shifted a little farther apart from one another. The boy had no idea what it all meant, only that the men seemed to share his fascination for Hugo, that they seemed also afraid. But these men, he had always considered fearless. Except for Krains, every one of them was big. Their powerful hands burst out of their shirtsleeves as their blunt fingers gingerly crowded the plates. Their faces were hard and square.

Chickens

"Look at that. Look at Ilse," Kowalski said. The group turned to the dancers. The boy watched as Hugo and Ilse swung out to the edge of the tangle. Hugo stared stonily over the top of Ilse's head. His quick feet whirled Ilse in perfect unison with the rhythms of the polka, but his arms, torso, and head were poised as if stilled within the thrall of violent motion. Ilse seemed to take two steps for every one of his. It was as if Hugo held her aloft and her feet merely mimed in the air the steps of the dance. The couple drove back into the center of the throng. "He's sucking her dry," Kowalski said. The words conjured an image in the boy's mind of a spider drawing the life from its prey. It was true that Ilse seemed thinner than he remembered. She had developed a stunned look, and something boxlike in the cut of her jaw.

❧

From his backyard the boy could look southward or eastward past Ilse's house into the grain fields. The fields were green in the early summer, blonde in the late summer, and white all through winter. In fall the blonde darkened because the black earth showed through the wheat stalks. Later in his life when he lived in another country, the boy's sense of the ocean would arise from the smallness he'd felt in the prairie, from the way the prairie's endlessness made him feel lifted outside of himself. His sense of the rightness of the rhythms of the ocean, the rise and fall, was an activation of the stilled rightness in the rhythm of the prairie.

Sometimes he rode out of town with his father in the family's Marmon to visit the other churches. When they returned, the boy would perch himself on the edge of the seat to look out for the town. From the distance, the grain elevator appeared first, then the fire station and church steeple, and finally the rest of the town in between, all of it looking like what he imagined a heavily laden ship at sea must look like. The town would grow larger until it filled the windshield. Details became visible: in the summer the fences around the houses, the bright red and yellow flowers and sometimes people in the yards, suspended divans on the porches, the glitter of bicycles, clothes fluttering on the lines, yellow fuel barrels, wheelbarrows, people in the streets, people at work, and everywhere in the town a certain darkness of earth and shadow. The boy would think of the harvesters, or of the Piegans, absorbed into the earth, or of Hugo Goettinger, arriving here from the mysterious, distant place. The boy wondered how this town – all he knew of the world – would seem to him if he were the newcomer, a stranger entering his own life.

Throughout the fall the boy caught only glimpses of Hugo. The man spent most of his time inside the barn. The boy found a sheltered place to sit on top of the coal chute at the back of his house. He was protected there on one side by the kitchen wall and on another by the brick chimney. Warmth from the fire in the kitchen stove crept through the brick. If he waited long enough, he might see the tall man walking between Ilse's house and the chicken barn, using the tractor with the cable-driven loader to move the steaming manure, or carting eggs to the panel truck, which was used to make deliveries on the new egg routes. Smoke trailed from the barn's chimney. One day the boy saw Hugo emerge from the shed carrying a chicken by its feet. An ax head appeared, glinting above Hugo's head, and as it came down, Hugo lunged. Hugo lifted the headless chicken. Blood streamed from its neck. The boy was inflamed by the display of power.

On another day when he'd not seen Hugo outside, the boy moved away from his house and into the field. He skirted the backs of the other houses. The turned earth was frozen in ridges. He stopped to look back and found no one watching him. He thought – Wrong! – and for a moment he was unable to move. Then he ran headlong across the corner of the wheat field toward the concrete barn and ducked behind Hugo's manure pile, which gave off heat and the smell of ammonia. He peered at the barn. It had grates in the windows. The steel vents in the roof revolved slowly. He stood up and edged nearer, thinking – Wrong! – then darted out and ducked beneath the engine compartment of the tractor. His breath tangled in his throat. He looked under the tractor at the barn. Abruptly a door swung open, and in the frame of light, Hugo's figure appeared. He bent deeply at the waist and looked back at the boy. "Gut," he said in German. He beckoned and smiled broadly. "Come."

Panic-stricken, the boy obeyed. When he reached the doorway, Hugo gestured for him to go in. "Schnell! The cold!" The boy entered. The door clicked shut behind him. Inside, the air was warm and satiny, and the boy found himself under a sheet of sound, the clucking of the hundreds of chickens joining to make one throbbing commotion. Hugo was behind him. The boy stared straight ahead down an aisle, and then as his fear increased, he desperately skittered his eyes this way and that. On either side of the aisle was a row of steel cages filled with white chickens. Beyond those were more rows, row upon row going to the walls. Beneath the cages were pans like cookie sheets that caught the chalky droppings. The concrete floor was scoured clean. The walls were white. Creeping plants grew beneath the windows, which they encircled, scaling the walls to the ceiling. Above the cages hung lines of electric lamps. Interspersed among them were kerosene lamps. Just to the boy's right stood a coal furnace with a complicated array of dials, valves, vents, and levers. It radiated heat. Hugo stepped between the boy and the furnace, and the boy glanced up, then watched as Hugo plunged one hand into the pocket of his striped coveralls. The man extracted a gold watch, popped open its lid, scrutinized it, and then, the boy. "Early" he said. The boy looked away in astonishment, now fixing on the pipe that ran from the furnace to the far end of the barn. It circled and returned to the chimney in the center. He looked back but avoided Hugo's gaze by staring at a water cauldron on top of the furnace. The cauldron emitted a cloud of steam. Even in his terror, the boy understood that the heat, light, plants, and vapor were like magic, recreating summer.

Hugo said, "Hier!" as he strode into the aisle. The boy obeyed again. The chickens had yellow legs, yellow beaks, and red eyes. There was one to each cage. Some pecked at their neighbors through the wires. The clamor was ceaseless. Running along the backs of the cages were two troughs – one for feed, one for water. At the fronts of the cages was a wire trough to which the eggs rolled. Hugo plucked up eggs as he passed. Sometimes as his big hand approached, a chicken fluttered and shrieked, and the chicken in the next cage did the same. The shrieking and beating wings made a snake of sound that slipped through the horde, exciting more knots of pandemonium. Hugo stopped and turned back. The boy stopped. Each of Hugo's hands was filled with eggs, the delicate things cradled by the powerful fingers. It was like a trick. Hugo grinned and gestured broadly with a handful of eggs, bringing them close to the boy's face. "Dey come quick," he said. "Die Eier. Eggs, you say? Die Eier? You come."

They reached a space at the far end of the barn where Hugo set his eggs in a basket. He showed the boy the equipment kept there – a dolly that was pushed along the aisle as eggs were gathered, shovels, feed sacks, the water spigot that fed the troughs, and a cupboard filled with medicine bottles. As he touched each thing, Hugo named it in his broken English. His teeth were as white as snow. For a moment it seemed to the boy as if his fascination for Hugo was part of a dream, as if now he had entered the dream and found Hugo awaiting him. But when it struck him that this might mean he would have to stay in the dream, terror rushed back at him. Hugo had large, chiseled-looking lips. His red tongue moved awkwardly, touching his teeth as he struggled to form words, but his aura of hard white light emanating from the pale skin remained undisturbed.

Hugo took out a syringe and squeezed the plunger. A thread of liquid shot out from the needle. He gestured toward the chickens and said, "Keine Krankheit. Sickness. Nein. Perfect!" The boy looked out at the racks of chickens, then back at Hugo's smiling face. He looked at the needle. A drop fell from its tip. The boy knew about sickness and needles, and hated them both. The man's eyes blazed, but his voice was soft and insistent. He leaned forward, plucked gently at the boy's sleeve, and said, "Jahre?" The boy didn't understand. Hugo said, "How many? So Klein. How old?"

"Seven," the boy said.

Hugo pulled back and frowned. He said, "Wie heisst Du?"

The boy stared at him.

"Name."

"Jim," the boy said.

"Jim," Hugo said flatly.

"Jim Blood," the boy said.

"Blood!" Hugo said. "Blut!" He leaned against a pile of feed sacks and began to laugh. The laughter was eerie and high-pitched. His ears turned red. The boy edged away, then froze when Hugo abruptly bent and placed his hands on his knees. He stared fiercely at the boy and whispered, "Jim Blood?" The boy turned and fled down the aisle, pulled open the door, ran out into the cold and straight across the wheat field toward his house. As he ran he heard his mother's voice crying out, high and thin in the cold air, "Jimmy! Jimmy!"

Later he understood that he'd been mistaken by Hugo for someone else, an older boy from one of the Goettinger farms who was to come into town to work for Hugo. This boy did come the next day. His name was Gus, but now Hugo, who hadn't even known who Jim was, would nod deeply whenever he saw the boy and smile as if he were about to break into laughter again. The smile chilled the boy. Gus sat next to Hugo in church on Sundays. The boy watched as Gus's face became more and more like Hugo's and Ilse's, the eyes wide as if shocked, the hair spraying out, and the grim cast to the jaw. He began to have a recurrent nightmare that ended with a voice like a raven's crying from the distance: "Die Eier! Die Eier!"

ॐ

Winter came. The boy's mother hung out his brother's diapers in the mudroom, then brought them into the kitchen. The diapers were frozen solid, and she carried them stacked in her arms like sheets of tin, the cold having shocked the moisture out of the cloth. When the diapers thawed, they were dry. Snow drifted to the bottoms of the windows. Only the upper walls and roofs of the buildings were visible. The earth was covered with snow, which the wind blew up against whatever would stop it.

Deep paths were shoveled from place to place. At the boy's house, one path led to the church. One led to the street. Another led to the outhouse and from it an offshoot led to the coal bin. All the houses in town had paths like these, and the boy knew the paths out on the farms were more intricate yet. The paths were maps of the lives passed upon them. Ilse's place, which the boy now observed from within his kitchen, was different. Hugo plowed every day. Only a skim of ice shone in the sun like moonstone on the grounds around the house.

The boy spent hours reading and playing near his kitchen stove. The year before, there had been the other baby, the sister who had died. The boy could recall that she'd been in the kitchen, that she was carried into his parents' room at night, and that then she wasn't there, that for weeks afterward his mother hardly spoke and that sometimes she suddenly burst into tears. He remembered the morning his sister died – his father rushing out of the house to fetch the doctor and his mother, behind the bedroom door, shrieking. It was a high, metallic sound that came again and again, falling to sobs and then rising to crash once more. It froze the boy to one spot in the center of the living room. Doctor Pruitt arrived, followed by Mrs. Pruitt, who took the boy away to her house. The baby had choked and suffocated. At her funeral his father stood straight at the head of the grave, his overcoat flapping in the breeze, his gray eyes the color of the sky. The boy's mother tottered at the edge of the hole as if to plunge into it, but Mrs. Pruitt came up behind her and held her arms. That was all. This was not long before Hugo came to town.

The boy had no recollection of his sister's face. He could remember himself looking at her, the way she wrapped a tiny hand around one of his fingers, and the feel of the bassinet's dry woven cane near the kitchen stove, but not her face. It was like peering into the grave: nothing, the nothingness of her in his memory became his own nothingness, a zero within him. Later in his life, he would understand that the loss of the child caused his mother's protectiveness and the grief that filled the house and raised in him his contrary impulses: the one to flee, the other to stay near his mother, to move to her, to try to find in her the heart of her panic, to fill up his zero with her.

He remembered better his mother standing at the stove the following fall and winter – this year. He remembered her still haggard face and dispirited words, her worry and wishing. He remembered her rushing off to attend to church business or fussing over his brother, who would soon turn two and now slept in the boy's room against the far wall. She would come upstairs late at night to make sure her sons were safe and warm. The boy remembered her hand touching his chest and her face coming near. There was a dark smell of coal smoke in her hair as it brushed his face and an incising scent of lilac in her skin. He inhaled her.

He remembered the eggs, which she'd left on a kitchen windowsill one night. In the morning the eggs were frozen, the shells cracked. It triggered something in his mother. Her eyes sparked as she raged. She said she didn't want to stay in this place a day longer. He remembered his father cradling her next to the stove and her eyes gradually softening. His father put the eggs in a white bowl with a red rim and set it up on the stove's reservoir. "We'll make Yorkshire pudding," he said. The eggs thawed. The boy stood on a chair to look. The bowl was filled with thick yellow liquid and the shells floated on top. He heard the voice in his mind, crying, "Die Eier! Die Eier!"

The eggs were Hugo's. He used the panel truck to deliver to his new clientele. He plowed the roads with his war surplus truck, but only far enough to clear his routes, which became a map of his success. In the past people switched to horses when the drifting was worst. Now, they could use cars on sections Hugo had plowed, but only so far. A cleared road might stop abruptly in a heap of snow. The pattern of plowed and unplowed roads allowed some to drive clear into town from the outlying farms, while others still used horses. The boy had heard one man say it was a wonder what Hugo managed to do. Someone else said that the plowing was a pressure upon them to purchase the eggs. After Sunday services the boy listened to the men in the church vestibule. Hugo had gone too far, some said. The boy was confused by these men who drove the roads Hugo had cleared and who then condemned Hugo for plowing. One Sunday Otto, the butcher, lowered his voice, leaned into the knot of men, and said that Ilse was buying quantities of meat. "It's like she's feeding an army," Otto said. The boy imagined Ilse's kitchen draped with great slabs of beef.

"Do you remember how she used to laugh? Always laughing, Ilse was," Otto said. "But not now."

Another man said that next year Hugo planned to start up a dairy, that the egg deliveries were just a beginning. Someone else said he'd heard it would be turkeys next. Krains, the stationmaster, began to speak. The boy heard dangerous-sounding names: *Schutzstaffel, Nazi.* Krains went on, speaking in his high voice of Germany, stolen money, and killing, and the boy felt a terror that the words would carry down the stairwell. Hugo had passed through the vestibule just before the men gathered in it. He'd led Ilse down to the basement where, at this moment, the ladies were setting out cakes and brewing pots of coffee. The boy thought of Hugo standing down there, nodding and smiling at anyone who came near.

As Krains spoke other men began to mutter angrily. The vestibule filled with venom. Stan Fassbinder spoke up, "Careful. Careful, boys." The men looked around, and the boy pretended to busy himself by straightening the candles in a candelabra that stood in the corner. No one marked him. "What has he done to any of us?" Stan Fassbinder asked.

Krains replied, "I hear he was an agricultural engineer."

"That means he knows his business," Louis Carpenter said. The others fell silent and Louis Carpenter went on, "The war is over. The drought is over. Farmers have power in the government now."

Louis Carpenter passed his eyes over the group then took a

step back. He had a broad, pale brow and fleshy, purple lips. His voice began again as soft and rich as his brushed tweed suit, the gold watch chain that passed across his vest, and the knitted, brown tie: "The devil's here, passing on the wind, seeking out weakness. He still has the Ottawa bankers in his thrall." Louis Carpenter's voice rose. "Get thee behind me! We have a kingdom to build! May our children never know the shame of poverty or the gall of being thrown from their lands." The floor creaked as Louis Carpenter leaned forward. His voice dropped almost to a whisper. "Look what Hugo has done – single-handedly created a home market."

The boy was transfixed by the words, which he scarcely understood . . . only that it was CCF politics that sprang somehow from his father's sermon on Christ's forty days in the wilderness. All the men in the vestibule had becharmed expressions on their faces, too, except Krains, who stared fixedly straight ahead and whose fists had turned white at his sides. To the boy, the words had a strange, spinning force that drove his mind to a recurring nightmare in which Hugo pursued him and trapped him in a corner. Hugo's hands were loaded with eggs. Eggs kept tumbling off, but each time, Hugo would snatch up the falling egg in mid-air and return it to the heap. His face was as white as death, but his eyes burned. He came nearer and nearer with his heap of eggs, shouting, "Die Eier! Die Eier!"

෴

He had the nightmare again several nights later and awoke and heard the shouts. He lay on his back in his narrow bed, drew his hands out from under the blankets, held them in front of his face, and moved each finger one at a time, counting them. He slipped out of bed, taking care not to disturb his sleeping brother. He knelt at the window and peered outside. At first, he saw only the snow-swept street, the houses, shops, hotel, and at the far end the towering elevator – everything bleached by moonlight. It seemed the cries he heard – "Die Eier! Die Eier!" –

were still sailing out of the world of his dream, and then he saw a figure, a black form struck against the white. It moved along the center of the street, past the hotel, the mercantile. . . . It kept coming, kicking its legs high. The figure was tall and angular. It wore a black uniform with glistening dots of light on the breast. The earth rang with each blow of the gleaming boots. It was Hugo. He held one arm outward as if to take command of all that fell before him . . . the street, the town. As he passed beneath the window, the boy saw clearly the white, frozen face and then heard the words differently. They confused him then, but later in his life, recalling the words, he would recognize them: "Sieg Heil! Sieg Heil!"

෯

In early March the cold relented. The snow remained, but on Saturdays townspeople met in the park for outdoor badminton matches. The boy's parents played. The Catholics came. The boy and his brother stayed in a three-sided shelter next to a stove made out of an oil drum. A fire crackled in the drum and the metal turned pink. The boy sat on a bench, and his brother sat nearly smothered under blankets in a wooden crate bolted to a sled. As the adults played, they stripped off coats, sweaters, and gloves. Their boot hobs squeaked on the packed snow. The shuttlecock flew lightly over the net. The breath of the players came out in white puffs as they sprang in the world of white, the bushes and trees weighted down with white, and the gently heaving fields, as far as the eye could see, and the white of the sky kissing the cold white earth.

At a pause in the games, the men and women came into the shelter to drink cocoa. The boy tucked his feet under the bench and cradled a warm mug against his chest. His brother's bright eyes peered out from among the blankets. The shelter grew dark with bodies. The boy smelled perspiration and the damp wool of sweaters. The people talked and laughed softly, and at times the group would spread out or rock to and fro. But then the boy heard a voice say something about Louis Carpenter, who'd taken his car out on the plowed roads during a storm and never returned home. The people stood still in silence. Finally a woman said that if the roads hadn't been plowed willy-nilly, Louis would never have driven his car.

The people fell into a deeper silence and then started in again. The voices growled. The bodies shifted closer together. The boy's sense of them was of tremendous, suffocating density. He heard the words – *Fascist, Criminal.* The Catholics spoke as one with the Protestants while the boy listened for Stan Fassbinder, the voice of resistance and calm, but didn't hear it. He didn't hear his father, either, nor his mother, although he caught a glimpse of her face, wrenched with strain. What he heard was the angry muttering spreading nastily, and then the voice of Krains, the stationmaster, sailed overhead like a rooster cry. Krains said it was time for Sergeant MacLeod to do something. A murmur snaked through the crowd, creating small whiplike explosions at its turns, and the boy wondered if this was the devil, now, who had found his way in to bind up all the hearts in a knot.

The next Sunday was the day for the boy's father to minister to the other churches out in the country. Since the snow was still deep, he planned to travel by horse-drawn sled and decided to take the boy with him. It would be an outing. The boy's mother disapproved, but his father said it would do the boy good to get out of the house. They drove down one of Hugo's plowed roads, then came upon an unplowed stretch. The clipping sounds of the hooves grew muffled, and as they arrived at another plowed section, they had to skirt a large bank of snow that had been left in the way. Suddenly the horses sank to their bellies right in front of the sled. Then the horses vanished entirely. There was a wild thrashing, the sled swung sideways, and the boy clutched his father's arm to keep from falling out. The heads of the horses reared back into sight, raising clouds of snow. The sled jumped forward, righting itself, but the snow came up nearly to the floorboards. The boy's father shouted and bent back, pulling the reins taut, making the horses stand still, deep in the snow with just their heads showing.

Chickens

"I drove into the dog-biting barrow ditch," the boy's father said. His face was blank. A new snow had fallen the night before, and as he'd negotiated the bank he lost track of the road. He adjusted himself now and touched the boy's leg and looked at him. "I guess we're all right, eh?" he said gently. He would have to wade chest deep into the ditch, unhitch the team, extend the line and gee up the sled, rehitch the team, and certainly be late for his services. For the moment he put his arms on his knees and gazed at the two horse heads that looked decapitated, resting there on top of the snow with their angry, flattened ears. He began to laugh. As he laughed his face grew fixed. Suddenly he whirled, facing the town behind them, shook his fist, and cried, "Damn you!"

The boy had never heard his father curse, and he felt something close in his mind: Even him, now, even my father, he thought. Then it must be so. Soon something will happen. For the boy this was at once personal and not personal because he knew – again, without exactly understanding it – that his father was trusted, that once his rectitude was broken, the town would lose what remained of its own. It was over. The boy felt the contradiction rising in himself because, although he was terrified of Hugo, the fascination remained. The fascination had become a form of love for the alien, the separate, and the wildly secret.

§≈

Not long afterward when the thaw began in earnest, the top of a car appeared in a ditch just outside town, beside one of Hugo's heaps of snow. People went out with shovels and a tractor. They knew who it was, and everyone was amazed that it had happened so near. The pool of red metal that slowly enlarged as the snow melted off the roof told them it was Louis Carpenter's Lincoln. Someone came for the boy's father. While his mother wasn't looking, the boy snatched up his coat and slipped out the door to follow. The men had already dug out the snow in front of the car and attached a chain to the bumper. When the tractor pulled, the

103

chain went taut. There was a sharp crack as the car broke free of the ice, then the tractor hauled it up to the road. The door had to be popped open with a bar. Inside the car the boy glimpsed a figure inclined toward the steering wheel.

He stood to the side but remained near enough to see. More people gathered. A car drove up and Mrs. Carpenter flew out. The boy's father leaned into Louis Carpenter's car and came out, pulling a body by the shoulders. Stan Fassbinder caught the legs before they hit the ground. One of the body's knees was kicked up crazily, its arms reached out as if to hold something, and the face was perfectly that of Louis Carpenter, though as white as snow. The body thumped sharply when it was set down in the bed of a truck. Mrs. Carpenter leaned into the truck, weeping frantically. She struggled to climb into the truck bed, but the boy's father said, "No," and firmly put his hands on her shoulders to keep her back.

The women drew Mrs. Carpenter away and closed around her, making a huddle in the road. Their ankles stuck out below their flapping skirts. Their heads and shoulders were bent inward. Mrs. Carpenter's weeping began to sound softer, a moaning. One or two of the women made a cooing sound as they tried to comfort her. When the truck's engine started up, the circle of women swayed, containing Mrs. Carpenter, and when the truck vanished, the women's voices rose and took flight across the prairie. It was a singing conjured from snow. "Aaiii! Aaiii!" the voices wailed.

The boy walked back to town with his father and several other men, who were turning angry. They said they knew who was to blame, that if the government didn't take him out of their town, they'd do it themselves. The boy heard the words "deport" and "demon." The bell at the fire station was ringing, making the air shudder. At the side of the parsonage, his mother beat at a rug she'd hung up on the line. One fire engine passed them slowly, its engine making a low, raw sound while ice snapped under its wheels. It was followed by Sergeant MacLeod on his motorcycle. The boy's mother kept hitting the rug violently again and again with a cane. Puffs of dust floated into the crisp air. His brother was out there, too, wearing his bright yellow snowsuit. He tottered toward his father and brother with his arms straight out at his sides. The pale blue sky was dotted with white, puffy clouds. The bell at the fire station stopped ringing. The boy's mother followed the three of them into the house and said, "I don't think I'd have taken the boy out there to see that."

"It's Louis," his father said.

"I know. I heard. Of course. It had to be him."

His father said, "The boy was there before I knew it."

"And now they're after Hugo," his mother said.

"I suppose they are," his father said.

"They'll have their way no matter what."

His father said, "They believe he's had his too long."

"Yes," his mother said. "That's the truth. But there are laws. They should follow the law."

"Yes," his father said. His voice sounded hollow. "They'll make use of the law."

"Make use," his mother said. "Then there's no law but what's to be as twisted as he is."

His father raised his hands, palms up. It was a preacher's gesture, which expressed the inescapability of pain. "It's gone past me now."

The boy stood in front of the cookstove, toying with the nickel-plated spring that hung from the handle of the oven door. The spring was not too hot to touch, and yet it was too hot to hold. He felt his brother's hand on his hip. A picture of Louis Carpenter's face and cocked up leg and reaching arms filled his mind . . . he of the magnificent voice who would soon have stood for Parliament.

"I want out of here," his mother said. "And the boy should not have been out to see what he saw or to hear what he heard. He's heard far too much as it is."

The boy thought. "But I'm here. I'm here at this moment. You're talking here. You're talking about what I saw. I'm eight now. I'm here."

Chickens

"I suppose he'll have to hear such and see such sometime," his father said.

"Not yet," his mother said. Her eyes flashed. "Not yet, by God." She stalked out of the kitchen to the living room, and the boy heard the piano cover slap up and then the first notes of a Chopin prelude. It stopped suddenly. "I want out of here," his mother called from the living room. "Now. Tomorrow. I want a train ticket tomorrow." There was a pause. His father stood still. Next, the chords of a hymn began, and then that stopped, too, followed by a crash of notes . . . his mother, in her rage, slamming her arms against the keys and holding the notes down.

The boy heard everything, every note, every cacophonous juxtaposition that defied the old, familiar gravity of chords and melody. He hung onto the cookstove's nickel-plated spring as if his life depended on it. It burned into his hand. He listened to all the notes, their overwhelming dissonance, and entered the heart within the heart of music – the hot, wild, chaotic heart of hearts. He couldn't let go of the spring, and then he heard himself screaming.

℘

The boy would always remember G—— as if it were his birthplace though it was not. He was born elsewhere, in another province, but that place didn't exist in his memory. Before G——, before his sister died and his brother came, before the eggs, the chickens, the howling wind, his mother's outrage, and the year 1949, before Ilse, before Louis Carpenter was believed to have been killed by a man the boy had strangely loved, and before Hugo himself – who remained always an intimate demon in the boy's recollection – there was nothing. After that he had enough. The people of G—— were first- and second-generation immigrants, most of them – Germans, Swedes, Poles, Finns, Yugoslavians, Russians, English, and Belgians such as Krains. They were farmers and merchants, a good people. As a man, he would wonder if there had been a Jewish family among them. He had no idea.

Chickens

The last thing he remembered of Hugo was not his departure under the escort of Sergeant MacLeod, who dressed him in manacles and took him away by train to Regina where, it was said, he was taken into custody by immigration officials. Nor was the last thing Ilse's death, which occurred soon after Hugo's departure. But it came even after that while his mother was in the kitchen . . . still there . . . when the boy walked to the far edge of his yard to watch the burning of chickens outside the concrete barn. Unattended, the chickens had wasted away. Goettinger men arrived from the farms and emptied the cages, used Hugo's loader to make a pile out of the bodies, then doused the pile with diesel fuel and lit it. That was the end, the white heap with the smoldering red eye of fire slowly swirling into black, and the silhouetted figures standing in a circle around it deep into the evening. Above them the stench of the smoke, unctuous against the darkening sky, drifted into the town.

I Could Love You (If I Wanted)

LOLA HAD DECIDED to move out of the apartment that nestled in the shadow of the hospital tower where her mother lay dying. A real estate salesman came and drove her and her two little girls out to see a rental house in the country. He said the owners had installed a new roof and paid five hundred dollars to have the interior cleaned. The salesman was skeletal. He wore a red vinyl coat and a blue ball cap that matched the color of the big blue Lincoln, which he steered with his fingertips. His name was Bob. When Lola caught him stealing looks at her, she gazed back evenly in order to thwart his interest. He glanced at her again, and then quickly away, which permitted her to inspect him. He had sallow skin, a mustache as thin as a pencil line, and a patch of stubble on the side of his jaw that he'd missed with his razor.

They drove through the trees and came out into the long evening light of autumn, then turned onto a lane that led to an old farmhouse. Bob told her that the place had stood empty for a year. The agency had stripped out the carpeting, he said. But there was a new space heater in the living room and a fresh coat of sealant in the basement. When Lola got out of the car, she had to step around a jackhammer that had been left to rust on the ground. Bob came up beside her, lit a cigarette, and brushed her arm lightly as they stared toward the house.

Lola looked at the wreckage: besides the jackhammer, the corrugated steel sections were blowing away from the walls of the huge hay barn up on the rise to the left, an acetylene welder leaned against a tree, and in a ring like battlements around the house lay hulks of cars and scores upon scores of abandoned tools. Her daughters, Yvette and Nikki, scrambled over the fire-scorched foundation of a milking parlor. The house had weathered, silvery siding. Its new galvanized roof reflected the sky. The narrow two-story building looked light, as if it were about to float away. Behind it were wheat fields. To the right the ground sloped into a pasture where a dozen Holstein cows grazed. Their black-and-white coats glistened.

An iron fence encircled the house. Bob opened the gate, and when Lola passed through, he leaned toward her and said, "We'll put in a new water heater, too." His coat squeaked in the cold. He blew out a cloud of cigarette smoke and the sweet odor filled Lola's nostrils. Inside the fence and up against the house, the flower beds were choked with weeds. The sinking sun glanced against the windows of the house, turning them into mirrors. Lola saw herself in one – black coat and hood, blonde hair, cream-colored face. It seemed as if she were glimpsing a stranger.

Bob said that if she took the place, he'd be pleased to come by to make sure everything was right. "I bet," Lola said acidly. She had never met this man before but believed she knew him absolutely. At her words his body rocked back, and she thought it remarkable . . . a man so thin his bones almost chimed against each other, so unlike her own Louis, who brimmed with life. Her daughters shrieked with mock fright as they swung inside the fence and ran toward her. Lola placed her hand on a wobbly banister, stepped up to the door, and peered inside through the window. She saw a dark plank floor and pale walls flooded with angular light, and to one side, another doorway leading to an obscure room.

Lola turned back and said, "Two-fifty a month is too much. Look at this place."

"The inside is fine. You haven't even seen it," Bob said.

"I'd give you two-fifty if I had the rights of salvage to all the crap that's laying around. Then you'd get it cleaned up. It's going to snow. If you leave it, what good would it be ruined? You'd have to pay somebody to haul it out."

৳৯

To Lola's surprise her proposal was accepted. After Bob returned her to her apartment, she walked to the hospital. She left the girls in the waiting room and went to see her mother. The old woman, Wanda, wanted out of bed, but her sickness had moved into her legs. They swelled and bled. She had hot and cold flashes. She had cancer in her liver. She wanted to have a tea party. She wanted to go out drinking. "Talk to me," she said. Lola began reading aloud from the *National Enquirer*, something about Kenny Rogers and his hundreds of women and then the one about the lady who gave birth to a salamander. "The sky's the limit with these things," Lola interjected.

"Shut up," Wanda said.

Wanda forgot who was at her bedside, and yet she began to moan when Lola prepared to leave. Despite her resolve to not judge her mother and to hold her old outrage in abeyance, Lola was angry. Her mother twisted the sheet in her hands and contorted her ashen face. She said she wanted to take a drive, and then she imagined she was in a car, traveling with a man. "Let's go to Reno," she said to the imaginary man. To Lola, she said, "Me and Johnny have to go to Reno to gamble. It's Johnny Carson, you know. Excuse us."

"He's off the air," Lola said, and thought further that for all she knew he was dead. When Wanda tried to climb out of bed, Lola pressed her back into the mattress and was amazed at how light her mother was, like a leaf. Wanda stared at Lola with her opaque eyes, and said, "Who are you?"

"You don't know? You don't know who I am?" Lola said.

It was a two-person room, divided by a white curtain. The high-pitched voice of the other old woman in the room spoke up from behind the curtain. "Yes, she does. Deep down truly she knows. You keep coming, honey. A mother needs a daughter."

༄

The next day, Lola rented a U-Haul trailer. Her friend, Fanny Blue, who lived on the same block, helped her carry her things to the street. Fanny was heavyset, kind, and a cousin of Louis'. She worked in a gift and secondhand shop owned by Louis' brother, Sam. Lola had worked in Sam's shop, too, before she got a better job at Sears. That was how she'd first met Fanny and then Louis, and through Fanny she'd found this apartment, close to the hospital for the sake of her mother's treatments. For a time her mother had lived here with her. That was over. Two weeks ago Lola lost her job. Fanny had said that Sam would hire her back, but Lola declined. Now, Fanny wanted to come along to help unload the trailer, but Lola lied, saying she would have help there.

"Of course. You have Louis," Fanny said. "Is he back in town?"

They stood at the rear of the trailer. Fanny had a low center of gravity, and the smile on her face seemed connected by a stem to the bottom of her belly. She seemed to grow heavier and heavier, as if to counterbalance Lola's lie, then her expression grew sad. Lola felt sad, too, because to refuse Fanny's help was to insult her, because to lie to accomplish this was a yet deeper insult. Lola felt trapped. It seemed as if the earth were tipping under the sheer weight of Fanny's generous nature, and yet Lola couldn't bring herself to say that all she wanted in the world just now was to be alone with her daughters, to get away to some place where she didn't have to look at the hospital tower every time she stood at her kitchen sink, not even to see Louis unless she chose to.

She grasped the handle that latched the trailer door and listened as the girls chanted from the front seat of her old Chrysler, which the trailer was hitched to, "We love our Mama. We love our Mama. Let's go. Let's go."

Lola stared at the sidewalk where someone had spray-painted a swastika. "I have to change my life, Fanny."

"Listen," Fanny said. "When somebody you love dies, their presence changes form. But they're still with you. You'll be all right." Fanny's face was broad, brown, and soft as flour. She had three red ribbons tied into her black hair.

Lola wondered why what Fanny had said alarmed rather than reassured her. "I'll come by," she said. "Right away. You'll see." Her eyes welled with tears because Fanny was her friend, and she was still lying to her.

She moved quickly to her car, started it, and drove out of the valley. In the distance the mountains stood against the sky. The trailer made her old Chrysler handle like a boat. Nikki and Yvette became still as spiders. Lola headed west. They crossed the river and entered the woods, then the road wound through the mound country. Soon afterward, Lola turned onto the gravel lane and parked next to her new house. The girls leaped out of the car and ran in ever-widening circles, farther and farther away until their delighted shouts sounded like the calls of crows.

Lola unloaded everything herself – boxes, kitchen table, easy chair. She pulled the mattresses out of the trailer and dragged them through the gate, up to the porch, and inside. She dragged the sofa to the porch and then jockeyed each end alternately up the steps. When she had it close to the door, she threw herself down on it, lay back, and stared upward. The sun turned the sky above the horizon a metallic lemon color. Otherwise, the sky was slate blue. Small, puffy clouds floated by. A flock of geese passed beneath the clouds, making a racket with their honking. She watched and thought about how they must have been talking among themselves, that what she heard might actually be an argument over the next, best place to stop and eat, although from the ground the flock looked like a highly organized V.

Nikki and Yvette had gone into the house. Their running footsteps reverberated in the rooms. The moldy odor of the ancient, flowered wallpaper wafted through the screen door. The footsteps of her daughters talked to her as if they were played upon a drum. This is how it should be, Lola thought as she listened to her daughters and the dwindling cries of the geese heading south.

※

People had always said Lola was smart. Back in high school, her counselor had asked why she got As one semester and Fs the next. Lola couldn't answer. The counselor told her she should think of college. "Look," he'd said in exasperation. "Your test scores are awfully high. What is it?"

It was the lack of hope. Her mother was a drinker. As a girl, Lola had lived in one place after another with one man after another moving in for a year, a few months, or sometimes for a week or two. She'd grown exhausted, seeking the father she'd never known in these men – seeking him not just for herself but also for a ballast, a counterweight to the wildly listing life of her mother. Sometimes Lola had to care for her mother as if her mother were the child, taking her cure of orange juice, toast, and long, heavy sleeps.

A year after high school, Lola was married. A year later she was divorced. In three years she'd had Yvette out of wedlock, and then Nicole. The fathers of the girls had also disappeared. Her mother came to visit, once, from her home a hundred miles to the north. Not yet ill, her mother announced that it had only taken one baby to teach her how to get an abortion. Stunned at first, and speechless, Lola was just now beginning to understand that it was a falsehood, a profound lie, by which her mother's life had been governed. Lola required her daughters. Although she had Louis, too, in his way, floating at the far edge of a whirlpool that turned slowly around her, it was the girls she held close in the powerful eye of the vortex.

Lola was good with numbers. The people at Sears said they'd never seen anybody learn the computer so fast. She'd been assigned to train new workers, but she was fired for absenteeism. It was because attending to her children and her mother became too much to manage. Lola told that to her supervisor, not to gain sympathy, but because it was the truth. The supervisor, a well-kept woman with many sharp edges – pants suit, crisp blouse, sharp chin, plucked eyebrows, and glasses with rectangular frames – said, "Maybe we can hire you back when you get your life in order."

"Whose order?" Lola said. "Where do you keep it?"

The supervisor's eyebrows went up. "I beg your pardon."

Lola liked numbers. She liked the certainty of numbers, the way they became a part of a day, as domestic as teaspoons, hours, and miles to go. She also felt drawn to the flimsiness of the world of numbers, the chaos at its heart. She saw numbers in her dreams, phosphorescent, and flooding from the mouths of the people in her life.

I Could Love You (If I Wanted)

🙠

She returned the trailer to town that evening, went by McDonald's, then drove to the Saddle Inn to meet Louis. He was a trucker. She saw his rig, the Loadstar tractor and his grain trailer, pulled up at the edge of the road. Lola parked near the front door where Nikki and Yvette could watch the lighted Hamm's beer sign in which a yellow canoe dropped again and again over a blue waterfall. The night had turned cold. She let the girls open the McDonald's bag, loaded with hamburgers and French fries, then dumped a heap of blankets over them and gave them strict instructions not to move, not to argue, not to unlock the doors for anybody. "Count the canoe," she told them. "How many times it goes over."

They began immediately: "One. Two."

Inside she found Louis in a booth against the wall. When she slid in opposite him, he filled a glass from a pitcher of beer, pushed it toward her, and said, "I'm surprised you came. Who do you think you are? The Queen of England?"

"I'm here," she said.

He had black hair and a dark, pockmarked face that looked like it was carved out of wood. He smiled. He often smiled, but his face could change expressions behind the smile. It was as if there was a river running behind the mask of wood. He wore a leather vest with big silver buttons and under it a plaid shirt that was open over his smooth chest. On the table to one side, his gray Stetson rested upside down on its crown. His eyes held points of light.

"I'm moving," she said.

"I'll help you."

"I am moved," she said.

He gazed at her. "I got a new run that gives me three days off a week. We could go up to the hot springs."

"Mama's back in the hospital," she said.

Louis made a silvery sound in his throat.

Lola took a sip of beer and looked away. From the beam above the bar hung old lanterns, bridles, harnesses, and dangerous-looking tools – shears, prods, hooks, branding irons, and hunks of chain attached to metal hasps. Behind the back bar was a gun display. Four men in cowboy hats sat at the bar. A man and woman were next to each other in a booth near the door. The woman was closest to the wall, but Lola could see that the man had his hand on her leg. An image of her mother flashed into her mind – the tall woman flat as a board under the sheets with the ravaged face like a tattered flower sticking out the top.

Louis placed five twenty dollar bills on the table and looked expectantly at her. "Maybe we need some fun."

She stared at the bills. It was more than she had to get to her next unemployment check. Louis made good money. He was thirty-eight, married, and his wife, Bird, kept the books for the hauling operation. Between Louis and Bird there was a complicated equation into which she – Lola – had somehow been entered. She supposed that Louis' play money was allowed to leak out in order to keep the relationship from hemorrhaging. For two years Lola had awaited Louis' arrivals, for the hardness of his body. She liked to submit to him. She had grown attached to the sadness that swept through her when he left, the way her other problems passed away as she dwelled upon the trouble he always brought, the way the trouble made her life stop and hang as if between heartbeats, the way it pushed her through that pause into the jungle of herself – deep into the thick of the dark, absolute wild.

The bench creaked as Louis leaned back. Lola sat poised, touching her arms lightly to the table. He squinted at her and slowly tapped his glass with a fingernail. They sat that way, eyeing each another, until Lola finally said, "I need to be alone."

Louis made the silvery sound again, deep in his throat. It was a sound like heavy coins shifting in a purse. Lola looked down at her hands, stretched out to touch her glass. She looked up at an old axletree nailed to the wall, then at the jewel-studded saddle hanging over the jukebox and wondered how much it was worth. Louis leaned forward on his elbows. "You think you do. But you don't. Not now."

"You don't know what I think."

"People in pain shouldn't be alone."

"Who are you to talk about pain?"

"It ain't natural to be alone like that when you're in pain. It ain't safe, either."

"You cause me pain."

"Look," he said softly. "Sometimes, it's damn hard to tell whose pain is rightfully whose. What do you want?"

"Nothing."

He smiled. "Everybody wants something." Behind the smile the waters churned.

"I could . . ." she began, then stopped.

"Could what?" When she didn't answer, he said, "Besides, I know where you're moving to. It's the Bodines' old place. Fanny saw the realtor's sign on the car that picked you up. I called the office. I want to help."

Lola's teeth felt huge inside her mouth. It was how she'd felt as a girl when her mother left her with the produce man who beat her with his pale hands that smelled of disinfectant and who kept telling her over and over to do as she was told. The tavern jumped around in her vision, swimming with hooks, prods, and chains. She looked at the woman in the booth by the door. The woman had a narrow face. Her head was thrown back and her mouth was open like a pit. Her partner was turned toward her, crouched like a leopard. Finally, Lola gazed fixedly at the broad backs of the four men at the bar. They were utterly still, heavy as iron on their stools.

Louis touched her hand. "Let me help." In his mouth a gold tooth glimmered, and his eyes glinted like shards of glass. It was as if light came from behind the dark beautiful mask.

"No," she said. Louis had never hurt her, and yet she knew that if she stayed here she would give in and travel back through the shadows to his jungle. At the same time, she wanted to touch the softness of Louis's skin between the scars on his face, to feel the smoothness of his chest, the fine hairs on his belly, to stroke the earth-color of his body, to feel his callused hands holding her, to make her pain pivot upon his flesh. She was filled with desire. Suddenly she stood. Her legs shook wildly. "Don't you see that I could love you?" she said.

"Easy," he said, looking up at her.

"I could love you, if I wanted to." Her voice broke. It seemed as if something within her were about to explode.

"Easy, honey," he said. His eyes glittered.

As she lurched away, she glimpsed him sliding out of the booth behind her. She stumbled through the tavern doorway to her car. When she looked back, Louis was silhouetted in the doorway. The light from within shone around his head and body and between his legs. Lola put the key into the lock, opened her car door, and slid in. The two small faces in the front seat tipped up toward her like plates.

"Ten million!" Yvette announced.

"It's Louis. Look!" Nikki cried. She sat up straight and waved frantically.

૪ૐ

The next day, Lola drove into the city to visit her mother.

"It's Rodney," her mother said.

"Rodney?"

"Hi, sweetie," said the old woman behind the curtain.

"Dangerfield, you idiot," her mother said, wheezing with laughter.

"Mama, please, no," Lola said.

"Get it?" her mother said. "The fields of danger. What happened to him? Where'd he go? My Rodney. He disappeared." She stopped and rolled her eyes slowly from one side to the other, then said, "We're having our drugs. We're taking our drugs." Slowly her mother reached over to her tray and lifted a cup of water. The cup trembled in her hand. "Drugs," she said. "More drugs. They've got us drugged. We want more drugs. We like our drugs." She dumped the water onto her face. "Drugs!" she shouted hoarsely.

A nurse hurried in.

"Drugs," Lola's mother moaned.

"You've had your medicine," the nurse said.

"We want more. The pain is killing us." Once again, Lola's mother began to laugh. "Get it? Killing us. Me and Rodney." She gazed at Lola. "What do you want, you little whore?"

The voice of the old lady behind the curtain piped up: "She doesn't mean it. She's not herself. She needs you."

Lola was filled with despair. A doctor came and took her out into the hall. He was a young man hardly older than Lola herself. Lola understood that in the medical profession the young were allowed to cut their teeth on welfare cases. He had a smooth, fleshy face, and probably drove a Porsche. He said her mother was fading quickly, that the best they could do now was ease the pain, that perhaps if her condition stabilized she might go home with Lola. The hospice people could visit to help, he said.

Home! – Lola thought. It's my home!

But for now, the doctor said, it would not be wise to move her mother. Until that very moment, Lola hadn't believed her mother would ever actually die.

It began to snow as she drove through the city. Darkness fell. The city had on its Christmas lights, the tiny white lights on the trees that bordered the streets. Snowflakes danced in light and swirled against the buildings. On the open road outside the city, the snowflakes raced by the windshield. Lola and the girls pretended they were in a spaceship and that the snowflakes were stars. The girls lost themselves in the phantasm.

Lola thought about the infinity of stars. She'd read that this universe was connected to another by a pipe, that the two universes were mirrors of each other, and that at any moment one might rush into the other. Only gravity kept everything just barely arranged. Infinity was chaos. She wondered how things would be if people just did away with it, if there were no infinity but only the known piling up higher and higher like wheat. Maybe infinity was nothing more than a bad turn taken after a pretty good idea, like the bomb. She wondered if the way her mother's life kept rushing into her own and taking over would end after the death.

৯৯

Lola did not want to bring her mother to her house, but that night she cleaned as if it were foreordained. It was doom she felt, made out of the old contradiction: the necessity that she care and her wish not to care. There were tack marks around the edge of the hardwood floor in the living room. The kitchen linoleum had tears in it. Dirt was still caked to the kick space under the counters and in the corners of the windowsills. Everywhere she looked she found dirt, and sometimes even bits of what she thought was dung. She scrubbed the crevices with a brush and washed the floors with bleach. She soaked the stovetop parts in the sink. Fumes filled the rooms. She played a Sound Garden CD on her stereo, and then an old Nirvana. The girls followed her about, filled with wonder at the fury of her energy. Angrily Lola told them to go play, but immediately she called them back, knelt, and hugged them, bringing her head down between their heads. "I'm sorry," she said. "It's not your fault."

She turned off the stereo, pushed the couch to the center of the living room floor, set up the TV for the girls to watch, and resumed her work. In the corners of cupboards, she found remnants of the previous occupants: a bowl, two dishes, a can of cayenne, cutlery, a shoebox full of jewelry. She gave the box to the girls. She cleaned her bedroom for her mother, who might or might not come, who Lola did not want here, who might die instead. She stacked her own boxes of things tightly against a wall. If necessary she could sleep on the couch. High on a shelf in the closet, she found a carton. When she opened the flaps, the scent of mothballs assaulted her nose.

She found a woman's sealskin coat within, wrapped tightly in oilcloth. She laid it on the bed, unfolded it, and tried it on. The crimson lining slid along her arms. The coat reached her knees. It had thick shoulder pads in the long-ago style. The collar felt luxurious against her neck. The black fur shone. When she stroked it, the fur coursed deeply between her fingers. She hugged herself in the coat and threw her head back. If she took it to Louis' brother, Sam, he could get at least two hundred for it. She walked to the living room and modeled it for Nikki and Yvette.

"Look at that thing," Yvette said.

"It's animal fur," Lola said. "Seal."

Nikki said, "They do tricks. They swim like nobody's business."

"It keeps them warm in the cold ocean," Lola said as she sat between the girls.

The girls touched the coat and pressed their faces into it. Lola liked the way their elbows and knees jabbed at her as they squirmed. The girls went to sleep against her, under her arms. Their birthdays fell in such a way that they would both start kindergarten next year. Lola liked to think of them being bound together forever as if they were twins. She reached out with her foot, poked off the TV, and sat that way for a long time, as warm as toast. Outside, the snow fell steadily. She could hear the wind in the trees and the snow hissing against the eaves. It's a storm – she thought. Thank God!

❧

It snowed all night and continued into the next day. By morning everything was white outside. The fields were white. The roofs were white. The limbs of the trees sagged under the white weight. Lola dressed the girls in their snowsuits and sent them out to play, then went out herself. She loaded the jackhammer in a wheelbarrow she'd found. The jackhammer lay there, a pig of a thing with its hydraulic hosing coiled on top of it. Laboriously, she pushed it up the slope to be stored in the hay barn. Nikki and Yvette followed her, pulling plastic sleds.

Lola unloaded the jackhammer in a dry corner where she already had a small cache – a set of socket wrenches, screwdrivers, battery charger, an electric drill, a power saw, an air compressor she'd dragged up on its broken wheels. . . . She'd wiped the small tools with oil and arranged everything in lines on a plastic tarp. It pleased her to see the tools, bright against the green plastic, the consequence of a deal cut on a whim. She intended to make money.

She tipped the jackhammer out of the wheelbarrow and put it next to the compressor, then rolled the wheelbarrow back to the bay of the hay barn and watched Yvette and Nikki hurtle down the slope. Their sleds careened away from each other, returned, bumped, and crossed paths. They skidded on yesterday's ice and plowed through today's snow, out of control. At the bottom the sleds crashed and the girls tumbled off. Afraid, Lola leaned forward, but then she heard the girls' laughter. Beyond them, beyond the house, lay the white hayfield from which the cows had been withdrawn. A sheet of snow abruptly slid off the steel roof of the house, and a small flock of finches that had been searching for seed on the ground fluttered into the air. Off to the side, she heard a truck laboring. The girls scrambled to their feet and ran toward the lane.

A gray flatbed with an orange snow blade appeared and stopped. The girls danced at its side. The door swung open and Louis stepped down, holding a shiny, aluminum case. The girls led him toward the house. Lola heard their excited voices rising and falling and Louis's low voice punctuating theirs. They were telling him about the house. The three passed through the iron gate and out of view. Lola heard the front door open and shut. For a moment Lola didn't move, and then she walked down, went inside, and found Louis and the girls sitting on the living room couch. They stopped talking when she entered.

"Thank you," Lola said. "For plowing, I mean. But I have chains." She had a sinking feeling. Although the chains would have done for today's wet, melting snow, she'd need to find a way to have the road plowed in the future.

Louis grinned. "I knew that name was familiar. Bodine. The old fart. He had a fire." He gestured over his shoulder. "Did you see the shit spread around out there?"

"I can give you some coffee," Lola said. She realized that if she told Louis about her salvage deal, he would want to help. And he could help. With his trucks he'd make it easy. He would take it over. If she kept it secret and he hung around, he'd start poking through the equipment for himself and take it over that way. She knew him and his endless wanting. She looked at her watch and said, "Then I have to go."

"Sure."

Lola walked into the kitchen.

Louis followed and said, "It was the wood chips the old guy used to bed down his cows. That's how I knew him – delivering wood chips a few years ago."

Lola poured the coffee and set it on the kitchen table. The girls came in and she poured juice for them. The four sat down. Louis placed his case on the floor, took off his Stetson, and carefully perched it on the table. "You got to watch those chips," he said. "Hay, too. It all rots. You get rot, then fire. Sometimes people don't care what the hell happens."

When he pulled the snaps of his leather coat apart, Lola smelled the whiskey in his sweat. He said he'd heard that once the fire started, the old man turned his cows loose and started throwing tools out the barn door. He kept going back into the flames to throw out more tools. "He lost his parlor, burned clean to the stubs, but saved the tools and then left them. I guess he never touched the tools again except what he needed for the boat."

"Boat?" Lola said.

"Boat?" Louis said, mimicking her. Yvette and Nikki squirmed in their chairs and looked up happily at Louis, whom they liked because he made them laugh. Lola stared at her hands.

"An old tug," Louis said. "He sold off his herd, bought the boat, and refitted it. He called and asked if I would haul it over to Seattle for him, but I couldn't. His old lady'd died and it broke him up. I heard he was planning to spend the rest of his life in his boat, fishing and floating wherever he wanted." Nikki reached out and put her small hand on top of Louis's weathered one. Louis got a faraway look in his eyes. "Claude," he said softly.

"That's it. Claude Bodine."

Lola looked out a kitchen window at the snow. She thought about a man who loved his wife with such steadiness that when he lost her, he left everything to rust and rot and set out for the high seas. She pictured such a man . . . his silver hair tufting out from beneath a seaman's hat and a craggy, resolute face set against the wind and spray, the eyes gazing past the crashing waves into the distance. "So?" she said.

Louis cocked his head like a crow. "Why did you move here?"

"I like the country."

"There's picnics for that."

"It's cheaper than the apartment."

"What're you going to do when your unemployment runs out?"

"Get work. Maybe go to school."

He squinted at her. "From here?"

"Look, my mother might be dead now," Lola said. "If I had a phone, they might have called by now to tell me she's dead. If she's not, I may bring her here."

Nikki and Yvette had fallen still. They gazed at their mother, then at Louis when he spoke.

"That's crazy."

"Maybe," Lola said.

"No phone," Louis said.

"The next time I go in, she could be dead. Maybe today. Don't you see?"

"You need a phone."

"I don't want one yet."

"Sure," Louis said. "You could get a mobile." He reached down for his aluminum case, set it on the table, unsnapped the latches, and opened the case. It was stuffed with clothes. From the bottom, he pulled out a binder and set it on the table in front of Lola. "There."

"I can't have you here."

He flipped open the binder. She looked down at a page that was filled with numbers written in a neat, round hand in black ink. "I'm out of my place," he said. "Bird said I could take my clothes, my truck, whatever I wanted, but if I took the titles and books, she was through with me. That was the line, and I crossed it."

"You cross the line with her all the time," Lola said.

"Not this line. Look, I got my car over at Fanny's place. My rig's at Sam's. What is it? You want me to beg? Fuck you."

They stared at each other. The mask of his face was as shiny as polished wood in the hard white light of the kitchen. He raised his arms and set his elbows on the table and cocked his head to one side again. He looked like a big crow, rustling as it adjusted its wings. He scrutinized her sideways. His eyes sparked with the rapacious intelligence of a crow, looking to see what could be taken. Lola had read that crows were as smart as dogs. If they were that smart, she thought, and since the cause of their intelligence was not known, no one could understand just how smart they really were. Louis was suddenly a complete mystery to her. A week ago Lola might have taken him in and been glad for it. Even now she felt the old trigger of her wildness about to be pulled. If it were pulled, she might accept him. She could feel his energy, electric and full, swelling across the table. She stayed as she was, rapt in her sense of being watched, waiting to feel the trigger in her cocking back. It didn't and suddenly the mystery of Louis was transformed into an emptiness. "No," she said. "I can't."

His expression didn't change.

"Please, Mama," Yvette said.

"No. Go home, Louis. Keep what you have."

ॐ

Lola drove to town. The packed snow squeaked under her tires. At the hospital, she led Nikki and Yvette into the elevator. The girls' eyes widened and they smiled as the elevator shot up the tower. Lola situated them in the waiting area, went to her mother's room, and found her curled up on her side, moaning, "There. Touch me there." Her mother writhed and moaned,

"And there." A nurse was in the room checking the intravenous dispenser. The other elderly lady lay in her bed over by the window, her form silhouetted behind the curtain. "Yes, there," Lola's mother said. "Touch me everywhere."

The nurse had thick eyebrows and a dark, downy mustache. Her eyes were set wide apart. She had acne scars on her cheeks and fat knees. She might have been the homeliest woman Lola had ever seen, but Lola envied her because of her job, her white dress, white shoes, and white hose. The nurse smiled at Lola. She had a husky, sweet, melodious voice. "Wanda must have been a player in her day," she said.

Lola thought, "Wanda was a waitress, a barmaid, and not a stupid woman, but she changed the sheets in motels, swept the floors, stood in the lines and served countless men. All she ever wanted was to be a player. She's my mother, for God's sake!" Lola's eyes shifted around the cream walls and steel fixtures of the room as she wondered how it was possible for a person in her mother's condition to have such fantasies. "Shouldn't I take her out of here?" she asked.

Her mother went on moaning, "Touch me there."

The nurse said, "Not yet."

"When?"

"She's not doing well."

"She's dying for God's sake," Lola said. "Should she die here?"

"The doctor will soon be up to talk to you."

Lola moved to the bed and placed her hand on her mother's bony shoulder, finding that the old woman stank of medicine and decay. The nurse trudged out of the room. Lola thought that along with Johnny Carson, Rodney Dangerfield, and whoever else from the old TV life – Tony Bennett, maybe, or Joe DiMaggio – her mother might be dreaming of any one of the actual men in her past life: the lumberman, logger, the lineman, the produce man with the decontaminated hands, or the hardware salesman. From each of these, her many fathers, and from her mother's inability to resist either them or the drinking, Lola had been taught to lose track of herself and be afraid.

I Could Love You (If I Wanted)

She looked into her mother's haggard face and wondered if all the men had entered together to make a complicated creature in her mother's mind, one piled-up morph of them all to carry her off into afterlife. As she had many times, Lola wondered about what went beyond what she could know, what her mother had done, or what had happened that caused her to be like this. The long, ravaged body was outlined like a rope beneath the sheet. Lola thought, "I would like her to be here just this once," and as if in response, her mother slowly turned her head and looked up at Lola. Her lips moved, forming the words, "Touch me."

Shaken, Lola thought, "Nevertheless, I might take you home to my wrecked house, you and your men. You could make as much noise as you want and fall out of your bed. What the hell. We could turn up the music."

"Touch me here," her mother whispered in her ragged voice.

Lola thought, "Nothing ever changes."

"Touch me," her mother whispered.

Lola held her mother's arm, the stick with skin emerging from the gown.

"Touch me."

Lola touched her cheek to her mother's head, inhaling the smell of death. She thought of the things she should get if her mother came with her, finding relief in the organizing list: a dresser, another bed, a tray for her mother to eat from. Wheelchair, maybe. A fucking bedpan.

Maybe flowers to place in the window against the light.

"Touch me."

A picture on the wall.

From the other side of the room, the other old woman spoke out in her little girl's voice, "If you ask me, she's lucky to have a beautiful daughter like you."

"Touch me."

"I could love you, Mama," Lola said. She wondered if her mother mistook her voice for the voice of the composite one. If so, she was where she'd always been, mixed up in her mother's craziness. Lola imagined herself in there, not here where she was standing next to the bed with her feet on the actual floor, but just another phantasm to her mother, in there without identity, wandering with the other shadows along all the mismapped routes. She thought it might be all right, just once more, to release herself to be in there like a child within the doom. After all, the life of the other would soon shed itself like a husk from its seeds. Lola felt free for a moment, thinking that, and said, "I could take you home if they allow me."

The Cross

ZETA AND I RENDEZVOUSED on a Tuesday, midway on the eighty-mile journey between his house and mine. I parked in a turnabout, and he drove us along the back roads, winding eastward at first. His old Travelall was decorated with hanging things – beads, thongs, and feathers. On the dashboard was a garden of dried plants, driftwood, and stones. The garden trembled in the early morning light. The Travelall was filled with the odors of wild things. Zeta's body was poised and his hands rested lightly on the large, plastic wheel. Soon we would turn north toward the K—— River, a tributary of the great Columbia, and the K—— River Dam, where we planned to make an adjustment to the landscape.

As we drove we gazed at the forestland, which in the watersheds grew so deep as to blot out the sun. In other places the clear-cuts opened gloomy vistas of stumpage and barrens backed by beetle kills. Our project would have made me anxious in any circumstance, but at certain intervals I also found myself seized with rage, still shot through by images of what had been – feasibly, yet unbelievably! – a threat on my life two nights before. There had been sounds in the dark outside my house, then silence, and at dawn I found a decapitated calf and an appalling message left in the cab of my truck. It was a dangerous time. Brutality was on the rise and intimidation, the order of the day. I wanted to speak of this to my friend, but as if stunned by the utter incomprehensibility of it, I couldn't find the words to begin.

Zeta and I each wore black sneakers and navy blue stocking caps. Our camouflage slickers lay draped over Zeta's day pack, which sat on the back seat, heavy with tools. The Travelall broke out of the woodland into coulee country, a place of steep canyons, buttes, and a pervasive color of beige from the dead ground cover left over through the winter and not yet quite overcome by this spring's green. It was a dry country. We each drank a can of v-8 juice. It left the taste of tin in my mouth. Our conversation traced the wiggly edges of a subject that soon plunged into a lacuna of mind: Paul Wittgenstein, the Austrian pianist and brother of Ludwig, the positivist who had asserted that the problem of meaning dissolved when it was cast into sentences.

It was Paul Wittgenstein who had had his right arm amputated after being wounded on the Russian front during World War I. A man of means, he then commissioned works for the left hand alone from several composers, including Maurice Ravel. I told Zeta that Wittgenstein had objected to Ravel's concerto because of its difficulty, but later in his life, after Ravel's death, he managed to perform it and therefore concede its greatness. Whenever I considered the concerto, I imagined the one-armed veteran at the piano with the pinned-up flap of sleeve exposed to the audience, a mournful and heroic figure. Now, I took a deep breath and told Zeta that I thought Ravel's menace and lyricism at once memorialized Wittgenstein's dismemberment and made it immaterial.

By late morning Zeta pulled off the road into a wash. The Travelall lurched and its hanging things swung. We put on our slickers, walked up the road, and crossed toward a white sign with black letters that said, U.S. GOVERNMENT PROPERTY. DANGER. NO TRESPASSING. There was a roar in the distance, ceaseless and throaty. We slipped between strands of barbed wire with impunity. We were also the government! We made our way through sage and stunted conifers. Native flowers were coming out, too, such as grass widow and adderstongue, along with European weeds – toadflax, thistle, and spurge. The weeds were remarkable for their adventurousness, as they had quickly gorged the cuts in the earth. Zeta took the lead. Under the slicker his shoulders swung according to the lightness of his feet, picking the places to step. In his pack the tools clinked softly.

It was early May. The ground was still damp from the rain and thaw but dry enough to resist the weight of a footfall. Following the first steep incline, the trail turned. The river roared and the dam came into view. Its line of concrete was interrupted by spillways and capped by steel grates. It had a plank gangway, iron handholds, steel wheels, and chain drives by which the spillways were cranked open and shut. Behind it, slack water the color of a thundercloud backed up the canyon. The dam had a vintage character, the instruments of leverage protruding from its insides to be manipulated by hand. It had been in place for a century. Hauling the turbines over an arduous course by mule teams had been heralded as a brave crusade in its time.

Across the way to the north stood the black rock of the opposite cliff. At its top were lawns and white buildings with red roofs that housed the equipment and the crews that came and went. A glass door flashed open, and a man in a blue jumpsuit and blue baseball cap appeared. He also wore a tool belt. The stainless steel handle of his hammer glinted as we watched him go to another building just above the dam. He mounted the steps, that door flashed, and he passed within.

Zeta glanced at his watch. "Good. Now he'll ride the elevator to the bowels."

We stepped to an outcropping and paused. Not far below was a larger outcropping on which a white cross was bolted to a concrete slab. A year ago it had simply appeared. No one was certain who had put it up but only that the power company, a public utility, had at first proposed removing the dam from service because it cost more to maintain than the value of the electricity it generated. Local business people and politicians had objected, while the deep ecologists were enthusiastic over the prospect of what they called the river's "outing." A small knot of them held vigils on the maintenance grounds in preparation for the river's release. The Army Corps of Engineers assessed the site. Archaeologists surveyed the banks. Biologists in diving gear explored the reservoir, where they discovered heavy silt cast in the shapes of dunes and a bizarre new dominion over which shiners, suckers, and huge, mutant carp held sway.

For months the controversy smoldered in the weekly newspaper of the region. It was featured in the daily, published in the city to the south. Senators and federal bureaucrats began taking positions on the question. Then five cases of dynamite disappeared from a nearby construction project. The FBI was summoned. All these things were thought to be bound together as is the way. The controversy had seemed on the verge of inviting civil disorder, but then the white cross materialized as if from nowhere.

The dissension abruptly subsided, but whether this was due to a natural ebbing of energies or to the effect of the cross was impossible to determine. People traveled to see it. The power company took the liberty of setting up picnic tables on the maintenance grounds, and on weekends groups gathered with their meals and bore witness by gazing over the canyon at the cross. An editorial in the regional paper praised the action of the anonymous party for reminding the citizens of the Lord's power to heal dissension. The dynamite was never recovered. In the months that followed, the power company quietly maneuvered for a rate increase to finance retrofitting the dam.

Forty feet below the cross lay the canyon bottom. It was high water and the dam's floodgates stood open. Great tubes of water poured through, plummeted straight down, cut through the surface of the river, then boiled up again a short distance downstream. A huge hole, bounded by a jagged curling wave, trapped entire logs. A cloud of vapor rose from the bottom and billowed around the cross. Looking down filled me with rue for what I must not do: fling myself over the edge and plunge into the river and come up and bob against the logs and be driven down again by the surge to the depths.

In my anxiety over our project – what we called "monument correction" – I had completely forgotten my particular sensitivity to heights. All my life an all-consuming terror has filled me whenever I stand at the edge of a precipice, but remembering it quite vividly at this moment, I found myself clinging to the branch of a gnarled fir that burst out of the face of the cliff. Cautiously, I raised my eyes and stepped back. Zeta cocked his head. He knew I'd been momentarily lost in a wild place. His thick hair was black. He had a mustache, beard, and dense eyebrows. His

face, which was a dark rose color, seemed to shine out from behind the black patches.

"Menuhin," he said. "Wasn't he really another amputee?"

I looked at my friend, startled but knowing not to take him
literally. Zeta had an admirable mind. He was capable of sweep-
ing into the most unexpected quarters one moment and of
mounting an inquiry akin to monomania in its singularity of
purpose at the next. But of course he was not a lunatic! We spoke
of the violinist, the prodigy Yehudi Menuhin. Although Zeta was
an aficionado, music was one subject about which I knew more
than he. As a child Menuhin's virtuosity had caused him to be
regarded, he himself had said, as a "sacred monster." But at another time in his late twenties, he found he couldn't play a note.

Menuhin has claimed that he played utterly without self-con-
sciousness until the breakdown. It was then the time of World
War II, and he was touring Europe. He was Jewish. His people
were marked, herded, enslaved, and exterminated. He had personal trouble, too, which led to a divorce. The sheaf of his prodi-
gious California child, inside which he'd remained safe, rapt with
his music, was ruptured. Suddenly he couldn't play at all. He had
to go back to absolute zero, relearn the most rudimentary ma-
neuvers, and reconstitute his spirit. Truly, it might be said in a
case such as his that the coming into awareness had severed his
body from his being.

"Too many messages about the true state of the world," Zeta
said. "Too many melodies. Not enough rhythm."

It was a joke. Zeta's face glowed. He rocked gently to and fro,
laughed softly, and touched my arm. We were hunkered against
the cliff, awaiting the moment of our descent. A week ago we'd
gone with our wives to a concert by the Ghanian drummer,
Dadey. Dadey's performance on a set of five congas was impec-
cable and majestic. Above the crimson shells, his dark hands
flickered among the pale skins. At times his playing was exquisitely simple, while at other times it filled the hall with a labyrinthine roar. The listeners were awestruck, knowing they were in
the presence of a great heart. Dadey made a remark with which
I'd been grappling ever since. "Melody is distance," he'd said.

The Cross

Zeta and I stared across the canyon. Between us a root of the fir snaked out from the earth. It embraced a heap of gravel. At the outer verge of the root a groove had been worn, and there was a small opening in the gravel, as if something had been entered there not long ago and chafed back and forth. I couldn't make it out. "It's the cry," I said, referring to Dadey's remark. "It's the melody that's heard over great distances. The drums send messages to each other; everything else, the intricate rhythms, is maybe a way of making sure the transmission is clear."

Zeta smiled. "But people also dance to the rhythm."

I thought about Ghana. I thought of drummers in trees sending messages across the savanna, of how in the old days the messages might bear upon questions of life and death – game migrations, army encampments. I knew nothing about Ghana. I thought about the slaves in the plantation days, how the masters had outlawed drums in fear of the messages they sent – the dangerous secrets, conceivably the plots of insurrection and escape. I thought of the slaves in the fields, looking up in recognition at the sentences the notes contained. I knew nothing about the plantation days. I could only imperfectly imagine the fervency of such messages. It was a shakily formed and yet dynamic phantasm in my mind.

Zeta rocked forward and scrutinized the shaft. "There," he said. The service elevator passed darkly by the lowest window. "He'll go to the generating room." We looked up at the top of the opposite cliff. No one was there, nothing – only the black rock, lawns, picnic tables, and white buildings with red roofs. "Now," Zeta said as he rose and moved for the trail. "Be careful."

We continued our descent into the canyon. The trail cut back and forth through a string of switchbacks. The air grew chill, and the way was steep, the trail narrow and wet. A fall meant death. I was afraid and didn't know where to look to calm myself – up, down, or straight ahead. As we negotiated a sharp turn, I clutched at the rock wall. Before us the trail straightened in a final incline toward the second outcropping. The cross stood in plain view, bathed in luminous mist.

The Cross

Zeta came to a stop. He gestured several feet ahead at a place where the trail angled downward toward the bottom. He pointed at a slot in the rock wall, leaned forward, put his hand into it, then held himself as he darted across. I reached out and slipped my fingers into the slot, which I found grooved as if designed as a handhold; later I would surmise that it must have been so. It was an ancient thing made for just such passage. I exhaled deeply then stepped. My legs shook. One foot began to slide out from under me. For an instant I froze. The foot slipped further. A terrible coldness rushed through my body. I moved, almost wildly, and Zeta reached out and grasped my wrist. I was across, safe.

Zeta knelt and quickly emptied his pack of the socket set, hacksaw, wire cutters, pry bar, cold chisel, rubber mallet, and can of penetrating oil. I knelt opposite him and inhaled deeply. Between us was the cross. Made of four-inch steel, it was six feet tall with a four-foot cross member, a *crux immissa*. It was heavy, beaded with moisture, and expertly welded. It was a Protestant, hard-edged thing to which one was obliged to reattach by imagination the impaled body of Christ. I reached out to touch it and felt overwhelmed by my history in this religion, as if I were a boy again: the night prayer meetings, the squared-off hymns, Sunday after Sunday attending sermons and scriptures, session after session filled with remonstrance against evil, and finally, most loathsome of all – though I didn't know it at the time, having been spun myself into a sheaf of childhood – the sinister requirement that believers evangelize the world, that the willing voluptuousness in every corner of the earth be brought under the pilotage of righteousness.

Zeta passed me the penetrating oil. The steel plate at the base of the cross was attached by three-quarter inch bolts. The heads were imbedded in the concrete slab. The slab had been poured into a depression in the rock itself. I doused the two bolts on my side with oil then looked around. We were perhaps two-thirds of the way down the crevasse. Straight across was the black cliff, the access tower. There was no sign of anyone. Below, the white froth boiled. We were now in thrall to a roaring envelope of sound. I looked back along the trail and straight up, wondering how the cross and its accouterments – bolts, cement, and water to activate the cement – had been carried here. I constructed imaginary scenarios that included managing a water vessel and negotiating that last stretch in the rail, bent profoundly beneath the cross. It seemed beyond possibility, but then it dawned on me that everything could have been lowered by rope, coming down perhaps from the outcropping above. I remembered the groove that had been worn into the protruding root of the fir and felt a grudging admiration for the perpetrators of the deed.

Each of the bolts had a hole drilled in it through which a loop of wire was passed and joined with a clamp. Zeta clipped off the loops on his side then passed over the wire cutters. I clipped the loops on my side, drew the wires through the holes, and tossed them over the edge. Zeta had the socket on the ratchet, and he started on the first nut. He had to put his weight into it. The nut broke loose with a crack. His body swung outward and back. He turned off the second nut. I braced myself and did the third and fourth. When we tried to rock the cross, it didn't move at all.

Zeta began chipping the concrete from around the edges of the base. It was painstaking and a good way to think through trouble . . . to engage in repetitive labor, to allow the flood of trouble to compose itself into rivulets that found their way through the work. Hand on the chisel. Hand on the mallet. Driving the chisel through the concrete. Then passing the tools over and watching Zeta work his side.

Now, suddenly, I told him how our dog had barked wildly in the depth of the dark two nights ago, how it then fell silent, how the other noises – a footfall, the click of a latch – formed an ominous music. I'd lain awake on my back listening.

I had known, sensing the alert consciousness next to me, that my wife had been awake for some time. Finally, she spoke: "Maybe it's nothing."

"Maybe."

She rolled over to her side. The bed rocked. Upstairs, springs creaked as our youngest son shifted on his bed. "Probably," my wife murmured. Now that I was fully awake, she fell asleep.

The Cross

For anyone to come to our house required a mile's drive from the county road. We slept easily most of the time. When we did not, we would sleep in turns, one sleeping and the other keeping vigil. I knew the shotgun was in the corner of the closet near the bed. I had timed myself because I worried about my inquiries into the neo-fascist organization headquartered not far from my home. They were building underground bunkers in preparation for Armageddon and to keep themselves safe for the Rapture. They stockpiled weapons and were suspected of running a counterfeit ring. They might well have the stolen dynamite. It took me twenty seconds to get from the bed to a fully armed condition and then ten seconds more to reach either the front or back door. A half minute. I finally fell asleep.

In the morning I found the dog closed up in a shed with a slab of meat. "And then I saw that one of our calves was missing from its pen," I told Zeta. "I felt like an idiot. We'd been complacent."

He looked at me. We had the cross free. When nudged, it rocked lightly. It was a question of prying it up over the bolts and letting it drop. I drove the cold chisel under the base. We moved close to the rock wall. Zeta put the tools away except for the chisel and bar. There was no sign of the watchman. "He should come out soon," Zeta said. "We want to know where he is – that's all."

It was remarkable how softly we could speak. It was as if we occupied our own pocket of quiet within the roar of the water.

"When I went to the pen, I found a heap of entrails on the ground and a carcass hanging from a corner post. Somebody had come in, baited the dog, killed and dressed out our best calf. I started back to the house," I said, "but I saw something on the windshield of the truck, pasted to the inside. And when I opened the door, I saw the hide draped across the seat and the calf head wired to the steering wheel, the eyes looking mournfully right at me, blood everywhere. I practically fell over trying to get out of the way of the thing. On the windshield was a note. It had a drawing of a gun sight, and it said, THE CROSSHAIRS ARE ON YOU. I told Zeta that the message also bore the red-and-black insignia – swastika, wings, and raptor talons – of the very organization I'd been researching. He already knew that my interest in the organization had to do with its professed fascism – mainly with the power of belief to mount a cover under which the faithful could creep like larvae, sealed from the light, carving out a scrabbled-up sanctum with their trails.

He held my arm and leaned near. "I'm sorry," he said. "No wonder you're edgy. We could have waited. You should have said something."

"I haven't been able to figure out what to say. It's so strange that it hardly seems like it happened."

"This was two nights ago? Have you called the police?"

"Yes. Two nights ago. And no, we haven't called the police." As I said that, I once again asked myself why: perhaps because then we'd have the police on our place, not that we had much of anything to hide; perhaps because, made a matter of record, we'd be drawn ever deeper into an imbroglio. "But maybe we should. I don't know. The kids have been driven to school the last two days."

"You bet," Zeta said.

"It's true that all day yesterday and last night I wondered if those people were onto what we were up to. Up until a few minutes ago, I wondered if it was a warning. Now I don't think so."

"Why?"

"Workmanship. I've been in their buildings and sat at their tables. They're rough-cut folks and close to incompetent. I've seen a bench collapse when one of them sat on it. They've got wires hanging out of their walls. Whoever made this cross and put it here is a different order of adversary."

"I'm sorry," Zeta said again. His commiseration was meant to strengthen me. He had perceived that I was more disturbed than I myself realized. "We could just leave now."

"No," I said.

"So," he said, "who put this thing here?"

I shook my head. "I don't know. Maybe they picked up a welder. The hell. Maybe it's a freelancer."

Zeta smiled. "Maybe it's the power company."

We laughed softly. Surely, that was an absurd proposition, yet it was funny because it seemed possible. But for the moment all that mattered was that this incidence of vandalism – the emplacement – be countered, its spell broken.

We fell silent. The elevator passed by the second window. Zeta slipped the tip of the pry bar under the base. The cross tottered. I moved the chisel. When the elevator passed the third window, Zeta levered the bar. Instantly the cross toppled and dropped from sight. The metal rang against the wall of the cliff . . . once, again, and a third time, calling out brilliantly and echoing with quickening clarity against the other side. Then there was nothing.

We didn't move. The elevator passed the fourth window. The door flashed open. The watchman appeared and started across the lawn toward the building where we'd first seen him. He glanced our way and went on, then glanced again and stopped. We didn't move a muscle.

"Does he see us?" I asked.

"Don't move."

The watchman didn't move, either. He was still looking. It was too far to make out his expression, but the inclination of his body suggested scrutiny.

"The question is," I said, "does he see what's not here."

"Right."

"He's taking a long time looking."

"Right."

"He's trying to figure out what's missing," I said.

"Or has figured it out, but can't remember how long it's been since he last saw it. He's thinking maybe it was yesterday, or maybe it's been a month. He doesn't know."

"Maybe he sees us."

"If we don't move, he can't be sure."

I looked from the watchman to the dam, that antique. It had been once an exercise of imagination and will, a form of prosthesis even, that drew into its engine the potential energy of topographical relief, of the "drop." It then harnessed the energy and articulated it out into the grid. It also severed the river from itself. There were now few trout here, the quick ones colored bright as birds, and no salmon at all coming up – blood red, filled with sex and death – to make the river talk to itself all along its course.

I looked back to the watchman. He removed his cap, ran a hand over his hair, replaced the cap, hitched up his tool belt, and walked on. He mounted the stairs of the other building, looked back again, then went inside. "Now," Zeta said. We got up, negotiated the slippery stretch with surprising ease, and went on around the switchbacks. When we reached the upper outcropping, we paused. There was no sign of the watchman. I put my finger into the groove that had been worn into the root and decided that it could well have been made by rope. I grasped the limb of the fir, moved to the edge, and looked down. I couldn't resist. It was all right. The cross was visible, a diffuse white shape just downriver from the foaming hole. A lone osprey cruised up the river, cut through the vapor, caught a draft at the dam, and shot high into the sky. We went on, pausing again at the top, and saw the watchman on the deck, cupping the brim of his cap with his hands and peering across the canyon. We froze.

"Now he sees us," I said.

"Maybe," Zeta said. "Or maybe what's missing just hit him. When he turns, move quickly." The watchman turned. We scrambled up the last stretch, ducked through the fence, and beat a path to the Travelall.

We took a different way out, along the wash to a logging road. Zeta told me about his grandfather, an old Obregónista, who'd come to this country after the Revolution and done field work in the southwest. He married and raised a family, then, when his wife died, returned to the homestead in Sonora that the Mexican government had granted him for his service. "Owning the land meant little to him," Zeta said. "But he told me how every night he fell asleep facing north where his children were. And he had his violin. Before I visited him last time, he wrote and asked me to bring four strings."

Zeta told me how when he'd arrived in the little town in the desert, his grandfather was in the hills. "Way out there with the rocks and snakes," Zeta said. "He was skinny as a rail. He had a ponytail and big curls of hair coming out his ears and nose.

"He played for me on the one string he had left. It was a tune with an offbeat in it. When he put on the new strings, he broke one right away by tightening it too much. He said it was a bad string." Zeta slapped his thigh and laughed. It was infectious and I laughed, too. Then Zeta went on, "So he had to put the old string back on, but it wasn't the right one. He had two strings of one kind.

"They were having a fiesta in the town, which was my reason for going at that time. Grandfather played in a mariachi band with three other old men. Guitar, guitarron, a trumpet, and Grandfather. They were very good. The people slaughtered a steer for roasting. An old woman killed it. Grandfather told me it was an honor for her, just like being able to play was an honor for him. She was a tiny thing, and the steer was big. But the young men had it roped up, and she popped it once between the eyes with a small sledge. It went right down. It was like she got suddenly big in the instant she swung the hammer. Grandfather broke another string, so he had to finish the night playing with three. It was clear he could play with one. Or if he had no strings at all, I guess he'd have scared up a piece of wire."

Zeta paused. The highway was in sight. My thoughts turned toward my wife and children, toward getting in my car and going home to the calf's head that was still in my truck, and the note and maybe to the sheriff's department, toward reckoning with the meaning of all that. At least I'd already hauled the carcass into the trees for the carrion eaters to have.

The hanging things in the Travelall swung, and the garden on the dashboard leaped crazily when Zeta bounced onto the pavement. He worked the Travelall up to cruising speed. We each drank another can of v-8 juice, but I wished we had a little tequila to go with it. "Did you send him more strings when you got back?" I asked.

"Of course," Zeta said. "It's my duty as a grandson. I send him some twice a year. He appreciates it, but really it doesn't matter to him. He's over ninety. All that matters is the music."

Nocturnal America

10/28/02 2330 Departure
2400 Pos   Lat 33°46' N/Long 118°37'W
Temp 63°   Lt airs/Brkn clds/Calm water
Proceeding in Nbound traffic lane

IN THE AFTERNOON, the Arco Transportation Company van picked Fay up at the airport and took her through downtown Long Beach and along the viaduct toward the harbor. They passed a tidal plain dotted with rocker pumpers that were silhouetted against the red sun as it sank into the Pacific. A few pumpers dipped over and over again like large drinking birds, but most had been shut off so that the plain looked like a statue garden, a reliquary to days gone by. The van skirted the refineries where the air was laced with aromatics – benzene, toluene, and xylene – and the dark, adhering odor of primordial tar, the bottom fractionate of the crude that was now delivered by ship. The smell conjured Fay's home in Valdez, where she'd lived most of her adult years. She found herself transported to her front porch there with its view of the Chugach Mountains, blazing ice, and the oil terminal on the slope across the harbor. She might have been waiting for her husband, Oz, coming from work, or for the school bus and her two children darting up the walk years before. Fay was gripped by sadness and a contrary sense of expectation since she was headed back to Valdez now. There was something alchemical in this outcome, the activation of the feasible by the wish of the dead.

She was let out of the van at a security station where a guard placed her suitcase on the counter and asked for her identification. He ran her card through a scanner and peered at his screen. "New hire. Felicity Harper. *Arco Spirit.* Almost a rhyme."

"Fay," she said.

"Snowshoes," he said, looking down at the pair she'd strapped to the side of her suitcase and then up at her with eyes the same gun-blue color as the barrel of the sliding action shotgun in the rack at his side. "That's different."

She murmured and gazed through a window to her left, watching the chain link gate automatically roll open before the van, and then back. Here she was, nervous and yet also feeling as though she were geologic, a cavity underground where memory dripped and things more ancient than she could fathom – things going far back beyond memory – were encrusted on the walls.

The guard pulled on a Latex glove, zipped open the belly of her suitcase, and bent to it, snaking his fingers among her personals. "Otherwise, you're traveling light," he said. "First-timers usually bring a trunk."

Fay again murmured and looked through the window on her right at her ship riding high fifty yards away. Spidery apparatuses stood in the tanker's shadow on the pier . . . *chicksans* . . . the mobile cranes that manipulated cargo lines between the ships' holds and the pipelines on shore. Near the ship's stern stood the superstructure, and before it, stretched an enormous deck, giving the vessel a rakish cut like a preposterous shark.

When she turned back, she found the guard holding the box she'd wrapped in silver paper and gazing at her questioningly.

"Ashes," she said.

He made a sound in his throat like a cat purring, like stones rolling in a can.

"It's my husband's ashes. Open it if you need to."

He squinted at the box, passed his wand above it, and gingerly turned it upside down, making Oz's bone chips rattle. He ran his wand over the box's underside and then set the wand down, returned the box to the suitcase, pulled the zippers shut, snapped off his glove, and slid her card across to her. "I guess not."

She pulled the suitcase on its wheels toward the looming ship, thinking it odd that the guard hadn't bothered with the stuffed crow, Lovecraft, whom she'd carefully packed in a corner of the suitcase. Once she'd climbed the gangway to the deck, she

144

paused. Before her lay the expanse of steel as long as a football field with its vents and cargo apertures, three of which were mated to the chicksans. Above, two military helicopters thudded by, slow as dragonflies. They patrolled the array of docked vessels, the piers dense with cranes, semitrucks, lines of train cars along the rails, and brigade upon brigade of stacked up shipping containers extending as far as the eye could see. It was the nation's cargo, incomprehensible in its quantities.

Entering the superstructure, she walked down a dim passageway to a notch in the bulkhead. In it was a console loaded with switches, dials, gauges, and levers, lit by gooseneck lamps. A woman stood there, and as Fay slowed, she turned: "Felicity?"

"I'm called Fay."

"Harley," the woman said. "First Mate. Right," she added as Fay's eyes fell to the winged Harley-Davidson logo on her T-shirt. Harley cocked her head, revealing a white scar that dropped out of her hair to her eyebrow, and then she spun back to the console to pull a lever. Fay smoothed the hem of her sweatshirt over her hips, having noted Harley's leanness and youth and her formidable manner. Harley was, no doubt, a match for the duty that Fay only roughly understood: The pumps that drew the crude from the ship's holds and drove it through the lines to shore were controlled from here. The holds, positioned along the length and breadth of the ship, had to be meticulously discharged and ballasted in synchrony so as to balance the stress upon the vessel. The ship was like an egg carton and its fourteen tanks like ponderous eggs. Overstressed, tankers were known to shatter at sea.

Harley turned back again. "There's three of us girls aboard. But a rack's open, so you get to sleep solo . . . deck two, number nine. Bring female issues to me."

Startled, Fay thought, "*Female* issues?"

"Do you smoke?" Not awaiting a response, Harley went on, "No smoking on deck. Nothing battery operated because even ballasted, she's a floating bomb." She jerked her head in the direction of the passage. "Report to Taj."

Fay picked her way through the officer's mess to the galley, where the man she took to be the chief steward, Taj Rashee, was slicing beef into cubes. Taj immediately set down his knife, wiped his hands on his apron, and took her hand, smiling. "You've arrived. Welcome aboard." He was her height, dark, and deftly built.

A second man leaned against a cooler in the far corner. He was tall and impressed her with his sullenness. The galley was bright – stainless steel stove and ovens, cupboards, lockers, sinks, counters, dishwasher, even the ceiling made of gleaming metal, white floor, and implements tucked into nooks. Besides blood, she smelled beans and the clay-like odor of chili.

"This is Mort," Taj said, gesturing at the tall man.

"Communications Officer," Mort said in a deep voice.

"Fay," she said.

He grinned down at her and, in a sardonic tone Fay was unable to decrypt, said, "Contact is my business. It'll be my pleasure to give you a tour of the ship, once you're settled."

"Thank you," Fay said.

The man had a bald patch and disheveled hair, a bony face, rubbery lips, and a round cushion of belly above a buffalo head belt buckle big enough to choke a horse. When he spoke his Adam's apple wriggled. "Starting over?" he asked.

For years Oz had worked at the oil terminal in Valdez. His former supervisor had facilitated Fay's hiring by Arco, and her time working as a hospital nutritionist had given her seniority. She'd been told that her duties would be those of baker and cook and that if all went well, she'd be upgraded to Utility I at the end of the tour. Taj would know some of this, but Fay had determined not to advertise her advantages, which had come with befuddling speed in the pit of her grief: Oz no longer at the table sorting through his fishing flies, no longer poring over the box scores, not at his computer running his calculations, not stroking the balls of her feet with his toes at night, not there inside his Buddha-shaped body in the bed's depression at her side, not breathing at all, not with her, not home.

Mort was well old enough to perceive that a seismic event had brought her here. His face bore traces of his having been crossed – a jagged lightening scorch in his gray eyes, something lost. She answered, but turned to Taj as she did so, "That is my hope."

10/29/02	
0600 Pos	Lat 34°21.9' N/Long 120°8'W
Temp 54°	Moderate seas

The *Arco Spirit* embarked not long before midnight, shuddering as it left its berth. Fay slipped out of bed and gazed through her porthole while the ship maneuvered through the harbor and the lights of Long Beach gave way to the dark.

The next morning, she cooked cornbread to go with Taj's chili, working within the compass of the ship's throb and twist, moving from locker to counter to stove, storage bin to counter to oven, and counter to sink to dishwasher to cupboard. Utensils went in and out of their slots. No more than four steps were required in any direction. She knew that negotiating the galley would become an adroit dance once she learned it, but now she bumped awkwardly against the others, causing them to chuckle and clear the way. Often, there were three, and sometimes all four: Taj, Fay, and the two utilities – a big one named Ed and Mike, the quick one. Water thudded into the sinks, pots steamed, and hands flickered here and there, carrying the food off to the mess and bringing back the plates. Ed reached over everyone, lowering the boom of his arm between them to put items in place while Mike slithered through the openings. Oz would have liked this, the magic of rabbit after rabbit leaping out of the little hat of the galley while astonishing numbers of objects clattered back into it.

That night Taj stayed to show Fay how to set up the galley for the next day. He had a lilt in his speech. When she asked where he was from, he told her that, though he'd been born in Jamaica, he'd grown up in Boston. Later, he had moved to Panama with his wife and children because it was cheaper. When his ship passed through the canal, he said, he used to be granted a day's furlough to visit his family. "But it's harder, now," he said. "Security."

Besides Valdez, Long Beach, and Cherry Point, the *Arco Spirit* had Panama City, Houston, and Seoul as ports of call. Fay had been told that she might be shipped off to the Persian Gulf, too, or the North Sea. These obscure itineraries chasing off to who knew where aligned with her feeling of being lost in herself.

"There isn't so much trouble with race in Panama, either," Taj said. "I love my country, but it made me tired to live in it."

Fay felt flattered that Taj would speak so openly. "I have two children myself," she said. "My son's in the air force. He's a surveillance pilot, stationed in Qatar."

Taj looked at her searchingly.

"My husband died a month ago. Cancer," she said, and suddenly discovered herself plummeting into her cavern: his prostate, lymph, kidney . . . chemotherapy, surgery, more chemotherapy . . . in the hospital, home, back in the hospital, back home . . . liver, lungs, bowels, even his legs . . . the morphine, the drool of death black as oil in a line from the corner of his mouth. . . . "His name was Oz," she said.

"I am sorry," Taj said.

"Thank you. We lived in Valdez but moved south to Arizona on his doctor's advice. Our daughter lives in Phoenix. Now, I'm going back north," she said. "I've never been on a ship like this, yet I used to see them every day. It's so strange. It's familiar, but I know so little. Oz worked in the ballast treatment plant in Valdez."

"For the galley, you know more than enough," Taj said. "You'll see."

Fay thought she heard something in his voice, a darkness, but when she looked he had the same smiling expression . . . smooth skin on his cheeks, white teeth and molars glimmering with gold. He placed a carton of stretch-wrapped chickens on the counter and went off. She cut and breaded the parts and put them on trays in the cooler. She turned to the bottles she'd brought from the mess and set in ranks on the counter – ketchup, mustard, Tabasco, vinegar, oil, salt, and pepper. Such simplicity as cleaning and refilling bottles, she found to be what she most needed.

When Taj returned he said, "Things are changing. Soon, we'll have prepackaged food like the airlines. Condiments in packets. The chicken will come cooked."

"It won't be as good," Fay said.

Taj laid out a stone and his knives and set about sharpening. "Less work. Less waste. Management wants one less utility in the galley."

They brushed elbows as they worked. "It'll be more duty for you."

"Maybe," Taj said. "They're downsizing. They're eliminating the communications officer. Mort's been given his papers and he's angry." Taj turned the first knife so that the line of the honing shone in the light like the edge of the moon. "But it's true that food is the crew's main pleasure. It's what keeps their spirits up."

Something shifted in Fay like the movement of a fault. It came from the relief in hearing such kindliness and care. "It's fine to think of it that way."

"I'll be taking retirement soon. I have over twenty years in."

"Back to Panama?"

"Home to Panama." His hands stilled, and he looked up. "My children will be teenagers. I have also a son and daughter. My daughter is learning the violin. My son is older. He plays baseball."

"Ah," Fay said. "Good baseball there, I bet."

"I believe my son will be very good. When I'm home we practice every day."

"I love baseball," Fay said. "My husband loved it, too." As she sucked ketchup from a gallon can with a syringe and injected it into bottles, it occurred to her that she knew nothing about Panama, except that it was equatorial and had had its canal returned during the Carter administration. She also knew that its president, Noriega, had been extracted by the first President Bush. She imagined Taj's family – a beautiful wife and two beautiful, brown-skinned children – on the porch of a stucco house, awaiting his return.

"Three days ago I was in Arizona," she said. "I was told it would be six months at least before a place opened, so naturally I've wondered what happened to my predecessor."

"Rodolfo was sending e-mails to his fiancée. He always told her where the ship was. But he is young and in love. He wanted her to imagine him being just where he was. Everything is being monitored now." Taj held up a piece of butcher paper and, with a quick gesture, sliced off a strip with the knife he'd just sharpened. The cut was as clean as if it had been done with scissors. He set down the knife and continued, "They made an example of Rodolfo by ordering him off in the middle of the three month tour. He was full of ideas and laughter. Everyone liked him. In my opinion it's a shame."

"And now they have a middle-aged woman in his place," Fay said.

"Oh, no. It's no reflection on you." She heard the darkness come back to his voice: "The communications officer has a social function, too. It used to be that Mort would let anyone send messages home as time permitted, but now, along with being given his papers, he's been reprimanded. We had the FBI on board, questioning us. Officers have a new list of irregularities to report. No one likes the distrust." He picked up a boning knife and added, "My wife and I are followers of Islam."

"Oh," Fay said. Taj bent over the stone, starting on the knife's arched tip. She imagined that his revelation was akin in magnitude to what she'd told him about Oz, that there was something torn open in him beneath which lay a shadow land. She was about to make the same response he had, to say she was sorry, but realized he might think she meant his choice of religion. Instead, she said, "You're free to be so."

"Yes, we are."

After a time working in silence, he told her how there was a time when he'd hoped to be the first black captain in the fleet. He'd been a bosun, taking classes during his furloughs to improve his standing, but he'd broken both legs in a fall and taken a year to recover. "Becoming chief steward was more realistic," he said. "Harley might be the first female captain, though. She understands men. She understands how to be like a man and stay a woman. She's only twenty-eight. She will be a good master." He smiled. "You should go. It's Ed's job you're doing. You need your rest."

Fay carried the bottles to the mess and distributed them. Afterward she stood on her toes to peer out a porthole at the sea. She saw the lightening-like whips of froth on the swells, the waxing moon, and the darkness beyond. "Soon," she thought, "Taj will go home to his house, to his waiting wife and his daughter practicing in her room, and to the games played on the vivid grass and black earth marked with white chalk at the edge of the jungle."

10/30/02

0600 Pos	Lat 39°14.9' N/Long 124°50.3'W
Temp 40°	Brkn clds/Mod seas

Toward the stern and off the main deck's passageway were several hatches, among them one to the engine hold and one to a video room. On her third night, Fay ventured to the video room, where in the obscure light close to a dozen men had rendezvoused. They were watching an old Charles Bronson movie in which Bronson marched up a snow-covered mountain slope with a pack and a rifle strapped to his back. Others pursued him. In the room eyes glimmered toward her. It was as if she'd stumbled upon a lair, dense with bears lolling upon the sofas. The screen switched to a shot of the snow again. The white washed over the men's faces. From the back of the room came Mike's voice: "We'll make room for you."

She stood still, tempted, but said, "I'm just exploring."

"Welcome to desperation row," Mike said. Ironic laughter swirled and then ebbed as the eyes shied back to the screen. Fay loved movies. In this one, she knew Charles Bronson was a trapper in the Yukon, falsely accused of a killing because the others envied his skill and independence. Therefore, they'd transformed him into a devil in their minds. Bronson moved into a stand of trees, going deeper and flickering in and out of sight among the trunks until he vanished into the wilderness.

Fay took a turn around the deck, stopping near the stern. The ship's wake laid out a fan on the water, turned phosphorescent by bioluminents. She moved to where she could see to the bow lights and grew transfixed by the ship's trajectory into the lengthening night, black as black velvet. The sea was dark, and the froth in it white as the moon and stars. The wintering bite of air seemed a beloved thing. The deck was alive under her feet, its great steel plates flexing at their tensile welds. The engine ran a pedal point against the beat of the crashing swells. The floating machine talked back to the sea by speaking its rhythm to the dream world full of unseen creatures below.

Back in her cabin, Fay sat at the table and took out her employee's manual, which she was required to study, but instead she gazed at the arrangement she'd made on her dresser. The box containing Oz's ashes was there, and beside it were pictures of her children – Paul in his air force uniform and Vi with her husband and her two little girls in their Easter dresses. There was a picture of Oz and herself, taken not long before he'd fallen ill. His curly hair lifted in the breeze and his round face was wreathed with a smile. Behind the pictures was Lovecraft, the crow, poised with outstretched wings.

Only once had she examined the contents of the box given her by the mortuary. She'd dipped a fingertip in the ash and touched it to her tongue. The ash tasted of lime. She had surprised herself by mounting her own reliquary on the dresser. It seemed that sometimes she lost track of what she was doing, that she had come to be driven by powerful obscurities, by something subterranean, an inscrutable, half-hidden ceremony played upon death and speaking a language beyond her comprehension. Once in a while, she would tip the box, listening to the sliding bits of bone as if to an African rain stick, hoping it would reveal something.

When Oz brought Lovecraft home, the bird was stunned from flying into windows in his effort to escape the treatment plant where he'd been trapped. With Oz's help the children nursed him back to health. Oz named him after his favorite writer of the macabre. Lovecraft became as indispensable as a cat, coming into the house, eating from a plate at dinner time, and stealing coins and bits of jewelry, which later might be found cached away in a shoe or other niche, or never found at all. Once, he unraveled a skein of yarn, creating a weblike labyrinth that ran up and down the halls. After his escapades he would perch on top of a kitchen cupboard, preening as if nothing had happened. The children delighted in his games. Other times, if let out of the house, he would disappear for weeks until everyone was sure he'd found a mate or been lost, but he always returned, appearing on his own time as if from nowhere.

One day, Vi found him dead at the threshold of the door. Because Vi had been so distraught, Oz took the bird to a taxidermist, but Fay knew it was his choice, too. His sensual Catholicism craved icons to tie him to the world's dark comedy. Fay had considered stuffing Lovecraft disturbing, even a little perverse, yet now it was she who kept him.

She had placed the pictures in a triptych to watch over Oz's ashes and her as she slept. Still, it was Lovecraft – with his shining feathers and yellow eyes, his beak open as if to caw, and his wings arched as if he were either about to land or leap into the air – who seemed most to bespeak her loss. It was the indirection of his being as she remembered it, his apartness and also his impish habits that she linked to her children's pleasure, and the ways in which his migrations mysteriously stitched her family together. When she gazed at him, she heard her daughter as a child, laughing, and Oz chuckling, and saw her son feeding him bits of bread, and felt an inconsolable ache. It seemed as if she were passing between two lives. From each life she could peer at the other. It was as if she'd flown off and was returning as a stranger, like a passenger on an airliner. But she would then be shocked to discover that she was here to meet another stranger, who was herself.

As she put on her pajamas, she felt the ship's throb slackening and a pull to one side. She took it as a course adjustment, a turn yet more dead ahead toward Alaska. She lay down under covers, cupping her body so that the north would flood into her.

10/31/02	
0600 Pos	Lat 43°42' N/Long 129°17.2' W
Temp 38°	Brkn clds/Mod seas

In the galley at mid-morning, Taj sliced cold cuts for lunch while Fay arranged the serving plates. Ed was off, but Mike was cleaning up after breakfast. There was a somber air because an F-14 had gone down the night before not twenty miles from the ship. They had the story from Mort, who'd said he'd been up much of the night sending and receiving messages. He'd come to the galley earlier to tell them how their ship had circled the site for three hours awaiting the Coast Guard.

"It is strange," Taj said. "It seems it has nothing to do with us. We only happened to be there. Yet it has everything to do with us."

"That's a sensation I know well," Fay said, feeling she was being drained of something. "And the opposite, too. It's hard to know where the mark is sometimes."

Taj smiled. "Just so."

Mike switched on the dishwasher, hot water thudded, and steam wafted through the galley. "There was a report," he said, "that it was shot down."

Mort reappeared, filling the hatch with his long body. His hair stuck out sideways on either side of his bald patch and his limp shirt had the look of having been worn for days. "They confirmed that it was a patrol," he announced.

"Homeland Security," Mike said.

"It's the air force, for Christ's sake." Mort said. He leaned toward Fay and looked directly at her as if she in particular needed instruction: "We're combustible, you know. We're the oil lifeline. We're vulnerable. Maybe it dawned on them that they'd better watch over us instead of coming aboard and accusing us. But all we get is ever-rising levels of incompetence. Now, there's a fifty million dollar jet in the drink. Two men dead." He pulled back and disappeared, but his voice could be heard echoing in the officer's mess: "All of a sudden, everybody was glad to have contact with a communications officer."

Taj turned back and resumed slicing. Mike intently scraped the griddle with a pumice block. Fay arranged cold cuts on plates like large, fleshy flower petals around little heaps of mayonnaise. Then, Taj paused and touched her arm, saying, "Mort doesn't mean harm. He's not himself."

Because of Taj's care for Mort and his delicate perception into what might worry her – her son, the air force pilot, the fright by association with the crash she had as yet hardly named to herself, and perhaps the synchronicity of secret menace out there and the seeming secret of Mort's trouble here – she discovered her eyes welling with tears. "I know. But thank you," she said, looking at her hands. "I'm going to keep working. It helps."

"Yes," Taj said.

It was true she worried about her son, whose absence hung like a cold spot in her cave. Her fear for him was intertwined with the pangs of remorse she still felt over his being unable to visit before his father's death. There was something very wrong in that, a door not thrown open to let in light. She could hear Oz's plaintive voice in the last days, saying, "I wish Paul were here. Be sure he knows I think of him every hour of every day."

Each time, her answer flew against her doubts: "You'll see him soon."

Of all things, Oz had loved his family best and then fishing, baseball, and his numbers. At the end, he'd had everyone near except Paul. He relinquished fishing when he left Alaska, but going to Arizona made it possible for him to watch his favorite team, the Mariners, in spring training. His numbers never completely left him.

He was a chemical engineer. His work had been to monitor the passage of ballast from ships through the filters, tanks, and holding ponds of the plant in Valdez, where oily residue was separated and the remainder treated with chemicals before being flushed into the harbor. He'd come to consider the process a droll testimony to the limitations of human powers: It was impossible to ever completely erase oil from ballast, and thus, it was necessary to accept this resilient contamination along with all the opportunistic organisms the tankers hauled in from their wanderings over the globe – bacteria, barnacles, crustaceans, and mutant fish. "It's like the oil itself," he would say. "Hydrogen and carbon released from pressure, fractioning off and bonding in all different ways to make God knows what next." One day he discovered a seal pup swimming in a treatment pond. As to it, he rolled his eyes and said, "How it got in there, nobody knows. It took a wrong turn somewhere. It was like Jesus, cruising about all alone, accepting the poison we pass to it."

What Fay learned to love best about baseball was its rhythm, the long pauses suddenly invaded by intense activity when the ball was put in play. It made the game seem like life, the continuum of dreaming leaping up into high alerts. She liked the slowly mounting tension, the patterns repeated like ritual, and the way the ball sailed, white against green, drawing everything to a bead. Oz had loved these things, too. But as his illness deepened, he grew agitated during the lulls and obsessively tapped his pencil on his score sheet . . . waiting, waiting for the next thing to measure . . . just as his preoccupation with his son's absence seemed a frantic beat set again the certainty of what was coming.

She had the cold cuts arranged. The plates of cheese and lettuce and sliced tomatoes and the bread she'd baked early in the morning were set out on boards. When Ed came to start his shift before lunch, she took her leave and walked into the passageway just as Mort appeared from the stairway. He caught her eye and strode toward her. "They're saying it's pilot error. But who knows what to believe, right?" He lurched to a stop before her and looked at his watch. "We might start our tour now."

Before she could respond, he jerked open the nearest hatch, showing her the fan room where the instrumentation for the ship's ventilation system was mounted, and several steps down the hatch to the electrical control room, and one to the foam room where fire fighting equipment was stored – axes, hoses hung from stirrups, and enormous stainless steel canisters. Jittery, he let that hatch suck shut, took plastic earplugs from a wall dispenser, passed two to her, stuck two in his ears, and threw open the next hatch. Fay was afraid of provoking him. She followed onto a platform above the cavern of the engine hold, where the thunder pounded straight through her earplugs.

From the deep emanated a fiery glow. Throughout, winding in and out of the slashes of illumination were labyrinths of pipes, ducts, cables affixed to girders, and gangways passing from one control station to another. She picked out crew members on the platforms; among them was Sarah, the third engineer, whom Fay had seen sitting with Harley in the officer's mess. Sarah was just out of maritime school, blond, and full of flowering body in the aching way of some young women. She was descending the ladders, her pale blue shirt like a flag as she went into the deep, down one flight, another, and another.

Mort bent toward Fay, touching her. "It's thirteen stories!" He was shouting, but his voice seemed remote. She could smell him through the odor of oil, his rank sweat and the peppermint on his breath. "Ten below the ship's draft!" He pointed sternward at a huge tank rising several stories. "Fuel oil!" He pointed the other direction at a pair of cylindrical tanks encircled with ladders. "Boilers!" He pointed into the navel of the dark where Fay picked out an iron mass. "Steam turbine! Under it the worm gear! Drive to the prop!"

He pointed again. "Backup engine!" He tugged on Fay's arm,

leading her out to the passageway. When she removed her earplugs, she felt as though she'd fallen into a tube. "It's all fail safe in there," Mort said. "Two engines, two props, two generators. Two sets of lines for the cargo tanks. There's a second worm gear in the hold." He grabbed his belt buckle and jerked, hiking up his pants, and rocked on the heels of his boots. His lips were flecked with white spittle. "But say a meteor takes out a satellite and there's a hole in the GPS. Say something breaks in the radio shack. The captain's supposed to fix it and run the system?"

Fay took a step back, thinking, "Here it is."

Mort stepped toward her. "The captain has time for that?"

"I wouldn't know," Fay said and, at the same time, asked herself, "Has he been drinking? Is it possible?"

"I guess he would not," Mort said.

Fay took another step back, and remembering Taj's troubled expression, she thought, "Or what? What is it? What?"

At the same time, she felt sorry for Mort. She understood that he must have loved his work, that obsolescence and downsizing had spoiled it for him. She felt for his pain yet realized that sympathy would make her a target, and thus, she felt absolutely compelled to not jostle his mask: lantern-shaped face, hair bursting out his ears, rubbery clown's lips, and his Adam's apple quivering like an impaled mouse.

"Look out you don't get squeezed," he said. "You might as well try to stop Godzilla." He reached up and snapped his fingers. "They want me to disappear. Poof! Just like the poor sons-of-bitches in that jet! God bless the corporation!" He lowered his arm and stood still for a moment, seeming to master himself. "I could show you the radio shack. And take you topside to the bridge."

"Thanks" she said. "But I'm going to rest during my break."

"You seem like a good woman," he said, leering at her.

"My God!" she thought.

Behind her she heard footsteps passing, what she guessed was the crew beginning to arrive for lunch.

"But I've wondered if you're a plant?"

"A what?"

"A company plant. An informant. Rodolfo was discharged and you were bumped over others on the waiting list, right?"

In disbelief, she said, "I beg your pardon."

He leaned toward her.

Alarmed, she thought, "Don't touch me!"

He straightened as if she'd spoken aloud. His eyes lifted above her head, skittered, and then returned to her. "Are you married?"

"My husband has passed on. Recently."

His voice turned to acid: "Myself, I've been divorced for years. My ex still gets half of everything I make."

"His name was Oz."

"Oz?"

"I'll have to go now," she said.

When she turned she discovered Harley down the passageway, standing with her arms crossed and leaning against the bulkhead next to the cargo control console. With her hip cocked and the light from the goosenecks at her back, she was silhouetted, angular, and as still as a mantis, watching. She nodded faintly as Fay passed but kept looking in Mort's direction with her hard eyes.

Fay escaped to the refuge of her cabin, where she sat on the edge of her bunk. Her mind spun with the intimations of intrigue aboard ship into which she was being drawn. Mort, she feared, was pressing his trouble and sure to be further reprimanded, even dismissed. She knew she was not responsible. She felt insulted by Mort, yet it aggrieved her to find this new world, into which she'd only half-willingly come, already marked with pain.

She stared at the wall above her dresser. The throb of the engine came through the deck to her feet. The sexual innuendo in Mort's bodily address to her was shocking. What did he think she was? Her longing to be somewhere else grew sharp, and memories flooded her – storms whirling out of Prince William Sound, snow piled high in Valdez, the children learning to tie flies in the basement, and going fishing in the spring, or flying the kites their father made, while Lovecraft darted about, daring to land on the lines, swooping down, and rising to weave pirouettes in the air.

She was aghast to discover her mind doing its own pirouette above Oz's six-month dalliance with a shipping clerk from work. She had forgiven Oz long ago but never quite released the idea that the woman had affirmed his passion for the fanciful in a way that was beyond her powers. She and Oz had met at a Catholic college in eastern Washington. He was from the coast and attended because he was Catholic, and she because the college was not far from her family's home on the hill above the city there. He studied science, and she theatre. He sought her out after seeing her in a play and from the beginning said he was fascinated by how she could be so expressive on stage and at other times so shy. But there was something alive in her, he'd said. He could see it in her eyes. It was true. As a young woman, she'd loved channeling herself into an invention of someone else's imagination and going into another world where she could discard the reserve to which nature had otherwise consigned her.

Oz had grown into what he'd intended – a chemist. She'd grown into mother and wife. For a while she managed a café in Valdez and then took classes at the community college and went to work as a nutritionist in the hospital. Her interest in theatre never died. It reposed in her like a ravening animal, taking its ration in her children and Oz, in the presentation of food, in stories, and in the way movies regularly made her weep, but it otherwise suffered through her preference for the plain, even in lovemaking – ever more plain as time went by, yet always heedful of offering satisfaction. Oz's dalliance had caused her to fear that she'd been wrong all along about what she believed to be the genius of their marriage – her steadiness matched with his sense of the antic.

As death approached, Oz became obsessed with their financial affairs. Huddled over his computer projecting moves in the market, interest rates, and amortization, he was transfixed by a future he would not share. He projected that a position with Arco and the benefits attached to it – if she worked for ten years, and when combined with his pension plan and their investments – would make her independent. She could buy another house in Valdez if she wanted, he'd said, or one here in Arizona. She never mentioned that she'd considered she might not be in either of those places but that maybe she'd return instead to the well-settled and austere place in the interior of Washington, where long ago the softly glimmering sparks of her childhood had been safe.

When his eyes failed, he began computing on paper, making the numbers large. He would ask that lamps and magnifiers be brought but soon began losing his path entirely. He attributed his loss of vision to his coming death, the growing dimness as the curtain dropped. More precisely, as the doctors told Fay, it was cataracts deepening their webs as they were nourished by the collapse of his body. During the final days, bedridden, he was nearly blind. On his last night, he said, "I can't see. Fay, I can't see. I can tell it's light, but I can't see anything in it."

But it wasn't light at all anymore, not in the room, not outside. Fay was in anguish over his weakening hold and yet relieved that he was releasing her.

After a while, he said, "But you'll be worth over a million. You'll be safe."

She hadn't told him that the market was volatile, that everything he projected might turn out wrong. She supposed she was grateful for the prospect of a job. She cared about money, but not as much as he wanted her to. Going to sea was surely not what she would have chosen. Yet feeling trapped between the pair of impulses – his line of expectation and her sense of the oblivion to which all paths seemed to lead – she couldn't bring herself to speak of these matters to him.

At the end, as he lay still in the pale morning light, his once unruly hair flat as if ironed upon his skull, his once nut-colored face a husk shining like parchment and his eyes silvery as dimes, he said, "I see Jesus beckoning. Fay, I see Jesus."

Fay believed in Jesus but doubted he would make a personal appearance to ease Oz's passing. She was Presbyterian. For her, religion was plain, too, practical, and filled with inescapability. Her daughter had become a Pentecostal along with her husband.

The several times Fay had gone to church with them, she found the shouting and hand waving disturbing but kept her silence. Her fear that Oz, a scientist and rogue Catholic, was now suffering a similar illusion and also her deeply held, muted fury at the possibility that he might not be deluded shook Fay's sense of mystery.

"Everything is here," Oz said.

"But you're not," Fay thought. "Where are you?"

"Everything," he said. "Jesus is in it." Next, he asked, "Fay, do you know how much I love you?"

His question only left her with her own:

Did he know that she had never wronged him? Did he know how much she loved him? Would he know to carry that with him? Would he accept its comfort? And, for the sake of her own comfort, how could she ever be sure that her love had been understood?

She felt as though they'd just had an argument without words in which their two worlds sheared apart.

Oz breathed his last in a rattling rasp. Fay sat beside him for a long time, holding his hand. Then she rose and stood at the window next to the telephone stand. The room was silent. She would begin to weep as soon as she dialed her daughter's number and heard her daughter's voice answering, just as her eyes had welled in the galley when Taj touched her arm in sympathy. After calling her daughter, she would place a call to Paul's commanding officer, and Paul would be granted his furlough several days too late . . . not in time for Oz.

For the moment, she gazed past the lights of the strip mall into the valley below and up across the desert, past the saguaros and above the cloud from the Navajo zinc mine to the mountains. The cloud had an elongated shape like an enormous cocoon. The sun cut through, irradiating the cloud to the color of a peach.

11/01/02	
0600 Pos	Lat 55°15.9' N/Long 139°39.5' W
Temp 35°	Clds/Mod to hvy seas

Taj arranged with the captain for Fay to go to the bridge as the ship entered Prince William Sound. When she asked Taj why he had done this, he said, "Whenever we pass through the canal, I go to the bridge to see the land unfolding toward my village. It always seems a ceremony, coming home. I know that my joy may be your pain, but I thought that if you wanted to go topside, you should be free to do so. That's all."

Moved by his kindness, she climbed the ladder to the top deck and stood quietly on the carpet near the landing, well back from the wheel and instrument panel. All around were windows. Soon, the barrier islands appeared like knuckles on the line of the horizon. They grew into hands, then gnarly arms, and finally into themselves – craggy, deep blue, and white on top from the autumn snows. The ship also seemed to enlarge as it approached them. Upon the captain's command, the helmsman – the third mate – carved a turn toward the Hinchinbrook Entrance that lay between the islands, drawing the ship away from heavy water and going into the calm.

"Five degrees right," the captain said.

"Five degrees right," the third mate repeated as he adjusted the trajectory.

"Ten degrees right," the captain said.

"Ten degrees right."

"Steering three-thirty-six," the captain said.

The ship shuddered.

"Steering three-thirty-six."

Harley stood beside the captain. The three made a line before the glass – Harley in her black T-shirt with the skull between a pair of big orange wings, the captain before the screens, and the third mate straight as a post at the helm. Hovering between them and where Fay stood was Mort, who had come to receive instruc-

163

tions for the message he was to send to port. On his way out, he sidled toward Fay, softly asking, "Will you go ashore?"

Harley's head twitched back.

"Would you need company?" Mort asked. "I know the town."

All edge, Harley turned. "Is this man worrying you?"

Fay took flight into rumination upon the meaning of "worrying," but Harley cut through, saying, "Back off, Jack. Send your Telex to port."

Mort turned to the ladder. Gangly legs, checked shirt, and the head with its shaggy hair and age-spotted skin in his bald spot, his body went down just to Fay's side.

Fay doused her impulse to touch him in sympathy.

"Most of the guys on the crew are not assholes," Harley said. She turned away, exchanging a look with the captain.

Through the glass beyond them, Fay saw sandhill cranes in a V as they winged southward. Hundreds of phalaropes, off starboard, rose like clouds from the islands' estuaries. Kittiwakes stitched through the phalaropes, and beneath them cruised gangs of gulls. What of the migratory birds remained in the sound were flocking up for travel.

Fearing that her presence had caused a disruption, Fay asked, "Should I leave?"

The captain, a short man with a purple birthmark that ran up one side of his neck, turned and looked directly into her eyes. "Stay where you are."

"Ten knots," the third mate said as the ship nosed into the entrance.

The vessel passed through, seeming to fill the opening to the brim. Two sea lions reposed upon the float of a marker buoy. Off portside, arising from the western horizon, Fay saw the jagged, snow-covered peaks of Knight Island. To that radiant place with its intricacy of bays, she and Oz had gone every summer to fish.

"Seven and a half knots," the third mate said.

"Steady as you go," said the captain.

They cleared the entrance. The pilot boat approached.

Mort's voice came in over the intercom. "They have a chicksan down for repair, but we're clear to berth."

"Then straight in," the captain said. Harley, who at port would have the duty of discharging ballast and loading cargo, spun and moved for the ladder. Without looking at Fay or speaking, she nevertheless lightly tapped Fay's shoulder as she passed.

Soon, the pilot arrived, and again, there were three in position before the controls. The pilot had come by Fay without marking her presence, but all of a sudden she recognized him as the heavyset man who'd lived a couple blocks down from her in Valdez and with whose wife she'd had coffee once in a while.

Beyond and just to the east of Knight Island, the white of the Columbia Glacier at the end of its fjord glimmered in and out of view. Icebergs drifted out the mouth of the fjord and made an arc across the shipping lane. Several times she and Oz had floated the fjord with the children, going deep into the chill where rock, pulverized fine as dust, drifted in the aquamarine.

"Twenty degrees right rudder," the captain said.

"Twenty degrees right."

"Ease to ten degrees. Rudder back."

"Ten degrees," the third mate said.

The ship came abeam of Bligh Reef, nosed into the Valdez Arm, and slipped into the Valdez Narrows.

Fay saw the pilot looking back at her through her reflection in the glass, and then he turned. "Fay?"

"Hello, Ned."

"I'm surprised to see you." He cocked his head and asked, "Oz?"

She felt her throat catch. "He passed on a month ago."

"I'm very sorry," Ned said, moving toward the starboard wing. "I'll let Gail know." When he opened the hatch to the wing and went out, a pillow of cold air floated through the bridge.

"Right ten degrees," the captain said.

"Right ten degrees."

"Twelve knots."

"Twelve knots holding."

The sky was darkening. In the narrows the land came close upon the ship. Soon, the lights of Valdez sparked and Fay glimpsed her old neighborhood. Here she was, now, coming in on one of the alight tankers she used to see from her porch. To starboard, the great egg-colored holding tanks appeared on the slope; below them, the terminal where Oz had worked; and up above, the pipeline running out of the mountains like straight pins laid in a line.

After the ship entered the harbor, the captain said, "Stop ship."

"Stop ship."

The vessel quaked as the prop was thrown into reverse. Three tugs approached, vanishing as they pulled near the hull.

"Finished with the helmsman," the captain said.

"Locked down." The third mate stepped back. Fay imagined the engine hold going quiet and all the crew members on their platforms pausing to take stock of themselves. The captain moved to the wing with the pilot, who issued rpm commands to the tugs by radio. The tugs swung the *Spirit* 180 degrees and then in ensemble nudged it across its slip stream from fore, aft, and midship on the starboard side until the vessel kissed its berth.

11/02/02	
Valdez berth 4	
Temp 34°	

The next morning, thanks to Taj, Fay received permission to disembark. She walked past the ballast treatment plant, which made her feel tremulous. She checked through the security gate, took a taxi, and having decided she couldn't bear to call any of her old friends – not this trip, maybe next time – rented a car. Understanding now what she'd wished for but had never quite named as her purpose, she drove by highway to the mountains and turned onto an access road where, from the distance, she had a fleeting view of her ship and three others floating like toys in the harbor. Once she reached the point where the road was no longer cleared, she parked, got out, buckled on the snowshoes, and hiked for two miles, carrying the box and Lovecraft in a day pack. The snow squeaked under her weight and icy air filled her lungs. Her feet knew exactly where to go along the trail to come out of the trees at a rock outcropping that overlooked Veil Creek, one of Oz's favorite fishing places.

Here, the creek cascaded into a pool some thirty feet below where she stood. She could see the edges of the rock shelves poking out from the snow along the banks and the ice skiffing from the banks to the center, where the water still ran. In the dark heart of the pool, a pale rope of silt twisted. She imagined Oz there and the children fishing from the shelves, sometimes scrambling over them, playing with little plastic boats, soap bubbles. . . . On the far bank stood an old spruce tree with gnarled, protruding roots, where they'd sat to eat their picnics.

Something else was there, some bark-colored mobile thing: A river otter rose on its hind legs and cocked its head to look up at her. The otter moved across the snow to the edge of the creek, stopped stock still for an instant, and then in a flash snaked its long body across the ice and into the water.

Shadows lengthened toward dusk. There was little time left before Fay had to return to duty on her ship. Because of the hazard of ice and loose scree on the slope, she decided not to try to climb down to the creek. She took Lovecraft from the pack and knelt and placed him far out on the outcropping. She stood again. The days at sea and the accommodation of her body to the ship's subtle and endless list and yaw had the effect of making the world of land rock to and fro. She took the box out of the pack, removed the paper and lid, and put her fingers in to feel the ash and bone. When she dropped a handful over the edge, it drifted toward the bottom. She struggled to form words, a memorial prayer of gratitude for having been given a life as good as it was, for Oz, Vi and her family, Paul, for this place, for all things in life, and even now for what was new and terrifying.

She tipped the box, allowing Oz's remains to slide free. The line of ash widened as it descended, slid laterally above the water, and curled back out of view. The action felt as mundane as dumping potatoes into a pot. After what seemed too long a time for the ashes to have stayed suspended – though somehow they must have, gingerly conjuring themselves among the air currents, low to the water, and played upon by a draft – they mushroomed upward nearly to her feet, and then bent downstream, parted into tendrils, and scooted off into nothing.

The world swayed. Two ravens passed above the cascade, croaking as if calling to their little brother, whose glass eyes glinted. His black, cocked, absolutely still body shone against the snow. He was there – that was all. A crease slipped along the surface of the pool below where the otter in its vigilance arched near the surface, not quite breaking it. Fay sought words again, hoping to draw forth some clarity, but in her cavern, spirits stayed pressed flat against the walls, declining to dance away into ideas. Words would not come. Fay stood still, tearless, terrified, and alone, holding her box and wrapping paper.

Freeing the Apes

Flamme flammet, rot in Gluten
Steht das schwarze Moosgestelle.

J. W. von Goethe, *Faust*

One

WHEN I CROSSED the cattle guard onto Jim and Diane Blood's lane, I spotted a green-and-white sheriff's cruiser fifty yards ahead, hidden in the shade of a lone hawthorn. At first, I supposed there'd been speeders on the county road, but next, since I'd just passed a school bus bringing children home, I wondered if there had been reports of a "school bus chaser," an exhibitionist or predator. Because of my long experience with the machinations of the perverse and more recent brushes with the dark, my mind was disposed to seek out the ominous. Yet it was true enough that lost souls were known to appear in the far reaches of rural school districts.

To the left of the cruiser and arching back out of sight toward a stand of ponderosa pines, lay the Bloods' front field. It was early June. Oats had been planted, and they showed three or four inches of bright green growth against the dark earth in the gently arching furrows left by the seeder, like the whorls of a great fingerprint. Planting oats, Jim had explained to me, was a way of cleaning opportunistic weeds from a field. He had an alfalfa seeding planned for the next year. I admired – or envied – the life Jim and Diane had come to, guided as it was by the protocols of hope: planting and harvesting, birthing and butchering, the storing of goods, and their three sons loosed to the world. Beyond the field, the tops of the pines rose above a ridgeline to rake the clear, high country sky. From the ridge, it would be another half mile to the Bloods' log house.

The cruiser's door swung open as I approached, and the deputy stepped out. I stopped and lowered my window. A young

169

man with honey-colored skin and a fuzzy moustache, the deputy asked for the purpose of my visit and to see my license.

I passed over my government card, saying, "I'm visiting the residents. Is there a problem?"

The deputy scrutinized the card, which had an embossed seal and a Washington DC address. I watched his expression shift to that of the naïf edging carefully into the thrall of authority beyond his compass.

"Federal," he said. "Is this military?"

"FEMA." He squinted at the card, and I added what was plainly written: "Federal Emergency Management Administration."

He looked my new Envoy up and down, and then back at me. "It says Investigative Division."

"That's right."

"No driver's license?"

"That serves as one."

He looked at the card again.

"You're a friend of the residents, you say?"

I hadn't exactly said that, but the question increased my concern – for the Bloods and for the possibility that the deputy would run a check on my ID which could prove problematic. Worse yet, he might get a wild hair to search my vehicle, and then I'd have to explain the Glock in the glove box and the police issue AR-15 under the back seat. I told the truth: "I've recently left government service and moved here, back home to Spokane, but I don't have residency documents yet. What is the problem?"

After handing back my card, he unnerved me by saying, "Crime scene." He then took his pleasure in pausing before adding, "Go on ahead. Your friends are fine."

I drove through the woods to the crest of the ridge and down, following the twist in the lane around the top of a ravine that dropped into a canyon. Ascending again to the house, I found county vehicles everywhere, including a government van. Jim appeared on the back porch. I parked, got out, and went to him, skirting the red extension ladder that had been laid out on the lawn and was the excuse for my visit. I had come to borrow it.

Jim led me inside along the hall, pausing in the living room next to a wall full of books, where he explained that a woman had been found the day before on his and Diane's property at the base of an eighty-foot cliff. Her skull was crushed from hitting the rocks. "Nobody's saying whether she slipped or was pushed," Jim said. "But look."

We moved to a bank of windows at the south end of the room that had a view of the ravine, the ridge just beyond it that broke into the line of cliffs, and the canyon directly before us. It is an unruly topography. I leaned near a window and saw spots of orange on the cliffs. Far down in the canyon, I picked out several more vehicles, more orange like pinpricks of fire in the distance, and other tiny figures moving here and there. I drew my scrutiny back to the highland above the cliffs. There, yet more figures in blaze-orange suits and vests emerged from the woods and moved toward the lane I'd just driven on. "They've brought out help for the search," I said. "They must think she was pushed."

"Boy Scouts and work-release prisoners if you can believe it," Jim replied. "The kids I don't mind, I guess. A gang of ex-cons, I'm not so sure about."

I followed him into the kitchen, where he took out glasses, a pitcher of water, and a plate Diane had left for us. It had cheese and bread on it and – what most drew my eye – a row of smoked salmon sticks. Diane was a musician, away at a rehearsal. The youngest son of the family, I understood, was due to return home from college but seemingly had not arrived yet. Jim's elderly parents lived in an adjoining building. I'd never formally met them but glimpsed them now through the side window in the kitchen seated next to each other in the sun on their deck. They were white haired, small, and still in their chairs. Jim's mother was an Alzheimer's victim and his father was providing most of the care. Jim and I walked back into the living room, where Jim set the food on a table near the windows. There is nothing in the world like the sweet, smoky bite of Diane's salmon sticks, and I couldn't stop myself from taking one straightaway.

Jim had a grim expression. Of course, such an event would

shake him, as would the trespass of police upon what for many years he and Diane had nurtured. They had their meticulous, small-scale farming operation on high ground – alfalfa and oat fields, pastures mixed in with woods, cows and a few chickens, a big garden – but they otherwise protected their property against disturbance.

Jim took a sip of water. "First, I saw vultures circling. I was missing a calf and thought maybe it'd wandered off and died, so I walked down. The woman was an air force colonel and neighbor of a sort . . . Singley, Colonel Singley. There she was, all decked out in her dress blues on the rocks. The vultures had ripped through her clothes to get at her. They'd eaten out her eyes and started on the gut." He stopped and looked away, beset, as I surmised it, with the image of what he'd seen. He went on: "The police say she'd been there four days. While one of the deputies was examining the body, he noticed that the ground had been disturbed further down in the meadow."

"Rose's dig," I said. I looked out the window and down where the figures moved in an opening. "That's the meadow we see?"

"Right."

Diane and Jim had adjusted their practice of leaving the canyon alone for wild plants and animals to allow an archeological excavation. This did not seem inconsistent to them – wild nature and, as it turned out, the romance of a lost history. By happenstance, the archeologist was an old acquaintance of theirs and of mine, a woman with whom I'd had a liaison in my college days but hadn't seen for years. Not long after I'd moved out here, Jim had taken me down to see the site, and I was astonished to learn that it was she – Rose Levant.

"They opened it up," Jim said.

Upon discovering skeletal remains in the dig – the bones of a child, calcified and shining in the ensconcing earth – Rose had refilled the hole in order to protect it and to avoid legal entanglements while she sought permission to proceed.

"Does she know?" I asked.

"I practically had to shout at them to get them to stop," Jim said. "I told them to call the archeological agency before they went any further, so she must know. Diane left her a message, too."

We were silent, standing before the window. I thought about Rose. I'd grown up in this region and had attended the state university a hundred miles down the highway along with her, Jim, and Diane. I'd completely lost contact with Rose, as is the way. Seeing her again provoked my own archeological probe into a disappeared sector of the days before the navy, before I entered my profession, before my marriage to Molly, before my daughter was born, before FEMA, before estrangement. . . . At first, Rose seemed charged with the alien in the way that alterations in the formerly intimate can effect, yet as I spent a little more time in her company, she winnowed back into the hard little germ of the irreverent person I remembered well. As to Jim and Diane, I've kept on and off contact with them, though we've grown closer during the last few years. I've held them in high esteem for a long time. Jim, in particular, I consider a counterpart, whose nature – what I've always construed as his reserve and acuity and purposefulness – had led him to succeed where I had failed in the sacred ordinaries of life.

I said, "Look. If the police think homicide is possible, a search like this is pro forma."

"There's more, Peter." Jim turned his head to me. "They brought in a dog. Twenty yards from Rose's dig, another body turned up. It's another woman, buried barely two feet deep and in an advanced state of decay. They're doing an autopsy and tests on the site."

I had just taken another salmon stick, folded a hunk of Tilsit in a slice of bread, and been pleasuring in the manure-like odor of the cheese, but now I stood still, holding the food. Jim turned back to gaze at the men in orange, who were working their way from the ridgeline toward the house. The light flooded through the windows and made his beard, pale as steel, shine against his sun-darkened skin.

Finally, I said, "Nobody saw sign of anything like that when Rose was excavating."

"Of course not. Diane and I were questioned, me especially," he said. "It's interesting how being interrogated about something you didn't do, or would never imagine doing, something totally out of the blue, nevertheless makes you start casting around for your guilt. They kept forgetting why I'd stopped them from going further into Rose's dig."

"It's their job. They try to tap into the guilt everyone carries, hoping they scare up something that matches what they're looking for. They're trolling."

"It's a damn sorry procedure, if you want to know what I think." Jim continued, saying he'd been asked about an altercation he'd had with Mrs. Singley's husband over a property boundary the previous autumn. "All I could tell them was that the day they think Mrs. Singley died, I was seeding the back field. The hell."

"It's a process of elimination. No one would seriously think you'd have anything to do with it." I meant to reassure him, but my words seemed so glib as to completely miss the mark. This came from the habits of my work, the hardening of the spirit from repeated exposure to depravity, the lost ability to be surprised by horror, and the belief at bottom that guiltlessness did not exist. Margins had been drawn to separate guilt from innocence – that was all. Codes, written and otherwise, created the margins, while guilt was bacterial, a lawless agent leaping nimbly from one habitation to the next.

Jim turned and clicked his water glass down on the table. "I'm upset. I'm sorry. I got the ladder out for you."

"I can forgo the ladder. You have a lot going on."

"There's nothing going on for me except hanging around and worrying. Let's walk out back."

Two

AFTER LOADING the ladder onto my Envoy's rack, we walked past Jim's machinery to the back field, well away from the activity toward a place where cows were watered from a tank just inside a fence in the shade of a stand of bush, chokecherry, and aspen. Jim checked the half-full tank and said, "I mean to dig a little well for them in there and pump it out here." He pointed over the fence at a damp place, thick with underbrush. "I think there's enough sub-surface water. That way I won't have to keep trucking it out."

We turned and looked up the field. Fifty yards away stood Jim's small herd of red cows with their calves, some of which skittered about among the mothers. Beyond the cows the pasture inclined gently across the next farm toward a series of irregular plateaus and then the Kettle Mountains. To the west a spine of land sloped down just above the house, blocking it from view. The Bloods' black dog, a wolf-like creature, had tagged along with us but disappeared for a time to scout the pine trees to the east. The trees laid a fringe going well up the pasture and then broke into blackened snags, the result of a big fire that had passed near the Bloods' house a few years ago. This was a dry country. Thus, any place where water ran or gathered, such as the canyon bottom or here where we stood, became electric with life.

"I don't mean to sound self-serving," Jim said. "God knows, it's terrible about Mrs. Singley and the other woman. Mrs. Singley was a nice enough lady. I wouldn't say the same for the husband."

He told me about his and Diane's relations with the Singleys, how they shared a stretch of north-south boundary that ran from the cliffs to the canyon bottom, and how for whatever reason the Singleys had bought their property landlocked. They had an easement to the high ground, but no way to get to the canyon because of the sheer drops from the bluffs. They lived in the city, and Jim guessed they'd bought the land as an investment. He'd first met the husband a few years ago when he came by to ask for an easement to the bottom. "Even if we'd have considered doing such a thing," Jim said, "which was unlikely, he settled it by coming through the woods on a dirt bike. Then he pulled right up to our house and tried to kick our dog, who didn't like him much, either."

There was a bare patch of earth in front of us from the cows milling around the water tank. Jim crouched and drew a straight line in the dirt with a stick. "There's the boundary. Here's the creek." He drew that, a ragged diagonal that cut across and then angled southwestward. "And here are the bluffs." He drew a set of scallops running alongside the boundary.

I crouched next to him, looking and leaning back against a fence post.

"The one Mrs. Singley fell from, or whatever happened to her, comes right up to the property line," he said, touching one of the scallops with his stick. "This one. See? She was last alive on her property and dead once she hit ours."

He marked the spot with an *X*.

"There used to be an access road that came in from farther south, but it got washed out years ago, so now the bluffs keep the Singleys from being able to get to the little bit of bottom they have. Here's our meadow." On his side of the line, inside the off kilter V made by the bluffs and creek, he drew an irregular oval and within it two more *X*s, which he also touched with his stick, saying, "Rose's dig is here. The other body was found just over there."

We stayed quiet for a moment, hunkered over the map. Up the field the cows had spread out in a line of their own making and had all turned to stare at us as if they'd decided it was time to give consideration to our presence. Even the calves were still, standing near their mothers. The mosquitoes that bred in the damp at our backs had found us, too. They were biting through my shirt and I was slapping them off my neck. Jim picked one from his arm, rolled it between his fingers, and then scrutinized the bloodstain.

"They'd bother us less if we moved into the sun," he said.

We walked over the top of the map, going several yards toward the cows, who didn't budge.

"Back when we were first getting mixed up with the Singleys, it wasn't them I was worried about," Jim said. "Instead, it was the horseback riders and dirt bikers coming in across the creek from the far side of the canyon. We have our rules about the bottom, as you know."

Indeed. I'd hiked down several times with Jim and Diane – the first time, early one morning in April not long after my return to this region. They told me that each spring they'd find scat and prints from an elk herd migrating back to the mountains, and we were on the watch for that. Every few minutes wild turkeys gobbled at each other from across the canyon. We visited the creek, stirring up the ducks out of the eddies. Brook and rainbow trout swam in the creek. Watercress grew in the shallows, and low on the bank wild mint. Higher up stood thickets of willow and wild rose and a tangle of chokecherry, service berry, saskatoon, gooseberry, and hawthorn spreading to a line of aspens and alders. In one tall alder, as Diane pointed out, a big nest of sticks had been assembled by a pair of blue herons. They'd begun seeing an eagle off and on, too, she said. Near the meadow were ponderosa pine and fir, and kinnikinick growing in the catch basins among the rocks. There were bitterroots, the exquisite little purslane that lifted its pink flower and spread its petals to greet the sun during the day and closed itself up and lay down to sleep on the rocks at night. And across the meadow near the bluffs at the far end of Jim and Diane's place was evidence of the fire in the form of a band of charred trees. Those trees – more pines and what Jim said had been their only stand of birch – had a stately quality, as if to mark the dignity of their death. A crazed florescence was all around them, popping out of the carbonized ground – grass widows and buttercups embroidering the new bunchgrass, fireweed, and well into the burn zone even birch saplings sprouting from the rhizomes that survived.

We had come back to the meadow where Diane stopped to say that once she'd been startled in this very place by a completely foreign thing. "I was here. It was there," she said, gesturing back at the burn zone. "It was about knee-high. It turned and fixed its eyes on me. The instant I realized what it had to be – a wolverine, for heaven's sake – it vanished into the rocks. It was like smoke, there one moment and gone the next. Of course, the cynic here didn't believe I'd seen a wolverine," she'd said, cocking an eyebrow at Jim.

"Not at first," Jim had said, grinning. "Now, I surely do."

It seemed a moment that held the delicate evidence of an altercation, what might have been born of their differing views of the world – his skepticism, her all-embracing idealism – but also what in their long marriage they granted in each other as necessary to the fit. I envied them this. My wife, Molly, and my daughter, Beth, now lived in Spokane with Molly's mother. Their moving out here had been the impetus for my return, but upon arriving I discovered that Molly's and my estrangement was far more extreme than I'd imagined. At times the very idea of Jim and Diane's vigorous, enmeshed love made me feel like eating out my own liver in fury.

Diane was a cellist and always held herself erect. When I'd remarked on her posture once to Jim, he said that she was actually in pain much of the time because of the toll on her body the hours spent poised over the instrument had exacted and that she consciously kept her body straight. She stood that way in the canyon just then, looking formidable in her pleasure, her face filled with light.

"I didn't know what it was at first because it didn't belong here. And they don't," she said. "They're high elevation animals. But they'll eat practically anything. They're one of the few predators that take porcupines. What hit me is that there are all manner of unknown creatures out there, weaving together their life codes in ways also totally unknown to us. Once in a while, they rise up to remind us of this."

Wolverine, I'd thought.

Gulo gulo.

The glutton, it is called.

Freeing the Apes

Diane had made me think of the ravaged places to which FEMA had sent me. In some, virtually all life seemed extinguished – whether by natural disaster, industrial calamity, or war. In one, a village of the Tanzanian interior near newly developed oil fields, there had been an explosion in a chemical plant, killing hundreds. All that was left were abandoned buildings and huts, defoliated earth, and two-inch long, iridescent blue beetles that rattled through the air and crept up the walls. From the distant bush, jackals pierced the eerie air with their cries. As the humans – the destitute survivors of the village, the pillagers, and the international teams, of which I was a member – ventured back into the site, I wondered what new system of life might be assembled in a place left so barren as to be rendered abstract, like the mineral Mars, like a heart stripped cold of its loving.

While Jim and I stood at the bottom of the pasture, he continued with his story. Normally taciturn, or even guarded, his part in conversations often came in thrusts and asides, but now he seemed to want to talk. He said he'd been amazed to realize that Singley might next try to simply appropriate his access. Jim had decided to mark out the property line with posts and barbed wire. He drove down with his supplies and discovered trees well onto his and Diane's property festooned with pink survey ribbons. When he went down again the next day, half his supplies had vanished, including three fifty-pound rolls of wire.

"But Diane always takes the direct approach," Jim said.

When he'd first started worrying, it was she, he said, who told him, "Put up a fence." When his supplies had been pilfered, she said, "Take the posts you have left and sink the fuckers in concrete."

Envisioning Diane's force in saying such a thing made me smile to myself.

Jim followed her advice, and then she tracked down the Singleys' phone number and invited them over for tea.

The Singleys came. The four of them, the two Singleys and Jim and Diane, sat around the table near the windows. It turned out that each of the Singleys – Bob and Helga – were lieutenant colo-

179

nels, though the husband was retired. "It's funny," Jim said. "She was striking, but I can never remember what he looks like. He's got a face like a zero. The two of them made you wonder how the hell the one ever managed to persuade the other to marry. And the way he talked was like he'd never given up his command."

When Jim asked about the ribbons on the trees, Singley said they were his.

When Jim said they weren't on the survey line, Singley said they certainly were.

When Jim asked whose survey line he had in mind, Singley said it was the correct one. He'd had help running it from an air force surveyor.

"A surveyor?" Jim said. "All those flags. It's like the Fourth of July."

"When you're in the trees," Singley said. "You have to triangulate."

Jim had almost said, "Somebody needs to triangulate you to figure out what you mean, my friend," but instead, he asked, "How many times?"

"As many as you need," Singley said.

When Jim asked about the missing supplies, Singley said he knew nothing about them.

Now, Jim looked down and poked a hunk of dirt with his boot toe and then went on, saying, "Mrs. Singley was quiet through that, except to compliment Diane on the food she'd prepared. She couldn't stay away from it. It was bread and cheese again. And a pâté and salmon sticks, which Mrs. Singley enjoyed about as much as you do. She said our house was like a restaurant."

I had two salmon sticks in my shirt pocket. Unchagrinned, I took one out, bit off the end of it, and chewed. "So, it is," I said. "At the slightest provocation Diane lays out a feast."

Jim smiled. "It's true. She likes people to be happy." He looked over to the right where the black dog had materialized from the woods and was coming our way, cruising the fence line. Soon, the dog sat, leaning her head against Jim's knee. He bent to scratch her ears and continued: "I'd guess Mrs. Singley was a few years younger than her husband and a few inches taller, too. She had to be six feet, and she was graceful. It made you think, 'basketball.' She was large and beautiful in a way with her shining hair and blue, Nordic eyes. At first, she had little to say. She was like a hungry animal, rising up every now and then to check for trouble while she fed. When Diane asked what she did in the air force, she said, 'Information systems.'

"Her husband said, 'She has a doctorate in Comparative Literature,' which came out sounding like it was his achievement, not hers.

"She said she'd got her assignment because she could write sentences, and then, as if her switch had been flipped, she started in on her service during the Persian Gulf War. Do you remember the letters? The first President Bush, trying to whip up enthusiasm at home, called on the public to send letters of support to the soldiers stationed abroad. Mrs. Singley was shipped over to take command of the mailroom. She said they had bag after bag of letters coming in, hundreds of thousands of letters, and most were addressed to nobody in particular.

"They were given a hangar in Riyadh. The mailbags kept piling up, but there was no one to send the letters to. They had to arrange photo shoots with soldiers opening mail, so they put up a bivouac outside the warehouse and brought in tanks and Humvees and an army detail to pose. They had lines of tables, stacks of filing boxes, and computers to keep the records. 'But it was a war,' she told us. 'Troops were moving around and getting hurt.' And then, she said, suddenly it was over, smoke blowing in from the oil fires, Saddam's Republican Guard buried in the sand, and the U.S. troops shipping out. She and her crew stayed for two months with the piles of letters, separating what was actually addressed to somebody. The rest, the bags and bags of dead letters mostly sent in packets from the schools, they burned. When she was done telling us all that, she said, 'What does it mean?'"

Jim stared up the pasture. The dog stood, took several steps away from us, and turned toward the ridge on our left. Her ears were cocked. At that moment all the cows, as if suddenly landing on a shared idea, moved off in single file toward the trees in the other direction. They went with great deliberation, switching their tails, while the calves gamboled to and fro.

"They're funny aren't they?" Jim said. He bent and plucked a straw from the ground, which he placed between his teeth. "The cows."

The dog growled and we looked at the ridge. A cluster of orange jump suits appeared from the direction of the house. They spread out and began moving along the top of the ridge.

"Shit," Jim said.

Feeling the hardness next to me, I gazed northward up the pasture to where Jim had been looking in the first place, toward the mountains that seemed like charcoal-colored cutouts pasted to the sky. Beyond them lay Canada.

Jim took the straw out of his mouth and finished his story: "I arranged to meet the Singleys at the creek. We ran a string line from a point where we agreed on the boundary all the way to the disputed corner, through the trees, over the bluff, and down through the trees again. I went up on the last cliff while Bob Singley took the spool down toward the corner. Mrs. Singley was with me. While we waited I told her I'd studied literature in college and asked how many languages she knew. 'Five,' she said. 'All Northern European languages, plus Old Finnish.' She told me she was a Finn but had lived in the U.S. since she was a little girl. It made sense with her looks. She said that was what got her started in her studies. 'But how many jobs are there for specialists in the sources of the *Kalevala*?' she asked. She said it's the national epic and that the story turns upon a stone that gives you whatever you wish. 'Things haven't changed much, have they?' she said, looking down into the canyon. Then she said, 'It's beautiful here, isn't it?'"

Jim gazed up at the ridge. The orange suits were alight slats moving through the trees. Just behind them, a guard turned toward us, precipitating another low rumble from the dog.

Jim continued, "Pretty soon, Singley had the line tied off on one of the trees that marked what he wanted me to believe was the corner. He came out to the edge of the trees and called up to us, 'See?'

"'It's bent,' I shouted back. And from our vantage point, it was clear as day, a good ten degree wow in the line that would give him part of the meadow and, while he was at it, about fifteen acres of our land, including most of the burn and our rejuvenating birches.

"Singley shouted, 'Do you see?' When I shouted again, saying the line was crooked, he said 'No, it isn't.'

"I pointed, showing him where to go to get the line straight. 'Go that way.'

"'No, I won't,' he said.

"Mrs. Singley had backed off from the edge of the cliff, and when I looked at her, she was staring straight across the canyon, not paying attention to him or me or anyone. It seemed she'd somehow disappeared right there with her eyes like stones. It was like she'd turned into a wall and only her blue eyes were peering out of it.

"We climbed down through a cut between bluffs. Mr. Singley had moved through the trees, and as Mrs. Singley and I walked along, a great horned owl appeared from the shadows, startled out of its roost. It sailed toward us in the way of its kind, gliding with its wings spread and as if powered by little jets, weaving around the tree trunks. It made the both of us stop in our tracks. When the owl came near, it pumped its wings, making them hiss, and it shot straight up into the sky.

"We found Mr. Singley in the clearing where the burn had started. I was still hoping that if I gave him a little rope, maybe he'd be reasonable. So just to make conversation before we started in on the tricky shit – namely his lies – I asked if he'd seen the horned owl. In his unequivocal way, he said, 'There are no horned owls here.' Why he would say that or what kind of fool he thought he was talking to, I have no idea. It made me look to Mrs. Singley, but she got swallowed up in herself again, leaving only her blue eyes.

"When I told Diane about this, she said, 'I think that man is beyond choosing anything. He's obsessed. He's dangerous. Helga knows that.' Diane always wants to give quarter to others, but every so often she surprises even me." Jim went on, saying that Diane thought Helga's story about the letters was told in desperation and that there was something very shaky about her. "'It seems like she's made them her letters,' Diane said. 'It's the messages sent out that got turned to ash.'"

Jim ran his fingers along the piece of straw, straightening it, and looked up the pasture. All the cows with their calves had disappeared into the woods to our right. In front of us, the black dog stood up, a sentinel on the orange suits who had turned around and were sieving back through the trees in our direction. Above, a red tailed hawk rode the drafts, searching for small prey. To our left the sun was descending. It streaked through the broken clouds, glimmered against the distant mountains, and made the shadows of the trees on the ridge reach across the pasture.

"That's it," Jim said. "I kind of liked Mrs. Singley. We hired a surveyor, though. The line's exactly where we thought it was. Once they get their graphs drawn up, we'll register it with the county." He put the straw back between his teeth, and his voice thickened with emotion: "Singley's got no access to the bottom and his wife is dead."

After a moment, I said, "So you think he killed her."

Jim murmured indeterminately.

I well knew that obvious explanations were often the truth but also that it was easy for information to be spun by strong feeling so the clearest answer gets tossed to the side. Then you have clean out the debris of wrong signals and rearrange everything. "Do they know where he was?"

"Out of town on business, he says."

"Can he prove it?"

Jim shrugged.

"This is outside my usual field of activity," I said. "But I have contacts. I could inquire."

Jim glanced at me. The harrowed expression on his face was

startling. I took it to mean he might have liked to ask that, but that he felt he'd left his feelings more open than was his habit and at this moment would not go further by prevailing upon me. Instead, he said, "What I think is that whatever was wrong between those two came to a head, and one way or another, the crazy son of a bitch forced her off the cliff."

Again we fell quiet. The sun irradiated the bottoms of the clouds with pink. The air around us had turned luminous. The last of the Day-Glo vests and jumpsuits passed by on the ridge and headed down in the direction of the house. They were finished for the day and would load up in the van. The black dog, relieved of her watch, had lain down between us with her head on her paws. In a moment, we heard the faint popping of gravel as vehicles pulled away.

"And how are you?" Jim asked.

"Fine."

"Any more crosses?"

"No," I said. "All's quiet on that front."

Three

THE CROSSES HAD BEEN appearing in front of my house. I had
my own ongoing intrigue, therefore – though in comparison
with Jim and Diane's, it seemed like nothing. The crosses were
about two feet tall, made out of steel, ornamented variously on
their fronts while each had the letter *H* inscribed on its back.
What their meaning was, I had absolutely no idea. Yet because of
them, I'd decided to install a surveillance system on my house. It
was so that I had driven out to borrow Jim's ladder.

A few days later, as I began my installation, I realized that it
would take much longer than expected and should buy my own
ladder. I called Jim to tell him I would return his, but he said to
keep it until I was done. He had another. He said that if I was
thinking of coming out anyway, though, he could use an extra
hand for a few hours. The prospect of being helpful pleased me. I
told Jim I'd contacted an old associate, an air force prosecutor,
and that he'd dug out a few things about Bob Singley. "Your man
hit the ceiling in the promotion ladder because of problems with
female subordinates," I said to Jim. "That's probably why he took
out his retirement after twenty years."

There was a quiet on the other end of the line.

I arrived at the time Jim and I had agreed upon, finding no
deputy at the gate and no government cars parked at the house.
As soon as I stepped out of my Envoy, I heard a din like machine
gun fire and walked toward the noise, finding Jim's flatbed
backed up to the fence at the bottom of the pasture, where we'd
stood and talked before. On the other side of the fence were
heaps of earth and stone, tools and supplies on the ground, Jim's
old backhoe parked near to the trees, and in the midst of it all a
deep hole from which the racket of a jackhammer emanated. I
eased between the strands of barbed wire and peered into the
hole. Jim was bent over the jackhammer, his body lurching violently as he broke up the rock around the edges. When he spotted

me, he switched off the hammer and leaned it against a wall of the hole.

"Hey," he said.

With his foot he nudged the end of a hose over to a pool of water in the center of the hole, and then he emerged, finding footholds on the rock protrusions in the wall. He was drenched to the thighs and splattered with mud all the way to his face. He bent to switch off the compressor, which along with the sump pump was plugged into a gas-driven generator resting in the bed of his truck. The generator idled. The pump hummed as it sucked water from the hole and ran it down a line of hose through the brush to dump it in a depression. Between tree trunks, I could see the little pool in the making, flashing in the sun.

"I think I'm as deep as I need to be," he said.

"You're making a hole."

He pulled foam plugs out of his ears. "A hole, you say? It's a well."

"That's a windmill." I nodded toward the parts of the thing – steel scaffolding, mounting boots, drive line, gear box, hub, and blades – that lay neatly arranged on the ground just beyond a pile of dirt.

"A farmer up the road gave it to me. It's something, eh?"

"Antique."

"Oh, no," he said. "It's cutting edge in this age of dissolution." A wry smile flickered on his lips, and then disappeared. He told me there'd been a dental match on the second body. "It's Margarita White."

At first, the name meant nothing to me.

"She disappeared when we had the firestorm. You were out here visiting."

"I do remember," I said. And I did . . . the young woman, a power company employee, presumably abducted from a transmission station several miles north of the Blood's farm.

My wife, our daughter, and I had regularly traveled from the east to see my wife's mother at Christmas and often early in the fall. That year, we were here at the beginning of October when firestorms raged over a couple hundred square miles and nearly jumped the river into the city. I ended up staying for a couple weeks to open a FEMA office. The threat to the Bloods' place became apparent as soon as I saw the maps of the fire's course, and I'd driven out to check on them. It was so that we'd renewed our friendship.

"I suppose it's a relief for her family," Jim said, "to have confirmed what they most feared. For us, it puts a name to the questions: Margarita White. How the hell did she get here? Who brought her? They say it's certain that the body was there during the fires, which raises all kinds of possibilities. It's the only other time since we came here that there's been vehicles and people all over the place."

"And you've been questioned again."

"You bet, and it still pisses me off. To you, I'd guess this all sounds like just another macabre local yarn."

I looked at the water in the hole that made a V-shaped riffle as it reciprocated with the suction from the tube. "The macabre is always local."

From behind his camouflage of mud, another wry smile glimmered on and off Jim's face. "The sheriff's investigator found me here and wanted to know why I was digging this hole." Jim bent to pick up a can of mosquito repellent, and said, "Take a look at this." He led me past the backhoe and through an opening in the brush and trees to a low hillock from which we could see the house over to the right and the canyon below. Just to our left was the depression filling with water. In the canyon bottom, I spied the fluttering of yellow police ribbons and a green van and thought it interesting how so small an adjustment in position could lead to such a radical change in perspective.

"It seems like they're permanently camped out," Jim said. "They come in to do something or other every day. They don't let us know any more. They just arrive and drive around where we never drive. Why don't people understand that in this country if you cut the ground, you've opened it for the noxious weeds?

They act like the place belongs to them. The people across the canyon are watching. Singley's taken to hanging out on the high ground of his place. I see him up there, watching, the skittery son of a bitch. I wonder if they know he's there."

"They know," I said.

Singley intrigued me because of Jim's description of him as utterly unmemorable, a zero. He'd be an outcast, a feasible killer, scorned, shunned, and yet scrutinized.

Jim sprayed repellent on his arms and passed the can to me. "I want the fucking police off my land," he said.

A haze of mosquitoes had collected around my face. When they bit, they raised welts. I sprayed my hair, and then meticulously abluted the cuffs of my jeans, my legs, waist, hands, shirt sleeves, chest, and neck. When I was done, I said, "They're looking for whatever else might turn up. Forensics. In the case of Margarita White, what they want is to put a perpetrator on the scene."

"It's a plague."

I was tempted to say, "Consider the rest of the world, my friend ... Afghanistan, Uzbekistan, Kashmir, Sudan...." It was true that I carried with me a shadow land of bestiality and mayhem that shaped itself into what might be called the macabre. I said nothing.

"So, Singley had troubles?" Jim asked.

"There was enough of a cloud to freeze him in rank. The wife was a different matter. She'd been approved for a bump to full colonel. She was going places. I might have contacts I could ask about Margarita White, too, if you want."

Jim looked at me without speaking. He had the harrowed expression again, opened-eyed and flat-cheeked, seemingly his own shadowy aggregate of misgiving, distrust, and curiosity that I couldn't quite piece together.

"Or I can just lay off it," I said.

"I guess it won't hurt."

"No."

We moved back through the brush. I set the can of repellent

down on a toolbox. Jim got on his knees at the edge of the hole and dragged up the jackhammer. The hose ejaculated a pop of air when he pulled it free of its fitting. He coiled the hose around the tank's handle and reached into the truck bed to switch off the generator, which left us surrounded with sudden quiet. A frog croaked from the pool on the other side of the bush.

Jim returned to the hole, pulled up the tubing, coiled it on the ground, and changed the subject: "It's interesting how different it is here from below or even up higher on the pasture where you could dig ten feet and still be in sand. Rose's midden is in sand." He gestured toward the distant mountains. "It's all downhill for miles, so we get the water riding through the fissures in the basalt. Here I am, too, opening the earth in a place that's been left untouched for so long. But look." He pointed into the hole and ticked off the layers. "There's a line of ash from Mount Saint Helens on the half foot of top soil, then loess, then a couple feet of sand mixed with stone. Then brown clay, another line of gravel, green clay, and the basalt in the bottom. It's a tight little typology. I guess it's the floods that make the ground seem so discontinuous."

He was referring to the floods from the sundering ice dams at the end of the most recent glacial epoch. A lake more than half the size of Lake Michigan stretched from what is now the Idaho Panhandle to the city of Missoula. It drained many times, and several times cataclysmically fifteen thousand years or so ago, releasing ten times as much water as presently flows through all the rivers in the world. The water, a thousand feet deep and rushing over seventy miles per hour, spread in three courses across eastern Washington, enough of it arriving all at once at a slot in the Cascades near the coast to curl a wave all the way back into Idaho again. This explains the tumultuous quality of the terrain in this region with its flattened off hills, huge gouges, tracts of exposed basalt from the volcanic epoch years before, the deep, tear-shaped lakes produced by cataracts, the boxcar sized erratics dropped like pebbles, and the sand and gravel deposits, which are actually river bars on an enormous scale. Everywhere, the irregularity in detail bears testimony to the effects of gigantic rivers passing by, even here on Jim and Diane's place. The large hole of the canyon below had been carved by floods. The two southerly running ridgelines were high ground, and the shallow soil in one place and deep sand in another were the result of scouring and backwash.

It was my home. My grandparents had settled here. My parents had died here.

It was the place Jim and Diane had made their home.

They came and embraced it with their love.

I considered that its discontinuity is what formed me, and then murmured, "Discontinuous, you say?"

"But only apparently. The native peoples have stories of the floods, which are disavowed by science because no proof yet exists that this place was inhabited at that time. But science is wrong. The stories are what remain of the flesh. They carry the mark of the wounding and of the pleasure, as well."

I stood still, digesting the statement, a seeming non sequitur, yet resonating with the trouble Jim felt.

"It's still Mrs. Singley I'm trying to understand," he said. "If she jumped, then what she was doing was bringing to a final end the story of her personal cataclysm. Diane believes this all started with the ancient child in Rose's dig."

"The mystic explanation."

"No, Peter," he said. "Apparent discontinuity."

"You mean unseen connections."

"Diane says it's like string theory."

"You mean everything happening at once."

"I think what she means is that we're not just dots. Everything is connected, but still we make what's useful into a measure and miss the rest of it. She loves that stuff." He moved to his old backhoe, stepped up on it, and looked back at me. "First, I need to scrape out the rest of that loose rock, and then I'll put you to work. Pascal's home and he'll be coming out, too."

He started the tractor. It was a two-cylinder diesel and made a racket as it expelled plumes of exhaust that drifted up the pasture. Jim drove the machine to the hole, unscissored the bucket, extended the armature, lowered the bucket, and fished the rock from the bottom. I stepped clear to watch. Each time the bucket came out of the hole and into the light, it streamed water in a glittering fan. The rock rang when Jim dumped it on a pile. He turned and plunged the bucket back into the pit and dug at the bottom, making the tractor's engine surge.

Four

MY SPECIALTY is resource economics. For several years at FEMA, I subjected all forms of loss, including human life, to cost analysis. Consider the obscurity: With the devastation of an earthquake in California, a hurricane in Florida, volcanic eruption in Mexico, or fire, drought, riot, insurrection, even war, not only the loss of infrastructure – buildings, communication systems, transportation networks – would be calculated, but also the value of lost cash flow from businesses, the projected earnings and contributions of the deceased, or conversely (and perversely!) the negative worth of certain blighted locations. If a convalescent home, crime-infested sector, or a terrorist haven were destroyed and the life within snuffed out, so much the better! The gains from terminating future medical bills, insurance payments, and either government support or military suppression would far outstrip the losses. What for me began years ago as an interest in having a positive – and perhaps corrective! – effect on the disposition of resources turned into a mummification within the staggering detail. The ever-arching estimates, their contingencies, graphs, actuarial charts, and the labyrinthine crochet of the civilized imagination around death and destruction wrapped me inside its cocoon.

When my position was upgraded, the cocoon turned subterranean. I became an on-site investigator for the bureau's international arm, traveling under false pretenses to far-flung points of the earth – Nigeria, Tanzania, Argentina, Serbia, Yemen, Chechnya, Afghanistan. . . . Never given full knowledge of the purpose of my missions, I nevertheless understood that they were directed toward U.S.-supported factions and that the elaborate investigations I conducted and the reports I filed were meant to vanish into the bureaucracy. Because of a recalcitrant Congress, siphoning off funding from the FEMA budget to further foreign policy objectives was the point for the Clinton administration. I carried a diplomatic passport and doubled as a courier, handing over documents and small fortunes to strangers in state buildings and dilapidated outposts and armed camps. In Rwanda once, I was driven to a bunker overlooking a quarry where scores of the dead had been scattered – a hole for a mass grave. Gangs of men in rags broke open bags of lime and spilled it over the bodies, whitening them, and then shoveled in the earth. From behind the closed door of the next room, I heard thuds and moans, what had to be the sounds of a beating. It gave me a feeling of disassociation, as if we were all one, but our heads only were in this room conducting business while our brutal bodies were hard at work on the other side of the wall.

Some years ago – well before the American election of 2000 and, thus, before the suicide attacks on the World Trade Center and the Pentagon – I delivered a diplomatic pouch filled with U.S. currency to Afghani "irregulars," who arrived at our meeting place in an old Toyota pickup with a machine gun mounted in the back, the type of vehicle that had come to be known in Somalia as a "technical." Out of the truck piled four shaggy, heavily armed men. I'd come in a Land Cruiser in the company of a driver, two private security guards, and a Pakistani interpreter. We'd driven from a helicopter pad in the hills, raising a tube of dust as we drove into a neglected agricultural region of the Kabul Valley and stopping to wait for the men at a bend in the road next to a dry irrigation ditch and a crumbling, stone irrigation tank.

When I handed over the pouch to the oldest of the four – Shakur was his name – he grasped the strap with both hands and, keeping his gaze fixed on me, bowed his pockmarked face. It was an oddly courtly gesture. He had a scraggly, gray beard, and his eyes were like this desert, all-encompassing and searing. Yet fearsome as he was, even more so was the man at his shoulder, a much younger and bigger man with a pistol squeezed under his belt and holding what I recognized – and immediately coveted – as an Afghan knockoff of a British Lee-Enfield bolt action .303. This man's eyes had the dead quality of a psychopath.

Through my interpreter, I offered to buy the gun.

Shakur spoke to his man, who muttered a reply. Shakur then spoke to the interpreter, who said to me, "He asks how much you would offer."

I said, "Three hundred dollars," knowing that was enough to buy several such weapons in this place.

The interpreter passed that figure on, and then Shakur spoke directly to me in heavily accented English: "Eight hundred dollars American."

I offered four hundred, saying that I could do no more. This was accepted. I gave the money in fifty-dollar denominations to Shakur, who peeled off several bills and stuffed them beneath his caftan and handed the remainder to his man. The man emptied the rifle's magazine and ejected the cartridge from the chamber. He kept the cartridges and passed the rifle to Shakur, who passed it to me. Shakur bowed again. I bowed back. They both studied me, the one with his leaden eyes and Shakur with his, which were so alive that it seemed all matter falling under his survey, including me, my money, and my newly acquired weapon risked being sucked in and incinerated.

We drove off in opposite directions. I sat in the back seat of the Land Cruiser, holding the rifle poised between my knees. We passed a group of a half-dozen women, walking along a dry streambed in the direction Shakur had gone. They carried burdens on their heads and wore black head-to-toe coverings. I turned to watch them, thinking about the ironies of economies: the small fortune in the valise for the purchase of arms, or so I assumed, the antique Lee-Enfield, and otherwise my pile of fifties to be used for sustenance and bribes and to pay my driver and interpreter, and then whatever hard-won material the women were carting – water, maybe, or seeds. Their robes fluttered as they walked a course that seemed melodic in its rise and fall upon the desolate flatland.

Beyond their vanishing figures to the north, I saw the blaze of an opium field, and well beyond it, the mountains. That would be a country of precipice and crevasse, and somewhere in it stood the massive eighth-century statues of Buddha that the Taliban were destroying. I'd hoped to see the statues, partly from simple curiosity but also from the all but submerged wish in me to take a sounding on such monumental spirituality and on the damning, reciprocal, equally monumental defacement.

Five

ONE NIGHT, upon returning to my Washington DC flat from a mission to Kosovo, I found the entryway lined with boxes. Molly, who was waiting in the living room, told me that she'd sent Beth off to stay with her grandmother in Spokane, that she herself was catching a flight out that night, and that in two days the movers would come to pick up the boxes and furniture she'd tagged in two days. She'd resigned from her position as an interior designer. I was exhausted, as I always was after my journeys, and barely capable of receiving this information let alone understanding it. I told myself that it was my long absences that caused her to lose patience. She'd said before that since I spent so much time away, perhaps there was little point in her keeping Beth here in a place they both despised.

I looked around, taking in the yellow Sticky Notes she'd affixed to the hutch, the easy chairs, the sofa I sat on, and the glass-topped coffee table between us. The coffee table had a collection of articles on it, including a stack of towels, ceramic figures, carving knives in a case, and a .38 revolver. It was the house gun I'd bought for Molly years ago in defiance of city ordinances. I was licensed to be armed. She was not. I picked up the pistol and opened the chamber. It was loaded.

"I'm taking it," Molly said.

"Loaded?"

She shrugged and retrieved it from my hands, snapped the chamber to, and set the pistol back on the table. She was wearing jeans and one of my old dress shirts with the arms folded up to her elbows.

"Protection," I said.

"We all need it."

I picked up the gun again, opened it, emptied the cartridges into my hand, closed the gun, set it down, and stood the cartridges on end in a row beside it. "I suppose we do. But maybe not right now."

She'd watched the procedure and now looked up at me, her eyes intent on either side of a slash of brown hair. "Are you all right?"

Her question threw me for an instant, but then I realized it wasn't my condition she was asking after but rather the prospect of carrying off her plan with as little interference as possible. I looked at the boxes lining the wall. "I'm tired, of course," I said. In fact, I was merely riding the edge of an incomprehensible adrenaline alert. Strangely, I remembered the voices of the women of Kosovo as a cluster of them had passed when I came out of my hotel to catch a ride to the air base. Among them several men carried a casket. The women's keening and wild ululation of grief for a lost husband or son filled the air and then slowly receded as the procession turned down an alley. It was a curiosity of culture and circumstance in which, at the time, I'd taken little more than passing interest. Why it came back to me as I sat across from Molly, I couldn't make out. Only later did I realize that it was an insurgency of my nature, a haunting struggle to break through my inability to feel grief.

Molly's voice came back at me: "I won't live in this hell hole any longer. I'm sick of the barricades and police, the infernal detours, the uppity clients, and the fear."

"I could resign," I said, suddenly filled with hope. "In a few months I qualify for a pension."

Molly picked up the pistol, snapped it open, replaced the cartridges, snapped the gun shut, and clicked it down just so on the glass tabletop, all the while keeping her lips in a line.

"You'll have to declare the gun if it's in your luggage," I said. "You don't want it loaded."

"Please don't condescend to me," she said. "And don't touch my things. As to your job, that's your decision."

"It affects you."

"It affects Beth. You should plan on providing for her support and education. I'm leaving you."

She was being quite clear, but I could neither absorb nor accept it.

The next day she was gone. The day after that, the boxes and most of the furniture were carted off. I stayed on with FEMA long enough to qualify for my pension, sustaining myself by imagining that the measured tone Molly took on when I called on the weekends suggested an adjustment in her position. I intended to move back home myself to be near my daughter. What other holdfast did I have! When the proper moment arrived, I had hoped to persuade Molly to reconsider. Sometimes I slipped into fanciful imagining: We might buy a home in the country. We'd take holidays to the mountains. I could teach Beth to ski. In the summer, we would drink coffee on the porch while the long light of the north slanted over the hills and glimmered through the pines.

I arranged for a moving company to transport my possessions and drove across the country to Spokane. When I arrived at Molly's girlhood house near midnight, she met me at the door and informed me that I was allowed one night on the living room couch. After a fitful sleep, I rose early and walked through the neighborhood, filled with misgiving. Upon returning I found Molly, her mother, and Beth at the kitchen table eating waffles. The coffee pot was empty. There was no chair for me. A hunk of leftover waffle lay on a plate on the counter. Molly's mother nodded at me and left the room. Molly sent Beth away. Beth was twelve, on the cusp of womanhood, and as she went she paused in the passage to the living room to give me a long look, as if she were surveying where that man might now fit in the puzzle of her world. She vanished. Her footsteps creaked across the old hardwood floor, and then the house fell silent.

"What now?" I said.

"You can't stay here."

"That's evident, but that's my daughter." I picked up the familiar blue plate from the counter and, suddenly angry, said, "This is my mother's fucking plate."

Molly stalked out to the back porch. She returned with a cardboard box, which she set on the counter. She opened a cupboard door to where the dishes my mother had left us were stacked. There was nothing distinguished about the heavy blue dishes that Molly and I had used for years.

"There," Molly said. "Take them. And please watch your tongue in this house."

I stared at her. She herself had always been able to curse like a sailor, not to mention the exotic sexual positions she favored. Whereas I'd had the unquenchable desire, she'd always known best how to dispose it. I backtracked, saying, "No. I'm sorry. I don't need the dishes."

Her navy blue bathrobe brought out a faint blue underlaiment of color in her cheeks. Now, the blue began to modulate into a rose color. "You don't want them?" She lifted a stack of plates from the cupboard, stepped to the sink, and in one violent motion, heaved the plates into it, shattering them.

She sat back down at the table, her face flushed in earnest. The dead silence elsewhere in the house grew profound, as if every room had a person in it frozen in position. Aghast, I stood stock still against the counter and looked away toward the porch. The morning light flooded through the windows. Out in the garden, neat rows of garlic had sprouted. I picked up the hunk of waffle, stuck it in my mouth, and chewed.

"As to Beth," Molly said. "We'll make our arrangements."

Not knowing how else to respond, I said, "Fine."

"You've become somebody else."

"Who else could I be?"

Molly revolved in her chair to face me. "The man I once knew is gone."

The skirt of her bathrobe had fallen open, and I found myself gazing at the outline of her knees beneath her nightgown, her thighs, and the body so well known to me. "What can I do?"

She drew the hems of her robe together. "Leave."

As I remember it, this was another of the moments in my life when I at once knew exactly what was transpiring and could not begin to fathom its meaning. It was like falling: I knew I was falling. Everything was lucid and quick, but I had no conception of what would happen when I hit bottom. I was frightened. To try to tell Molly how I clung to her – the hank of hair falling across her cheek, the cut of her eyes, the endearing cleft in her chin, her hip, leg, knee, even the intimacy of her fury – was beyond me.

Six

SEVERAL WEEKS AFTER the scene with Molly and just as I was settling into the house I'd purchased, I caused an accident. It seems now like the insurgency of nature, once again, triggered by happenstance. To this day, before I fall asleep at night, the seconds before the collision replay themselves in my mind: the skiff of spring ice on the back road, the velvet slide of my Envoy, the rearing headlights, the arms in the other car like blades flailing before the face, and the concussion of metal.

My Envoy was hardly damaged, while the car, a small Honda, careened sideways into the barrow ditch and rolled. The car had to be craned back onto its wheels and cut open to extract the driver, a young woman. Two men, struggling for footing, hauled her out of the ditch on a gurney and then snapped the gurney up, one of them shouting, "Hoist! Hoist!" A fractured arm slipped over the edge of the gurney as the woman was rolled to the ambulance. She was thin and long, like a plank laid under the blanket, and the outline of her face, which I glimpsed under the stroboscope of emergency lights, came to be seared into my memory – aquiline nose and bloodied, high, dome-shaped brow. There was something patrician in it like a Jeffersonian death mask.

In no mood for dissimulation, I admitted everything to an officer – how I'd dropped an apple and had been fishing for it between my feet just as I came upon the curve, how I'd drifted into the oncoming lane, and how, though I didn't believe I was inebriated, I'd had a drink before setting out. As I disencumbered myself, I actually felt my spirits lightening in a religious way. Maybe it was the moth in me fleeing its cocoon. The officer scrutinized me and then walked to his car with my ID to run a check. When he returned he addressed me with a changed demeanor, his face set as he requested (requested!) that I report to the sheriff's headquarters the next afternoon.

Once there, I was interviewed by a lieutenant named Joe Bradley, a lean man with an equine jaw. He looked across his desk at me and told me the woman was a Russian immigrant and that she was one of the Pentecostals who had come to this region since the collapse of the Soviet Union. He said she had no known immediate family. She lived alone. They'd checked at the church, but no one claimed her. She might be a sole survivor, he said. All this was delivered with an odd combination of detachment and familiarity, which I at first ascribed to Bradley's thinking that he and I were compatriots in our service.

"Or the ways of the Russians may be keeping them back," he said. "They're tight-knit. They have an underground economy, but they're the least of our worries. We've got the meth labs, the gangs, the gypsies, sexual predators on probation that Seattle ships over, and the mafiosi the Secret Witness Program deposits here. Ours is a funny little mainstream city, staid and conservative, but with more than its share of vermin just under the skin. Like scabies laying eggs in their own excrement, and every so often they break out." Bradley picked up his coffee cup, took a sip, set it back down, and squinted at me. "You have a security clearance. We can't access any records on you. I guess you know why."

I didn't. It was news to me. "I worked for FEMA," I said.

"We know that, and I know FEMA people. They don't have clearances like yours." He leaned back. "You don't remember me, do you?"

"Should I?"

"We were in the same class in high school. You were class president."

I looked at the man closely, trying to conjure his image from the past, but came up with nothing. It was a blank.

This made him smile. "I guess you wouldn't. I was in ROTC and ran cross-country."

"I'm sorry," I said.

He shrugged. "No matter. You went on to a position of importance, as we expected."

After a pause, and once again feeling the prospects of my confession slipping away, I said, "As to this accident, I've admitted guilt. I've said I'm responsible."

"I know you have. My advice is to walk away from it," Bradley replied. "The accident didn't happen." He picked up a paperweight, moved it to another location on his desk, and then said, "I'm a church member myself. Methodist. I'd be happy to bring you to a service. Sometimes that can help."

I'd been raised an unruly Catholic, had long been a non-practitioner, and I was put off by Bradley's proposal, though I myself had engendered it. At the same time, though just for a moment, I did feel drawn to the idea of group support, a gathering of believers who might take my troubles to heart, like a backup choir behind a blues singer. "Thank you. I'll keep that in mind," I said, knowing I would not.

The next morning, I called my former superior at FEMA and was told that my records had been sealed while I was in service and that there must have been a vetting problem before they were cleared. He promised to check. "We'll let you know," he said. Each time I inquired, I was told the change in status was "in process." Whether by device or mishap of system, that the agency had nevertheless sucked what little air I had in my life, as if to turn me into dross and thus affirm Molly's view of me, was of no importance to it. From my experience as an apparatchik, I understood this. Yet as one who had exiled himself from the cover of government in order to walk the earth as an ordinary mortal, I became increasingly mystified, and realized that in fact I'd completely lost my hold on the meaning of confession and similarly the meaning of evil. When I went to public places – the grocery, hardware, or gas station – or carried on conversations with my next door neighbor, Josephine, I grew profoundly bewildered by people's acceptance of my presence and of their willingness to ignore the fact that shades like me might be lurking everywhere.

I discovered the first cross on the strip of lawn near the street in front of my house. Puzzled, I examined it. It was about two feet high; its steel cross members were three inches wide and a quarter-inch thick. The ends of the members had been cut to make points. On the front a vine with several blossoms had been implanted from a welding rod, and on the back a single, Gothic

H had been neatly inscribed. I carried the cross inside but thought little of it. Despite its heft and the care that had been put into its making, I reasoned that it could have been left for any number of reasons by anyone – perhaps a proselytizer of our new national order. I believed it could not be anything more than a happenstance that carried ephemeral ironies. The second cross was positioned next to the walk halfway between the street and my front steps. This one had a slightly more elaborate decoration of vines and blossoms and affirmed that the first was not a random occurrence.

My house is in an old, upscale neighborhood on the hill south of the city and a mile from Molly's mother's house, which was my first consideration in the purchase – a reasonable but not excessive proximity. On Wednesdays I would drive Beth to her piano lesson and return her to her mother. On Friday afternoons I would pick Beth up after she got home from school and return her the next evening, since Molly's mother insisted on taking Beth to early Mass every Sunday, or so Molly said. To this day, even in winter, I make the two round trips on Friday and Saturday by foot. The walk seems to set Beth at liberty to talk freely, much of the time about her school. She is beginning to show an interest in boys. In Molly's mother's neighborhood, there are more children on the streets. The sidewalks have buckled and heaved from the roots of the huge maple trees planted decades ago. As I pick my way along them, I invariably wonder at the wanton, swelling force beneath my feet. Beth meets me on the porch and waves good-bye from it. Molly rarely appears. My mother-in-law shuns me. The closest I've come to seeing her since the morning in the kitchen is the surreptitious movement of a curtain in the far corner room.

A couple of weeks before bodies began appearing at Jim and Diane's farm, and as I returned from leaving Beth off, I found the third cross in a little garden plot next to the stairs that led to my porch. It was just like the first two, except that the decoration was yet more ornate, the vines now twining out onto the arms and giving the cross a distinctly Byzantine look. I stood staring at it in the light from the porch, recognizing that whoever had left it was not only familiar with my movements, but growing bolder, too. The next one might appear inside the house, I thought, which brought me to an alert as I considered that someone might be waiting in there now. I walked to where my Envoy was parked in the drive, got my Glock, put it in my pocket and returned, unlocked the door, went inside, and warily roved the rooms. No one was there. There was no sign of a stranger having been there, neither downstairs nor upstairs nor in the basement.

I came back to the dining room, where I kept a table with two chairs – one for me, one for Beth – and the two ceiling-high safes that held my gun collection. I set the Glock on the table and stood listening, hearing nothing but the hum of the refrigerator in the kitchen. I went outside, pulled the cross from the ground, carried it inside, and placed it next to the other two so that the three of them leaned against the wall in a row near the safes. Though certain that no one had penetrated the safes, I worked the combinations and threw the levers. Each door made a kissing sound as the rubber seals parted and I was saluted by the scent of solvent and gun oil. The guns were there, undisturbed, what had begun as a modest collection of World War I- and II-era military long arms left to me by my father, and which I'd expanded to include a sixteenth-century hatchlock, several flintlocks, a nineteenth-century Houiller pin-fire, a later Mauser, Civil War-era Winchesters, Remingtons, Lees, Spencers, and Henrys, a Kropatschek .433, the Afghan copy of the Lee-Enfield, and several military rifles of British design and Indian manufacture. . . . In the felt-lined drawers at the bottoms of the safes lay an array of side arms. Surveying the collection always gave me the satisfaction of the hoarder, something of the glutton finding surfeit, and of the obsessive connoisseur pleasuring in the woodcraft and exquisitely machined metal. These were instruments of killing, quieted in my safes.

I called Lieutenant Bradley that Monday and told him about the crosses. I asked if the like was known to be happening elsewhere in the city. He thought not . . . graffiti, yes, and sometimes hate messages were left at the Temple or Mosque, but not crosses, certainly not crosses like the ones I'd described. He sent a deputy, who filled out a report and carted off the three crosses. I found that I missed them for the way they cast their angular shadows against the white wall next to the black safes. I regretted parting with the reminder of another unknown person's obsession, a consensual stain upon being. It was then that I decided to install a surveillance system.

As I did that, I came to know my neighbor, Josephine Chandras. She was divorced and had a high school aged daughter. They made a winsome pair – the daughter willowy and longhaired like her mother but tawny skinned, while the mother was fair. One was just arriving at the fullness of her pulchritude and the other dallying at its nether reach. They were always dressed to the teeth. The daughter played the clarinet, but not well. In the evenings I heard the screech and yowl of it from the belly of their house. Josephine and I soon began having casual exchanges on the weather and local politics when we encountered each other out front. One day we fell into conversation while I was vacuuming the interior of my Envoy, which was parked in the drive between our houses. I had told her previously that I'd worked for FEMA, which seemed to make me a point of interest.

"Emergencies," she had said.

"Lots of them," I'd replied.

She was a structural engineer and worked for an architectural firm. Now, she told me about her husband, or ex-husband, a securities broker who was from Delhi and had immigrated to this country with his parents as a boy. He'd worked out of an office in Spokane – because of her work here – but spent nearly half his time in Seattle. And every two or three months, he traveled to New York. He'd been in New York on the day of the World Trade Center bombing but not in either of the towers. He'd been at the airport waiting to fly home and was stranded there, and then he was detained and questioned because of his itinerary, his name, and the color of his skin. It took him over a week to get home, taking cabs, buses, and finally renting a car in Salt Lake City. "Something shattered in him after that experience," Josephine told me.

"We had our problems," she said. "After 9/11 he was in a fury, and terrified, and there was no way to resolve things."

She paused, standing motionless.

This all seemed a little personal to me, yet I listened attentively.

"Then he drove to Seattle and never came back," she said.

A few days later, she was out front raking grass clippings while I, with the aid of Jim's ladder, attempted to install the surveillance cameras under my eaves. We began talking about her work, and I asked if she thought it was true that al-Qaeda had studied the structure of the World Trade Center's towers, if it was known that explosions from the airliners would cause the floors to sheer away from the outer skins as they fell one upon another and that the overwhelming kinetics would cause complete collapse into the pits.

"It's possible. It's true that kind of impact and the fire over-taxed the structure. It was over two thousand degrees. But, of course, I don't know about al-Qaeda," she said. "Were you in Washington DC?"

"No," I said, looking over at her from my position on the ladder. "I was in the Philippines."

"The design is straightforward enough," she said, pulling a pile of clippings toward her with the rake. She was wearing a loose-fitting top and an ankle-length skirt through which the sunlight outlined her legs. "The impact blew the fire protection off the steel, and then the fire softened the trusses and welds. The design had no structural fail safe for that kind of assault," she said. "Every structure has weakness in its relation to gravity. If explosives are used, what can happen in an instant, from a structural point of view, is a wild hunt for the weakness. The towers came down just as you'd have wanted if you were razing them."

She went away. I resumed my work, thinking about how it rarely seemed difficult to find ways to get weakness to express itself. I had my battery-powered drill and was attempting to screw in the camera mounts. One mount was before me, dangling from a stretch of conduit with the wire and video line strung through. I'd begun to realize that this was a bigger project than I'd envisioned.

After a few minutes, I heard her voice behind me: "We don't have much crime here."

I looked back at her, twisting around on my ladder. "That's good."

She had a bulging, plastic garbage bag by the throat and was smiling at me. "Are you expecting trouble?"

"Did you see the crosses in my yard?"

"I saw one. You had more?"

"Three. Somebody's leaving them."

"How unusual," Josephine said, and then with what seemed genuine feeling, she added, "Feeling watched is not fun."

I indulged in a mild braggadocio, saying, "To be honest, I'm probably more curious than afraid."

"I thought you were religious."

"Not that way," I said, remembering Bradley's invitation and suddenly wondering, as has become inescapable in our age, if how I might be irreligious or religious, and if so in what way, or what denomination or sect, if any, that I might belong to, or whether or not I'd been saved yet, or born again, or if, as I did, I eschewed the stamp of redemption, might provide Josephine with a measure for judging me.

She pulled the cinch of her bag tight.

I turned on the ladder and reached with my drill. It had a magnetic bit, and the first screw for the mount dangled from it. In the corner of my eye, I saw Josephine come nearer, stepping down the ledge that separated our yards. The screw fell off the bit, and I had to pull back to fish in my pouch for another one.

Now, she was next to my ladder. "I hope I'm not bothering you."

"I'm pleased to talk with you."

"I have a friend from college who works in New York as an architectural modeler," she said. "She lives just a few blocks up from the World Trade Center and helped make the models for it. She went up to her roof after the first tower fell and saw the second one. She says the time she spent working on the models came vividly back to her, as if her fingers were at the pieces again, putting them together. She dreams about the models coming apart."

I had another screw stuck on the bit. I reached with it, leaning out and inserting the screw through the opening in the camera mount. I pushed the mount up against the wood with the drill chuck. My arm was quivering from the strain. When I squeezed the tool's trigger, the bit immediately stripped the screw head.

"Be careful," she said.

"Yes." I reversed the drill and tried to turn the screw out. The bit whirred, obliterating the notches. Exasperated, I squared myself on the ladder, hung the drill on the hook of my tool belt, and flexed my arm. I told myself I should be more deliberate like Jim, beginning with not pressing things and paying attention to detail, such as climbing down and moving the ladder to a better position, yet I stayed where I was, resting for a moment.

"What I remember most from the news clips is the couple who leaped from one of the top stories," Josephine said. "They were wearing their business garb, and they fell through the air holding hands. Do you remember?"

"I saw the newsreel in a bar in the Philippines. I imagine everyone remembers that." As I spoke I looked down at her, discovering that I had a full view of her breasts through the top of her blouse. Embarrassed, I looked away quickly. I'd been celibate for months, numbed as I was by Molly's renunciation and otherwise lacking in options. Now, I was amazed by the flush that rose entirely on its own power to my neck. It was as if there were an erotic impulse like a small engine inside me that had merely been quieted, awaiting the click in the ignition.

Josephine continued: "I wonder – did they just happen upon the window at the same time? Were they complete strangers or casual acquaintances? Were they friends who gave each other courage by agreeing to jump together. Or were they married, and had they searched desperately for each other before going to the window? Did they have children? Or were they work place lovers? And if so, what about their families otherwise? What would their families, consigned to remain among the living, think? What fears were confirmed? Just imagine the worlds that collapsed around the couple in that two or three minutes as they fell. What were those worlds? What chaos was left to grow among the living, what terrifying stories, and what utter clarity for the dead at the end of their lives?"

"I think I've wondered something like that," I said, looking hungrily down at her. She seemed unaware of my vantage point, or she permitted it.

"Everyone must have wondered," she said. "Maybe the horror all around them collapsed into a perfect compact with everything that had made them and everything that lay unknown before them when they gave up together."

This seemed a stranger, truer, and more unnerving thought than I could have ever had. "I don't know," I said.

Seven

ONCE JIM FINISHED scraping the loose rock from the bottom of the hole, he dumped a layer of gravel into it to make a bed. Then he attached a choke chain to the culvert so that he could lift it with the loader. The culvert was ten feet long and three feet across. He'd fabricated a screen on a steel hoop and welded it to the bottom of the culvert to make a filter. The culvert rose up, twisting in the air. Carefully, he lowered it into the center of the hole, screened end down. I held it steady while Jim climbed off the tractor and unhooked the chain.

I leaned to look into the culvert that now stood balanced on its end. Within, the circle of water was visible like a huge eye. It reflected a chokecherry bough overhead and the sky. Jim came over to look. His son, Pascal, now appeared, making his way through the opening in the trees. He'd grown into a young man since I'd last seen him a couple of years before. Lean looking in his T-shirt and Carharts, he had Jim's dark hair, something of Diane's flash in his eyes, and was outfitted with gold hoops in his ears, a stud under his lower lip, and a tattoo of a killer whale on his arm. He stood with us and looked in. Slowly, the water rose in the culvert.

"Looks like a good little well," Pascal said.

Jim moved to his pile of tools and came back with a level, which he handed to me. "We'll need to keep that thing straight."

Pascal had his hands on his knees and was peering at a rock shelf that protruded into the space between the culvert and wall of the hole. "A newt," he said.

Jim and I looked. The thing was absolutely still and caught light reflected from the steel culvert. It was olive green with a blood-colored spot on its shiny rugose skin.

"It's a male," Jim said. "See the crest on its neck. It's been breeding."

"They're good luck," Pascal said.

"Salamanders are, so it is said," Jim replied.

"Associated with fire," Pascal said.

"Yes," Jim said. "It's a non-existential symbolic extension of their actual amphibious nature."

Pascal laughed softly, the echo of his voice bouncing between the walls of the hole and culvert.

"Things call up their opposites," Jim said.

"You never see these here except in a hole," Pascal said.

"Grubs," Jim said. "They eat grubs."

He moved back to his tractor and started it up again.

Pascal found the shovel and rescued the newt by carefully slipping the blade under it and lifting it out. He set the shovel at the edge of the brush, near where the frog was croaking. The newt stayed poised on the blade, but just before we started in again, as Jim was coming over with a loader full of gravel, I glanced over at the shovel and saw that the newt had vanished. Jim went back and forth with the gravel, dumping it in while I went around the culvert with the level, tugging and shoving on the culvert to keep it straight. Pascal spread each load of gravel with a rake. Soon, we had the space filled to within a half foot of the top.

Jim switched off the tractor and came back and tugged on the culvert. It was solid. He checked it with the level and smiled at me. "Not that I don't trust your judgment," he said. "Now, we have to tamp this down." He passed a long bar with a tamping plate to Pascal.

Pascal tamped the gravel. Jim started up the generator again and plugged in the cement mixer that stood just this side of the fence near his flatbed. He had his water tank in the truck, too, and cement sacks piled up at the end of the bed. Jim mixed cement while Pascal wheelbarrowed it to the hole and dumped in the loads. I spread the cement around with the rake, filling the cavities in the wall, and then tamped the cement and got on my knees and smoothed it with a trowel. It was an admirable thing, the sense of ensemble Jim and Pascal had and the way I could fit in, and the scent of the bush, soil, and limey cement. It was not long before the cement had risen to the level of the ground. Jim switched off the mixer and carefully washed it, the wheelbarrow, rake, shovel, tamping bar, and trowels. He bent and turned the hose on his face, washing off his mask of mud. The cows appeared as if from nowhere, standing in a line on the other side of the fence and looking in at us.

"They've had water in their tank all day, but they came anyway because they heard the compressor start up," Jim said. "The sound makes them sociable."

"That must be an existential extension," Pascal said.

Jim chuckled and carried the hose over to the fence and let it run a while. Some of the cows began drinking, sucking up quantities of water through their teeth.

Jim worked around what had been a hole, giving the cement doughnut one last troweling, and then washed the trowel again and switched off the generator. He'd made a template out of cardboard that marked where to set the brackets for the windmill boots. He'd welded bolts to the brackets. He slipped the template over the top of the culvert, which stuck up three feet from ground level, and eased the template down to the cement. Through the slots he'd cut in the template, he set the brackets in the concrete. There were three brackets, each with a set of three bolts, and he ran the level across them two at a time to make sure they were set right. I was impressed with the order of it all, the planning that facilitated the work.

Jim peered into the culvert, saying, "There's four feet of water. This is good."

I looked in at the rising, reflective eye with the cherry bough and the sky in it. The image of a bird flitted across the surface and landed on the bough. When we both looked up, the actual bird shot away, flashing the white band on its tail.

"Flycatcher," Jim said. "The first I've seen this season."

Also known as the eastern kingbird.

Tyrannus tyrannus.

A curious name for such a trim and stately looking creature.

Jim placed a lid he'd made over the top of the culvert. "We don't want the critters falling in," he said.

Freeing the Apes

Pascal had gone off ahead of us. The cows were strolling way, too, slowly making their way up the pasture. Jim and I loaded the tools into the back of the flatbed and walked through the trail in the brush back to the clearing. We stopped there again before advancing to the house, which was in full view, now. The flycatcher reappeared, flying across. A pair of magpies winged from behind us, soared overhead, and landed to strut along the ridge of the shake roof.

"More luck, maybe," Jim said.

"Two. It's good luck," I said, referring to the saying about magpies. "But whether it's existential or not, I'm afraid I have no idea."

"They've given me fair warning to get up there and sweep the needles out of the valleys," Jim said. "Pascal's going to help me replace the roof with metal."

"Fire," I said.

"Right. Fire season is coming."

It was true. Even the twenty yards we walked away from the damp on the other side of the bush and trees had brought us out to a place where the ground cover was desiccate.

The magpies leaped into the air and cried out raucously as they wheeled in an arc and flapped away in a line above the pines, their white wing markings making whirligigs on the sides of their dark bodies. They cruised toward the first in the line of bluffs, and their diminishing forms sank like diving fish into the canyon.

Along the canyon's opposite rim, a mile or more away, the boxy shapes of several newly built houses poked into the sky. For several miles beyond the houses – to the south and east – stretched the flats known as Indian Prairie. An obelisk stands there, one of the two that commemorate the site of the Battle of 1858 between the U.S. Army and the Allied Tribes. The other obelisk, nestled among the hills fifteen miles south, marks the beginning of the battle. The nearer one, just six miles southeast from Jim and Diane's place, marks the end of the battle on level ground where the cavalry, with its superior arms, picked off the

Indians at will. In yet another synchronicity, or irony, just across the highway from the obelisk is the air force base with its survival school, the squadron of refueling tankers, and the nuclear-tipped warheads stored in bunkers from the days when B-52s had been stationed there. Recently, the entrance to the base had been sanctified by numbers of armed police, concrete barricades, and surveillance cameras bristling from signal poles. Another twelve miles to the east lay the city where city hall and the federal courthouse were also barricaded.

Down in the canyon, we could see the cordoned off place in the meadow, a solitary sheriff's van, and just beyond and to one side, the hook of blackened snags from the fire four years ago. In the trees coming up the slope and on the tops of the bluffs, the ground was still littered with what would soon become dangerous tinder. Hanging in Jim and Diane's living room is an aerial photograph I'd procured for them from the FEMA office before I returned to Washington DC four years ago. It shows toy-like fire trucks parked along their lane, a vaginal shape of unburned woods and fields through the smoke, and their house in the center of it all. Jim and Diane had been very lucky once already. They were lucky people.

The fire had begun with eighty-mile-per-hour winds that blew trees into power lines, snapping them. The fallen wires started over a hundred blazes in the fields and woods. The separate fires, spread and driven into each other by the wind, turned into a firestorm with its own weather, its rushing crosscurrents sucked into the voids created by the explosions at its superheated eyes. In the way of such fires, it became a living thing running on a chaotic course. It ripped across the fields. In the pine stands, it crouched, replenishing itself on dry matter and inhaling oxygen, and then leapt up the slopes and into the crowns of trees. Armatures of gas from the pines sailed hundreds of feet upwards, igniting in midair. North of here, houses were heated past the kindling point by the mere proximity of the fire and they burst into flames.

The window in the back door of Jim's house flashed as the

door swung open. Pascal appeared with a young woman. They spread out on the lawn and began playing catch with a hardball.

"It's Agatha," Jim said. "His girlfriend from college."

Agatha had a long ponytail that whipped each time she threw. She threw well. The ball sailed back and forth, white against the trees, and it thocked each time it was caught.

"She seems a fine young woman," Jim said.

"You approve of her?"

"We're glad to see that he has good judgment."

The windows to the house were open, and from inside, Diane could be heard practicing her cello. The sound was of something rhapsodic and dissonant.

"What is that?" I asked.

"Kodály."

"Ah," I said. "It's the unaccompanied sonata?"

"Right. It's filled with the dark of folk tunes."

As former practitioners, Jim and I shared an interest in music. I'd played the piano and still fooled with it off and on. Jim had played the violin, which he'd given up. I envisioned Diane with her sense of theatricality making the sounds she was. The music seemed like a long, organized cry of pain, punctuated by the back and forth impact of the baseball in the mitts.

The door opened again, and a wheelchair rolled out with Jim's mother in it. Jim's father followed, guiding the chair down the ramp and across the yard toward his car. The old woman was talking and gesturing. I could barely hear her high-pitched voice decorating the other sounds. Every few steps the old man stopped and leaned toward her with a puzzled expression. Pascal caught a throw from Agatha and then stepped to the car, opened the passenger door, and helped his grandmother in. The old man loaded the wheelchair through the hatchback and moved to the driver's side. In a moment, the car pulled slowly away. Pascal threw the ball back to Agatha. The sounds of Diane's cello kept coming, and now, too, it was laced by the plaintive calls of quail, who had moved into the place Jim and I had vacated just behind the trees. I thought of the women in Kosovo, shrieking as they followed the coffin into the alley.

"Mother has talking jags," Jim said. "Other times she won't respond at all. My father doesn't hear well. They make a pair. She hears everything and either won't talk or doesn't make sense when she does. He can't hear, but always wants her to be making sense. He's desperate to find reasons to believe she's still who she once was." Jim fell silent for a moment and then asked, "Do you remember those two little girls?"

Strangely, my thoughts had been gravitating to that exact place. "From the fire? How could I forget?"

Often enough, trouble and catastrophes rub the grain of people, drawing out the good in them. In the aftermath of the firestorm – the charred yards, scorched hulks of cars, the remains of homes and farm buildings set against the spiky trees and the blackened slopes – people established funds, donated clothing and shelter, and served a moveable feast to the victims. By the time I'd arrived to visit Jim and Diane, the heart of the fire had passed them to the east. They were fine, if frazzled, and busy keeping things running. Everywhere, power lines were down or burned out. Diane and some of the neighbors had set up a telephone tree to get help to those who needed it. Our mutual acquaintances from the old days, the Zetas, lived at the northern extreme of the fire's compass. Diane had tried to reach them repeatedly. Jim and I drove out along the back roads and found their house burned to the ground. No one was there. The desolate sight of their stone chimney against the smoky sky and the singed foundation of a beloved home shocked even me.

I also knew that catastrophe can bring out the bad from people's bottom nature. It calls imposters, the corrupt, and the deranged to the surface. Protracted catastrophe creates a bandit class. Even here there'd been acts of vandalism, thievery, and arson in the fire's aftermath. Then there was the case of the two little girls who were abducted. One escaped, but the other was raped and strangled with barbed wire. The predator, carried deep into his obsession by the opportunity of fire, tried to obliterate the evidence by burning the body in a fire he set himself. Thinking of that, I suddenly remembered that the fire in Jim and

Diane's canyon was suspected of having been started by an arsonist.

"And the fire you had in the canyon," I said.

"Right."

"Margarita White," I said.

"She was a grown woman. Those others were children," he said. "But I've wondered."

"Singley."

"God, I hope not. But the fire in the canyon started on the Singleys' place, on the uphill side, which was one of the reasons the firefighters got it out in time."

"It was thought to be arson."

"Yes."

"She disappeared not long before the fire?"

"Less than two months."

"So, you're thinking what?"

"Either I can't puzzle it out, or I don't really want to."

There'd been no evidence of a struggle in the lot at the substation up the road where Margarita White's company pickup was found and not a trace of her. I'd heard that certain imaginings crept into the public mind: There had been more than one serial killer in this area. Maybe this was another depravity, some thought. Or maybe she'd had a lover or there'd been trouble at home that caused her to fly off to oblivion.

Small billboards had been mounted by her husband. I remembered seeing them along the roadways when I was here, some charred by fire. They had Margarita's name, a telephone number to call, and the words in red: *Lost! Missing! Reward for Information!* In the blown-up, black-and-white photograph that also appeared on the billboards, Margarita had high cheekbones, melancholy eyes, and black eyebrows and hair. The photograph, with its indistinctness of line, gave her the quality of an enchantress, as if the image arose from another world.

The billboards along with the full page ads her husband took out in the city newspaper and his public pleas through reporters led some to wonder if he himself had killed her. But at the same time, considering that a loved one might simply have been spirited away, pulled from the earth like a plant, carted off, and then feasibly discarded, the husband's aggrieved obsession was plausible. One might consider the loss of the breath so long near him, the rise of her hip in their bed, the call of her voice, the lingering scent of what she'd baked early in the morning.

"First, it was her abduction," Jim said. "We had a few searchers then, too, but really nobody thought they'd find her here. Then we had the fire four years ago and people forgot about her."

"I could go back into the records to see what was said about the cause of the fire in the canyon," I said.

"They knew all along that a propellant was used. It was clearly arson."

"I've got an FBI contact here and the lieutenant in the Sheriff's Office. I could see if there's more."

Jim murmured noncommittally and looked away. As before, I found his response to my offers difficult to interpret. My first guess was that he was still declining to impose, though to me it was nothing to shake the trees with a few phone calls. But I also worried that my wish to help would be an intrusion.

Over toward the house, Pascal and his girlfriend had stopped playing catch and were throwing a stick for the black dog, who returned it, prancing and wagging her tail. The girl laughed at something Pascal said as he bent to take the stick. Diane's cello sang through the windows. In the distance an engine started up. Soon afterward the police van could be heard laboring up the old logging road.

"What they've told us," Jim said, "is that they found soil in the grave from another site. So she was moved here."

"And maybe the fire down there was started to scorch over the digging. It's the husband?"

"Which one?"

That stopped me for a moment. "You're thinking Singley?"

"Maybe. But either one of them is a reach at this point."

Thinking of this made me feel the pull of voyeurism as if into the center of a whirlpool where lay the zero of Singley, as Jim had described him.

Jim drew a jackknife from his pocket and opened it. "Diane still thinks the body in the midden has something to do with all this. I think it's Margarita White's abductor who somehow opened up the path of demons. That's just my opinion, though." He crouched and etched a line in the mud.

I knew that metaphors were real to him, a part of the metaphysics he also held to be real. He knew I was at once skeptical and yet susceptible to his belief that the world and human mind had their actual demons, not mere phantasms. I waited for what he was going to say next or what map he was about to draw. He stayed where he was, looking at his line. Then he looked into the canyon, and I felt my scalp prickle . . . the goose on the grave. I had the foreboding that the line marked what he knew and I did not about the demon that had already crossed over.

Eight

ON ONE OF MY EARLY visits to Jim and Diane's farm last May – after Molly's rejection, after Jim's imbroglio with the Singleys over the property line, a month before Mrs. Singley's and Margarita White's bodies were discovered, not long after my accident, yet before the crosses began appearing in my yard – Jim told me there was an archeologist in the canyon. He proposed that we walk down to see the site. "You came on a good day," he said.

Then, too, we were standing in the living room near the windows. It was bright outside. The aspens in the draw that led to the canyon had leafed out, making stretches of intense green on the slopes. Puffy clouds cast their mobile shadows. I felt grateful for what I took to be Jim's effort to cheer me.

On our way to the canyon, he told me that artifacts from a seasonal hunting and fishing camp were emerging: the half-rotted remains of a willow fishing weir, digging sticks, stone implements. He said that Diane, who'd studied anthropology in college along with her music, had made it a condition that she be allowed to assist before agreeing to let the archeologist dig. Nobody was supposed to talk about the site, Jim said. Secrecy was mandated by the law in order to prevent plundering. In addition, the sovereign claims of tribes had to be honored. "The project will be skewered if word gets out prematurely."

Of course, I would understand that – how in a government career one's deceptions had to be impeccably groomed. We were just then making a steep descent along an old logging road, and I said, "But you're taking me down, anyway."

"Look," Jim said. He pointed through a break in the trees at the meadow where a white awning and two figures bent over a hole were visible. "There, too," he said, gesturing at the houses along the opposite rim of the canyon. "They all have spotting scopes. They're watching, so secrecy seems relative. Voyeurism is undying. What the fuck."

I also understood that secrecy was regularly modulated into levels by its practitioners. We moved through a stand of ponderosas near the bottom and came out into the open. From there we could see the slope to the west, rising toward the bluffs. Coming along the incline were the pink flags of the line left by the surveyors Jim and Diane had hired.

Jim smiled. "Besides, the archeologist says it's okay to bring you down. They've found something. The archeologist knows you."

"Oh?"

"Rose Levant?"

That brought me to a halt. "Are you serious?"

"Doctor Rose Levant?"

"A doctor?"

Jim shrugged. "She's still a character, though."

Back in the days we'd all known her, Rose had been a member of the radical fringe, an animal rights activist ahead of her time and the last person I'd have expected to run the academic gauntlet and end up working for a state agency. In my own youthful trifling with radical action, I'd joined her in an act of sabotage, after which she vanished completely from my life.

Jim and I came up to the white awning mounted on poles and a rectangular three-foot-deep hole beneath it. A tarp lay on the ground beside the hole, and above it stood a screen, also under the awning. On this tarp were small heaps of sifted earth; and over in a corner, what I guessed were artifacts – small bones, little stone things, bits of basketry. The two women were there – Diane perched at the edge of the hole, bending to scoop out earth with a trowel and placing the earth on the screen, and the second woman lying on her belly in the grass and reaching far into the hole, carefully moving earth aside with a brush. It was Rose, decked out in overalls. When she twisted to look up, I saw a person I'd never have recognized. She'd put on weight and added thick glasses that made her eyes seem protuberant, like a gargoyle's. She had a downy moustache and blue tattoos encircling her wrists.

She rolled over and sat up. "Peter?"

I knew the voice, as clear and sweet as an English horn.

"The world gets small again," she said.

"Indeed."

"We'll have to catch up," she said, grinning. Then she put her weight on both hands, deftly lifted herself, slipped down the wall of the hole, and leaned to probe at something with a long dental pick. In her way of moving, I discerned the vestige of the unusually agile woman I remembered, which raised a flickering melancholy for what had passed so long ago. Diane set more earth on the screen and stroked it with her hand, causing dirt to filter to the tarp while puffs of it floated off in the breeze. Where Rose worked in the whitened light under the awning, a narrow, amber-colored thing took shape. She stopped and looked over at Diane. "I've got another piece." She bent again, delicately wielding her pick and brush. The narrow thing came to arch toward another crescent-shaped thing.

Jim and I moved to the very edge of the hole. Diane put her feet in and slid nearer to Rose. We were all silent as Rose freed the outlines of the two shapes with her brush. Gradually, a set of flattened-out ribs appeared, followed by the opposite side of the pelvis and a femur. With a larger brush, Rose swept away more dirt and then went back to the small brush. Soon, several vertebrae emerged, along with the knee joints and small bones of the feet, the dome of a forehead, the openings for eyes and nose, and a mouth full of dirt.

Rose abruptly straightened, reached for a pack that lay on the grass, and dragged it to her. She took out a vial, tissue, camera, and a notebook. She set the camera and notebook on the bank and looked at Diane with an intent expression, and then at Jim and me. Finally she looked away from all of us down along the canyon to where the creek twisted. "My God," she said, seemingly to no one, or to the apparition the bones conjured in herself. "This is absolutely as much as I could have hoped for." Then, fixing on Diane again, she said, "It's a child. A little girl. It's unbelievable."

She went to her knees in the hole, carefully brushed away more dirt from the bones, and bent near. "Nobody saw this," she murmured.

Diane shot a glance at Jim.

Rose shaved a few slivers from the femur with the knife, placed the slivers within the tissue, and pressed the tissue into the vial. "There," she said, rising to her knees again. She screwed in the lid until it squeaked, secured the vial in one of her bib pockets, and sat up on the bank so that she and Diane were sitting on either side of a corner of the hole.

Softly, Diane said, "We might prefer to leave her as she is."

"I know," Rose said. "Next is to take some pictures, pack up our specimens, and cover everything up."

"I don't think you understand," Diane said. "I don't mind the pictures, but you've taken a sample. That's what I mean."

"It's an intact skeleton," Rose said. "We have to date her."

"Who do you mean, 'we'?" Diane replied.

Even in the quiet of Diane's voice, the formidability had crept in. Jim and I stood silent. Before us in the hole lay the bones, exquisite in their detail, an intaglio calcified to a slightly lighter shade from the earth into which it was pressed. The two women were looking at the bones, too, not at each other, though their faces had grown grim with what they were saying to one another.

"I guess I mean science and me," Rose said.

"It's against the law," Diane said. "You said so yourself before we started on this. Not that that necessarily speaks to my point. We'll withdraw permission for you to be here."

"I'm not sure you can do that, now, since you've agreed," Rose said. "You signed a release."

"Not for that, we didn't. I'd like you to put back what you cut off."

"I won't do that," Rose said.

There was a pause. The breeze could be heard sifting through the ponderosas over toward the ridge. Then Diane said, "I respect what you do, but I don't like this. The child was buried here by people who loved her."

Rose kept staring at the bones from behind her thick glasses. "Actually, from the looks of her position, she fell, or since it's a midden, she might have been tossed here."

"That doesn't matter," Diane said.

"I have my science," Rose said. "I do it with care."

"I know you do." Diane looked up searchingly at her husband. Rose's eyes followed, going to Jim, then darted to Diane, and returned again to the bones. It was a moment when matters of which I had only inklings were balanced against each other. There was the depth of Diane's feeling about the evanescence of the canyon and of whatever it held, almost as if a monster resided here, protecting its treasure, and who, if disturbed, might go on a rampage. Jim was seemingly acquiescing to her (and indeed, he would later tell me that, though he shared Diane's view in its fundamental, had he been in Rose's shoes he would have done what she was doing; but when he saw Diane's passion rising in this fashion, he knew from his years of marriage that it was a time to get out of her way). Then there was Rose, who had dropped quite completely into the complicated person I remembered so well. She had tenderly uncovered the bones. Clearly she felt empathy for the long-dead child, and yet she was compelled to chase down the path of her single-mindedness.

"In this case I don't like it," Diane said.

I looked away and took a step back, instinctively increasing the distance between myself and the vortex. Up on a cliff in the sunlight above the diagonal of survey flags, I saw a flash and two figures facing our direction. One was a woman, judging from the skirt that fluttered in the breeze. The other scrutinized us through binoculars. I touched Jim's shoulder and gestured with my head.

Jim came next to me and his jaw tightened. "It's the Singleys."

Diane swung back on one elbow to see from under the awning and then looked over at Jim with an expression of extreme annoyance.

Rose gazed quizzically at me.

I tipped my head, meaning to communicate that I knew far too little to explain anything.

Nine

WHEN A PARTICULAR RESULT is strongly desired, the world
regularly arranges to place it beyond reach. The hunter can tell
you how a quarry, no matter how strategic and exacting the approach, often fails to appear. The geese have flown off to another
pond. The buck has drifted to another meadow. Or for a soldier,
the enemy chooses that day to position himself at an unexpected
crossroads, through a conspiracy arising from the secrecy of
mind and event not completely understood even by him.

Patience, an improvisatory state of readiness or what an old
friend of mine calls "the rage to conclude" (after Claude Levi-
Strauss's *la rage de vouloir conclure*), must all be summoned to
overcome the evasion. The bureaucrat knows this in his or her
own way, as does the business person, who must stay with the
plan and sometimes hammer shut all passageways out of which
the components to success might escape or through which im-
pediments might enter. This can be cruel, as I well knew from my
travels as a government agent – communities, villages, and even
nations were destroyed, and not always by disaster, but sometimes by the zealotry of the "other." The frustrated lover knows it,
too. He knows that patience has its dark side and how the tick in
the trigger of his yearning could change him into a stalker.

I admired people with capacious minds and fluid enough na-
tures to keep true to their purpose while staying alert to the
shiftiness of the world. Jim and Diane had these traits. Much of
the time, they remained calm in the face of the evil that had
snaked into their garden of possibilities. As sages advise – Jesus'
conversation with the woman at the well comes to mind – it's
often better to look away and cultivate what serves no immediate
purpose than to keep on staring down the trouble. It's wise to
mark what lies at the peripheries of vision. Good scientists pay
attention to the borders of their fields of inquiry, the froth kicked
up by the action at the edges of the transepts. Good investigators

do the same. I understood this despite my difficulties with grasping my personal troubles, my homeward trek after the path of my child and a woman who no longer loved me. To my surprise Lieutenant Bradley – the old high school cross-country runner – understood it, too.

I went in to see him on impulse, and he made time for me. My reasons for visiting him were first to ask if anything had come up with the three crosses and second to inquire about the Singleys and any records that might remain of the arson in Jim and Diane's canyon. I was conscious of the need to be careful with Bradley so as to hold the balance among his natural skepticism of a freelancer such as I was, his friendliness to me, and the illusions he seemed to have about my importance. I underestimated him.

He told me that the fire in the canyon was formally listed as arson and that his department had looked into it recently. He led me down a staircase to the evidence room. We passed through a steel doorway into a caged-off area. The entry was secured by a deputy on a stool, who looked like a large frog. As we went by, his eyes darted to me, and I had the sensation that his tongue might come next, whipping out to snatch me. In the room stood rows upon rows of steel shelves loaded with sheaves of paper and filing cartons.

"We have three sectors," Bradley said. "The dead, the inert, and the lively." He gestured at a far wall at the end of the main aisle, where I saw the crosses leaning in a stack. "They're here. Waiting." He smiled, the chevrons in his cheeks bracketing his lips. The rest of his face didn't move – bony jaw, cheekbones, and brow. He kept talking as he moved down an aisle: "There were a dozen or more arson fires during the firestorm. It's the psychos, using a disaster as cover. Most of those files are inert, but the one for your friends' canyon has been moved back to active."

He stopped and slid out two file cartons from a shelf. I followed him back to a table on which he set the cartons next to each other. "Here's this," he said, removing a report on the fire investigation of four years ago from the carton farthest from me.

He pointed at a line that said traces of propellant were found at the fire's starting point. "And there's this." He took a sheet of soiled notepaper from the second carton, which I could see was labeled "Col. H. Singley" and dated this last June. He laid the paper on the table. It had two lines of poetry on it:

Flamme flammet, rot in Gluten
Steht das schwarze Moosgestelle.

Bradley leaned over it. "German?" When I murmured, he said, "Can you read it? Does it say flames?"

"I don't know German well enough," I said. "There's fire in it, and red and black. *Moosgestelle* and *Gluten*, I have no idea."

"It was found in Mrs. Singley's pocket." He reached into the same carton again, extracted a metal medallion on a chain, and laid it on the table. "She was wearing it."

The medallion was an odd thing with a half-black, half-white face on its front, a variant, it seemed, of the Yin and Yang. I turned it over and read the inscription on the back:
Antiquarian Reproductions, Essex, UK. Hel.

Bradley had gone off down the aisle, and he returned with a third carton from which he removed a second medallion and laid it next to the first. The two were identical, but the second was far more tarnished than the first. I turned the second over and saw the same inscription.

"What's that word, *Hel?*" Bradley said, bending near.

I shook my head.

Bradley straightened, smiling again. "It's not part of the place name."

"Call the company."

"Of course. They could have sales records. We've got somebody on that and on the German. This one," he said, touching the tarnished medallion, "was found with Margarita White's body. When she disappeared, almost five years ago now, it wasn't long after she'd finished her stint in the air force. She was Colonel Singley's subordinate for a while . . . Mrs. Singley's subordinate, not Bob's. The husband . . . Margarita's husband . . . says he's never heard of the Singleys. But the Colonel . . . Bob, that is . . . knows who Margarita was. He says Helga befriended her."

"Does he know about the medallions?" I asked.

"The one from his wife he recognized immediately. It was a favorite thing of hers, he said. He was surprised when we produced the one from White. He says maybe his wife gave it to her. You have to think there's something here. The autopsy shows that Margarita White was killed by a blow to the head. We're waiting on a full-blown forensics report. As to Helga Singley's death, we still don't know the cause. Without a witness it's hard to prove whether somebody was pushed off a cliff or fell or jumped. And we don't know what we have here, otherwise. Killers will make stupid blunders, like McVeigh running the stoplight. But we haven't found anything like that yet." He touched the second medallion again. "The perpetrator of White's death was either smart or very lucky."

I was taking it all in, now understanding why the police presence on Jim and Diane's farm had persisted for so long.

Bradley looked straight at me and asked, "Your relations with the Bloods have always been good?"

"We're longtime friends."

"And you were here during the firestorm?"

I had an odd feeling then, as if I were the flying creature again, about to be plucked from the air. "Yes. Visiting family. I set up the FEMA office since I was on the scene."

"Right," he said. "I'm sure it was appreciated." He put his foot up on a chair and leaned on his leg with his elbow. For his age he had a lithe body. I'd begun to wonder if maybe I did remember him from high school after all, but whether this was an actual, emerging memory or a trick of our present association, I wasn't sure. He looked at me and then to the side down an aisle, saying, "There's the matter of the *H*s on the backs of your crosses."

It took me a moment to catch his meaning – the commonalities between the *H*s and the word *Hel* on the medallions. Next came the *H* in Mrs. Singley's name, Helga. My first, lightening-quick rush of indignation that Bradley might consider me a player in the scenario was immediately replaced by a half-amused appreciation for his excursion into the far reaches of the mystery. Later, I would conclude that his intent was not to implicate me but to take me as a collaborating mind out there with him to the edge.

His gray eyes, which were soft in his bony face, watched me. They lit up as he tracked my expression. "See what I mean?"

"I guess you never know," I said.

He straightened and stood on his two feet again. "No. You surely don't."

Ten

ROSE LEVANT AND I finally succeeded in meeting for lunch in late June. I brought my own medallion of Hel with me, which I'd ordered from the manufacturer. As I had been trained to do, I'd committed to memory the address in the evidence room and the four lines of German poetry, as well. A woman in the state university's German department translated and identified the poetry for me. The lines came from near the end of Goethe's *Faust*, Part II, and are sung in the depth of the night by the warden of the castle tower as he overlooks the burning of an elderly couple's house. Given her playful intellect, I was sure Rose would be interested in these arcane artifacts of calamity.

She had chosen a Greek restaurant in the city and was waiting for me when I arrived. As I slid into the booth opposite her, she immediately said, "Well, this whole business with the remains has scrambled up into the worst possible tangle." She'd just come from a meeting with the Kootenai. She was having trouble getting the tribal councils, her agency, and the Sheriff's Department to talk to each other about not further disrupting the midden in the canyon.

I refrained from asking if she and Diane were back in each other's good graces yet.

The window next to our booth gave us a view of a busy corner. A downtown mall had been recently built. Some of the city's old buildings had been razed and others refurbished. The restoration of a railroad-era hotel was in progress. Just down the street, a crew was assembling a crane, and across from our window, another crew and a backhoe were at work excavating a hole. Each time the bucket scraped bottom, the floor under our feet trembled. Two men in blaze orange vests stood there. When the bucket came out with a load of earth, they leaned over to contemplate the pit.

"It's a hole," I said.

232

She chuckled. "It's amazing how many of us depend on them."

As we began our meal, we touched upon the similar tracks we'd followed, starting from our nefarious escapade back in the seventies from which we eventually leaped into mainstream work, the surprise of our lives. I was careful with this conversation out of politeness, but then she said she'd had a few short-term relationships with men after the one we'd had. "Actually," she said, "there were fewer than I can count on one set of fingers." She laughed deeply. As her voice was clear, so, too, her laugh sounded like a cluster of ringing bells. "And to call them relationships is a stretch. More like little land mines going off. What man that I might find acceptable would want the likes of me?"

"Well . . ."

"Look at me."

I did so, tempted to say that I had once found her acceptable and might again. I was enthralled by the animal quality of her presence – moustache, tattoos, bulbous eyes, body as cylindrical as Jim's culvert, and her way of spilling rice and salad greens down her breast as she ate. She'd always been a geode, or a Silenian bust – a beast on the outside but ever more sweet and beautiful the deeper one went.

I said, "It took me the whole day to clean my apartment after our night. Things were broken. There was blood."

"I was menstruating. You don't remember?"

Even coming from her, the bluntness took me aback. "All I remember about that part is driving back to my apartment and then waking up to find you gone."

She settled back to chew on a hunk of bread. "I left because I had no idea what we could have said to each other. I was embarrassed and scared." She laughed again, tipping to and fro like a barrel in the booth. "I was just beginning to accept that it's women I love."

"Oh," I said.

She snapped a wing bone of her grilled chicken in half, sucked noisily on the marrow, and raised her eyebrows and pointed at me with the shattered end of the bone. "Surely that doesn't surprise you."

"I suppose not." It was a lie. I couldn't see how I'd missed something so obvious.

As graduate students, Rose and I had met at a coffee shop where the politically minded gathered. The leftist buzz then was all about post-Vietnam, Salvador Allende, Kissinger, and Nixon. Rose first attracted my attention because of her passion and theatrics – gesturing wildly from her table or standing up in her then Janis-Joplin like body, striking comic poses and shouting slogans: "No! No! Death to the nabobs!" Her favorite target was the university's experimental program with animals, in particular the Primate Center. After all the time that had passed, I still vividly remembered one of her statements, what may now sound passé but was then astonishing: "It's a charade. The researchers are deviant pleasure seekers. They're sadomasochists and imposters!"

In an effort to impress her, I proposed that we drive to see the Primate Center, which was out in the wheatlands of the Palouse. I had a packet of cocaine. Starting out after dark, we pulled off on a farm lane in the hills, laid out a line on a notebook, and snorted through a straw. It was early autumn. The vast tracts of blonde wheat stubble upon the hills rolled one after another under an ascending moon, the endlessly repeating curvature and slope made Escher-like by the drug. We drove on. The center was locked, but the next thing I knew I was picking the lock, a mundane skill I'd learned in navy intelligence. We went inside, threw on the lights, and heedlessly began opening cages.

The apes, one of whom had a heavily taped wound in its abdomen and another of whom had a metal device with a blinking red light screwed into its skull, lumbered into the lab. There were five. Yet another had wires poking out of a shaved patch on the back of its neck. The one with the metal case, the bull among them, rose up and stared at us. His brown eyes were soft and liquid, and his expression was as disconsolate as any I've ever seen.

We backed away. He shuffled near, bringing his overpowering pungency of scent mixed with the odors of defecation and disinfectant. Now fearful, we pressed back against the wall while I desperately racked my brain for a way to undo what we'd just done. There was nothing to do except flee, but the ape was between us and the doorway. He took another step, cocked his head, displaying his yellow teeth under the blinking red light, and then, as if some matter known only to himself had been settled, turned to join the others. They milled about the lab tables, ignoring us and sometimes lifting themselves to examine an object: a canister, a tray full of papers, a jug filled with liquid, an electronic monitor. . . . One knocked over a microscope. Another spilled feed out of a bag to the floor and scooped up handfuls to eat. Two, as if they were lovers long kept separate, began grooming each other. In the whiteness of the room, the dark, massive bodies swelled. They seemed quite accepting of this turn of events, but while Rose and I waited in trepidation, the sedateness of the apes grew ever more unworldly, as if soon out of the furious calm a lightening bolt would flash.

Instead, the apes found the ajar door and passed outside. In a moment, we followed, quickly making our way to the car. The apes gathered in a cluster at the edge of the gravel lot. They moved into a wheat field and fanned out, then converged into a single file. The blonde hills shimmered a froth color in the moonlight. For a time, we could see the blinking beacon on the one's head and the glint of his metal box. The group found its way into the mouth of a swale and then with great deliberateness began climbing the hill. I glanced at Rose, who was gazing through the windshield, completely rapt. The apes grew small, like a serration in the landform.

I have never told anyone about this, not even Molly. When I awoke in my apartment the next morning, I found bloodstains on the sheets, a half-empty bottle of tequila, a Fritos bag, and an overturned can of salsa on the floor. The kitchen was in disorder. Pictures hung crookedly on the walls. Rose was gone and nowhere to be found. It all became a dream-like enigma, driven by the spectral clarity of the drug's effect. I gave up all drugs years ago. . . . Indeed, I'm loath to fill prescriptions. . . . But at times I still long for the luminosity of cocaine, its whiteness, and for the wild idyll of the old days.

In the restaurant, Rose gazed at me intently. "What I remember is that the apes were kind to us."

I'd ordered a lamb kabob, which I finished off, and then said, "It's true. Maybe they knew we were friends."

"Four returned to their cages."

"That's what I heard, though there was no news report. The other was lost, I guess."

"It was all kept under wraps because they didn't want other people getting ideas. It's still there, the Primate Center. They do chimps now."

"So I'd guess."

"The other ape was shot by a farmer. It was in with his cows. He said he thought it was Sasquatch."

This made me smile, despite myself. "So he shot it?"

Rose smiled back. "If it's strange, you kill it, right?"

She devoured what remained of her bread, dipping it alternately into bowls of hummus and sour cream. "I got the carbon dating back on the remains," she said. "The DNA test will take a while. The bones are older than I expected . . . early sixteenth century."

Now, I asked if she'd been back in touch with Diane.

"Not yet." Rose looked toward the street with a troubled expression. "But I will be. I mean to talk with her."

"That's good," I said. "Is it Kennewick Man that makes you so wary of being shut down?"

"The little girl in the canyon will never generate the passion Kennewick Man did . . . not near as old. But Kennewick Man has certainly made everybody jumpy." She returned her gaze to the street. "I keep remembering what one of the Umatilla elders said . . . that we white people are like the ants, never resting, forever building our dirt mounds. I suppose Diane would agree with that. I guess she'd think building a data base is another dirt mound."

This put me in mind of my FEMA bureau – the reams and reams of paper, the files upon files in the computer banks, the information heaping far beyond the capacity of the staff to keep track of what was there. Paradoxically, the more of it there was, the more emphatic its nothingness became. It multiplied into a monumental zero. "Most likely," I said.

The bones of Kennewick Man were found with a spear point lodged between two ribs in the shallows of the Columbia River a couple hundred miles to the southeast. Several tribes, including the Umatilla, protested the dig, arguing that by law the remains should be given over to them for burial. They also objected to manipulation in any form, including carbon dating and DNA testing. Nevertheless, the remains were quietly dated at 841 BC and were, several archeologists had stated, either *archaic Mongoloid* or *proto-Caucasoid*, therefore predating the existing tribes. The find attracted enough attention for me to follow it in the East Coast newspapers. Some archeologists belittled the Umatillas, who had claimed that since their oral histories told of the land covered with ice, there was proof that their people had been here during the post-Glacial Age when Kennewick Man prowled the moraines. The Umatilla and other tribes filed a suit. The Army Corps of Engineers, which had jurisdiction over the site of Kennewick Man's discovery, entered the fray, as did the Department of Interior.

I told Rose how this had fascinated me, and I found myself echoing Jim's sentiment on the ancient accounts of the great floods by saying that the oral transmission of the stories and the information they might contain seemed to have been relegated by science to a vast limbo where all human utterances through the eons roiled upon each other like millions upon millions of shepherdless sheep.

"Science isn't interested in that," she said.

"Maybe they've forgotten how to listen."

"Not all of them have. But it's true that a lot of them only hear and see what they can make fit. What doesn't fit makes trouble. No scientist wants to get caught looking antiempirical."

I pressed on: "It's not unlike your apes."

"My apes!"

"With them, the unuttered, or what would seem to us to be the inexpressible primitive also ran willy-nilly beneath the research protocols. Remember what you used to say about research animals, how they were prisoners, stripped of their nature, how, as a cover for what they were doing, the researchers believed animals had no being?"

Rose smiled broadly, revealing her peg-like teeth. "And no humor, no thought, no subconscious life. Insensate. It's quite convenient to consider them so."

I pictured Shakur's henchman's vacuous eyes, behind which lay concealed the full cache of unspeakable treachery. For reasons turned inside out – the backspin nature can put on a psyche – his eyes were as arresting and mysterious as the disconsolate tenderness in the bull ape's eyes when he approached us.

"The white identity movement got into that one, too," Rose said. "They used the absence of DNA results as their entry point, though, of course, there are DNA results for Kennewick Man. It's just that nobody can say so publicly."

"I remember." I'd seen it written up, how several groups, choosing to misunderstand the meaning of *proto-Caucasoid* and making their own antic construct, claimed that if the bones were given a DNA test, they would prove to be of Aryan origin. This, they argued, would confirm that the lost tribe of Israel had settled here, that God had set North America aside long ago as the promised land for white people.

"Then there were the futurists," Rose said, again laughing deep in her throat.

It was infectious. I laughed, too, remembering how other groups with an equally fanciful bent became inspired by the way the artist's mock-up of Kennewick Man's head, which was widely circulated, looked like Patrick Stewart in his Star Trek role as Jean Luc Picard. "Oh my God," I said.

I finished eating my rice and salad, and we both settled back against our cushions. The waitress came for our plates. We ordered coffee and baklava, which Rose said was prepared impeccably here – made from a rolled-out sheet and drenched with honey. I took out the medallion of Hel and laid it on the table.

Rose glanced at it but carried on with her own thought: "My

find would never attract the attention Kennewick Man did. I wanted to know how old and, if possible, what tribe, that's all. The little known truth is that there are scores of sites like it in the state, although finding a complete skeleton off on its own like that is unusual. I'd have liked to have had it the way it almost was ... open up the midden, run a couple tests, and then fill it back in and leave things as they were, rather more mysterious than not."

She paused when the waitress set dishes with baklava in front of us and poured our coffee. The waitress was a young woman in a tight skirt, and as she walked away, I found myself checking the way her hips arched down in a heart-shape to the softness of her buttocks.

"By dating and doing a DNA scan, we'd have something to add to the record," Rose said. "Almost certainly, we'll confirm that the remains are Salishan in origin ... you know, an ancestor of the Spokanes, Coeur d'Alenes, Kalispels, or Kootenais. The artifacts suggest Kootenai."

She cut off a corner of her baklava and, holding it before her, said, "This is why I come here." She placed the morsel in her mouth, leaned back, closed her eyes, and chewed. She looked like a squirrel with her twitching moustache and lips pursed as if around a nut.

I took a bite of mine, crunching through the layers of pastry. The sweetness of honey bolted to the corners of my mouth. I followed it with a sip of coffee, which was bitter and fine.

"I really like Diane and I'm sorry about our difference," Rose said.

"It's a question of how knowledge is gained, isn't it? She'd say there are different ways."

"I suppose. It seems a little over the top. It's not clear to me how the bones came to be sacred to her."

I let that rest, took more baklava, and slid the medallion nearer to her – the lozenge-like rhomboid with the enameled face, divided down the middle, black on one side and white on the other with the features and background for each side reversed, black upon white, white upon black. It shone against the linen tablecloth. "Does that mean anything to you?"

Rose looked. "It's a yin and yang. The dual distribution of forces. Birth and death." She grinned at me, turning impish at her own pedantry, and then angled her eyes back at the medallion. "It appears to be a woman. So, it's the female principle, thank God, embracing the universal storm of opposites."

I turned the medallion over so she could read the inscription.

"*Hel*," she said. "Isn't that Scandinavian? Are you testing me?"

"You're doing well." Besides talking to the German professor, I'd done some research into northern European myth. The word was Old Scandinavian for *Hell*, I told Rose. "In German it's *Hölle*," I said, "which is interesting, considering our fascinations of late. The German for hole is *die Höhle*, while *Hölle* is also our holy. Hel was the Scandinavian goddess of the underworld, represented as a polarity this way. She prepared banquets for the shades when they arrived, filled with hunger from the travail of their passage. Everyone went there, as with the Greeks. But in Scandinavian hell there was celebrating each time somebody came down, and then everyone went back to their work just like in this world."

Rose's eyes had lit up. "What a fine way of thinking about death. Personally, I wouldn't mind carrying on as I am in the next dimension." She tipped her head and stroked her hair, posing. "Except I want to be beautiful." She snorted and tapped the medallion with a fingertip. "And the occasion for this is?"

"A medallion exactly like that was found on each of the two bodies . . . Margarita White and Helga Singley."

Rose gazed at me. "Helga? The colonel?"

"Her background was Finnish. She was a literary person."

"An air force colonel?" Rose said. "Her namesake, the goddess of the Underworld? Literary? Get out of here."

I shrugged and took the paper from my pocket that had the lines of poetry on it, unfolding it for Rose to see:

Flamme flammet, rot in Gluten
Steht das schwarze Moosgestelle.

"It was found in Helga's pocket. I had it translated," I said, turning the page over:

Freeing the Apes

The flames burn, red hot
In the black moss.

"The medallion ties the two women together, but otherwise the police still lack physical evidence. There has to be something here . . . the name, Helga, the other woman's name, White, the black, and the fire."

"The light and the dark," Rose said. "Hot and wet. So, they think what? That it's some kind of directive, or suicide note?"

"They don't know. It's from *Faust*, Part II. In the kingdom Faust received from his pact with the devil, an elderly couple refused to relinquish their hut with its linden trees. Faust wanted the trees. To mollify Faust and in his trickery, the devil turned the couple out by burning down both the hut and the trees."

Rose pushed back against her cushions. "So, you're back in the intelligence business."

"I am surely not a detective. More like a technical wool-gatherer. For years my job was to ascribe value to the lost and immaterial."

The grin crept back onto Rose's face. "Another thankless task. You always had a mind for puzzles."

Suddenly, I wanted to tell her how my government job had ended up as a messenger service delivering documents and cash to foreign mercenaries and, thus, to expiate to her my own deep puzzle, but I held fast to my instructions not to divulge that secret. Only with Molly and Jim and Diane had I violated the caveat.

She said, "Didn't I hear there was property dispute between the colonels and the Bloods?"

It took a moment, but next, I was thunderstruck by what I'd failed to put together – the meshing of elements yet more startling than I'd imagined, and far more obvious: the old couple, the hut, the warden in the tower, the house like a tower on the bluffs with their overlook like one, the underworld, the disputed corner of the meadow in the canyon, the fire, the birch trees.

Rose laughed rambunctiously at the expression on my face.

"Yes, but what does it mean?" I said. "There's a pretty strong element of the fantastical in all this, too, don't you think?"

Rose was still chuckling. "Isn't there always? Built up over bone like the flesh. That's where the wild ideas hang out, circling the totems of the world like buzzards."

"But what was Helga's idea?"

Rose dipped the last of her baklava in her coffee and put it in her mouth, closing her eyes with pleasure, tonguing the morsel into her cheek and sucking on it, slowly chewing, and finally swallowing. She opened her eyes. "That's always the question. What madness? What would I know?"

We sipped our coffee. It was a fine thing to be eating well-prepared food and having a conversation with a person of such energy. I should have been grateful, yet looking across at the roguish face, I felt washed under by a wave of loneliness.

Eleven

QUITE EARLY THE NEXT Sunday morning, I was upstairs, having just showered and dressed, when I heard the doorbell. I went down and found Josephine. When I went out, she pointed at the cross tilted next to the door and said, "I saw him!" She pointed down the street. "He went that way. I saw him from my front window."

I moved to the edge of the porch and peered down the street. No one was in sight.

"He went around the corner," Josephine said. "It was a young man."

I carted the heavy thing inside and examined it, finding it just like the others in its heft and with the *H* etched into the back, except that the ornamentation of vines, blossoms, and tree on the front was yet more elaborate, running nearly the complete length of the vertical and horizontal members. I leaned the cross against the wall next to my safes where the others had been and contemplated it, feeling a mixture of curiosity and affront.

Josephine had followed me. She bent and ran her fingertips along one ornamented arm to the weld at the joint. "This is very well done," she murmured. Her meaning, spun out of her expertise, was to reiterate that there was nothing casual about the crosses, neither in their making, nor in the leaving of them. Her bare feet squeaked on the floor as she straightened and revolved to face me. She wore a dark red bathrobe that set off her hair and fair skin.

"Let's see it," she said.

I didn't understand her. "See?"

"Peter! Your surveillance cameras. What are they for?"

"Oh," I said. "Of course."

"It's in the kitchen?"

She headed off through the living room to the kitchen, which struck me oddly, her familiarity with my house. As soon as I ar-

243

rived behind her, she turned to the monitor I'd mounted in a corner on top of the control panel.

"Let's look," she said.

I switched on the monitor with the remote control. The screen was set to the default vantage of the camera trained on the porch and walkway. I skipped the CD backward past the point where a figure first appeared.

"May I ask how you know where this is?" I said.

She smiled. "The monitor? I have a view of it from my back yard. It's in color. I've seen it turned on, usually on Saturdays when your daughter's here."

"She does her homework to it," I said. It was true. Beth enjoyed sitting at the kitchen table with the view of the street on the monitor. I indulged her with my electronics. She loved the Beatles and Mozart. She had all the Beatles's albums and watched the films *A Hard Day's Night, Help*, and *Amadeus* over and over again. She listened to Mozart CDs and knew his music, *Koechel* numbers and all. I realized that such fascinations were a way of countering the turmoil she felt, but I loved the twelve-year-old sagacity in them, too. Every once in a while, I would hear her calling out in her upstairs bedroom, "Oh, Wolfy!"

Josephine and I watched the screen, seeing the empty porch, walkway, and the street behind. The figure appeared in the upper right-hand corner and grew larger as he made his way along the walkway, carrying the cross over his shoulder. He came up the stairs to the porch, leaned the cross against the wall, and backed away to the edge of the porch, where he bowed deeply with his hands clasped before him, as if in prayer. He held his position for a full minute before lifting his face into view: It had the aquilinity and darkness of an East European. He was young. He had a wisp of beard and dark, pensive eyes. An embroidered shawl was draped from his shoulders. He turned to the stairs and walked out of sight in the direction he'd come from. It was the figure of a stripling going lightly away, without hurry. The whole of it took three or four minutes.

"I saw him just as he was coming down the steps," Josephine said. "When I came outside, I saw the cross."

We stared at the monitor that again showed the empty porch and walkway and, a moment later, Josephine herself moving rapidly up the walkway. I stopped the video and we stayed still, standing with our shoulders almost touching.

"Let's see it again," Josephine said.

The intensity of her voice made me glance at her. When she looked back, I saw that her eyes were moist. "What is it?" I asked.

Customarily nothing if not direct, Josephine seemed momentarily lost. "I don't know. I can't say. It's something haunting in his face. I'd like to see it again."

I replayed the video. As the man reappeared, Josephine slipped her hand into mine. The man came up the walk and placed the cross next to the door. As he moved to the edge of the porch, bowed, and then lifted his face, Josephine's hand tightened and I felt her holding her breath, as if she were about to leap. When the man retreated, she slowly let her breath go. The man disappeared. Josephine still had my hand, and when I looked at her, she looked back straight at me. Her eyes were like profound wells, and I felt as though I was about to tumble into them.

"Do you see?" Josephine said. "There's no meanness at all in that face. It's sadness. He's leaving you a gift."

This seemed a strange, not impossible, and inviting interpretation. Josephine was still looking at me. Her red robe had slipped away from one pale shoulder, and I caught myself about to put my hand there – what, for one pure moment, seemed perfectly natural but then, once realized, degraded into a risky impulse. I turned my head away, knowing she had read my inclination. When I looked back, she was smiling faintly.

"My apologies," I said.

"No matter," she replied.

Twelve

A FEW DAYS LATER, Jim called to say that Singley had asked to meet. "He says he wants to talk."

"About what?"

"I don't know," Jim said.

"You didn't ask?"

"He wouldn't say."

I'd already told Jim about the medallions and the note. His reaction had been stronger than I'd expected, though I should have understood how further turns without resolution in the crimes played out on his place would be galling to him.

"I don't think I'd do it," I said.

"We agreed to meet him. Here."

"Then you should tell the police. Tell Lieutenant Bradley."

"Maybe so," Jim said.

"You should."

"Maybe."

"Maybe I should come."

"If you can."

"As a fair witness, maybe."

"That would be fine." His tone suggested I'd hit on his reason for calling.

"When?" I asked.

"He's coming in an hour."

Taking the opportunity to return Jim's ladder, I loaded it on my Envoy and then, well aware of Jim's propensity for independence, took the liberty of calling Lieutenant Bradley myself. I left word about the meeting with a receptionist who assured me she would notify Bradley.

"It might be good if someone checked in," I said.

"I'll tell him," she said.

I set out and an hour later parked next to what I assumed was Singley's pickup. Pascal and Agatha were up on the near westward slope of the roof, pulling off cedar shakes with a roofing shovel. The nails shrieked as Pascal pried them. Agatha swept with a push broom, and when she shoved a heap over the eave, it landed on the ground with a crash. Dust filtered upward and whipped sideways in the breeze that circled the house. It had been dry and hot for days, and a whiff of smoke hung in the air from fires a hundred miles to the northwest. Much nearer and to the southwest, dark clouds amassed above the highland. Everyone was waiting to see if they would bring the comfort of rain or the threat of heat lightening.

I walked to the back of the house where Diane, Jim, and Colonel Singley were seated in lawn chairs in a copse of grass and trees. Jim introduced me to Singley, who stood but did not step away from his chair. He was about five feet eight, clean looking with close-cropped hair, and enveloped in a thin pad of fat. He wore a light jacket over a blue shirt, while the rest of us were in short sleeves. It was true that he would have made the perfect mole – once seen, immediately forgotten. There was nothing remarkable about his ovoid face, except for a tightness of skin above his lips and the eyes, which had a cast I'd seen many times, especially in military people – a screen thrown up to filter pain and conceal feeling.

In her incorrigible sense of hospitality, Diane had set out food on a red-and-white checkered cloth on the picnic table – celery and carrot sticks, deviled eggs, bread, a pitcher of iced tea, and a few salmon sticks, which I eyed keenly. Singley had a glass of tea. I poured one for myself and sat. We were positioned like passengers in a railroad coach, Singley and me facing each other near the table with Diane next to me, facing her husband.

"You've started on the roof," I said to Jim.

"Some of us have." He gestured with his head toward a pair of long pallets loaded with sheets of roofing material twenty yards behind him. "Steel."

Singley spoke: "It's a good idea in this country. For fire."

There was a moment of silence, a gulf into which I presumed our various, eddying thoughts on the fire in the canyon plunged. Finally, Diane said, "It is a good idea."

Jim had a shipping tube, which he passed to Singley, saying, "That's a copy of the survey. We meant to send it to you a couple months ago. It's registered with the county."

"It was for Helga, really, the property," Singley said, taking the tube. "She loved it."

There was another pause. Jim's face stayed set, and then he said, "We're sorry about what has happened."

Nails howled from the roof. The sound of shakes crashing echoed against the far wall of the canyon. A wind could be heard twisting up from the bottom, hissing in the pine needles. When it reached us, the hems of the checkered tablecloth lifted.

Singley shifted in his chair. "She had her transfer orders for Baghdad. She was about to ship out when she died."

In her politeness, Diane asked, "Information systems again?"

"Yes. I guess they need it." Indifferently, Singley leaned the survey tube against the arm of his chair.

After yet another pause, Jim said, "The property line is where we said it was."

Singley bent forward with his elbows on his knees, holding the glass in two hands. There was something odd about his position – his left arm was slightly askew as if he were nursing an injury. He stared at the ground. "Her dream was to build a house on the creek bottom. It broke her heart that we had problems with access. As good as she was with her command, her mind didn't always work like other people's. Sometimes she was unrealistic. She let her emotions take her off. She never understood the access problem."

Jim's eyes cut to Singley. "It won't be a problem again. I'll be putting in a fence." He sounded as though the project had already begun – each word he spoke, a post punched into the ground.

"I'm a practical man," Singley said.

Jim's eyebrows twitched upwards.

Singley crossed his legs and lifted his gaze over my head in the direction of the first ridgeline and the lane that came over it. "I'm going to sell the property. I'd be willing to divide it and sell the top and bottom separately. Are you interested?"

It seemed Singley had just stated his reason for being here, but the offer reeked of capitalizing under bad circumstances upon Jim and Diane's proximity and desire.

Finally, Jim said, "Maybe."

"I wanted you to know," Singley said.

"I see," Jim said.

Singley's veiled eyes turned to Diane. "Isn't it what you've wanted all along?"

Diane's body jerked lightly in her way of cocking herself before letting loose. "What we wanted," she said, "was to leave the creek bottom alone, not even to know it more than we should." I could feel her caution right next to me, and the passion rising against that check as if against a breakwater. "And maybe not even to assign names to the things in it," she said, "but to let it do its own naming in its own language, and as much as possible to let it move on its own terms. Obviously, it was too much to ask others to feel the way we do about it. Then after all, maybe it did move on its own. It's a violent world." She leaned toward Singley. "Things went out of control, didn't they?"

An expression snaked across Singley's face, what seemed amusement, and I waited to hear how his laugh would sound, squeezed through his vise. But the expression faded and his voice came out flat: "What's that supposed to mean?"

"It means you're an asshole," Jim said.

My blood lurched and Diane pulled back straight in her chair, flashing a look at Jim. Yet the insult seemed to have no effect whatsoever upon Singley. He said, "My daughter will be handling these affairs – Brenda Singley. She's a realtor. She's in the phone book, if you're interested."

There were more crashes as shakes were shoved over the eave, after which Pascal and Agatha could be heard moving to another position, their voices lilting in the breeze. I couldn't make out the words, but the tone – the pleasure and solicitousness of young love – seemed completely at odds with what was going on here below.

As I continued to scrutinize Singley, who uncrossed his legs and pushed back in his chair, I puzzled over how, when a person of interest is described by someone else, the actual encounter with that person nearly always reveals a nature that differs from what was anticipated. There's always a surprise. No one at any time had mentioned a daughter. And although Singley in some ways fulfilled my expectations – his snug layer of fat, the Wal-Mart garb, and unmemorable face – he was nevertheless not quite the hollow creature I'd imagined from Jim's description. I wondered about Jim's experiences with suffering, how his contact with it had to be slight compared with mine. His benchmark for the human zero – the nothingness of being, reduced to a clutter of primal impulses – would be set higher, while my brushes with depravity had certainly torqued my view toward the darkest depths of the shadowland. In my profession of calibrating calamity, later of tendering booty to the desperate, and yet of never actually doing anything of import, I'd been drawn toward what I witnessed. I'd cast myself into its mold and had yet to break loose from it or even to know how to begin. Just a week before this time, while returning Beth to her grandmother's house, I'd found Molly sitting on the front veranda, and judging some openness in her by the way she glanced at me from behind her knife of hair, I asked if we might soon talk. I was well aware – of course! – that a formal divorce filing had still not appeared, and so with that, too, I was left in a limbo of uncertainty. Once Beth had passed inside, Molly turned to me, as formidable as ever, as unflinching, and said, "I told you I stopped knowing you. I'm not having a tête-à-tête with a stranger."

As to my friend, Jim Blood – the discontinuity of perception between him and me, or the more, the unaccountable and frightening discontinuities of the world – awakened me to my desperate need to bind my spirit to people I trusted. My ability to do that seemed obliterated. The thought of Jim's sense of demons as complicated creatures – quite different from my uninflected romance with evil – provoked a terror of the damage I'd done to myself. And as to Singley, the barricades he'd thrown up around himself, his wooden posture across from me, his opportunism, all of the oppression of his nature upon himself and of his presence upon us, and his utter untrustworthiness made me want to sink back into my cocoon of unfeeling voyeurism. I was afraid of who he was. At that moment and while in that state of fear, my view of him – as he, strangely, looked straight back at me – shape-shifted into a doppelgänger, fashioned from behind my own screen.

Jim said, "Is that it?"

Singley sat stock still, ignoring Jim. To me, he said, "You're an investigator, I hear."

"My God!" I thought. "Or a secret agent of perfidy!" Yet the words came calmly out of my mouth, "I once was, in a manner of speaking."

"You know Lieutenant Bradley," he said.

"I've met him." I then wondered if Bradley might soon appear. I wished I had a way of telling Jim and Diane I'd made the call.

"You aided the investigation."

"Not in the least. I've been aware of it."

This was true. I'd done nothing to help but had merely been a taster.

"Not with the fire?"

I should have expected that, while he was encircled and scrutinized, Singley would examine all his adversaries. I was curious to know if he'd gone far enough in his inquiries to discover that I actually didn't exist.

"No. They had that information already," I said, and then – as best I can reckon it, wildly seeking an antidote to my own unease and fear – I lurched out from under my cover and satisfied Singley's probing by taking on the guise of a provocateur. In my pocket was the medallion of Hel, which I'd picked up after calling Bradley from my house, intending to show it to Jim and Diane. I took it out and set it on the wooden bench of the picnic table between Singley and myself. The medallion seemed exotic and yet like nothing at all – a bit of shining metal with the Scandinavian yin and yang face on it.

"That's Helga's," Singley said.

"Actually, it's mine."

His face didn't move. "Helga had one."

"So did Margarita White."

251

There. But I couldn't believe I'd said it.

Jim and Diane were utterly still, their state of high attention palpable, while Singley set his chin and stared fixedly over my head at the ridgeline, revealing nothing. It was clear that the storm cloud was approaching. The air had cooled. A heavy gust blew one end of the checkered tablecloth straight up and folded it over the plates. A pair of ravens careened overhead toward the pasture, croaking at each other. I thought I heard the distant sound of gravel popping under a car at the far end of the Bloods' lane, which could be played along its length like a drumhead, but the sound vanished.

Singley kept staring in that direction.

Jim glanced at me – quizzically, I thought.

Diane looked to the roof, on the far side of which Pascal and Agatha pulled shakes and pushed them to the ground, the noise rising and falling and sometimes almost disappearing in accordance with the direction of the wind. "Those two need to come down," Diane said. "It's not safe." She was rattled and, while clinging to her sense of decorum, also wanted to bring the conversation here to an end. She turned to Singley and said firmly, "We're sorry for all of this. It's not easy to lose a loved one."

Singley chose that moment to try his tea. His motion of woodenly raising a hand and tipping his head to drink revealed a leather strap that passed across his chest beneath the jacket. He was wearing a shoulder holster.

That he would sit in this company with a weapon was astonishing.

Yet considering his circumstance, it was not astonishing at all.

The outlandish possibility that he might mean to use the gun pitched against my doubts that he would and against my still resurgent preference for waiting to see what he would do – the sullen solace of my inertia and of not venturing, like the apes returning to their cages. Many people carry guns in this region. They are commonly seen poised on racks in pickup trucks. I had guns in my Envoy not thirty yards away. I had a hundred guns in my house. Jim and Diane had a holster with a revolver hanging from a peg next to their bed.

Singley then answered Diane: "There's no undoing any of it."

The steeliness of his tone and the way his face was absolutely void of emotion made me feel a chill. Something was shifting, something as delicate as leaves in winter, piled on the ground, being nudged away from a fetid place . . . the black moss, the fire deep within. Suddenly it struck me that Singley, the "practical man" clinging to his tactical world of procedures, pronouncements, and cinched-down fastenings, was quite mad.

And again hardly knowing what I was doing, I stood up. My first thought was to go to my Envoy to arm myself, but immediately I dismissed that, thinking further, "Show him your Glock? Then what?" Instead, I excused myself to the bathroom and went to the back door of the house. I felt like a sleepwalker climbing the steps, barely conscious; yet as soon as I entered the hall leading to the kitchen, I pulled out my cell phone and pressed the 9-1-1 key.

The back door creaked open behind me. Diane's footsteps approached quickly. She came out of the hall and headed for the living room, stopping when she saw me standing there. Gesturing upwards, she asked, "Did you tell them to come down?"

At that instant the operator answered, and when I said, "I need to reach Lieutenant Bradley," Diane turned toward me. When the operator informed me that I'd called the emergency line, I said, "That's right. We have a man with a gun here."

Diane marched right to me. "We have what?"

The operator asked for my name and location. As I told her, I heard a keyboard clicking. "One moment," she said.

"Singley does?" Diane asked.

I nodded. Past Diane and through the windows on the far wall of the living room, I saw that the wind had delivered towering, black clouds. Horizontal flashes of lightening sheeted the sky.

The operator asked if the person was threatening anyone.

"Not yet. He's outside. I can't see from where I am." Appalled, I pictured Jim there and Singley next to him with his rigid face. From her expression it was clear Diane was having a similar thought. "Should I look?" I asked. It seemed stupid, putting myself under the operator's bidding. To my surprise my hands were shaking. When she didn't respond, I said, "We want you to send a car now. I want you to contact Lieutenant Bradley. Tell him it's Colonel Singley."

"Who?" she said.

"Lieutenant Bradley. He knows the case. I called him earlier."

"Yes," she said. "The other name again, please."

My teeth ground. "Robert Singley."

"One moment," she said coolly. "Stay on the line."

To Diane, I said, "I'm on hold."

Diane opened her mouth. She was about to say something, but then instead she stalked off, going around the corner into the living room. I heard the front door open and her voice calling out from the deck, "Pascal." Through a window, I saw Pascal and Agatha up at the crest of the roof, looking out to the ridgeline. Their shirts and Agatha's long hair streamed in the wind. "Pascal. Do you hear me?" Diane said.

"Somebody's coming," Pascal said, looking down.

"Yes. Come off the roof, now," Diane said.

"It's a sheriff's car," Pascal said.

There was a pause, after which Diane said, "All right." Then her voice grew formidable. "Get off the roof. It's a storm, for God's sake, you two."

Even in the kitchen, I heard tires in the gravel, coming near on the lane. I thought I heard a second car, playing a distant staccato behind the first, and as Pascal edged down the roof behind Agatha, he stopped once more to crane his neck back. "There's another one," he said.

"Come down, now, and stay there," Diane said. Once Pascal had stepped onto the ladder, she returned to the kitchen, moving quickly through the living room back to the kitchen. "What the fuck is going on?"

In my ear, the operator said, "Lieutenant Bradley is on patrol. He's going to that address. There should be a cruiser there now."

"Yes," I said. "Good."

"Good, what?" Diane said.

I lowered the phone. "They're here."

At this confirmation of what her son had just told her, delivered by an operator on the air waves from thirty miles away, Diane's face gave a little. "All right, then," she said, turning to the hall.

Her face showed precisely what I felt: relief that matters were passing into competent hands, wonderment that this thing had been allowed to transpire, and the apprehension born of the anxiety that we weren't done yet. I followed her, and as soon as I stepped into the hall, shouts rang out from the back of the house. Then came a blast of gunfire – a succession of ear-splitting, reverberating reports, sounding like rim shots on the drumhead now, slamming back and forth between the house and the ridgelines. Diane jerked to a dead halt at the door. Her arms went up and she suddenly got big, her entire body bristling and electric as if she were about to sizzle right out of herself. She screamed, "Oh my God! Jim!" Then she was running, crashing through the door, and hurtling down the steps out of sight.

When I reached the porch, my gaze stuttered over a surreal montage. Diane was at the far end of the picnic table. With both hands, she clutched Jim's arm, and her face was wrenched with emotion. Jim stood stock still with an aghast expression. Two sheriff's deputies were just on the other side of the chairs, one of whom stood, cradling a shotgun. The other, holding an AR-15, knelt over Singley's prone form. Blood gushed from Singley's side. Next to him lay a nickel-plated .38 snub nose. A second cruiser sped up the end of the drive and jerked to a stop at the edge of the grass. Lieutenant Bradley stepped out. Singley's leg rose, bending at the knee, and collapsed sideways.

I recognized the standing deputy as the one who'd been out at the end of the lane when I'd first come to borrow the ladder two months ago. His face was ashen. He shifted the shotgun to one hand and began fiddling awkwardly with his radio, which was strapped to an epaulet. "I should call EMT," he said.

The other, older deputy had his fingers on Singley's neck. He looked over at Bradley and said, "He's gone."

Thirteen

A MEDICAL CREW ARRIVED, put Singley in a black zip-up bag, and loaded him in an ambulance. It was strange to think of Singley inside the vinyl, carted off with his secrets. Lieutenant Bradley took statements from us, but mainly from Jim, who'd seen it all. "It didn't seem like he panicked," Jim said. "He seemed calm and never did shoot, though he could have."

"He could have," the older deputy said. "He surprised us."

"I thought he wanted to." The voice of the younger was raspy. "He kept coming toward us."

"It definitely was a surprise," Jim said. Diane stood next to him, still holding his arm; and he, too, was visibly shaken, though his words came out with his usual rectitude. "It seemed like he wanted to be shot."

All of Jim's statements supported this: Singley produced his pistol, told Jim to get away, and advanced on the deputies, refusing to disarm even though the younger deputy had emerged from the cruiser with a shotgun leveled on him and the older deputy followed with the AR-15. When Singley raised his pistol, he was shot.

Bradley said, "It's not as unusual as you might think."

"I'm sorry this happened," Jim said.

"It's good you let us know he was coming," Bradley said to Jim, which told me that Jim had called, after all. "You, too," Bradley said to me and then added, "Though, one of you said to come in and check, and the other said 'be near, but don't come in unless you have to.'" He smiled faintly. "A mixed signal, I'd say."

"Meeting him was a mistake," Jim said. "The whole thing was a damn mistake."

"Look," Bradley said. "None of you pulled a weapon." He smiled again, a little more openly, crinkling his cheeks back in the way he had of putting people at ease.

"I provoked him," I said. "I brought out the medallion. I shouldn't have done that."

Bradley glanced at the bench where the medallion still lay. "That thing isn't a weapon either."

The deputies departed in their car. The black dog appeared and smelled the grass where Singley's blood had spilled. The dog curled away, growling, and, with its hackles up, stopped to sniff at a hunk of Singley's gore that was dangling from a tree trunk. Pascal sharply called the dog off and it slinked up next to him. Together with Agatha they hovered near the wall of the house. In the dark square of the window above them, Jim's father's face peered out like a skull, bony and white with obscure eye sockets.

Bradley explained that all police shootings were investigated and that there would be a follow-up with us. "We'll send a truck for Singley's vehicle." He looked at Diane. "Otherwise, I'd guess you're done with this."

"You mean it's closed?" Jim asked.

"I think we're finished here," Bradley said. "I don't suppose we can close the case yet." He looked down at the ground while we waited and then up again. "We suspect Mrs. Singley took her own life, but we're not positive. There was an affair, it seems, between Singley and Mrs. White, which nobody affirmed, not even Mrs. White's husband. There are the medallions. The one found on Mrs. White had to come from one of the Singleys, somehow. They knew each other. It's possible that both ladies had them at the time of their demise by chance, though Mrs. White's wasn't fastened to her clothing, so maybe it was put there . . . an odd memento. That takes you back to the Singleys again. Mrs. White's body was moved here during the firestorm. Soil samples suggest from somewhere up near the Pend Oreille River. But from where exactly and why she was moved, we don't know. To conceal her better than wherever she was left at first? And starting a fire to hide the digging? Or what? There is evidence of a struggle with Mrs. White. She was killed by a blow to the head from a tire iron or some such. The blow came from the front and an advantage of height, maybe by somebody pretty tall, taller than Singley. Or maybe he was standing on something. Maybe she was crouched. We don't know."

Jim's thoughts had run into the same path as mine: "Helga."

Bradley shrugged. "Mrs. White's husband is six-four. He's never been especially cooperative, but otherwise, there's not much to point to him. Truth be told, for all the information we have, there's a notable lack of useful evidence in this thing. No DNA traces, nothing." He put his foot up on the picnic table's bench next to my medallion and with great deliberation untied and retied one shoe lace. He glanced at me. "That's the intelligence we were talking about. The answers are out there, but there were brains in the cover up. We've been monitoring Singley for two months now, but he never gave us anything."

Bradley put his foot on the ground and straightened, making the gear attached to his belt creak. He spoke to Diane: "It'd have been good if we could have spared you this. I'm sorry."

After Bradley drove off, we all stood quietly, each of us wrapped in our own thoughts, and then Jim said, "I should go talk to my father."

A moment later Diane followed him into the house. This left Pascal, Agatha, and me standing near the table, held in what seemed an interminable silence. Finally, Pascal turned to me and announced that he and Agatha were about to walk up to the near ridge to watch the sunset. I became aware that while we were otherwise engrossed, the storm clouds had passed. There seemed something antic in this – a rainless, whirling, theatrical mountain storm cloud, flying off to the east, utterly without result.

"That was quite something," Pascal said somberly. "It's pretty hard on my folks."

I agreed.

Pascal gestured toward the ridge. "Tell Mom and Dad we won't be long."

Agatha picked up the folded tablecloth by its edge and laid it back down flat on the table, revealing the untouched plates of food, including the salmon sticks. This was the first time I'd seen her up close, and it was evident why everyone liked her – with her attractive and serious face, her lively green eyes, and her caring hands. The pair moved off, picking their way uphill among the stones and bush – Pascal slouched forward while Agatha's hair shifted above the small of her back. The black dog pranced ahead of them.

Diane returned with a bottle of mescal. Jim followed her, saying, "I'll go back later. He's busy with Mother. She's talking about trains coupling. He thinks she's returned to Saskatchewan, where we once lived near a station. He's trying to make out the why of it, but it makes no sense to him. Trains coupling? Think of it." He set his gaze on the mescal bottle and smiled. "What's that?"

Diane passed it to him. He uncorked it, took a slug, and passed it to me. I took one and gave it back to Diane, who took a long swallow.

"There." She wiped her mouth with her arm.

Unable to resist any longer, I took a salmon stick and bit off a hunk, which was perfect, sweet, smoky, and oceanic like nothing else in the world.

There are gravitational places on the farm. Two of these were the meadow and a hollow in the creek where the water pooled above the beaver dams. Now, the canyon had the midden, Margarita White's former grave site, the rock tailings where Helga Singley's body landed, and the ruts from vehicles passing up and down. I guessed it would take time for Diane and Jim to settle into its recomposed state. Another place was the bottom of the pasture where Jim had dug his well and mounted his windmill, and that was where the three of us walked. We stood at the fence line next to the stock tank, facing the pasture. Once more, we passed the mescal among us, and then Diane set it on the ground. She'd brought the remaining salmon sticks, too, and offered them.

The dark cloud plowed further eastward with its spectacular show of horizontal electric flashes. Off to the west, trails of cumulous clouds in long wisps and filigrees were lit up from behind by the sun as it descended toward the ridge. In this rare glow, the cows stood nearly half a mile away at the far end of the pasture. They had turned to look at us. A solitary flycatcher was poised on a post near us. Inevitably, it would fly out into the field, whip in the air to snag what we couldn't see, and return to its perch.

Tyrannus tyrannus.

The windmill at our back squeaked softly with each revolve.

"I have to fix that," Jim said.

"I brought your ladder back," I said.

"I saw."

We were left with plenty to speculate upon, despite what Bradley had said about the thinness of evidence. We began to inch into the empty spaces, weaving our theories. We wondered if Helga Singley might have killed Margarita White out of jealousy or rage, either meeting her by arrangement or just coming upon her at the substation up the road. Maybe it was feared that where the body had first been left would not suffice, as Bradley had suggested. Maybe out of warped commiseration or complicity, Bob Singley had stepped in to help conceal what Helga had done. They had their careers, she especially. They were military people, officers, with their sense of dignity and comportment. How that might be, I felt I understood perfectly, since I had once been a military man and in effect had become one again during my stint with FEMA. But why would they have transported the body here? This raised another set of questions: Most likely they were taking advantage of the confusion during the firestorm, but otherwise, why? To keep an eye on her? Out of a warped proprietorship over the dead?

"I still say he killed his wife in some fashion," Jim said.

"It's frightening," Diane said, "to imagine how things could go so wrong among people that one would be murdered and the two remaining would depart thus in their separate ways . . . and with the Singleys, none of it would have come out of a shared sense of pain, or even rage. Rage, at least, would have given them something to take with them. The coldness of it! They must have been horribly alone in their deaths."

"He certainly was," Jim said. "My God!"

We were all silent for a moment in what seemed an appalled prayer.

Then Jim said, "The person I saw telling bald-faced lies in order to rip off ten acres of land where Margarita was buried is maybe a person who'd drive another to egregious acts."

"Yes," Diane said. "And all of it so weirdly arranged in his head that he had to make a spectacle of his own demise on our land."

Jim said, "I think he made his decision the moment the sheriff's car pulled up."

"But he had to be wired for that."

"Of course," Jim said. "He was improvising on his nihilistic track."

This exchange made me look away because of my own tangled-up condition. In a clearing on the same ridge where Jim and I had spotted the searchers in their Day-Glo suits a couple months ago, I now picked out Pascal and Agatha's figures silhouetted against the outlandish sky. They stood still, probably reaffirming their psychic space in this turmoil. They moved into the trees where the ragged scrap of black dog scouted ahead. They might be retreating, yet a line that was palpable tied them to Jim and Diane. Soon, they would turn and the reel would draw them home. To my surprise this rumination upon connectedness, affirmed by what Pascal had said – "Tell Mom and Dad. We won't be long." – brought tears to my eyes.

"Peter?" Diane said, touching my elbow. "Are you all right?"

"I think so," I said. "Yes."

Diane reached around my waist and hugged me, making my eyes well all the more.

"What it is," I began, and then I stopped. For once, I felt more astonished than confused. Perhaps it was what I'd been seeking . . . to be affected by horror and its opposite, to clarify myself . . . for my daughter, Beth . . . maybe even some day for Molly.

I tried again: "It's gratitude." Again I stopped. "I want to thank you two for being my friends. You let me be here when I needed it, even though you had this trouble. I feel like I'm waking up."

"You were helping us," Diane said.

"I didn't do anything."

Jim leaned forward so he could see me. "Hey. You pulled out that medallion."

Diane rocked back and came forward again. "At least he didn't call him an asshole."

This made us all laugh softly. As if on cue, the quail in the trees behind us commenced with their clownish calls . . . *ChiCaa-go, ChiCaa-go.* The flycatcher darted out, executed a whirligig in the air to snatch a bug, and returned to its post.

I sighed, heavily letting out the air, and said, "I keep thinking about what Singley said about Helga's mind not being like other people's. Why should it be? She had an inventive mind, obviously, loaded with possibilities."

"To him, those would have been irrational phantasms, hopelessly lost in himself as he was," Diane said. "But to her, being with him, they must have been more dead letters. If we have it right . . . we could have it all wrong, you know. It could be a totally different story. . . ."

"It could be they had marital troubles and she fell off the cliff and that's all," Jim said.

"I don't think so and neither do you," Diane said. "If it is the other way, if Helga killed Margarita, do you suppose that by helping her hide Margarita's body, he was really and finally blotting out his own wife?"

This was a powerful thought, and we fell silent again.

Pascal and Agatha had picked their way down from the ridge toward the far end of the pasture. The dog shot ahead, stirring up the cows, who began to move in our direction. Diane scooped up the mescal bottle and took another swallow. She handed it to me. I took a swallow and passed it back. Diane delivered the bottle to Jim.

Jim tipped it to his lips and was about to set it down, but Diane snatched it and, holding it aloft, said, "To Helga! Rise up and feast!" By an unspoken agreement, Jim and I had consented that a little mescal was in order, but not too much, while Diane seemed to be of a different opinion. She took another swig and made us chuckle again, and it felt good for the vividness of its effect, like the drink itself.

"Whatever happened with those crosses?" Jim asked.

"It was one of the Russians." I told them how the fourth cross had appeared, how we had seen the video, and how Josephine, remembering what I'd told her about my accident and seeing the way the man in the video looked, had suggested I take it downtown to the Russian Pentecostal Church to ask about it. It happened to be a Sunday morning, anyway.

"Josephine?" Jim said, raising an eyebrow.

"Yes. My neighbor."

"Oh?" Jim said.

I told them about the fifty or so people who came out to the sidewalks after services – the men in their thrifty blue suits and the women in long skirts and head coverings – and how I'd spotted the young man I believed was in the surveillance video. I asked him about it, but he knew no English. The cross I'd brought with me seemed to frighten him. Then, an older man joined us. I showed it to him and explained how all these crosses had been appearing at my house.

He took the cross and turned it over in his hands. He and the young man spoke back and forth, and then the older man said to me, "Yes. It's for Natasha. They were to marry." I asked why the young man – whose name was Pyotr, or Peter in Russian – had been leaving the crosses and if he meant to threaten me. "Tell him it was an accident. It was my fault. Tell him I am very sorry," I'd said.

Other people gathered, making a circle and sometimes murmuring among themselves. The older man told me that Pyotr did not mean to frighten me but that he wanted to give me a cross as a . . . and the man hesitated, searching for the word.

"Memorial?" I asked.

"Yes!" he said, but I still wasn't sure if that was the right word. It seemed as though consensuality might have been in it. What the young man might have desired was consensuality between the bereaved and the perpetrator of loss. "For memory," the older man said. "And to forgive you. Pyotr does not understand the ways of this country. He is new here. With us it's custom to do the best thing, which in such a case is to forgive. He knows it was an accident. It is not a threat. He is an artist, a machinist still looking for work. Natasha was a poet. In our home country, she was well known. She was our poet."

"Tell him I am terribly sorry. Tell him thank-you. Tell him I will put the cross in front of my house and leave it there," I said, even though – as I said to Jim and Diane – I was a little wary of the prospect of having the thing in my yard forever.

When the older man translated this, Pyotr leaned toward me, nodding, and all around me I heard the approval of the circle.

"It's been a strange homecoming," I said to Jim and Diane. "And I forgot how, in the Russian alphabet, their *H* is our *N*. The *H* that so threw me off is for Natasha. The crosses are incredibly well crafted."

"And what now?" Diane asked.

"I don't know."

"You should go to their church."

"Oh?" The idea had not occurred to me.

"What is it about the cross?" Diane said. "What power is in it for him? They're Russians. Think about that. Your fate was to kill his fiancée, and he forgives you. You should learn more about the meaning of that."

This startled me. What she was suggesting, I'd all but posed repeatedly to myself. Then, it had been handed to me, but I still wasn't answering its call. It was the very principle of consensuality she was talking about, my need to come up out of my dungeon and to stay out and to do the obvious and simple acts such as having the courtesy to visit the Russian church, maybe even to help Pyotr find a job.

The cows ambled toward us in a ragged line. The dog had swung over by Pascal and Agatha, who hung behind the last tailings of the herd. Agatha was gesturing and talking, while Pascal looked at the ground, measuring his steps. It seemed as though an agreement had been struck among the unlike creatures to come see us. Further behind, a cocoon of dust rose, catching the rarefied light of the sun reflecting off the clouds. It was invigorating to consider how one could behold the tailings of thunderclouds, distant flashes, moisture in the air and yet no rain, setting sun, and dust all at the same time.

"The child in the midden," Diane said. "Rose said it was unusual to find remains, especially a child's, in a junk heap."

When I looked at her, I saw Jim looking, too, smiling at her.

I wanted to ask if she and Rose had begun talking again, but I didn't.

"I mean it," Diane said.

"I know you do," Jim said. He cut a line in the earth with his boot heel.

"More demons?" I asked.

Jim said, "It's just a line to let Diane know that I'm over here on this side of it if she goes where I think she's about to go."

Diane looked into the sky. She had swallowed yet another slug of mescal while I was telling my story. She said, "I walked down to the canyon yesterday evening. The little girl is still there, of course. She has something to do with all this."

"This is where I start having trouble," Jim said.

"String theory," Diane said.

Jim said, "That's mathematics. I'd rather just call it demons and leave it at that."

"But mathematics given sound is music. It can be ethereal and frightening. The math is just offering a proof for what we'd have already known if we'd been listening. There are other dimensions right here that we're not seeing. It's hard to give the other dimensions body." She paused to catch her breath and then went on, "The two colonels had their trouble, which was going to be expressed somehow, somewhere. The question is why in our meadow. Why not at their place in town, or why not leave it up on the Pend Oreille? If it was them, why did they cross over to us? The little girl has something to do with it. Rose said it was like she was just tossed there, thrown away and left. Her unsettled condition is part of the mix. And that's why she must not be manipulated. I'll do battle with Rose if I have to, but the Kootenai must take her and bury her properly, or come here and do it. I'm going to see to that.

"I saw something else down there, too," Diane said. Her voice grew yet more intent as she told us she'd picked her way through the willows and thorn bushes near the creek, and just as she was about to come out, she saw a heron in the shallows, standing on one leg with its head cocked. "It made me stop," she said. "I still had cover. Then a bald eagle appeared, dropping right out of the sky. I hadn't looked up to see it beforehand, so it seemed like it came from nowhere, suddenly hissing in the air. It slammed against the heron and forced it into the water. The heron struggled, flapping its wings furiously, but the eagle dug in and reached around with its beak and tore open the heron's neck. It ate the fish stored up in the heron's gullet."

Diane rocked back and gestured, holding out one hand palm up and in the other the mescal bottle, making the liquid slosh. Her voice softened: "The eagle flew off. The heron feathers and its stretched-out body floated downstream. It was a nocturne, violent and then quiet and delicate, played to call out the night."

All this time, she had remained turned toward the length of the pasture and the approaching cows, as if she were addressing it and them and at their far reach Pascal and Agatha as much as Jim and me. It hit me how she'd been carrying much more of the burden of this entire affair than I'd thought. That might have been what Pascal was intimating.

"It took abstract reasoning for the eagle to know the heron had fish like that, didn't it?" she said. "Following observation and coming out of the culture of cohabiting predators. That's what I mean. There's a lot more dreaming and thinking going on out there than we know about."

On her other side, Jim was silent but smiling wryly, as he also looked up the pasture. The cows were nearly upon us now. Though I had more inclination to think in Jim's way, I found Diane's position compelling. Certainly her keen penetration and her resolve with the remains in the canyon, which I knew Jim would respect, were impressive. I was struck by how eccentric the two of them were, and I admired and envied the way this eccentricity, like a cam swinging off-center, brought them to strike so sure a balance.

266

Pascal and Agatha arrived, edging along the fence line so as not to press the cows. I thought the cows would stop, but they kept advancing. In an instant, we stood in their midst, the twenty or so twelve-hundred-pound creatures milling around. All were gravitating toward the water tank. One or two sucked from it, followed by another, and the first went back for more, while the remainder queued up, awaiting their turns. When two or three cows drank at once, the water level visibly dropped.

"Now watch this," Jim said, gesturing at the float in the tank, which was attached to a spout at the end of a line that ran from the driveshaft in the windmill. When the float went down just so far, a valve clicked, and water flooded through the spout, refilling the tank.

"That's really something," I said. "It's really clean."

"Yes, it is."

In the *Prairie Schooner Book Prize in Fiction* series

Last Call: Stories
By K. L. Cook

Carrying the Torch: Stories
By Brock Clarke

Nocturnal America
By John Keeble

The Alice Stories
By Jesse Lee Kercheval

*Our Lady of the Artichokes and Other
Portugese-American Stories*
By Katherine Vaz

Call Me Ahab: A Short Story Collection
By Anne Finger

Bliss and Other Short Stories
By Ted Gilley

Destroy All Monsters, and Other Stories
By Greg Hrbek

Little Sinners, and Other Stories
By Karen Brown

Domesticated Wild Things, and Other Stories
By Xhenet Aliu

To order or obtain more information on these or other University of Nebraska Press titles, visit www.nebraskapress.unl.edu.

CPSIA information can be obtained at www.ICGtesting.com
Printed in the USA
BVOW02s1328060913

330484BV00002B/2/P